RULES
FOR
HEIRESSES

D0029244

AMALIE HOWARD

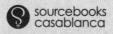
sourcebooks
casablanca

Published by Sourcebooks Casablanca, an imprint of Sourcebooks
P.O. Box 4410, Naperville, Illinois 60567-4410
(630) 961-3900
sourcebooks.com

Printed and bound in Canada.
MBP 10 9 8 7 6 5 4 3 2 1

For Cameron, my forever home.

One

LADY RAVENNA HUNTLEY, UNWED SISTER TO THE DUKE OF Embry, was in the biggest pickle of her life, and that was saying a lot, considering she'd been a fugitive on one of her brother's ships across the Atlantic. Now, she was about to lose a substantial fortune playing vingt-et-un while disguised as a man…unless she did something she'd never considered before.

Unless she *cheated*.

This win was a matter of survival. She was almost out of money, barring her last pair of earbobs. Notwithstanding her previous exploits, her brother would have her hide if his precious sister ended up getting thrown into the stocks on an island in the British West Indies.

But she wasn't a cheater and never had been. Ravenna could understand how desperate times made people consider unpalatable options because at the moment, she truly *was* out of options. She hadn't fully thought through her plan. Yet again.

She *could* win if she bluffed her way through it, but if she lost… Well, better not think of that. Why was it so bloody sweltering? It felt as though sweat was pouring down her back in rivers. She eyed the men gathering around the table in the gaming hell at fashionable Starlight Hotel and Club and tugged at her collar.

Jump first and think later had served her marginally well over the past six months.

Not now, naturally.

Her overwarm skin itched beneath the scratchy fabric of her clothing. Men's fashion, while practical, chafed unbearably, especially when sweat was involved. And right now, she was boiling like a hog farmer on a blistering day. A part of her—a sad, whimsical, minuscule part of her—missed the silks and the satins of her gowns, but those times were behind her. These days, she went by Mr. Raven Hunt, young nob and ne'er-do-well who enjoyed a spot of gambling...especially when finding his amiable, charming self in need of quick, easy coin.

Though said coin at the moment was neither quick nor easy.

She'd lost count of the cards ages ago...because of *him*.

Ravenna gulped, her heart kicking against her ribs, currently restrained beneath a starched band of linen. Despite its functional purpose of keeping her identity as a female hidden, the stiff, restrictive layer made it quite hard to breathe. And at the moment, she needed to capably inhale, exhale, and focus, mostly because of the inscrutable gentleman across the felted table who watched her with hard, piercing eyes.

Mr. Chase. Shipping magnate. Undisputed local sovereign.

Ruthless, cold, powerful.

Her one remaining adversary.

His sinful looks didn't help. Lips, luscious and wicked to a fault, were framed by a square jawline covered in a dusting of dark shadow, and an aquiline nose was drawn between high-bladed cheekbones. A pair of thick slashes for brows sat over an onyx gaze that was so mercurial it was impossible to read. His eyes reminded her of a churning ocean at midnight, lightning flashing over its surface. Those storm-dark eyes were a study in temptation alone—she'd only ever seen such intensity in one person before. She shook off the unwelcome near miss of a memory. It had been a very long time ago, and that boy was dead and gone.

This *man* made parts of her sit up and take notice.

Forget his looks, you twit, and think!

Ravenna shook herself hard, hoping to knock some sense into her own head. What were the odds that he would be at her table, over this pot? As far as she knew, Mr. Chase wasn't known to frequent the exclusive gaming rooms of the Starlight Hotel. On occasion, he'd have dinner at the exclusive restaurant there, a beautiful woman on his arm, but Ravenna had only glimpsed him from a distance.

It would be impossible to live on an island and not know who wielded the most influence here or the man who ran most of the trading ports in the islands. But powerful people made for powerful enemies, and she'd hoped to avoid him and escape his attention.

No such luck, however.

He did not resemble a soft, displaced Englishman in the least. Ravenna narrowed her eyes and fought the urge to yank on her sweltering, suffocating collar. While he didn't seem to be an expert gambler, she could tell he wasn't used to losing. She frowned. Had he *meant* to play poorly early on so she wouldn't suspect him… and then lure her into this final snare? Or was she reading into things?

Blast, her own sharp instincts were failing her.

She peeked at her excellent hand—possibly a winning hand—unless her opponent held a natural of twenty-one. The last round had seen all of the other players overdrawn, except for the dratted Mr. Chase who claimed he was content with his two cards. Ravenna eyed them and ground her jaw in frustration. She was so close. She needed the money for lodgings and food, or even passage back to England. And besides, Mr. Chase didn't need it. He was richer than Midas, or so the rumor mill proclaimed.

A bead of sweat rolled down her skin, beneath the linen drawn mercilessly across her breasts. She wished she'd left an hour ago, her pockets well lined and heavy. But no. Greed, overconfidence, and plain stupidity had taken over.

And she might as well admit it: smitten lady parts.

Not just because Mr. Chase was beyond a shade of a doubt unnervingly gorgeous, but because her shocking attraction to him—to any man—was something she had never, ever experienced. His arrival had thrown her off her game.

Ravenna didn't fancy gentlemen; she didn't fancy *anyone*.

In London, suitor after suitor had been foisted upon her—rich, titled, handsome fellows—and she'd felt nothing. Even when offers had been made, she had found a way to thwart them.

After all, she'd been engaged twice and almost compromised into a third betrothal.

The first had been arranged in her infancy, but that betrothal had been squashed by her father when her future groom had taken off for parts unknown without so much as a by-your-leave. Ravenna didn't know what could possibly have made Cordy do such a thing, but she hadn't dwelled on it. She'd been glad to be rid of the pesky menace!

Over the years, the two of them had been occasional friends but mostly enemies, having childhood adventures between their adjoining country estates in Kettering. He had been obnoxious and arrogant, and he had thrown it in her face that when they were married, she would have to do everything he said. He'd sported a blackened eye for weeks after that declaration.

Much later on after his disappearing act, she'd been saddened to learn from his brother that he'd perished from illness.

Betrothal number two had been a momentary blip in sanity. After her brother Rhystan's love match, Ravenna had felt the first stirrings of indecision. Didn't she *want* a family of her own? She would have to wed…eventually. Perhaps she could attract the ideal sort of gentleman: old, bored, maybe on his deathbed, and willing to let her live her life. Lord Thatcher had ticked all the boxes—widower, older, quiet—and after he'd proposed, she convinced herself she might have been content. But in the end, Ravenna couldn't go through with it.

Her third and final *almost* engagement, though it could hardly even be called that, had caused her to flee London on her brother's ship. Ever since her come-out, the Marquess of Dalwood had been persistent in a way that had made her skin crawl. She'd barely escaped his slimy clutches.

"Are you going to play, lad?" The low, lazy drawl drizzled through her chaotic thoughts like thick, smoky honey.

She peeked up at Mr. Chase through her lashes and grunted a noncommittal response. Drat, he really was stunning...stunning in the way she imagined a fallen angel would be. A sultry, terrible, beautiful angel meant to lure poor innocent souls into doing depraved things. Her skin heated with what could only be a surge of primitive lust. Ravenna opened her mouth, not even sure what was going to come out—a breathy *Take me now* or a much smarter *I withdraw*.

"What's it to be then?" Mr. Chase asked, idly tapping his long, elegant, tanned fingers against his cards in a repeated sequence that made her stare. His little finger tapped followed by the ring finger, then the middle, ending with his index finger. Those hands looked familiar and strange at the same time. Ravenna felt she might be hallucinating. His voice recalled her with a snap. "I haven't got all night."

"A man has to think."

"I could have sailed to England in the time it takes you to think."

The other gentlemen at the table had long since backed out, and now it was down to the two of them. He reminded her of a proud, terrifying dragon sitting atop his treasure, daring anyone to come take it. And here she was...attempting to do just that. "You can forfeit if you're in a hurry," she grumbled.

"Why would I when I have the winning hand?"

"I'm sure you think you do, especially as quite a bit of money is at stake," Ravenna remarked, keeping her naturally husky tones low. A man like him missed nothing, and while her disguise of a young, rich, well-born chap had served to fool many, she had the feeling it would not trick him so easily. She had the advantage as dealer, but if she took one more card, she could easily overdraw and lose. Twenty was solid and she doubted he had a natural. Those two cards under his drumming fingertips taunted her.

Mr. Chase peered at her. "What are you called?"

Hiding her sudden dread, Ravenna sketched a cheerful bow from her seated position, hand tipping the brim of her hat. "Mr. Raven Hunt, at your service. Seventh son to a seventh son seeking his fortune, friendship, and a fine adventure." She cringed. It was a smidge too dramatic, but she held on to her charming grin as though it were a shield.

Eventually, one side of his full lips curled up at the corner into a half smirk. "You're barely wet behind the ears. What's a whelp like you doing here?"

"I'm old enough to seek my own way."

"Is that what you're doing?" She was still contemplating how to respond when he leaned back in his chair. "I make it my business to know everyone who comes onto my island."

"Is that a fact, *Your High-Handedness*?" she shot back.

"Careful, puppy." His lips tugged into a full smile, though it didn't make her feel any better. This one was a downright threat. Ravenna bristled. No one, not even Rhystan, had ever spoken to her with such condescension. Who did he think he was?

A duke's heir, her brain interjected. If local gossip was to be believed anyhow. But the rumor mill on the island was unreliable at best. He had money, certainly—the cut of his clothing revealed that—but Mr. Chase didn't carry himself like elitist British nobility. Notwithstanding the delicious layer of scruff covering that hard jaw, his attitude was relaxed and unconcerned as though he didn't *need* an English title to flaunt his power. No, that came from within…from someone who had earned his place in the world and reveled in it.

Even now, a muscle in his jaw flexed with impatience, a slight tell that there was a good chance he was bluffing and held nothing. Besides, she had three of the aces and the last had already passed. *Hadn't it?* Angry at herself for losing the count in the first place, she considered the odds. There was no way he had a natural. Even if he had twenty, she would still win as ties paid the dealer.

With a grand flourish, Ravenna set down her cards. She shot him a wink. "What do you know, old man, you just got trounced by a pup."

—————

Courtland Chase sat back in his chair.

Old man? The lad had balls, he'd give him that. Word of the boy's winning streak had filtered up to him, mostly from grumbling members. This was his hotel and his club, and he made it his business to know what went on. At first, he thought the boy a cheat, but his skill with the cards was extraordinary. Closer scrutiny revealed that the lad didn't *need* to cheat to win; he simply kept track of the cards that had been dealt. It was bloody genius.

A fascinated Courtland had kept a watchful eye on the young man from afar for a few weeks, the boy's natural baby-faced charm making him a popular addition to aristocratic circles. There was something uncannily familiar about that stubborn jaw—the arrogant tilt of that head—but Courtland couldn't figure out what it was.

The lad was so young he barely had any hair on his pallid chin, but aside from his skill, something about him had rubbed at Courtland. It wasn't anything more than a feeling that something was out of place, but his instincts had never served him wrong. The boy was hiding something. Not that many of the gents here didn't—half of them had run from responsibility or duty in England.

Technically, Courtland himself had been run *off*, but what was in the past was in the past. This was his life now and this was his domain.

Which brought him back to his current predicament.

Disappointment warred with admiration. Skill didn't mean the boy hadn't practiced some clever sleight of hand. Nine cards adding up to twenty was incredibly lucky. Or extremely resourceful. Courtland didn't know how, but the more he thought about it, the more it was likely that the boy had probably cheated. He had to set an example or thieves would run roughshod all over him. *No one* had that kind of luck.

Courtland set his cards down—without disclosing them—and steepled his fingers over his chest. "We don't abide cheaters at the Starlight."

"I'm not a cheater."

Courtland's brows rose in challenge. "Aren't you?"

"No."

"Nine cards and not overdrawing is more than sheer skill."

"Sore loser?" a confident Hunt shot back. "I wouldn't have countenanced it."

Courtland blinked. What an odd choice of phrase. It tickled at his memory. Not that the local toffs didn't speak the Queen's English, but it wasn't as common a saying on the island. It was a pretentious expression, typically wielded by some censorious tongue in a London drawing room. His own stepmother had been fond of it.

A boy like you, better than my Stinson? I couldn't countenance it.

Swallowing hard, he shrugged off the old anger and rush of unworthiness. His mother had been born a free woman of mixed heritage. His father, a duke's spare, had loved and married her and, when she died in childbirth, brought his infant son back to England to be raised in his family home. When Courtland was barely a few months old, his father had remarried—most likely to secure him a replacement mother—but it became apparent by the time he was five that his new stepmother didn't care to raise another woman's child.

Who his own mother had been didn't signify...until it did.

Until Courtland was deemed a *hindrance* to the new marchioness's ambition.

And once his father died, she'd made it her mission to get rid of Courtland. It was obvious she wanted the dukedom for her own son, born shortly after him, though Courtland couldn't imagine how she intended to accomplish that, short of murder. Primogeniture was a devil of a thing.

She resented that he was heir as the firstborn male and despised him for it.

Her son too.

At home, his younger half brother had made life intolerable, and when they were away at Harrow, life had become unbearable. He'd fought and was bloodied every day by his so-called peers, including Stinson, whom Courtland suspected was behind a lot of the hostility and certainly relished his older brother's torture. He'd defended himself. Who wouldn't? Eventually, they'd kicked him out at sixteen, citing rebelliousness and belligerence.

The marchioness—by way of Stinson—had offered him passage anywhere he wanted and enough money to live on and support a small retinue. He was young, but he did not return to London or to the ancestral seat in Kettering. He'd boarded a train to Europe instead. He'd then apprenticed to a Spanish railway industrialist and paid his own way to finish his education at the Central University of Madrid.

Blessed with a keen mind, he invested heavily in shipping and trade, and he eventually migrated to the West Indies to see if he could locate any of his maternal family. When he had arrived, it'd been a shock to his system. A *wonderful* life-changing shock—one he'd sensed in the air he'd breathed into his lungs and felt to the marrow of his bones. *This* was home.

The British gentry had welcomed him with open arms, but they'd always been swayed by pretty faces and prettier fortunes. The islanders had taken longer, but he'd been determined to earn their trust. And he had. Now, Courtland belonged here. He'd built his fortune and reinvested in local infrastructure. The Starlight was his kingdom, and here, he reigned.

This bold, cocksure boy who was testing his patience needed to know his place.

"I never lose," he told the smug Mr. Hunt.

"Everyone loses sometimes," the lad shot back. "Get used to it."

Courtland smirked. "Not me."

"'Pride goeth before destruction, and a haughty spirit before a fall.'"

An unexpected chuckle burst out of him. "Let me guess, you forgot to mention you're the seventh son of a vicar?"

From beneath the wild sprigs of auburn curls poking askew from beneath the boy's hat, sharp eyes the color of polished pennies narrowed on him. They shone with intelligence and suspicion. Good, the brat wasn't foolish. "Something like that. I'll just collect my winnings and be off, then."

Hunt stood and pulled his coat tight, his fingers darting up to the inside of his waistcoat. Courtland noted the garment was well stitched, though the edges along the coat cuffs had seen some wear. It seemed like normal wear and tear for such fabric, but Courtland suddenly felt sure there might be a card hidden in one of those sleeves. "Wait," he commanded in a deadly soft voice.

The young man froze. Courtland could care less about the money, but the principle mattered. His gaze glanced to the crowd standing a few feet away and those seated at the table. If he didn't act and Hunt had indeed cheated, it would encourage others, and that, he could not permit.

He nodded to one of the men behind him and the porter

stepped up to the boy, grabbing him by his arms. Hunt tried to pull away without success. "Unhand me at once, sir!"

"Remove your coat," Courtland ordered.

"What? No!" The boy's coppery eyes rounded with panic. "What kind of establishment is this? I'll have you know I will seek out the owner of the Starlight and have you thrown bodily from this hotel. How dare you, sir? You cannot do this."

"You're in luck, *puppy*. I'm the owner so feel free to state your grievance at any time. Now, remove that coat."

"This is an outrage," the boy insisted, his thin shoulders trembling with indignation.

His mouth opened and closed, a rivulet of sweat trickling from his temple to the hairless apple of his cheek. He was a baby. Courtland wouldn't put him at more than seventeen, if that. The thin brown mustache over his lip seemed out of place on his face, and it also seemed to be traveling of its own accord and curling away at the corner. The more the youth struggled, the more it shifted. Courtland's gaze narrowed on the brown stubble along the lad's sloping downy jaw where sweat mixed in with the chin hairs.

What in the hell? Was that *ink*?

"Remove your coat or Rawley here will do it for you. Or break your arms if you don't cease struggling."

His man of affairs and second cousin, Rawley was a large local with a razor-sharp wit, a quick brain that outmatched many, and enough brawn to deter the most hardened of troublemakers. Courtland had hired him years before, and now, he trusted him with his life.

"No, wait," Hunt pleaded. "Please."

Someone in the crowd jeered. "If you have nothing to hide, take it off."

In the next moment, Rawley yanked the coat off the boy's shoulders, buttons popping. A high-pitched yelp tore from the boy as the plain waistcoat went next, leaving him standing there in a linen shirt, hastily knotted cravat, and trousers. His narrow frame shook, shoulders hunching forward, arms crossed over his middle.

"Please, cease this," he begged in a plaintive whisper. "You don't understand."

Courtland hesitated at the hushed desperation in the boy's voice. It wasn't in him to publicly shame someone this young who might have made a mistake and could learn a valuable lesson, and besides, he liked the boy's spirit. However, before he could order Rawley to take him to his private office, his burly factotum, Fawkes, shoved through the crowd. He was closely followed by a perspiring, balding, well-heeled man.

"What is it, Fawkes?"

"Mr. Chase. An urgent messenger has arrived." The man was fairly bursting with news, and a dribble of unease slid down Courtland's spine. "From London. From—"

"Your Grace," the unknown man said in a loud voice, and every muscle in Courtland's body solidified to stone. "I'm Mr. Bingham, the private solicitor of the late duke, your grandfather, His Grace, the Duke of Ashvale, God rest his soul. As your grandfather's eldest heir, you've now been named duke. However, the will is being contested, claiming you are deceased, though clearly, my own eyes attest that you are not."

Thunder roared in Courtland's ears. This was not bloody happening.

For all intents and purposes, Lord Courtland Chase, the rightful Marquess of Borne and heir to the Ashvale dukedom, *was* dead. But the damage was done. Amid the chatter now soaring to the rooftop, he opened his mouth to say what Bingham could do with the title and the rest of his message, but was thwarted by the young thief who now seemed to have lost half his mustache and was gawking at him with wide, incredulous eyes that burned with an unnaturally disturbing degree of emotion. Not shock

or wonder or even awe like everyone else in the room, but...
recognition.

"Cordy?" the boy whispered.

Courtland hadn't heard that name in well over a decade, but it
was a like a punch to the chest, more powerful, deadly even, than
the wallop about him being duke. No one had ever called him
Cordy...no one except...

His jaw hardened, confusion pouring through him. "Who the
fuck are you?"

Two

RAVENNA FORGOT THAT SHE'D BEEN ACCUSED OF CHEATING and almost stripped down to the altogether in front of a crowd in a popular local hotel and club. Not even the whispers of *Your Grace* and the *Duke of Ashvale* could take away from the fact that her childhood friend and nemesis, her once-upon-a-time betrothed, whom she hadn't seen in eleven years and also thought long dead, was standing in front of her.

Hale, healthy, and cold as a winter ocean.

And so obviously alive.

No wonder he'd seemed so familiar. The last name was common enough, but her brain hadn't connected the mister with the lord. Ravenna blinked her shock away. His family had mourned him. Stinson, Cordy's younger half brother, had been devastated and inconsolable after his death, even taking to burning down the woodland fort she and Cordy had built. Ravenna had let him, guessing it was due to his inconsolable grief. A breath shivered out of her tight lungs. If Cordy was alive and living here all along, why wouldn't he have let his family know?

"Answer me, damn you!" he demanded in a growl. "Where did you hear that name?"

The terse command shook her out of her memories. *Blast it.* If she admitted to knowing him, he might know who *she* was. And well, she wasn't exactly dressed as Lady Ravenna Huntley at the moment. Revealing herself as the daughter of a duke and an unmarried female in the midst of a gaming room full of men would be the pinnacle of stupidity, not that her decisions leading her here hadn't been foolishly reckless. It didn't matter that she wasn't in England; the scandal would be swift and inevitable. She had to deflect somehow, at least until she could run.

Piercing dark eyes held her prisoner, but Rawley, the enormous and handsome man with deep brown skin who had several stone of muscle on her, had released her arms. This was it! Her moment to escape. Her nemesis must have seen what she meant to do in the sudden tension of her body because he snarled a denial and lunged across the table for her.

For once, her small stature helped as she snatched up her fallen coat—it had her winnings in it, after all—and shoved through the dense crowd. She could hear a predator's frustrated roar, and even as she reveled in her almost victory, a part of her quailed at the savage sound.

Luck was finally back on her side. She let out a soft whoop. Thankfully, everyone in attendance wanted to congratulate the new duke, which gave her plenty of opportunity to slip away. She'd lost her hat and she was certain half her face paint was now a sweaty mess. Oh, well, it was about time for the fantastic Mr. Hunt to abscond to another island anyway. She'd danced with the devil, nearly gotten caught, and the near discovery of her identity had tested her every nerve.

Lengthening her strides toward the exit without breaking into a sprint that would draw attention, Ravenna could taste the sweet, fresh tropical air on her tongue, just beyond the wide paneled doors of the hotel. It was a far cry from the smog and foul scents of London, and one she'd grown to love.

"Not so fast, you slippery little scamp," a gravelly voice seethed into her ear, a huge hand encircling her upper arm in an unbreakable grip. Ravenna gasped, though it wasn't pain that forced the air from her lungs.

Horrifyingly, the rush of hot breath against her skin and the sultry tenor of his words sent heat flooding through her body and her knees went rubbery.

What on earth was wrong with her? He was going to strangle her, and she was falling to pieces. Her breath was short, her stomach was weak, and her heart was racing like a horse on the last leg of a race. This wasn't a swoon, was it? She'd never swooned a day in her life!

A powerful frame steered her into a receiving room off the foyer and manhandled her into a chair. The salon wasn't empty, but Ravenna had much worse to worry about, like the incensed male looming over her whose face could be carved from granite. His mouth, which she'd thought so full and supple before, was a flat, furious line. His stormy eyes had gone full tempest now.

She couldn't believe that *this* man was Cordy. It was unfathomable! For one, he was huge. Cordy had been scrawny with nary a muscle in sight. Built like a Roman gladiator, this man looked nothing like the rangy boy he'd been. His complexion was a much richer hue now, after being exposed to the hot sun of the islands, and his face…his face was even more dangerously beautiful up close. Ravenna had the sudden, inexplicable urge to run her hands over him.

A muscle flexed in that lean, stubble-dusted cheek, his intense gaze not veering once from her. "I'll ask you once, brat, who are you?" The ruthless snap of his voice raked across her mind, reminding her that his good looks weren't the problem. The fact that he was going to toss her into jail was. She had to get out of this mess somehow! "Speak or I'll make you regret disobeying me."

This was *not* good.

"I was a friend…of Lord Richard in Kettering," she blurted out, fear of discovery making her quiver.

Was that too close to the truth? Richard was her second oldest brother who died years ago in a fire along with her father and eldest brother. *Blast*! Richard had been a bit of a loner, preferring his books to actual people. Mr. Chase—*no, the Duke of Ashvale*—would see right through her falsehood and ferret out her identity in an instant.

"Richard Huntley?" he said. His dark gaze scoured her, fingers still clamped over her arms, though not cruelly. Ravenna forced herself not to fidget or break eye contact. She needed him to believe her.

"I saw you once at Embry Hall," she rushed out, panic overtaking her explanation. "His sister called you 'Cordy' and he said you were the duke's grandson."

Her body quivered when his eyes narrowed. Why on earth had she brought up a sister? Ravenna almost swore aloud and clamped her mouth shut, well aware of the obvious relation between her fake male name and her real one. It wasn't much of a stretch to connect Raven and Ravenna. Deuce it, how could she have been so stupid? The real question was: Would *he* notice? The Cordy she'd known might have been lacking in muscle as a boy, but he'd never lacked for acuity. She doubted that would have changed as an adult.

"Sir," a harried-looking man with his hair askew, who Ravenna gratefully recognized as the factotum, burst through the door and interrupted them. "It's madness in there. Bingham is waiting."

Rawley, following on his heels, entered the room with a nod. "I'm afraid you can't hide much longer, Cousin. The gossip is like a bushfire…already rampant and impossible to contain." His gaze came to rest on Ravenna. She peered back, not hiding her surprise that the two men were related. "What will we do with this one?"

The man who clearly did not want to be duke ran a palm over his face and nodded to his factotum. "Fawkes, escort Bingham to the library adjoining the office first. I'll be along shortly." He then turned brutally cold eyes on her. "It doesn't matter who you are or how you know me. Cheaters are a disgrace, and the piper must be paid. I have to make an example of you, young buck, and I reckon you'd much rather a harmless night in the stalls than the loss of a finger."

"Take it," Ravenna blurted out, though her body trembled

almost violently. A paltry finger was much less of a price to pay than being unmasked as a lady of quality or being thrown into a filthy jail.

"You jest," he said with a long-suffering look.

"I do not. Take. My. Finger."

"No."

"Then let me go. You cannot accuse me of thievery without proof." In response, Ashvale skimmed up her forearms as if attempting to feel beneath her sleeves for evidence. "I didn't cheat, *Your Grace*."

She spat the title with a mouthful of mockery, enjoying the tightening of his face and the ashen cast to his sun-kissed skin. A part of her wondered why he was so against being duke. It was his birthright, and one of privilege and power. No gentleman of sound mind would refuse a coronet, and yet, he seemed to loathe the very idea.

"I don't require proof. I'm judge, jury, and executioner here." He released her arm and handed her over to his man who had returned. "Rawley."

"No, wait, please," she said in alarm, her fingers catching on his coat. "You can't. I can't go there. Anything else. I'll do whatever you want me to here in the club, scrub pots and clean carpets, not the jail."

"It won't kill you, boy," Rawley muttered. "It's a damn sight better than losing a body part."

Ravenna ground her jaw. If he only knew that she was in danger of losing much more than that should her secret be discovered by a bunch of criminals who wouldn't care that she was nobility. Or female. She suppressed a shudder. "I'm begging you. Please."

When the duke made to leave, Ravenna panicked, yanking her arm from Rawley and heaving herself between him and the door. Hushed gasps from their avid onlookers reached her ears, but she had no choice. She would not survive a single hour in the local jail.

Her reputation might turn to tatters, but she wasn't about to give up the last of her dignity.

"Grow a pair of ballocks, Hunt," the newly minted duke growled.

Her voice lowered. "I can't." She peered up at him, though she kept her chin tilted down. There was still a chance she could salvage everything by not giving away *exactly* who she was, at least in public. "I'm female."

The whispered confession seemed to stump him for a second, but then his face hardened. "Being female doesn't win you leniency."

Gracious, he truly was without a heart, but enough was enough. Ravenna drew up her shoulders, channeled her mother's hauteur that had been drilled into her since birth, and met his burning gaze. "You are making a grave mistake, Your Grace," she told him with clipped diction that left no doubt that she was female and of unquestionable high birth. "Either release me at once, or you will not like the consequences, I assure you."

A menacing growl ripped from his throat. "Don't threaten me."

She'd never met such an autocratic man in all her life. One would imagine he was made of fire and brimstone with a clockwork heart beating in his chest. A chill settled over her—this was it, the point of no return. She should have known her freedom or anonymity wasn't going to last. She had one last hope.

"Then in that case, I doubt the Duke of Embry would appreciate you sending his precious sister to jail, regardless of any error in judgment on your part."

"Embry's *sister*?" he echoed, dark eyes glinting.

He studied her, his face giving away nothing as the chatter in the salon around them grew, the whispers of her identity a delicious on-dit. Scandal tended to have its own decibel level, after all. Ravenna breathed out. "What a delightful surprise to see you alive and well, Cordy."

The little hoyden from the neighboring estate in Kettering had grown up into a spitfire. Wearing men's clothing and cheating at cards in *his* hotel. What were the odds?

Lady Ravenna Huntley.

Courtland didn't doubt she was who she claimed to be. When he'd thought her a young gent, something about her face and swagger had struck a vague chord of recognition in him, and when she'd brought up Richard Huntley, it had clicked. He'd assumed her to be a distant relation or some such. But now, as he took in her heart-shaped face, blazing eyes, and that stubborn jaw, he saw distinct signs of the girl he once knew.

Though she wasn't a girl anymore—she was grown.

In spite of her clever disguise, that much was obvious. His lip curled in irritation. What the devil had she been *thinking*?

As if she could sense his thoughts, her chin lifted and she met his gaze with defiance.

"Does Embry know you're here?" he demanded.

"What do you think?" Her tongue was as cutting as he remembered.

"I think he should put you over his knee."

She rolled her eyes. "My brother is not a barbarian."

"Then perhaps the task should fall to me."

A furious copper gaze slammed into his. "Touch me and you will be the one missing a finger, I promise you. I've learned a few things since we were children."

His brow dipped. He didn't doubt that, considering she was *here*, and not tucked away in a ducal residence somewhere in England, being waited on hand and foot like the gently reared lady she was. What the hell was she doing here? And come to think of it, did she have a lick of sense left in that idiot head of hers? She had just announced her identity in a public drawing room while scandalously dressed in men's clothing. And yes, it was a far step away from London, but oceans didn't stop gossip.

Swearing under his breath, he shrugged out of his own coat, draped it over her shoulders, and shepherded her from the room to his personal offices, which he should have done from the start. Then his own ill-timed ducal news as well as her revelation would have occurred behind private, closed doors. Too late for any of that.

Bloody hell.

"Drink?" he asked her.

"No, thank you."

In silence, he poured two fingers of imported French brandy into a tumbler and took a healthy sip. Coppery irises of the same changing hues as the brandy met his. Had her eyes always been that color? He'd remembered them being brown. Her shorn hair was a surprise, the close-cropped curls lying flat beneath the copious pomade. As a girl, her long hair had been braided tight to her scalp and gingery-red—to the point where her brothers had called her *gingersnap* mercilessly—and not such a dark auburn.

It was no wonder he hadn't recognized her outright, though some instinct deep within him had sensed…*something.*

"Why?" he asked.

"Why what?"

Thick russet lashes lifted and he questioned how he'd ever thought she was male. Even with smudges of dark ink on her chin and cheeks, she was comely. *Too* much so. Courtland shrugged. The now defunct mustache, obviously fake, had been a damned convincing touch.

But now, he couldn't stop thinking of her as a woman—scrutinizing each of her features—including those copper-bright eyes and the wide, rosy pout that he *hadn't* noticed before. The meddlesome, nosy little Lady Ravenna had grown up to be a beauty, one whom gentlemanly suitors in London drawing rooms would have been fawning over.

Speaking of, why wasn't she married? *Was* she married? He was only two years older than she was, so she should be three-and-twenty or thereabouts. Long past marrying age.

"Why are you here?" he asked, enunciating each word.

"My grand tour?" she replied. "A pleasure trip?"

He couldn't help noticing that the huskiness in her voice stayed that way. Put together with the fact that she was an adult woman, the raspy just-waking-up-after-hours-and-hours-of-sex sound of it shaping the word *pleasure* arrowed straight to his groin. Scowling at the reaction, he moved behind his desk. "Ladies don't do grand tours."

"Hence my ingenious disguise," she said. "At least until today."

"You would have been found out eventually. Be glad it was by me and not someone else." He cringed to think that he'd nearly sent her to a public jail. "So I take it Embry doesn't know you're here then?"

Courtland wasn't close with the duke though they were close in age. The sons of the Duke of Embry had all gone to Eton when he'd been fighting for his life at Harrow. Even in Antigua, however, he'd learned about the tragic fire that had made the youngest Huntley duke, and then the news had come about said duke's nuptials with an Anglo-Indian princess.

Good for them, he remembered thinking.

If only the marchioness and his own brother had been that accepting, the path his life had taken might have been vastly different, though the final destination had turned out to be inevitable. While his grandfather had written steadily over the years, always knowing exactly where he was—first in Spain, and then Antigua—they hadn't cared.

Courtland had received all of the late duke's letters but had refused to read them. He'd instructed Rawley to dispose of them. If he was being summoned to Ashvale Park, he didn't want to know. He had no intention of going back to England.

Without Courtland's presence, his ambitious stepbrother would no doubt have led a charge to prove he was the Duke of

Ashvale's true heir. Courtland wondered idly if his stepmother had tried to have him declared dead through the courts. He also wondered what his grandfather might have had to say about that or if he even knew of their plans.

Scowling as fresh feelings of bitterness rose, Courtland stalked forward to refill his glass, lifting a brow and waiting for her answer. Her brother would never have condoned this, that much he knew. He glowered at his mutinous quarry who had yet to reply.

"Stop trying to think your way out of this and answer me—what does Embry believe?"

"He thinks I'm in Scotland with Clara."

"Clara?"

"A recently married dear friend. She wed a Scottish earl."

Courtland frowned. "How is Embry not worried?"

"I wrote several letters in advance, which she will mail out at monthly intervals, and swore Clara to secrecy as long as I was in good health." She gestured to herself. "Which as you can see I am. No need to trouble my brother."

"And this Clara considers you a friend?" He didn't hide his sardonic tone.

Her eyes narrowed on him. "The best kind."

"Forgive me if I've been out of London society too long, but friends don't force friends to lie on their behalf. Much less lie to a respected and rather formidable peer of the realm."

Turning pink, Ravenna tossed her head. "What Embry doesn't know won't hurt him, and besides, he's just had a new baby and deserves every joy. If he knew where I was, he'd be frantic with worry instead of focusing on his own happiness."

"For good reason, you daft girl!"

"Because I'm female?" she shot back. "Why should men have all the adventure and women be forced to sit at home tending the hearth? We are *not* possessions or brainless biddable toys designed for male consumption."

He almost choked on his drink at the images her provocative words produced, but the hostility beneath was clear. "Because it's not safe or smart for a woman to be traveling on her own."

"I know how to use a pistol, Cordy," she said. "I was a better shot than you, remember? Or perhaps you choose not to remember how many times I bested you just to preserve your insufferably delicate male pride."

He didn't remember her being this…caustic. Silent laughter rippled through him. Who was he fooling? She'd always been a hothead.

"We were children then," he said. "And my name is Courtland, not Cordy."

"Apparently, it's *Ashvale* now," she reminded him.

The sound of the ducal title set his teeth on edge. He was going to have to deal with that complication as soon as possible, too. "How did you get here anyway?"

"I took one of Embry's clippers." She lifted an ungloved hand to sift through the pressed strands of her shorn mane. "Hacked off my hair and disguised myself as a boatswain. Learned a lot over the last few years from my brother and his old quartermaster so it was easy. Kept my head down, did the work, and no one was the wiser."

Courtland balked in horror—she'd spent close to five weeks on a ship full of male sailors? His hands fisted at his sides at her foolhardy actions. "Why not an ocean liner?"

"Too easily tracked. I didn't need luxury, I needed to disappear."

"Why?"

Her lip curled. "None of your deuced business."

"If you were mine, I'd definitely put you over my knee." Courtland regretted the words as soon as he said them. The thought of her lying across his lap, her pert bottom bared to his gaze, was not something he wanted to envision, not while she already had him clinging to his temper by a thread. She busied herself with her gloves, but he could see more color flare into her pale cheeks.

"Good thing I'm not then."

Not yet. Courtland had no idea where that thought came from, nor did he want to know. He had no time for a smart-mouthed, self-centered heiress who knew no better than to traipse willy-nilly around the world with no regard for her own welfare. When he thought of the misfortunes that could have befallen her, his anger surged again. "You got lucky, you know. How could you have been so foolish? Things could have been so much worse."

"But they weren't."

He was going to throttle her. "They *could* have been."

"Let's agree to disagree. Are you going to send word to Embry?"

Controlling his irritation, Courtland shook his head. "I won't have to."

He heard her sharp exhale. They both knew what his answer meant. Lady Ravenna would be disgraced just from being in the West Indies on her own without a chaperone. If word got out about her travels on a ship with a bunch of rough-and-tumble sailors, her reputation would take an unrecoverable thrashing.

But that was none of his business. Her virtue, or lack of it, wasn't anyone's concern, but he more than anybody knew the exacting nature of the *ton*'s rules. Upon her return, they would shred her to ribbons. Any hope for a suitable match would be lost. Courtland felt an expected stroke of pity for what she would face, even if she'd brought the storm upon herself.

They fell into tense silence.

"What would it take for you to forget you ever saw me?" she asked after a while.

Courtland blinked—she couldn't possibly be asking what he thought she was. "I couldn't in good conscience do that."

"Yet you were willing to throw me in jail an hour ago."

"You weren't *you*!" He glared at her.

She cleared her throat. "Look, I'm serious. You know what awaits me if I'm sent back to London in disgrace. What will it take? Money? You are welcome to whatever I have. My body? Though I don't know what good it'll do—it's as frigid as they come, or so I've been told."

He ignored the bolt of pure lust at her wicked offer, even as her face flamed. "I'll protect you."

"How? Trust me, you can't."

"Bloody hell, woman, I will not let you go off on your own." He pinched the bridge of his nose, closed his eyes, and sighed. "Embry would pulverize my bones to meal and my father would turn in his grave if he knew I abandoned an innocent girl to her own foolish devices."

"I'm not innocent or foolish."

"Your actions prove otherwise," he said.

"Then I'm sorry for this."

A noise that sounded uncannily like a cocking gun made his eyelids snap open. He was right—a loaded pocket pistol was pointed right at his face.

Three

Courtland didn't question her skill with the weapon—he knew it firsthand. And the truth was though he'd known the girl, he didn't know this brazen woman who'd lived the life of a man for the past six months or who held the pistol with such unwavering confidence. By age eleven, she'd already been a crack shot. "Are you going to shoot me, Ravenna?"

At the sound of her given name, her fingers flexed on the handle but her eyes hardened. "I will if I have to." A loud knock banged on the outer door to the office. "Or whoever comes through that door. Get rid of them."

"Your Grace?" Rawley called out, making Courtland wince. He was sure his cousin was delighted to take the piss with the title. "Bingham won't leave without seeing you."

"Not a good time, Rawls."

There was silence. Perhaps, he'd get the message. Perhaps not. Courtland wasn't a man given to nicknames. "Very well, I'll try again later," Rawley said.

Rounding the desk to where he stood, Ravenna waved the pistol and set her eyes on the safe resting behind it. "Open that up and put the contents in that satchel."

"Stealing is as bad as cheating, you know." Squatting down, he obeyed her demands. She was close enough that he could probably tackle her and wrestle the gun away, but if the weapon discharged, she could get shot. He wasn't willing to take that chance, no matter how much fury filled his blood.

"I've never cheated, and at this point, it's survival." Her voice sounded resigned. "It's my mess, and I have to clean it up. I always knew it would come to this. I'll pay you back someday, I promise."

Huffing a breath, he stared up at her, the sack full of banknotes in hand. "It's not a crime to ask for help, you know."

Her smile was small. "How can you help me? You pretended to be dead to your own family for eleven years, hiding out here in Antigua of all places. And now that you're a duke, you don't even seem to want the title." She blew out a sigh and reached for the bag. "It doesn't matter. Honestly, I don't think even an army of dukes could help me right now." A dark laugh slipped from her lips. "I can see the headlines now: Lady Ravenna Huntley, plowed by a shipload of sailors, all hail the Hussy Heiress."

"It has a certain ring to it."

"Not funny, *Ashvale*." She backed away toward the door, the pistol trained on him. "Grant me this one answer then for old times' sake. Why don't you want to go back to England? You're a duke now. You'll be celebrated."

For the first time in his life, he didn't shy away from the question though his gut churned with the usual ugly combination of shame and rage. He rose slowly and inched round the desk, propping his hips on it. "Who'd celebrate me as duke? Not my brother." He lifted a hand. "I am of mixed blood. One single drop corrupts the whole, or so the dogmatists say."

Confusion crossed her face. "I don't understand."

"My mother was a mixed-race woman. Granddaughter of a French silk merchant and his *placée*. She was a free Creole."

"So?"

Surely she couldn't be this obtuse. "So *I'm* not a blue blood."

"I realize that you are of mixed origins," she said slowly. "But you still bleed scarlet like the rest of us."

"I'm glad *you* think so," he said, not disguising his sarcasm.

Flushing, she paused as if considering her reply. "Clearly, I'm not one to judge or offer sage advice. I can't claim to know what you've been through, but I saw my sister-in-law stand up to a ballroom full of bigots, and I witnessed my brother fall madly, hopelessly, irreversibly in love. And she's of mixed heritage." She exhaled a breath. "Eventually, you'll have to go back to England and be the duke. I hope you do it on your terms, Courtland, not because someone with a dried-up excuse for a brain told you that you weren't good enough or you didn't deserve it."

In an ideal world, perhaps such a thing would be possible, but this was reality, and his reality included a stepmother who wished him gone and a younger brother who would prefer he had never been born. Courtland didn't want to ponder the soft earnestness behind Ravenna's words, not right then as she moved away from him toward the door. At best, she might make it through the hotel, but would be stopped by his men. At worst, Rawley would be waiting to eliminate the threat. "Lady Ravenna, please stop before you get hurt."

She'd nearly reached the door. "Have a nice life. Don't look for me." She smiled at him. "And for posterity, I've always loved the color of your skin, even when we were children. Me, the color of paste, and you, so beautifully golden-brown as if you were lit from the inside with pure sunlight."

The sweetness of the sentiment moved him, but Courtland couldn't savor it. He would later, if they got through the next few seconds. She twisted to turn the doorknob, her attention slipping from him for one heartbeat, and he dove, launching himself across the room. His attention was on the pistol in her hand and making sure neither of them accidentally got shot if Rawley did come through that door as Courtland suspected he would.

Sure enough, the door shoved open at the same time that she unlocked it, the force propelling her body in his direction as his cousin attempted to barrel his way inside. By pure luck, Courtland managed to shield her with his frame and knock the gun upward in the moments it took for the two of them to tumble onto the plush Persian carpet.

The pistol discharged into the wall with a boom, making his ears ring. The scent of spent gunpowder singed his nostrils as he wrestled the weapon out of her grip when they collided with the floor. He absorbed most of the impact, the breath whooshing from his body, and he grunted, but he didn't release his hold on her even as they rolled to an ungainly halt in a lewd tangle of limbs.

Chest to chest, hip to hip, her heart galloping wildly against his, they'd landed in an obscene heap, his thighs wedged indecently between her trouser-clad legs, his body sprawled over hers in mimicry of an act he was beginning to crave with every rapid beat of his pulse. All of Courtland's hard edges cradled into her softer curves…perfectly as if they'd been crafted for each other. In that moment as he collected his absent breath, even though she'd very nearly put a bullet in him, all he wanted to do was kiss her.

The fall had damaged his brain, clearly.

A breathless moan breached those tempting, parted lips, the sultry sound daggering through him. It wasn't a sound of pain, but one of unguarded pleasure, and all of his marauding senses distilled to one thing—*her*.

Courtland was already at half-mast; now his lower body leaped to painful, rock-hard attention. She felt him. He could see it in her widened pupils and hear it in the tiny hitch in her breathing. Heated copper eyes peered up into his, and a pink tongue darted out to swipe at her plump lower lip. That hot gaze slid to his mouth. Did she *want* him to kiss her? Her hips shifted infinitesimally as if in silent answer. He narrowed the distance, hovering over her mouth and leaving the last millimeter up to her.

Hell, he'd die if she didn't want it as much as he did.

But the daring hoyden didn't hesitate, her lips surging to meet his.

The feel of her was sublime, the demanding pressure nearly making his eyes roll back in his head as she fused their lips together. She smelled of lemon balm, but beneath the citrus, he detected the slightest hint of plumeria. Courtland breathed in, curving his arm up behind her shoulder to cup her nape, parting his lips and coaxing her to do the same with an urgent flick of his tongue. Moaning into his mouth, Ravenna opened instantly for him.

Not wasting a single second, his tongue delved in and found hers, seeking her warm, pliant depths, another sound of pleasure escaping her. A hint of wine from earlier at the tables clung to her lips and tongue, but beyond that was a taste all hers. Like dessert and decadence. Honey with a hint of hot island peppers. *Intoxicating.*

Craving more, he thirsted for every silky inch of her skin. Dragging his lips away, he dropped heated kisses down her jawline to the poorly tied cravat that hid the length of her elegant neck. Her pulse fluttered madly, echoing the equally frantic thud of his.

"May I?" he muttered insensibly, fingers hooking into the knot.

She sighed *yes*, eyes dilated with need, and he wasted no time in removing the offending fabric gathered at her throat. He'd barely tugged it off before his lips descended again in nips and brushes and desperate licks against her fragrant skin. His busy fingers anticipated his wants and moved to the opening of her shirt. Courtland was a hairsbreadth away from ripping the damned thing in half when the clearing of a throat halted him midmotion.

Ravenna froze beneath him, and they wrenched apart to stare at the gaping door, where half the hotel stood, including a grinning Rawley and one red-faced, utterly aghast Mr. Bingham.

"There's no hope for it. They'll have to marry at once."

The solicitor's solemn proclamation broke the spell that was holding her body in place, pinned like a rag doll beneath the Duke of Ashvale's very muscled, very hard bulk. Ravenna could feel every last inch of him, including the straining ones pressing lewdly—*deliciously*—between her thighs.

Despite being untouched, Ravenna wasn't *that* innocent. A girl didn't pretend to be a man and live on a ship without hearing about more than a few filthy things. But for the first time in her life, she wanted to experience all the erotic stories she'd overheard. Why had no one told her what kissing a man could feel like? That a tongue could be so sleek and persuasive? That teeth could scrape and nibble and tease into a frenzy. That the world could end and she wouldn't even notice.

She'd felt that kiss in her breasts, in her belly, and between her legs…taking over her every nerve like a tidal surge. Suddenly, she wanted him to kiss her again, their uninvited audience be damned.

Deuce it, there was an *audience*!

Her cheeks flamed anew.

"Get off me," she muttered, shoving fruitlessly at the duke's hard chest, but attempting to move him was like trying to move a boulder. Mortification spread like a tide through her body at the sight of the somber solicitor. The late duke's man of business, and from his appalled expression, a very proper, stick-in-the-mud, all-for-propriety-and-blue-blooded-decorum Englishman. Blast her dratted luck.

"I won't marry him," she blurted out, finally wiggling away and scrambling to her feet.

"I don't intend to wed," Courtland said at the same time, rising and moving to his desk.

Good, then the matter was settled.

Mr. Bingham stepped into the room, nodding to one of the prune-faced ladies at his back to accompany him. He closed the door to the office behind them. Ravenna blinked. The woman was older and clearly nobility, given her gown and stance. It was obvious Bingham intended for her to be a chaperone, though Ravenna didn't know what dregs of modesty she'd be expected to protect. The ruined cat was well and truly out of the bag.

A resigned expression passed over Courtland's face, a

suffocated noise leaving his lips as if he was realizing the same. "Lady Holding," he greeted. "Good to see you."

Ravenna's heart sank. Good Lord, could her luck get any *worse*? Lady Holding was a denizen of local society. In addition, she was a passing acquaintance of her mother's from when they were in finishing school and they still kept in touch. It was the reason Ravenna had chosen Antigua in the first place. She had read her mother's correspondence with Lady Holding and the island had felt familiar. Any remaining dregs of hope she'd had to get out of this unscathed died a sad, swift death.

"Not so nice on your end, I'd wager, Your Grace," Lady Holding replied with a toss of her well-coiffed head. "The tongues will be wagging after today."

Her eyes moved to Ravenna, who met the lady's stare evenly, though the weight of judgment made her skin prickle and itch. "I've heard a lot about you, Lady Ravenna, and your wild, unseemly exploits, so much so that your poor mother has despaired of ever finding a proper match for you."

"I'm not ready for marriage," she said calmly. "Embry knows this."

"Then the fault lies with your brother, the duke, for not taking you firmly in hand."

Ravenna almost snorted. The day when any man felt he could take her *in hand* would be the day that hell became a wintry wonderland. The irony wasn't lost on her that Rhystan's wife was also an unrepentant hellion who did not live by any man's rules, least of all her brother's. Ravenna nearly giggled at the long-suffering expression on Courtland's face, a look she recognized. He'd thought her unchecked and *out of hand* for years.

"Your mama writes that Dalwood approached Embry with an offer for you," Lady Holding went on.

A wave of pure disgust buried Ravenna's amusement. "Dalwood is a revolting pig I wouldn't let near my worst enemy."

Lady Holding huffed, face going purple. "Well, I never. The marquess is well connected and an acceptable match for a girl of your station." She peered down the length of her hooked nose at her. "Though at this point, you'd be lucky to receive any offer from anyone worth his salt, and the fortune-hunting scoundrels will come out in droves." She tossed her head and stared down her long nose at the solicitor. "Mr. Bingham, I cannot help the chit if she refuses to be helped."

"Lady Holding, with all due respect, I would rather marry a disease-ridden, money-loving cur than that man," Ravenna bit through her teeth.

The incensed lady started to reply, but Courtland lifted a palm with narrowed eyes. "Did he say or do something untoward?"

"Planning to defend my honor, Your Grace?" Ravenna asked.

"Stop it. Answer the question."

Ravenna's jaw clenched. Fine. He wanted to know? Then she'd tell him. She'd tell all of them. "Said *and* did. Lord Dalwood's singular obsession led him to corner me in a locked room at a banquet. It was only by a miracle that I managed to escape unscathed and in possession of my cherished virtue." Even as Lady Holding gasped with outrage at her plain-speaking, Ravenna saw Courtland's eyes go wide in understanding and then darken with fury, a muscle beating wildly in his cheek. "Don't worry, I left a mark on him that he won't soon forget," she added with a shark's grin. "Right in his cursed, tiny ballocks."

Dalwood had gone down like a sorry sack of shit. Her sister-in-law, Sarani, had imparted that valuable instruction: a knee was always best, but when severely limited by skirts and petticoats, a swinging fist released with as much force as possible could do as much damage to those tender parts. But with the manhandling marquess, Ravenna had gone one step further, not that she'd admit to exactly *what* she'd done. Suffice it to say that Dalwood got what he deserved.

"Well, I *never*!" Lady Holding screeched. "Such lies. You are a disgr—"

A low growl erupted from the man beside her. "Not another word, Lady Holding, or you will find yourself removed from my presence."

Heart hammering, Ravenna wanted to stare at him, but she kept her gaze averted. She'd anticipated no one would credit her for speaking the truth, but Courtland's rebuke sounded like the opposite. Unexpected warmth slid through her veins. He *believed* her.

Mr. Bingham gave a discreet cough into the tense silence. "Let me be clear here, Duke and ladies, and state the obvious. You were witnessed on the floor in an extremely compromising embrace. Lady Ravenna, you are the daughter of a duke and sister to one, and are yet unmarried. As such, the damage to your reputation will be unsalvageable." He took a measured breath, letting the impact sink in. "Your Grace, it is your duty as a gentleman to make reparations. In the most placid way I can say it, you have compromised the young lady."

"No, he categorically did not—" Ravenna began.

"He's right," Courtland interrupted. "We might not be in England, but the rules of society and civility still apply."

"Well, I disagree," she fumed, all earlier warm thoughts of him slipping away. She glared at Bingham. "I kissed him as well. If anything, *I* compromised him, yet you don't see me flinging marital platitudes at his head. We were both at fault and now we can each go our own separate ways like reasonable adults."

But they were angry and utterly useless words. A gentleman of honor—even one with scruples as skewed as the hard-nosed Courtland Chase—would never let a lady face the consequences of ruination alone. She saw it written all over him…the silent and martyred acceptance of his fate. Of *her* fate.

Devil take him.

Wasn't he rumored to be hard-hearted and cold-blooded?

"I won't," she said again, louder this time.

He lifted a brow. "Such protestations. Afraid you'll fall head over heels in love with me?"

"As if that would ever happen, you arrogant clod. I don't enjoy being entrapped."

"Imagine how I feel."

Bingham cleared his throat again, and they both stared at him, she in impotent wrath, Courtland with amused restraint. "Even with a marriage to a man well respected in local society here, the gossip will not be curbed. Lady Ravenna will still be spurned."

"I don't care about any of those blockheads in the *ton*!" she bit out.

Lady Holding sniffed. "You mightn't, but what about your mother, the dowager duchess? What about Lord Ashvale's younger stepsisters, the elder only months away from making a suitable match herself? Your actions have much broader consequences than you can imagine, you selfish girl."

Helpless tears stung at Ravenna's eyes, even as her lips tingled at the memory of their kisses. She should never have entered this stupid club! She should never have played cards with him. None of this would have happened.

"Why couldn't you just have let me go?" she whispered.

Courtland's jaw clenched at the accusation in her tone, but he addressed his words to his late father's solicitor, no amusement in his tone now. "I gather that a duke will have greater success than a mere mister at silencing the chinwaggers and the tide of gossip."

Bingham nodded gravely. "I fear it is so."

"Then, fine, a ducal wedding, it is," he said with a martyred sigh that made Ravenna want to scream. Because there was nothing she could do besides watch the trap of wedlock snap taut.

Not a deuced thing.

A grand wedding was the least of Courtland's problems. At the top of the list were his family and the storm he knew would be coming from his stepmother and Stinson in particular. After all, he was well aware that Stinson had been falsely pretending to be the Marquess of Borne for a number of years, while everyone— except their grandfather—presumed the elder brother dead. Even in his bedridden illness, the late duke had kept regular tabs on Courtland's life.

The steady arrival of the letters had been baffling. Why write? Why keep track of his grandson's whereabouts? Why the *interest*? Courtland had been gone for eleven years. Surely Stinson would have done his due diligence to secure his position as their grandfather's heir. Make it legal and binding. His brother would have stepped up to the role in a heartbeat. Hell, he'd already adopted the title of marquess.

Even from a young age, his half brother had sought to discredit or beat him at everything. If Courtland did well in lessons, Stinson would insist that he had cheated. If Courtland won an archery tournament, Stinson would demand lessons from a private instructor. Courtland's stepmother had always indulged her precious son. The only time Stinson hadn't dogged his footsteps was when Courtland had left England.

Jerking at his collar, Courtland barked a dry laugh. Engaging in a public war with his family by returning to London to claim his ducal birthright wasn't something he wished to do. Because now the venom-filled Marchioness of Borne and her rotten son would crawl back into his life…all because of one willful chit he hadn't been able to resist. If he could turn back time and do as Ravenna had asked—let her walk out of the Starlight—he would have done so in a heartbeat.

None of this was ideal.

Hissing softly, Courtland raked his palm through his hair. The little brat had always been more trouble than she was worth.

Cordy, let's climb this tree. He'd broken his wrist from the fall.

Cordy, I dare you to steal the pudding from supper. He'd been thoroughly caned.

Cordy, kiss me. And now, wedlock.

To be fair, she hadn't asked him to kiss her, but she might as well have. The touch of her lips beneath his had been explosive. In a handful of breathless seconds, he'd wanted her more than he'd ever wanted any woman. In the heat of the moment, he'd have given up every penny of his fortune just to finish what they'd started.

Courtland scowled. No woman in his life had ever been able to get to his marrow and burrow under his skin the way she had...the way Ravenna *always* had. His scowl deepened.

Like an aggravating, flesh-mongering beetle.

As if summoned by some divine or darker force, the door to the chapel opened and there she was: Lady Ravenna Huntley in the flesh. Nothing at all like a beetle, of course. In fitted men's clothing, Ravenna had teased his senses, but in a frothy, feminine wedding gown, she struck him senseless. The dress clung to her in filmy ivory layers, fitting snugly to her breasts—now that he could see them—and cinching down to a narrow waist before flaring out in pearl-trimmed, embroidered panels to the hem.

Courtland's stunned gaze drifted back up. A cap of glossy auburn curls, pinned away from her brow by a pearl-encrusted tiara, framed a face of such unexpected beauty that he couldn't stop gaping. His bride looked like a magical creature from some other realm.

But the closer she stepped, the mirage of a beautiful, happy bride fell away. Huge eyes of burnished copper sparked with vexation, and her naturally plump lips were flattened to translucency. Gloved fingers strangled the bouquet of local lilies and hibiscus gathered between her palms. Perhaps she imagined it was his neck.

She doesn't want this.

Well, neither did he.

Regardless of what he had to do now for honor's sake, keeping his distance would be necessary, lest he let his guard down and have his heart skewered. This was to be a marriage of convenience, a marriage in name only for his bride's sake and his sisters' sakes. But for him to prevail, it had to be a marriage of *less* than convenience.

And if Ravenna wanted the future she desired, it had to be a marriage of abstinence.

Four

THE CEREMONY HAD BEEN SHORT AND EFFECTIVE, UNLIKE THE interminable days before and the inexorable march toward her doom. Four swift weeks were all it had taken for her to become Her Grace, the reluctant and bitterly unenthusiastic Duchess of Ashvale.

Once the application for an ordinary marriage license had been made, arrangements had to be sorted out. Her family had to be contacted—which she'd left up to her competent fiancé because she was in no hurry to face Embry's wrath. She did not require his consent to wed, being over twenty-one, but he was still her brother. And there was no telling how furious he'd be to learn of her whereabouts. Or her sudden marriage.

Besides, she'd had her hands full. Bridal clothes and a full wardrobe had to be ordered and fitted, considering she only had a fine but impractical array of gentleman's clothing. Scandal had to be mitigated, including the planted rumors that Lady Ravenna's unconventional dress choices at the Starlight had been on a lark from the local theater, and that she and Lord Ashvale had been betrothed in secret for months. Society ate it up—everyone relished a mawkish love story. All lies, of course, but people believed what they wanted to believe.

Especially when the title *duke* was thrown about.

Or said duke falling head over heels in love with his long-ago childhood sweetheart like some whimsical fairy-tale.

What a crock!

Given that she'd been practically bludgeoned over the head to reach the altar, Ravenna would much have preferred to marry an untitled suitor than a duke. She was all too familiar with the exacting pressures and responsibilities that came with a dukedom. After all, she was the daughter of a duke, sister to a duke, and now wife to one.

It was emphatically depressing.

Her mother, of course, had been mollified, despite how the wedding had come about. Titles mattered in England. The dowager did not have the constitution to travel for the nuptials, though she'd thrown an apoplectic fit that her only daughter would be married on an island without the proper fanfare befitting the Huntley name. She'd only been placated after being promised she would be allowed to host a formal wedding ball in London when they returned.

Thankfully, Ravenna had experienced that tantrum via correspondence and not in person. She'd kept the details of her reply spare—once more, the word *duke* had worked like the flick of a magic wand—with no need to let her mother know that she'd been the hare caught by a clever wolf. Not that the brainless hare didn't go and throw itself like a desperate, passion-starved creature in front of said wolf and demand to be consumed.

Clearly, she had wool in her brain! Because the boy from her childhood was not the man—her *husband*—who now stood beside her, face in rigid lines, mouth hard and unyielding, as he surveyed the colorful crowd in the packed ballroom at the Starlight.

Courtland Chase was a devil she no longer knew.

If she'd *ever* known him.

After the lavish wedding breakfast, the evening ball was the event of the decade—a local gentleman, one of their own, becoming an exalted English duke and choosing to marry his duchess on the island instead of returning to England's shores. Her husband, as she'd gleaned in the past few weeks leading up to the wedding, was hard-nosed in business, but admired and respected among locals and British nationals alike.

As such, his astonishing change in station was feted by everyone—from the shopkeepers to the governor—and the unbridled, joyful response of the islanders filled her to the brim. British aristocrats would never display such pure, unchecked emotion.

"I wish we didn't have to leave." To her surprise, the wistful sentiment had fallen from her mouth.

The duke inclined his head, eyes unreadable, as he peered down at her. "Oh?"

"I love it here," she murmured. "It's so real and…honest."

A puff of humorless air escaped his lips. "Said by a woman who has never endured a moment of hardship in her entire life."

His disdain could not be more obvious. "You don't know a thing about me, and that's not what I meant at all."

"Tell me, then."

The words were soft, unthreatening. She stared at him, wondering if he was merely humoring her or truly wanted to know her thoughts. Or perhaps he'd ridicule her for them. She was more than aware of what the word *freedom* meant to the people of the island, with the foul, unforgiveable shadows of the past ever looming.

While it'd been three decades since abolitionism in the British colonies, liberty was a hard-won human right that many of her privileged set took for granted. Ravenna knew that from her brother, who worked tirelessly in the House of Lords to fight against such injustices.

She blew out a slow exhale. "I meant their honesty of feeling. Joyful in this moment and not afraid to show it—that's what I meant. The lack of artifice is refreshing. Even the English ladies seem to be enjoying themselves."

"For many of the women here, it's all they have," Courtland said, his eyes casting over the crowd. "The balls, the dances, the diversions. Island life is not as it is in England, though many of them would wish it to be."

"Do you?" she asked.

"No."

Ravenna blinked. It wasn't a happy *no*, but it wasn't angry either. "Why don't you want to go back?" she asked.

Lean, tanned fingers tapped on the marble balustrade in that familiar little-finger-to-index-finger motion she'd intuitively recognized during their card game, and for a protracted moment, Ravenna thought he wasn't going to answer. "I don't belong there."

"You're an English duke."

"On paper." A cold smile pulled his lips. "And if Stinson had anything to say about it, he'd be duke, not me."

"Primogeniture matters, trust me." Ravenna gave a low laugh, drawing his gaze to hers. "I've heard Rhystan curse it enough. He never wanted to be duke, you know. His mistress, until he met the love of his life, had always been the sea. I suppose he and I share the same deeply rooted sense of adventure."

Courtland's brow shot high. "Or, in your case, one might call it absurdity."

One might, but not her. "Why? Because I'm female? Because of my sex?" She tapped one ivory-gloved hand to her chest. "Women face impossible standards to uphold the virtue of an entire nation, and honestly, it's infuriating. Not to mention illogical!"

Stormy eyes blazed at her provocative words—she knew exactly *which* provocative word—and an answering spark ignited inside of her. Ravenna sank her teeth into her bottom lip, and a muscle leaped to life in his cheek, his nostrils flaring wide like a predator scenting prey. The rawness of this…thing between them was madness.

Heat drizzled through her and she was suddenly reminded of their kiss in his office…his hot fingers at her throat, unloosening, untying, *undressing*… Gracious, she hadn't even thought beyond the ball or what would happen later tonight when she would be stripped and bare before him. When he would claim his husbandly rights.

Her wedding night. Perish the thought.

"You're a lady," he said slowly, his voice a low, masculine rasp that did unconscionable things to her. "You can't be gallivanting all over the world."

"Why? Because my virtue, and perceived inherent value, will come into question? Because a man deemed it so?" She let out a tight breath, mingled with equal amounts of waning fury and sharp-edged desire. "I am not the sum of my physical parts, Your Grace."

Silence descended between them and Ravenna feared she might have said too much. She was much too outspoken and free with her opinions. In England, even with the rise of the suffragettes, there was still the notion that aristocratic ladies should not entertain such controversial views of women having—*gasp*— rights over themselves. She sucked air through her teeth, desire cooling swiftly. Oh well, better he knew early on what kind of woman she was than be surprised later.

"No, you're not," he said eventually.

Her jaw almost fell open. "You agree with me?"

"I agree that you are your own person, physically and otherwise. However, rules and customs are in place for a reason. Even I, humble male that I am, must pay obeisance to the laws of society."

"Humility is the last thing you should credit yourself with, Your Grace. You left and no one stopped you," she said with a wave of her arm. "To live here. In this place of uncommon wonder."

"You would be in the minority with such an opinion."

"It would not be the first time."

Courtland turned fully to her then, the first genuine smile she'd ever seen curving his mouth. It fascinated her—that rare glimpse into a different man. Warmth tempered the usual storm of his intense gaze as he lifted her right hand to his lips. "I am not surprised in the least. Shall we join our guests then, Duchess?"

As he led her down the grand staircase, Ravenna did not stop to acknowledge the rapid staccato of her heart, be it due to the inflection of his address, his commanding touch, or the appearance of that smile. She did not *want* to like any of those things. She did not wish to like *him*. Marriage brought with it its own traps, even when couched in pleasure or passion.

Or unexpected affinity.

Because according to English law, despite her earlier views of choice and rights, she now belonged to him. She was the Duke of Ashvale's property, legally and entirely, and running away to chase a life of adventure as her brother had done was no longer an option.

The irony was painfully obvious—she'd come full circle.

Born and raised to be a peer's bride.

Leading his bride into the first waltz should not have felt as natural as it did. As if he'd done it his entire life. As if she *belonged* there. Courtland did not want to dwell on what that meant. Even if she'd taken his name and said her marital vows, Ravenna didn't want to be his. Not truly.

She wanted to live a life on her own terms, and he found that he didn't have it in him to deny her those dreams, despite the tangle in which they found themselves. Even when they were young, he'd admired her stalwart insistence on carving her own path. She'd scoffed at the rules that said girls shouldn't race in the woods, cavort with boys, or build tree houses. She'd muddied her dresses without a care in the world, and thrown the hardest punch he'd ever felt. Everything her brothers did, she'd wanted to do better.

And she had.

He bit back a smile. The unconventional little imp had even followed in Embry's footsteps on the high seas. It made him see red whenever he thought of the dangers she could have faced. But she'd survived…and one could argue *thrived*. It was patently obvious she hadn't planned to find a husband. Courtland swallowed. When appearances had been made and the *ton* was on to the next scandal, he would offer her the choice: live in England as a duchess while he returned to Antigua, or if she chose to be alone, he'd find a way to dissolve their union somehow.

"You waltz well," he murmured, aware of all the eyes upon them.

"I suppose I should thank my mother for all the years of torture, I mean, dance instruction."

His lips twitched. "You must have been quite the hellion during your come-out."

"You have no idea how many toes I demolished. In fact, in secret, I believe the gentlemen nicknamed me Lady Toe Crusher." She grinned up at him, and it was like a bolt of lightning crashing through his body. "I'm surprised yours are yet intact, but that's more to your credit as a partner than because of my tragic lack of skill."

"Years of practice," he said, turning her expertly in his arms. "If you are so poor a dancer, how do you acquit yourself so well then?"

"Counting." Her smile was cheeky. "Steps, much like cards, are easy to keep track of, Your Grace."

This time he did laugh, twice in the space of minutes. "Not for everyone, I assure you. That is an uncommon gift."

Once more, a pair of narrowed copper eyes met his as if she mistrusted his compliment. But Courtland meant it. The more he discovered about her, the more she intrigued him. She'd always been clever as a child, but now, that sharpness of mind had evolved with maturity. He was starting to see why she'd be bored sitting in a drawing room with nothing but an embroidery hoop for entertainment. A woman of her fiery spirit and fierce temperament would be better suited to leading a revolution than practicing dull needlepoint. It was no wonder she'd run.

Ravenna Huntley—*no, Chase now*—was a rare breed of woman. Despite her claims to the contrary, she was light on her feet, her slender form deftly mirroring his every step with each beat. When the distance closed between them and her soft skirts brushed the fabric of his trousers, he could feel the heat of her body beneath, and his own was quick to react. After six or so turns, Courtland was barely holding the guise of civility together. He settled for conversation that would lessen his growing arousal.

"Tell me, Duchess, why did you run from London? You were surely a sought-after prize."

She let out a puff of air, eyes narrowing. "A *prize*?"

"A beautiful heiress bred to be wed," he said, holding back his smirk.

"That's rather insulting."

"No less true."

The look she speared him with should have left him bleeding. He had no idea why he enjoyed poking at her and provoking a response. "It was suffocating, if you must know."

"And look what being so fussy got you—trapped in marriage with a duke."

"I am *not* fussy."

He twirled her around. "I don't think you quite know what you signed on for, Lady Ravenna, with me as your husband instead. A plebeian island duke is hardly a catch."

"There's no so thing as a *common* duke, Your Grace. I think you undervalue your own significance."

"A duke of disagreeable origins, then," he tossed back.

"To whom?" She sent him an arch glance as they spun in a well-executed twirl. "You would be surprised at what some women would overlook for the title of duchess. Old, stunted, pox-marked, gout-ridden. Your heritage would hardly signify."

"I forgot how bloody naive highborn ladies are," he said. "You live in a bubble of rainbows and ribbons with no sodding concept of reality."

"Do you have to be so vulgar?" she shot back, cheeks reddening. "It's our wedding dance. And besides, it's no wonder no one has taken you for a husband if that's your dreadful opinion of women."

"Not all women, just ladies of *quality*, though quality is a matter of interpretation, isn't it?" His stare was deliberately condescending. "Your privilege allows you to make such an erroneous statement. You see, Duchess, the same heritage you speak of is the very reductive and despised thing that dehumanizes. According to aristocratic sensibilities, that is what make me *common* in society's eyes. While well intentioned, your estimation is irrelevant." Ruining the dance or not, the unpleasant turn of the conversation was certainly helping to cool his remaining ardor. "It's the truth, ugly and spare, but true nonetheless."

"You're an arse, Ashvale. I am not like them."

"Now who's being vulgar?" he asked silkily. Ravenna's face went beet-red, and she moved to wrench out of his arms, but his fingers tightened about her, bringing her dangerously close to his chest. Her eyes went wide with alarm, even as chortles and loutish whistles reached them. "Finish the dance, Ravenna," he said.

"Why?" she snapped. "So you can insult my intelligence some more?"

"I wouldn't have to if your views were."

"Were what?"

He smirked. "Intelligent."

"Oh, you, you unspeakable—"

She was gloriously indignant. He had no idea why he loved riling her up so. Her coppery eyes fairly shone with rage, cheeks blooming and full lips parting. He wanted so badly to kiss her, to swallow the furious tirade trembling over that lush pout, modesty and decorum be damned. His arousal returned in full force.

Well, he was Duke, wasn't he?

An *island* duke…and island dukes did whatever they pleased when they pleased, especially in their own domains. And besides, they weren't in London yet, and most of the guests in attendance were his acquaintances. As the last of their waltz drew to a close, Courtland grinned and yanked her close…scandalously close, enough so she could feel the unyielding evidence of his lust. Her gasp was gratifying, even as answering fires lit those expressive eyes.

"What are you doing?" she blurted out.

"I *am* unspeakable," he said. "Ruthless. Hard. Selfish. Not like those senseless fops in London you can control with a crook of a finger and the flutter of an eyelash. But I will always be honest with you, even if it stings."

Then he dipped his bride, cupped her nape, and set his mouth to hers in full view of everyone. *That* should give his contrary little vixen something to ponder.

———

Thank heavens his big hands were holding her upright because if Ravenna had to depend on the strength of her own body, she'd be sinking into a very fashionable pool of ivory skirts on the ballroom floor. As it was, she could barely hold a coherent thought in her head. All she could focus on was the persuasive heat of her duke's kiss.

Courtland's mouth sealed to hers, his tongue darting out in a wicked flick against her upper lip, the sinful and utterly masculine taste of him invading her senses. Everything and everyone fell away—their guests, the musicians, the ballroom—until it was just the two of them suspended in a universe of their own making. As far as kisses went, it was mostly chaste for the sake of their chaotic hooting and hollering audience, but there was nothing decent about the lewd images currently hatching in her brain.

Or the fact that she wanted *more*.

Grinning, he broke from her, but still held her cradled in his strong arms. Her husband's eyes gleamed, their fathomless depths fraught with fervid promises of what he intended to do to her later, and every bone inside of her went liquid. His desires matched hers, it seemed, not that she wouldn't know it from the hard male organ grinding into her hip. A needy whimper escaped her lips, and Courtland's smile was positively corrupt.

"Ravenna."

"Yes?" she said, breathless.

"I will always value your opinion."

On that shockingly solemn pronouncement, he hauled her gracefully upright amid deafening cheers, and Ravenna let out a shuddering breath. Not even Lady Holding's enormous scowl could detract from her daze. While the duke's earlier words had pricked her pride and made her bristle, she felt a curious sense of wonder. He hadn't dismissed her, nor had he humiliated her. Instead, he'd explained how her words had caused injury instead of ease. It was rather...illuminating.

With an uncharacteristic smile to their audience, the duke took her palm in hers and kissed it. "To my beautiful and utterly singular bride," he said aloud to everyone. "The Duchess of Ashvale."

When the fresh round of cheering subsided, they moved toward the refreshment room. The man was mercurial at best. One moment he was taking great pleasure in schooling her during their dance, and the next he was kissing her senseless and parading her around on his arm like the greatest treasure known to man. Her head was spinning. Even now, she could feel the coiled tension in his body, while he smiled and greeted guests with unfailing civility. He was a conundrum, her husband.

A ripple of excitement rumbled through the room, and Ravenna turned just as the majordomo revealed the source of the interest. "His Grace, the Duke of Embry!"

Oh, damn and blast, no! Her stomach rose and dipped with a curious combination of alarm and happiness. She loved her brother dearly, but Ravenna knew Rhystan would not take to her recent escapades with any kind of calm. Hopefully, he wouldn't take her to task her in public; he was much too well bred for that.

Wasn't he?

She held her breath as he cut a path directly to where they stood. Her brother and her new husband were of a height and somewhat similar in build, but where Rhystan was all broad-shouldered bulk from living and working as a ship's captain for years, Courtland was narrower and rapier-strong. The two men acknowledged each other with polite if wary nods. Both of them stood rigid. Ravenna hoped they wouldn't come to fisticuffs, but with her brother's hardened sailor's background, one never knew.

"Embry, I'm glad you could make it," Courtland said.

"I must say it's good to see you alive and kicking with my own eyes, Ashvale," Rhystan said, eyes narrowing. "I could scarcely believe the letter I received, fearing that my poor sister had wed a ghost or an impostor, considering you're supposed to be dead."

The corner of Courtland's lip curled. "Life has yet to do away with me, I fear, despite conjecture."

"I am glad of it. Congratulations, I'm pleased I could be here," Rhystan said as Ravenna let out a slow, relieved breath that no blood would be spilled, at least for the moment, and then her brother scrutinized her from head to toe. "Hullo, sister, you look better than expected."

She bit her lip at his droll expression and gave a tiny eye roll. "Did you expect me to be trussed, bound, and dragged to the altar?"

"Something like that, though my wife firmly insisted that if you had indeed agreed to marry *any* man, it wouldn't have been that bad. I'm glad to see it's so."

Ravenna felt a stroke of emotion at her sister-in-law's steady support, though couldn't help remarking how wrong she was. Sarani would be horrified to know that Ravenna had simply gotten caught in a trap of her own making rather than her choosing. "Did Sarani not come with you? And my niece, how is she? Is she well?"

Rhystan laughed. "Everyone is well. My duchess sends her love. She was unable to travel—still recovering from the birth, you see. Nothing serious, just exhaustion so the doctor prescribed her lots of rest and fresh air. Our little arrival, Lady Anu, is healthy and hale, and just as beautiful as her mother."

"What a lovely name," Ravenna crooned, a rush of warmth filling the gaping hole in her chest. She hadn't let herself feel how much she missed her family, until this very moment. She fought back a sniff. "I can't wait to meet her, and I miss Sarani terribly."

"She misses you."

Ravenna drew in a breath, her eyes smarting. "You must be tired. Have you only just arrived?"

"Yes, but I refreshed on the ship, marvelous contraption that she is."

Courtland inclined his head at the praise. "I trust everything onboard was to your satisfaction."

"She was swifter than expected. I must admit some of the innovation in steam travel is fascinating. I'll have to have Gideon, my former quartermaster, speak to your engineering men about some of the developments on your ocean liner. The speed was astounding. Six days from port to port across the Atlantic. Astonishing!"

"Ocean liner?" Ravenna blurted, her gaze panning between them and then settling on her husband. "You own a ship?"

Courtland nodded. "Several actually, though not a shipping fleet for goods, more designed for passenger travel. I offered to bring your family across, though only the duke took me up on my offer." Ravenna blinked her surprise. She had known he was wealthy, but this kind of fortune bordered on the realm of the absurd. He misread her expression. "Don't worry, Duchess, you'll experience it for yourself on the way back to London. It won't be like being on Embry's clipper at all."

"I *beg* your pardon." The voice was low and full of menace. "Embry's *what*?"

Ravenna didn't have to turn around to know that her brother was glaring at her with the fire of a thousand suns. And it was all Courtland's fault, the loose-lipped, no-good, devilish-as-sin traitor.

Five

THE NEXT AFTERNOON, COURTLAND SAT IN THE UPPER restaurant at the Starlight, sharing an amicable meal with his brother by marriage. The Duke of Embry, sitting across from him in the tastefully appointed dining room, finished his meal with a gratified sigh.

"Now, that was spectacular."

"Thank you. Our chef is French Creole and has a decided flair for spices in his dishes."

"I've never tasted anything so delicious."

Courtland canted his head. "I'll pass on your compliments."

When all had been said and done—stories told, explanations given, and apologies made—his wife's brother had been surprisingly reasonable. Instead of blaming Courtland, he'd seemed resigned to the caprices of his sister. Apparently, Courtland's new duchess had a long history of going beyond the pale.

Not that that surprised him in the least.

Like a shooting star, she was…an unstoppable flare. She'd either be the death of him, or somehow bring him back to life. It was as though he was of two minds. One moment, he wanted her with every desperate beat of his heart, and the next, reason warred with lust, thrashing it into submission. He'd desired women before, but this kind of driving, primal need to claim and consume alarmed him. This woman would shatter him into a thousand pieces if he let her.

They'd spent their wedding night apart, though they'd been in his private apartments at this very hotel. Ravenna had been distressed after spending a fair amount of time with her brother explaining her whereabouts over the past few months and had returned to his chambers with red-rimmed eyes. While she desired comfort, Courtland knew touching her while she was in such a state would derail all his thoughtful plans, and he simply didn't trust himself not to give in. And so, he'd put her to bed. Alone.

Cold, yes, but necessary.

"You've built quite the life here, Ashvale," Embry said. The duke stared at the decor of the lavish room that rested adjacent to the equally extravagant gaming rooms. "The restoration you've done is remarkable."

"Thank you. It's my home," Courtland replied, one shoulder lifting in a noncommittal shrug, though bone-deep pride sluiced through him.

The hotel was one of the first properties he'd acquired, and it meant something to him. When he'd first moved to the island, it had been in disrepair, but the crumbling relic with its sprawling porches and elegant gables had struck something within him. He'd named it for his mother—the star that he fancied watched over him from the heavens, a sentimental and perhaps foolish way to form a connection with her. His father had met her here, perhaps in this very dining room. Fallen in love with a woman far beneath his station.

"My *grandmère* said I was born in this building," he murmured. "In one of the upper chambers."

"You have relatives here?" Embry asked.

Courtland canted his head. "Some cousins. My man, Rawley, is my second cousin. My *grandmère* passed on three years ago."

"I'm sorry for your loss."

"Thank you."

His chest ached at the thought of the woman who had welcomed him with open arms. Courtland had come to Antigua with one flimsy hope—to find his mother's family. Armed with a last name of Roche and not much else, he'd managed to locate his maternal grandmother and a handful of rambunctious cousins who now worked in one capacity or another for the family business he'd built.

The old woman had taken one look at him and enveloped him in her arms with a keening cry. "*Oh, mon petit chou, que tu es beau!*"

Either his French had been rustier than expected, or she'd called him a handsome little cabbage, but being held in that warm embrace had felt like coming home. Like the piece of him that had been missing had suddenly been found.

He'd blinked his surprise at the welcome. "You know who I am?"

"*Mais, oui!* You have the look of my Annelise...*les yeux*, in the eyes, you see, and the hair, too." Tearing up a little, she'd yanked him inside her well-kept house and proceeded to heap a mountain of food in front of him. "Eat. You're a growing boy and you need your strength."

"Thank you, Mrs. Roche."

She'd given him an affectionate swat. "Grandmère Lucille will do. Now eat before you waste away."

She'd always been fond of feeding him, no matter when he came to visit. In truth, he missed her cooking, her unconditional love, and her stories. Grandmère Lucille had died not long after he'd found her, but he'd had a few wonderful years at her table, learning about his mother as a girl as well as the day she'd been swept off her feet by a dashing young British captain whose ship had docked in port for emergency repairs. She'd been a hotel clerk.

His *grandmère* had even shown him the small chapel where they'd said their vows and written their signatures in the vicar's record book.

"Did you know me as a baby?" he'd asked her.

Her smile had been sad and full of loss. "I was the first to hold you. After your mama's funeral, your papa felt it was best to take you with him to England. I wanted to beg him to let you stay, but your place was with him."

Courtland had often wondered whether his life would have been different had he been left behind. Rawley treated him more as a brother than Stinson ever had, and once Rawley had made it clear that Courtland was his cousin by blood, other locals had become less wary. He would undoubtedly have been surrounded by love and the joyful chaos he'd come to esteem.

He was profoundly grateful for the time he'd had with his grandmother, however. After Grandmère Lucille's death, he came to realize that perhaps his happiness didn't lie in the past. It lay in the future. And so, he'd begun to build.

He took the money earned from engineering in railways and shipping, and he started procuring real estate and property. Acreage in the Americas, railroads, mining, hotels across continents, and ocean liners. He invested in anything that turned a significant profit and then reinvested his returns in the island. As his wealth grew, Courtland hired his cousins and anyone who was willing to work for fair wages. It wasn't by chance that his business connections called him Midas because everything he touched turned to gold. A small, gratifying irony for a boy whose stepmother had told him that anything he touched would turn to shit.

Embry cleared his throat after the efficient footmen cleared their plates and refilled their wineglasses. "So about my sister."

"As my wife, she will be afforded every luxury, Embry, that I can promise you."

The duke let out a sigh. "That's not what I'm concerned about. Even with her dowry, I've looked into your finances and know that you're more than capable of providing for her." Courtland arched a brow at that, but he should not be surprised. The Duke of Embry was not rumored to be a fool or dismissive where his family was concerned. "Ravenna is…headstrong."

"Is that what you're calling it these days?" Courtland smothered a laugh. "Not much has changed from the vales of Kettering then. She was muleheaded to a fault, if I recall correctly."

Embry gave a rueful shrug. "I suppose growing up with three older brothers didn't help." He took a sip of his drink. "After the accident, when I became duke, I should have returned home. I blame myself for not being there when she needed me the most. She sentimentalized my absence and convinced herself that she also belonged out on the seas. Needless to say, she approached every London season like a hardened general marching to make war upon her enemies."

A laugh burst from him. Courtland could see just see her, glaring down every suitor, mutiny in her gaze. Her hair would have been longer then, looped and coiled in whatever the popular women's fashion was. In truth, he rather liked the short, velvety-soft curls that sprang and entwined around his fingers.

"She refused every single offer," Embry went on. "It drove me mad, that stubbornness. But my wife insisted that some flowers bloom in their own time, and that she would wed when she was ready. Until I received your letter, I'd thought she was in Scotland with Lady Clara. I was shaken to learn that she was here. *Alone.*" His voice tightened, and for the first time, Courtland realized that the self-possessed duke was overwrought. "Thank you, Ashvale, for what you've done. My sister alluded to some actions on her part that were…reckless, and I am well aware of what could have transpired without your intervention. You have my everlasting gratitude. Anything you should ever need, please ask."

Discomfort filled Courtland. He was not the hero in this story. He'd been willing to toss Ravenna into jail, and then he'd been the one to maul her in his office like a sex-starved cad. A marriage between them was the *least* of what he should have offered. He kept his mouth shut on the subject, however, not knowing exactly what Ravenna had shared with her brother.

"It might have been better for your father to honor the

childhood betrothal agreement after all," he murmured, the barest hint of bitterness in his tone. Not that he'd ever wanted to marry in his youth—his younger self had viewed the engagement as a fate worse than death. Much as his young nemesis Ravenna had.

Marriage? I'd rather be coated in honey and left on an anthill.

Her insults had always been cleverer than his.

The duke leaned forward. "I wish he had. My father believed you dead. We all did."

"The marchioness knew why I'd left. I suspect she hoped her son would take my place. You see, in her highborn opinion, my bloodlines weren't of ducal caliber."

Embry's eyes narrowed. "While the *ton* might agree with her limited views, your grandfather didn't think so and his opinion, even posthumously, carries weight."

"My grandfather was addled because of the advanced state of his illness. I expect he wasn't in his right mind for many years." Courtland sighed. "And no doubt Stinson will use that to discredit me, dispute the terms of the will, and take what he believes to be his. The only reason I'm going to England is for the sake of your sister and the future matches of my half sisters. The gossip surrounding our union was enough for my late father's solicitor to insist on me showing my face as duke and putting to rest any questions that I am well and alive."

"That is sound advice." Embry blinked, frowning as if something had just occurred to him. "I admit I've been away from town for some time, and more recently in the past handful of years, my wife and I have spent most of our time in Hastings, apart from the demands of Parliament." The frown deepened. "Stinson has been calling himself the Marquess of Borne for some time. Which is *your* rightful seat, not his."

"I did not care, to be honest."

Embry scowled. "It wasn't lawful!"

"Men will do whatever they want when they feel they are owed something, and the law cannot be trusted to be upheld when those very men are the ones who wield it," Courtland said. "When our father died, Stinson was raised by the marchioness to believe that he was the rightful heir. I was simply an inconvenient obstacle that needed to be removed, and the only way for her to do that is by questioning my legitimacy." He shrugged as they stood and walked to the foyer. "My parents were wed here on this very island. I saw the register myself. My birth had to have been recorded by my father, though I'm sure mistakes could have been made."

"If your parents were legally married, then you are Ashvale's legitimate heir."

"So it would seem."

Embry smirked. "Welcome to the club, my friend. I assure you being a peer is not as bad as it's made out to be…as long as you stick to what you believe in and ignore all the noise."

"It's the noise that worries me. Not that I care what people think. I worry for Ravenna's sake. I wouldn't want her to be hurt by ugly gossip because of me. The marchioness is uncommonly driven."

"Ravenna is stronger than you think." The duke shot him an inscrutable look. "Remember, call on me when you get to London. We should be there for at least a part of the season while Parliament is in session."

"I will."

"And take care of my sister. While strong, she's also not as hard-edged as she pretends to be." He grinned, his blue eyes sparking. "Hurt her and this time your death will be more than a rumor."

Courtland lifted a brow. "Safe travels, Duke."

He watched as his new brother-in-law climbed into the waiting carriage and headed toward the local port. Anxious to return to his wife and infant daughter, Embry would not wait to go back to England with him and Ravenna in a few days, but would leave today. Courtland envied the easy way he spoke of his family with such love and adoration. He could never hope the same for himself. He did not intend to have children. He hadn't even intended to get married, but here he was.

He'd been honest with Embry. Ravenna would want for nothing, and he would protect her as best as he was able, for as long as he was able. If she wanted a separation in time, he would offer her a divorce on any grounds—cruelty, desertion, or adultery—no matter his own public indignity. It was only fair. He would do what was required of him and stay the course.

London and his marriage were necessary evils, simply a restitution for breaching the rules. Because no matter how well suited he and Ravenna seemed to be on every single level, no matter the intense physical attraction between them, and no matter how easily she'd reached inside and found forgotten tenderness in his granite heart, there was no real future for them. There would *never* be any true future for them.

She didn't want it—and neither did he.

═══════════

Escaping the packed and stifling ballroom, Ravenna slipped outside. The evening was overwarm, not offering much relief as sweat trickled down her nape. She fanned herself with some type of broad palm frond she'd broken off from a nearby pot, gulping in the fresh air on the wraparound balcony, desperate for a huge glass of the thirst-quenching lime juice and water the local ladies here favored.

While the gentlemen preferred their liquor, the ladies were rather more sedate than she'd expected…especially after reading Charlotte Brontë's account of Bertha Mason in *Jane Eyre*. Not that a fictional account of an island Creole woman had any bearing on reality, but it had created quite a stir some seventeen years before when it was first published.

The peerage, particularly, had always looked down on their

counterparts living here, seeing them as somehow lesser. The hot climate, apparently, was at fault. It apparently made people violent, per the account in the book. Lady Holding's letters to Ravenna's mother had conveyed a similar tone and judgment, bemoaning the absence of proper civility among the local gentry as well as the dreadful climate.

The old harridan was categorically wrong on both accounts.

For her part, Ravenna loved the heat and found most of the white Creoles, as they were called, to be quite fine in temperament, though a few of them had looked down their noses when she'd befriended a few of the island women. Ravenna did not care about anyone's narrow-minded opinions—she would make friends wherever and with whomever she pleased.

Life beyond England was a plethora of vibrant culture. Peoples from Africa, India, Asia, and the Americas. She'd never seen anything like it. Several of the island women she'd met, and who were currently in attendance at the dinner and dance, were wealthy shop owners or businesspeople in their own right, married to powerful men in the local government.

Her husband welcomed them all at the Starlight. In that, Courtland was much the same as other English lords of her acquaintance who owned exclusive clubs in London—if one had the means, one was allowed entry, regardless of station or circumstance of birth. It was not a novel concept. Wealth opened doors everywhere. Ravenna wondered if that was why Courtland had so much of it. Had he felt a need to insulate himself because of his background?

In the few weeks she'd been on the island, she had learned much about him, though always from other people. He was fair. He was shrewd. He valued loyalty and honesty, and he was not a man to be crossed. Ravenna formed a wry smile. *That*, she'd learned firsthand. But Courtland rarely spoke about himself. What had caused the estrangement in his family? As far as she knew, Stinson had adored his brother and had mourned him when he thought he had died. Yet, the moment she brought up Stinson or Lady Borne, Courtland grew stony and cold.

The night before, she'd asked her husband if he intended to see his family in Kettering and said she hoped his brother might be in London for the season.

"Are you well acquainted with Stinson?" he'd demanded with diamond-hard eyes.

She'd stared at him. "We live on neighboring estates. You know this. Of course we are well acquainted."

"You won't see him or seek him out when we get to London." It was a stark command, expressed through his teeth as though the very thought of his brother angered him, and the ferocity in his tone had surprised her.

"Ashvale, be reasonable. He's your brother. I don't know what happened between you, but he has always—"

"You will heed me on this, Ravenna."

Bristling, she'd opened her mouth to snap back, but the brief flash in his eyes had stopped her. It was a deep-seated, aching pain, visible but for a single instant that had made something inside of her fissure. It was a look that spoke of considerable hurt, of tremendous injury. So she'd clamped her lips shut and nodded.

Stinson had always been quite amiable and pleasant to her. Perhaps what had happened between the brothers was born of a misunderstanding. Siblings quarreled all the time. Her own brother had been estranged from their family for years because he'd felt disparaged by their father, when that hadn't been the case at all. Perhaps she could find some other way to help bridge the rift between them, but she'd have to tread carefully with any attempts at reconciliation.

Ravenna fanned herself harder, hoping for some relief from the heat. Normally there was a lovely evening breeze, but tonight the tropical air was dead still. Usually, that meant a storm was brewing on the horizon, not that anyone in attendance would care. The revelry hadn't stopped since their wedding night, continuing on into the wee hours when she and Courtland had retired. At breakfast the next morning, she'd blushed at some of the knowing, sidelong glances. Little did they know that nothing had happened.

Courtland's care had surprised her, but after Rhystan's awful reaction to her grand tour, which he'd called *grand codswallop* among other things, she hadn't been in the mood for company, much less a husbandly deflowering. Not that she hadn't obsessed about the act more than a dozen times. Her own mother had been vague about relations between husbands and wives, and while Ravenna had been exposed to enough bawdy talk from the sailors that would shock a seasoned harlot, she couldn't countenance that some of their lewd stories were true.

People weren't animals in the bedroom.

At least, Ravenna hoped they weren't.

She recalled one boatswain's account of mounting a jade from behind like a stallion with a mare, and blushed hot when the image of her husband in such a lewd position stole through her thoughts. Biting back an indelicate gasp, Ravenna fanned herself harder. Ribbons of heat that had nothing to do with the weather crawled up her damp neck, and she forced the wicked and thoroughly wanton vision away. Shame bit at her cheeks. She was a fool. Fantasizing about the man was useless and served no purpose other than frustration.

Because she was certain her husband wasn't remotely interested in bedding her.

Two nights had passed since Rhystan had left, and they'd maintained separate rooms. The rejection chafed. She was well aware that their marriage had been one of convenience, if not necessity, to save her reputation, and matrimonial vows didn't mean their spoken vows had to be consummated. Sex was not a requisite in a marriage like theirs, though clearly, some deeply desirous part of her wished it was.

She couldn't stop thinking about him.

Another heated shiver lanced through her to land right between her thighs.

Maybe Brontë had the right of it after all—the heat was turning her into a trollop.

Fanning with futile force, Ravenna caught sight of her husband through the massive balcony doors, speaking in earnest to the governor. Likely, it was about some amendment or local bill he wanted passed. He was very passionate about working conditions for the local laborers as well the influx of people migrating from nearby American cities in the turmoil of the country's civil war.

Giving herself one last swat with her makeshift fan and depositing the palm frond back into its pot, she made her way over to where the duke stood in animated discussion with a small group. Conversation slowed as she approached, but her husband did not ignore her—something else that set him apart from other men of her acquaintance.

Instead, he took her arm, drawing her against him. "Gents, may I present my wife, Her Grace, the Duchess of Ashvale. This is Sir Stephen John Hill, governor as you know, and Mr. Brent Sommers."

Both men greeted her with smiles and pleasantries, though the second man stared more at her breasts than her face and his lascivious expression made her feel mildly uncomfortable.

"A pleasure, Governor," she murmured and then turned to the other, detecting his accented drawl. "Mr. Sommers, are you American?"

"You guessed it, little lady."

"The correct form of address to a duchess is Your Grace, Sommers." The quiet assertion came from her husband even as Ravenna bristled. "Though I might not care how you address me, she is as aristocratic as they come."

"Marrying up, eh?" Sommers said with a loud laugh, slapping Courtland about the shoulders. Ravenna decided she instantly disliked the man. How *dare* he?

"Still a duke, Mr. Sommers," Ravenna chided softly.

Pale-green eyes met hers, then insolently ran the length of her body. "Forgive me, Your Grace. The aristocracy is English, not American. We make our own way, regardless of what we're born to." The last was said with no small amount of derision. "Money talks, everything else walks."

Seeing that Courtland and the governor had resumed their debate, she pasted a polite expression on her face. "What do you do, Mr. Sommers?"

"I own land in the Carolinas."

Ravenna blinked. The American Civil War was at its zenith, and tensions were high, particularly in the South. Though Britain had not publicly supported the American war as they did not want to become caught in a costly conflict, she'd seen accounts, mostly from private correspondence sent to her brother, that some British officials had secretly supported the South in their efforts and were still doing so.

"The past few years must have been instructive for you."

His smile was indulgent as though he didn't expect her to possess a brain or any ability to form an articulate sentence. "How so, darlin'?"

"'Your Grace' will suffice," she said crisply. "The reason for your civil war. We made sure to end that vile practice thirty years ago."

Sommers looked like he'd sucked on a lemon. His sour expression said it all: he was not in agreement. It made her dislike him even more and she opened her mouth, though at the same moment she felt a gentle pressure on her arm, drawing her away from her impending outburst.

"Excuse me, sirs, while I interest my new bride in a dance."

"What are you doing?" she asked Courtland as he steered her in the opposite direction, away from the men and away from the dancing.

"Sommers is a dangerous man."

"I'm a dangerous woman."

Her husband smiled at her furious answer. "I am well aware, but I'd rather not shed blood on my imported Italian marble because my fierce wife gutted one of my guests for his intolerant views."

"Why is he even here?"

"There are many men like him, not just in the United States, my dauntless little vixen, and I have my reasons," he murmured, running a soothing hand along her back and then up through her damp hairline. She resisted the urge to curl into the caress like a cat. "We must choose our battles."

"Is that what you've been doing? Choosing your battles?"

He stared at her, his gaze immediately shuttering. The question was not related to Sommers, but to the dynamics of his family, and he knew it. "You don't understand. It's complicated."

She flinched at the short snap of his reply, and Courtland blew out a breath, pinching the bridge of his nose between his thumb and forefinger. Her heart ached at the strain she could see on his handsome face. He could have a discussion on all manner of principles and policy, but the mere mention of his own family turned him mute. *Why?* Perhaps he might trust her, but she knew he would not when he shook his head and his eyes went cold.

She reached out for him, but dropped her hand at the last second. "You can talk to me."

"Leave it, Ravenna," he replied tiredly. "Trust me, the saga of my tragic adolescence is not worth a single moment of your time or anyone's. I've put the past behind me and that's where it will stay."

"Burying the past is not the same as moving on."

"It is for me. Hurt me once, shame on you. Hurt me twice, and

I am the fool." He stared at her, those eyes that had been so warm now as cold as ice. "I will never be any man's fool."

Or woman's.

He didn't say it aloud, but his meaning was painfully clear.

Six

COURTLAND'S PRIDE AND JOY WAS HIS OCEAN LINER, APTLY named the SS *Glory*. Not only was it unrivaled in terms of building material, technological innovation, and luxury, but it surpassed the speed and utility of many of its competitors from other shipping companies.

He was especially proud that some of the innovation his engineers developed was to be used in the conversion work for the *Great Eastern* steamship, currently being refitted with machinery to lay the a new submarine transatlantic telegraph cable in the next year or so. It was gratifying to be part of modern advancement.

While the SS *Glory* occasionally ferried passengers across the Atlantic, for the most part, it remained docked, constantly being tinkered on and improved. However, today it would be used to transport them to England and serve a second function as a honeymoon location. While it wasn't as extravagant as a trip to some far-off holiday destination, Courtland hoped it would impress his bride.

The carriage came to a stop at the private dock, and Courtland watched as his wife's eyes went round. "That's *your* ship?"

"One of them, yes," he said, basking in her open awe. He knew the *Glory* was spectacular, but something about Ravenna's reaction made him feel a deeply satisfying thrill. Given that Rhystan was her brother, she wasn't unfamiliar with the shipping world. He wondered whether her knowledge was empirical or more superficial.

"Gracious, Ashvale, she's magnificent!" She stalked to the edge of the wharf so quickly that he had to grab her to keep her from going over. "Is her hull iron? Do you use screw propellers? What kind of engine is it? What's her top knot service speed?"

Empirical, then.

Courtland had the sudden urge to savage that erudite mouth.

Every nautical term falling from it made his body tighten with instant, excruciating lust. He focused on answering her questions instead of pandering to his suddenly raging libido. "Not iron, composite with experimental steel. Yes to propulsion, and it's a combination of steam and sail, with multiple boilers powering a triple-expansion compound steam engine, and a service speed of nineteen point five knots."

"Marvelous," she murmured, her copper eyes shining with excitement. "So under a week to England."

"Just about." He offered her his arm. "Shall we?"

Her admiration continued as they boarded the massive vessel. He employed over a hundred people on the liner, and it was designed with seventy first-class staterooms, but there were to be less than two dozen passengers on this voyage. Perhaps that was an extravagance for the journey, but Courtland did not care. He'd spared no expense on the design and construction of this ship, combining his investments in shipbuilding, engineering, and steel-forging to build a liner that surpassed any other.

While she was exceptional in performance, the *Glory* was equally impressive in indulgence. Nothing was spared in comfort. Furnishings were burnished mahogany and rich leather with gold accents. Ravenna exclaimed at the sheer size of the promenade decks, the huge glassed portholes that let in tremendous amounts of light in the first-class common rooms, the richness of the floors, and the unrivaled opulence of his private apartments.

When they arrived at his personal suite that boasted several rooms, including a library and reading room, a private dining area, and a full bath with running water, she shook her head in wonder. "It reminds me of your rooms at the Starlight," she exclaimed.

They were much grander than those, but Courtland nodded because the design was nearly identical—reminiscent of a beautiful sixteenth-century French château. "Similar."

"It's incredible."

"I'm glad you like it," he said.

"Are you joking? It's the most fantastic ship I've ever been on." She twirled in a circle in the middle of the room in a flurry of navy-blue skirts, and grinned. "Don't tell Rhystan I said that, though he's more interested in sailing ships than passenger liners." She peered out of the gleaming-paned glass porthole to the docks beyond. "Are we to be joined by others?"

Courtland nodded. "Some. Dignitaries and businessmen, mostly. A few peers wanting passage as well, I believe. Rawley arranged it."

His efficient man of business had taken care of all the details of their guests. Courtland had intended the trip to be an extension of their wedding celebrations.

"Anyone I'm acquainted with?" she asked, pulling off her hat as the servants started putting baggage away. He'd employed a lady's maid for her. She hadn't had one for the months she'd spent in disguise. Thinking about it made him feel sick at the risks she'd taken, and yet, reluctant admiration for her sheer mettle.

"Perhaps. The Earl and Countess of Waterstone—I can't recall if you met them or not. They're acquaintances of mine. Mr. Bingham will accompany us back to London, of course. And our resident dragoness, Lady Holding, who has taken it upon herself to be your sentry."

Ravenna pulled a face that made his lips twitch. "Lovely. I'll be sure to be on my best behavior, and by that, I mean the most vulgar tart ever."

"Not too vulgar," he said. "You have a reputation to maintain, remember."

She feigned a sulk. "Reputations are for the weak."

"Not in London, they're not."

"Town is stuffy to a fault," she went on with a theatrical moan, her antics making him smirk. "So many rules and regulations. I must always be of pleasant countenance and wear a smile, but not too large, just the perfect amount with no teeth."

"God forbid," he said with an exaggerated shudder. "No one wants to see *teeth*."

"I must speak when spoken to, and only in appropriate situations. I must never have more than one glass of champagne. Never be seen in public without the finest of gloves. Oh, and don't get me started on clothing. Corsets and petticoats are devilry in disguise! Crimes against women, I call them. Down with undergarments, I say!" She gathered her skirts in one hand and displayed a hint of a trim ankle. A *shoeless* trim ankle. Courtland blinked at the sight. When had his wife's slippers gone missing? Ravenna grinned wickedly at him. "What would dear Lady Holding think about that, hmm?"

Courtland's gaze rose to hers, noting her flushed cheeks before it fell back to the hitched skirts of the lovely walking dress she wore. The sight of that delicately arched foot made him salivate, and the thought of what else lay under those yards of striped fabric blanketed his brain. In that moment, everything—all his careful plans to avoid temptation and stay away—evaporated.

He glanced at the lady's maid—Colleen or some such—who hovered in the corner. "Out."

"Was that necessary?" Ravenna asked as the young maid scurried away with a squeak, shutting the door to the sitting room behind them.

Every one of his reservations, his qualms, and his warnings went out the door with the maid. All he could think of was getting under those skirts. "For what I have in mind, yes."

He prowled toward her, watching her coppery eyes go wide

with alarm and then brighten with desire in the same instant as his intent became clear.

"What are you doing, Your Grace?" she asked, breathless.

"Conversing in private with my wife."

"*Conversing*?" She licked her lips, and he felt the stroke echo in his groin. "Then why does it feel like I'm being stalked by a hungry wolf?"

"Is that what it feels like?"

He reveled in the full-body shiver that rolled through her. "Quite."

"I am rather famished. I haven't hunted in some time."

"Haven't you?"

No—he'd starved himself of female company, so much so that he was ravenous. Lust bled through him, more powerful than any hunger. Her eyes widened, and his smile was indeed all wolf. Courtland shook his head. "Will you run, little hare?"

She met his stare head-on. "Does it look like I'm running?"

God above she enflamed his blood. Even as he closed the distance between them, his wife was no meek prey, no damsel in distress. Chin high and eyes bright, she held his gaze. She was bold and fierce, and by some random twist of fate, she was now *his*.

As two consenting adults, why shouldn't they indulge in a bit of harmless fun?

Not harmless if it clouds your judgment or purpose.

Courtland ignored that. He wasn't clouded, he was distracted. Deliciously so, and distractions were best handled quickly.

For every step he took forward, she took one back, until her legs bumped up against the sideboard propped beneath the glass porthole. Her chest rose and fell in shallow pants, but she made no move to escape as he bracketed her in with his arms. Breathing deeply, Courtland inhaled her scent. She smelled delicious, like lemon and sugar drizzled over hot buttered scones. His mouth watered. He'd barely gotten a taste of her, and now he craved more, plans be damned. It was a dangerous game, but she did not seem to care either.

"What were you saying about undergarments?" he rasped.

Molten eyes met his. "I dislike them?"

"Don't you know answering a question with a question is quite rude, Duchess?" His nose trailed along the column of her neck, above the very modest neckline of her dress. Her pulse hummed like a bird's wings beneath her flushed skin. "We shall have to work on reminding you of the rules, shan't we?"

"I might require a refresher, Your Grace."

Smiling, his lips feathered over the impossibly soft skin of her jaw to land at the corner of her saucy, smart mouth. Just recalling her questions about his ship made him as hard as stone. The fact that she was intelligent and shared similar interests only made her more attractive to him. In truth, he despised the edicts that governed their society. He'd always enjoyed a woman who wasn't afraid to speak her mind.

"Rule number one: you will always say what you think in my presence."

"Even if it's not the done thing?"

He nipped at her earlobe. "Especially then."

Ravenna let out a moan when he took the lobe into his mouth and then traced the pale-pink shell of her ear with his tongue. Moving back south, he lapped at the corner of her lip, the barest hint of the sweetness within making him groan. Hands rose up to clutch at his lapels.

"What's rule number two?" she asked.

Courtland couldn't answer. The pouted lips beneath his were far too much temptation. He crushed his mouth to hers with a groan, palms moving from the sideboard to her hips, fisting handfuls of her skirts. Without taking his lips from hers, he lifted her easily to sit on the piece of furniture. He licked into her mouth—sipping, tasting, devouring—her own sleek tongue hungrily tangling with his. A hint of mint tea greeted him along with that ambrosial taste that was naturally hers.

"Two," he rasped, eying her swollen mouth and passion-blown stare. "As my duchess, you will act as you please. You answer to no one."

"Except you."

"Only behind bedroom doors." Ravenna blushed as if the very idea enflamed her, much as it did him. He wondered how biddable she would be. Not very, he was guessing, given her proclivity to challenge everything and anything. But perhaps in bed she would be different. Perhaps in his arms she would yield to the pleasure he would give her. "Does the thought excite you? Answering to me?"

"I don't know," she said, her slender throat working, her heated sherry eyes never leaving his.

"Will you?"

Insolence and fire erupted in that liquid gaze. "With the proper incentive, Duke. Surely you wouldn't wish me to give in so easily? It's not worth the chase if I toss my skirts over my head at the slightest provocation, is it?"

Courtland chuckled, his fingers flexing on her curved hips. Her spirit was a breath of fresh air, and he could never imagine robbing her of it. She was not a creature meant to be tamed, and he never wanted to. In that moment, he swore he would never do anything to diminish that *fight* in her eyes. He loved the bold way she stared at him, as if he was already hers, with not a drop of bashfulness in her gaze. Her desire for him was plain to see, with no coyness or pretense.

How many lovers had she had? He frowned at the thought of any who had touched her before, but struck the pulse of pure jealousy from his head. She was his now. Courtland did not blame her, of course. He'd had lovers before; why should he not place the same standards upon himself? If she was experienced, the better for it.

Gliding up her corseted sides, he filled his hands with her breasts, kneading the soft fabric-covered flesh gently. Her eyes dilated with want, a desperate pant escaping her parted lips. Hell, he couldn't wait to see more of her.

"Rule number three: you will wear what you wish when you wish." He sank to his knees, one hand brushing against her shoe-less stockinged soles. She swallowed her small gasp when his fingers wrapped around her foot. "Or what you don't wish to wear, as it were."

Her feet were beautiful, much like the rest of her, with delicately sloping arches and slender, fine-boned ankles. His hands slid up her rounded calf just as her fingers slid through his hair as if she needed to touch *him*. She traced one eyebrow with her finger, staring down into his eyes, and something deeply possessive passed between them with that single shared touch. His hands upon her, and hers upon him.

"Courtland."

The whisper of his given name on her lips moved him to action, his palm tickling the sensitive spot behind her knee. He gave an involuntary grin at the feel of her many petticoats brushing against his upper arm and her ferocious opinions on them. "Petticoats *are* the devil's work. I want to rip them off you."

Her throaty laughter filled his starved soul. "On that, we are categorically in agreement."

Courtland held her gaze as his fingers skimmed up her thigh to the slit in her drawers where he hovered uncertainly. "May I, Ravenna?" he asked hoarsely.

He'd die if she said no. Hell, he was so hard already that death felt like it was upon him already. Every breath, every strained beat of his heart echoed in his cock. His gorgeous wife turned deliciously pink, bit her plump lip, and nodded. He didn't need her to tell him twice, his greedy hand sliding past the embroidered lace edges of the fabric.

A groan tore from him as he encountered bare skin, his own arousal ratcheting to excruciating levels, moisture leaking from him to bead against his trousers. Her skin was hot to the touch, the soft thatch of her maidenhair rustling against his fingers.

He slid a fingertip down the damp seam of her, and her hands dug into his hair in reflexive response. "You're so silky, so soaked for me, Duchess." She went crimson, eyelashes dipping in embarrassment, and he chuckled low in his throat. "As it should be. You're perfect."

Drawing his fingers through her slick sex from her entrance to the swollen bud of nerves above, he rose to catch her sweet gasps with his mouth, closing his lips over hers. She sucked at his tongue and clung to him, soft cries escaping her as he cupped her, relishing in the heat and wetness, stroking relentlessly until she was writhing in his arms.

"I can't wait to taste you here," he murmured, staring at her while giving his thumb a purposeful flick across her saturated flesh and making her moan. Ravenna sucked in air, surprise flashing through her eyes. "Does that shock you?" he asked.

"Yes."

Courtland couldn't help the beat of satisfaction that she wasn't as schooled as he'd expected, that there were still things he could teach her. "I'll make you burn," he promised.

"I'm already burning," she whispered.

Her head fell back, nearly knocking into the glass of the porthole. No one could see inside of course, but people walked up the footbridge a stone's throw away, and here he was pleasuring his wife in broad daylight without a care in the world. She wasn't the only one on the edge. He was so hard he was surprised he wasn't drilling past the fly of his trousers.

"Come for me, love." His thumb worried the hidden pearl at the apex of her sex, coating his fingers in her copious, silky arousal.

"Where?" she mumbled.

A low, husky laugh burst from him as he took her lips in a sweet kiss. Hell, she couldn't be *that* untried, could she? Courtland redoubled his efforts, gently pinching her sensitive flesh between his thumb and forefinger. When she arched back with a cry, her nails piercing into his scalp, he shifted to insert a finger into her. Her sheath clamped around him, making him wish it was his cock buried in her depths instead.

"You're grasping me so tightly."

She gave a helpless moan. "Please."

He knew what she wanted, and he had every intention of giving it to her. He wanted to give her wings, to make her rush over the edge with the confidence that he'd catch her when she fell. He wanted his duchess to soar.

He worked his hand faster, adding a second finger and stroking in and out, his thumb circling the neediest point of her, until her body went rigid. Huge copper eyes met his, scarlet flooding her cheeks as her mouth parted soundlessly on his name.

"Fly, Ravenna."

When the cataclysm struck, she broke around him...so beautifully it took his breath away. Her body clenched and rippled, her beautiful eyes going wide and glazing over with such palpable passion it awed him. What would she look like when he was buried to the hilt inside her? Rosy color stamped every inch of her porcelain skin, her lips releasing such a delicious sigh that he couldn't help but claim her mouth again.

"So lovely, you're so damned lovely."

His duchess came back to herself slowly as he removed his hand from her clothing, and ducked her heated face into his neck. He laughed. "Rule number four: never be ashamed of your body's responses. Not with me, and not when you reach your peak so prettily. Pleasure is to be celebrated, not scorned."

"That was...incredible."

"Yes, it was," he agreed, setting her skirts to rights and gently lifting her off the sideboard. He watched as her gaze darted to the porthole where the incoming guests were visible, and she turned instantly scarlet. "They can't see us," he assured her.

"What about you?" she asked, her soft gaze dipping to the noticeable bulge at his crotch. She slid a palm down to his waistband. "I could—"

Those eyes…they eviscerated him. Arousal and need swam in them, and so much melting emotion, it made him weak. Courtland stalled her, gently removing her fingers and lifting them to his mouth in a kiss, the insistent voice of reason finally penetrating his lust-fogged brain.

"Another time, perhaps." He ignored the barest flash of hurt in her eyes as he turned around and adjusted his mongrel of an erection before putting some much-needed distance between them. "Get yourself settled. I'll send Colleen back in to help you get ready for dinner. Your rooms are just beyond those doors."

She blinked. "My rooms?"

"Yes."

Now that the blanketing haze of desire had lifted enough for him to function, the truth was glaringly obvious. He *couldn't* be trusted, not even to pay heed to his own conscience. Clearly, being in any kind of proximity to her, especially with a bed anywhere in the vicinity, would only spell disaster.

Seven

THE CUISINE ONBOARD THE *GLORY* WAS BEYOND SUMPTUOUS. They could have been partaking of a ten-course dinner in any fancy dining room in London. Their every culinary need was met, from imported wines, to perfectly prepared and served courses, to melt-in-the-mouth desserts. It was delightful, and except for the fact that she'd barely seen her husband, Ravenna would have been having a wonderful time.

Right now, however, she was intent on drowning her fury at the bottom of a bottle in this very nice, very well-stocked library. Being foxed was vastly preferable to dealing with her *feelings*.

"A pox on marriage," she toasted, taking a healthy draught of the liquor and spluttering through a cough as the book she held nearly fell from her lap. "A pox on men everywhere."

She'd met most of the guests onboard the ship, including, to her intense dismay, the prejudiced and very persistent Mr. Sommers. Lord knew why *he* was going to England and with them to boot. Ravenna decided to keep her distance the minute she recognized his leering gaze in the breakfasting room, and she had been moderately successful at avoiding him thus far. Her wretched husband could have warned her that the man was onboard...if she even knew where *he* was.

She'd cornered Courtland's valet, a very nice man by the name of Peabody, but he'd been unable to string two words together at the sight of her. And now whenever he saw her, he scampered away like a mouse afraid of being trapped and mauled by the house cat. She didn't want to hurt the man; she simply wished to know where the dratted duke was.

Ravenna had tracked down Rawley, too. To her frustration, Courtland's man of business, and cousin as she'd learned, was his usual stoic and tight-lipped self, saying that Lord Ashvale had much to do before arriving in London and he was *busy*. If busy meant keeping himself away from her like a spineless coward, then yes, he was. The parting look of pity in the man's eyes had been rather too much to bear.

The rotter wasn't busy. He was *hiding*.

It vexed her, she had to admit. The fact that he would rather run than speak to her after what had happened left her in a state of confusion. The way he had touched her and brought her to such pleasurable heights was never far from her mind. What had *she* done? Had she frightened him away with her overexuberance? Had she been too forward or too bold? Too impassioned? With gentlemen from her past, she'd feigned indifference, but with him, she had been honest. Perhaps too much so.

He'd seemed to be as immersed in the deed as she'd been, but then he'd refused her offer to reciprocate. She had seen the jutting evidence of his arousal herself. A quiver coursed through her. The thick, hard length of him had been obvious through the fine wool of his trousers. She didn't have much experience with men's anatomy, but that part of him had been straining against the fabric as if it intended to burst through at any moment. She wouldn't have minded if it had. Ravenna had been desperate to see more of him. *Feel* more of him. To make him *come* as she had. But Courtland had snubbed her, and then he'd run from her.

Why?

Perhaps she didn't suit him in the bedroom, after all. Men seemed to be particular about their preferences from what she'd gleaned on Rhystan's ship. Then again, what did a bunch of randy old sailors know? She wished she had Clara or Sarani to speak to. They were both married women and certainly would have some helpful perspective, but neither of them was here.

No, she was alone. On a ship in the mid-Atlantic. With only a bottle for a friend.

Ravenna sighed. She could don men's clothing and cross an entire ocean without blinking an eye, but put her in a gown in front of a man who made swarms of butterflies spawn in her belly, and she was at a loss on how to function. But then again, that could be because she was shockingly drunk.

The fact that she rarely imbibed was evidenced by her atrocious state.

"Do you mind a spot of company, Your Grace?"

Ravenna glanced up from the book she'd been pretending to read, her gaze unfocused for a second. She swallowed a hiccup and recognized the arrival through slitted eyes. "Mr. Bingham, of course." Why did her voice sound so strange? "Please, have a... seat. Read or whatever."

She smiled at him fondly as he found a chair and reached for a book. The kindly solicitor was one of her few favorites onboard. Apart from the Earl and Countess of Waterstone, who were good fun for a game of whist and charades after dinner, she preferred to keep to herself. Lady Holding had taken it upon herself to point out each and every one of Ravenna's many flaws ad nauseam—her shoulders were too slouched, her smile was too bright, her gait was too choppy, her face was too splotchy and freckled.

In defiance of the last, Ravenna had taken indecent pleasure in sprawling across one of the lounging chaises on the promenade deck without a bonnet and lifting her face to the hot mid-Atlantic sun. She hoped she added a dozen more freckles! She'd thoroughly scandalized the meddlesome harridan when she'd had the audacity to kick off her slippers in public.

The duke himself had told her to do as she pleased, damn it, and he hadn't even been around to see her defying decorum so splendidly. Those bloody rules of his—she could hardly think of them without going into a full-on visceral quake—each one of them punctuated by the feel of his hands and lips coasting over her skin.

Say what you think.

Act as you please.

Wear what you wish, or not.

Never be ashamed of your body's response.

Ravenna took another unladylike gulp, spilling droplets down her chin. Sod his sodding rules! How dare he treat her so? Her fury had been the catalyst for stomping back to her quarters after yet another extravagant dinner and indulging in a lengthy sulk with a bath and half a bottle of French liquor in a nondescript green bottle she'd pilfered from her absentee husband's study. The drink had been terribly bitter at first, but after the first few sips mixed with water, she'd ceased to care.

Her husband was a blackguard of the worst sort. She'd cursed his revival from death, calling him every name in the book and then some. *Craven bastard.* She'd sat in the bath until her fingers and toes turned to prunes and the water had become cold against her overheated skin.

Ravenna peeked over the book that had long ceased to be readable to peer down at her bare toes and wiggle them. How were toes so scandalous? They were just *toes.*

"This pig went to market," she murmured, wiggling her big toe. "That pig stayed home. This pig had roast meat. That pig had none. This pig went to the barn's door..." She hiccupped. "And murdered a dastardly duke."

Her version was much better than the original.

"I beg your pardon, Your Grace?" Mr. Bingham asked. "Did you say something?"

"Oh no, dear Mr. Bingham," she said with a wobbly wave. "Don't mind me."

Just plotting the murder of a duke. Death by toe.

Feeling sorry for herself, Ravenna sighed again. She'd only

done as instructed and been condemned for it...for breaking with propriety and doing the unthinkable. They were shoes, for God's sake, not her petticoats! *Those* dratted things belonged in the lowest reach of the underworld!

And besides, this was the duke's ship, which meant it was *her* ship. Lady Holding was a nosy busybody. She had half a mind to tell her so...if only she could manage two steps without toppling over.

How she'd made it to the library, she'd never know.

Ravenna supposed she had Colleen to thank for making sure she was at least clothed before leaving her stateroom after her bath. They weren't even on English soil, and already she felt the burden to be the perfect English lady bearing down on her shoulders. *That* pressure was why she'd run away in the first place. It was why she hadn't been able to marry some titled prat of a gentleman and become his perfect, biddable, dutiful wife.

It wasn't in her to be what anyone expected her to be... She simply wanted to be herself.

To be *alone*. To make her own choices.

But as she was, she would never be good enough...not for the Dowager Duchess of Embry, not for Lady Holding, not for the *ton*, and maybe now not even for her new husband.

Sod him, then. Sod the bloody lot of them!

Ravenna reached for the glass of brandy that wasn't there and scowled when she saw the book in her hand instead. Where had her tasty liquor gone? Someone had bloody stolen it! She'd have their hide if she could remember who she could make her grievance to.

The Duke of Ashvale, no doubt.

That was the name of the cad who was to blame for all her tribulations. She shook a fist at the ceiling, noting the lovely mural of flying cherubs. She squinted up at it. How did cherubs fly? They were much too plump for those tiny wings.

"Your Grace, are you well?"

Her gaze flopped back down. "Oh, Mr. Bingham, hullo! I didn't see you there. Where on earth did you come from?"

He shot her a queer look. "You invited me to sit with you, Your Grace."

"Call me Ravenna, or Lady Ravenna, if you please." She waved an arm and nearly smacked herself in the eye with the spine of her book. "Her Grace sounds like a terribly stuffy kind of person." Her mouth formed a wry twist. "And while I'm at sea, I'd rather be me."

"And who is that, er, Your Grace?" Mr. Bingham regarded her with curiosity before murmuring something to a nearby footman. A glass of something cold was pressed into her hands. "It's water," the solicitor said.

She gulped gratefully, the cool liquid soothing her parched throat. When had she become so thirsty? Or when had water ever been so refreshingly delicious? What had Bingham asked her? Oh yes, who she was.

Who *was* she?

"A daughter. A misfit. A sailor. A gambler. A wife." She peered up at him through a lock of damp, springy hair that had fallen into her eyes. She blew a stream of air upward, but it did little to dislodge the clump. That didn't stop her from trying again and again—futilely, she might add. Hair was so bloody stubborn! Like men. Like *dukes*.

"Have you known the duke long?"

"Perhaps only as long as you've known him."

"Oh, I've known Cordy all my life. He was my neighbor," she explained helpfully. "We were engaged once, you know, but he was a dreadful bore. So bossy and such a know-it-all. He was insufferable. Everyone liked him, except me. He was the thorn in my side." She trailed off with an indelicate hiccup. "Oh, I do beg your pardon, sir." She sipped her water, noticing that the glass had been refilled. Her voice grew soft, heavy with memory. "But I think

I rather loved him. He looked out for me. And then one day…
poof!…he was gone."

"What happened?"

She smiled sadly. "He died. Or at least that's what Stinson told
me." Ravenna brightened at the thought of one friend she had in
England. "Do you know Stinson? He's lovely." She lifted a hand
and separated one blurry finger to point at nothing in particular.
"I think he might have fancied me. But now he's too late. I married the not-dead, cruel, heartless brother. He'll be so crushed, my
poor friend, because he *has* a heart." She let out a sorry sound. "He
said I couldn't see him."

"Who said?"

"Ashvale." She spat out the word as if it burned her mouth.
"The portentous Duke of Ashes and Despair."

"That's enough."

The harsh command wasn't Mr. Bingham's. No, it came from
the entryway to the library. Ravenna's vision was starting to blur,
so all she could see was a menacing, *looming* form that looked
uncannily like what she imagined Hades, the mythical lord of
the underworld, would look like: godlike, grim, and sinfully hot.
Her stupid thighs quivered. Gracious, had he come to take his
revenge because she'd cursed her petticoats to his realm? Surely he
wouldn't be so petty?

"Petty…petticoats." She giggled as Hades-in-the-flesh strode
toward her. Mr. Bingham rose and she reached out blindly for
him. "Don't leave, dear friend, I haven't finished telling you about
Cordy and our magical woods."

"Perhaps tomorrow when you're feeling better, Your Grace."
The solicitor bowed and took a rather hasty leave. No doubt it was
because of the fearsome god's arrival.

"I'm as fit as a fiddle, sir!" she screeched after Mr. Bingham.

"Are you foxed, Ravenna?" the new arrival demanded, dropping to one knee in front of her.

"Quite," she replied, thinking that Hades was extraordinarily handsome. "Quite, quite, *quite* foxed. I stole the liquor, you see."

"I'm going to sack that lackwit of a maid."

"Don't you dare blame my lovely Colleen! She's the one who kept me from coming out here in my chemise and nothing else!" She poked Hades in his chest and winced. His earthly form had to be made of bloody rock. "I'll tell you who you should blame...that Ashvale fellow. He's a scoundrel and a liar and a rotten, abysmal husband."

She'd had better adjectives in the bath, but she could hardly recall all of them.

His reply was soft. "Oh?"

Ravenna sniffed morosely. "He left me alone for days." She dragged her legs up, nearly kneeing the stern god in the face— though he would deserve it after chasing poor Mr. Bingham off— and arranged them beneath her. She tucked her head into the crook of her arm and closed her eyes. This would be a lovely place for a nap. "Good night, Hades."

The laugh was dry and humorless in the extreme. "You think me the lord of the underworld?"

She blinked one eye open. "Aren't you?"

"I suppose I've been called worse."

Strong arms scooped her up, one bracing beneath her knees and the other cradling her back. Hades was strong. He was also hot under her cheek and he smelled good, like lemon and verbena and something else that made her insides squirm. *Too* good. Was that what drew unsuspecting maidens to his underworld lair? Something wasn't right. Faces blurred together as he moved quickly down several corridors. Inexplicable panic took root.

"Put me down this instant, sir! I insist!"

The reply was quick. "No."

Seized with alarm, she began to struggle in earnest, the comfort of her captor's arms suddenly becoming a pair of heavy brackets that trapped her in place. She did not want to be confined!

"Ravenna, cease! It's me, Courtland. You've had a bit too much to drink. I'm taking you to your room."

"I hate my room."

"You hate your room?"

She wanted to weep. "I hate you, too."

The softest of kisses feathered over her brow, so soft that she could have sworn she imagined it. "I know."

"Why did you leave?"

"I needed to think."

The fissure in her heart widened. "Did I do something wrong?"

"No."

Courtland paused for a second, exchanged words in a low voice with someone, and then she was being gently set on top of a feather mattress. Blearily, she took in the details of the magnificent stateroom, noticing that it was not hers. For one, the mural on the ceiling was quite different. She'd studied hers for hours when sleep had eluded her, memorizing every bend and line of the ornamental cornices, every tender stroke of the artist's brush. This was not her chamber or her bed.

"Where are we?" she mumbled.

But Courtland was gone. In his place was Colleen, that darling maid of hers. "Come now, Your Grace. Let's get you into your night rail." Within a few quick moments, her clothing had been deftly switched out.

Ravenna reached out. "Don't be afraid of the duke," she told the girl.

To her surprise, Colleen sent her a shy smile. "I'm not, Your Grace. In fact, he's rather dashing, isn't he, rescuing you as he did?"

Rescuing her?

Ravenna blinked through her muddled mind. Surely she wasn't so much in her cups that she couldn't remember having to be rescued. Had there been cutthroats? Pirates on the high seas? A fire-breathing dragon, perhaps?

When her lady's maid gave her a quizzical look, Ravenna realized she had asked the questions out loud. Her poor maid backed out of the room so fast it was a miracle she was ever there at all. Ravenna's mind spun as she settled back against the fluffy pillows. Her limbs felt quite strange—like they were sinking into a cloud.

Good heavens, she was never drinking French brandy again!

"It wasn't brandy," that voice that did unconscionable things to her insides said. Drat and blast, had she said that aloud as well? "Yes, you did." There was laughter in the reply. She groaned. A familiar green bottle waved in front of her face, and she fought the urge to make a grab for it. "Brandy is brown. This is pale green. You consumed nearly a quarter of a bottle of absinthe."

"Absinthe?" she repeated somewhat dimly.

"La fée verte."

"I know what absinthe is, you big lump," she told him with an imperious look, though it was ruined by the indelicate slurring of her words. "The green fairy, *everyone* knows. I assure you, sir, this is not it."

"I assure you it is."

"It turns white when you mix it with water, did you know?" She wrinkled her nose. "No, no, it's brandy. Really terrible, possibly spoiled, dreadful brandy."

"And you still consumed it?" he asked, a pair of dark thundercloud eyes drilling into hers.

Ravenna did not want to admit that it was the first bottle she snatched, nor that she'd set out to get completely sotted so it hadn't mattered which liquor she swigged. "Heavens, Ashvale, are you always this fatalistic? I'm fine." She attempted to stare him down and failed. "As you can well see, I'm here in my chamber, safe and sound."

"These are my rooms."

"Why am I in your rooms?"

The duke groaned out loud. "Confound it all to hell, woman!

You're *not* fine. You were prowling around the ship with no idea where you were. How you ended up in the library is anyone's guess. If Bingham hadn't stumbled upon you, Lord knows what could have happened to you. You could have gone overboard!"

He stared at her after his outburst. So many emotions ran across his face. Anger was the most obvious, even to her fuzzy senses, then exasperation, followed by anger again. Fear was there, too, as well as resignation of some kind. But at the heart of it, he was clearly very angry with her. She didn't want him to be angry. She wanted him to hold her. To gather her into his arms and hold her tight, and never let go. But first, she wanted to erase those deep lines of worry and strain from his brow.

"Cordy?" she whispered.

"What?"

"I'm glad it was you."

His brow furrowed more. "What do you mean?"

"I mean I'm glad I found you again." She burrowed into his blankets, inhaling the clean, comforting scent of him into her aching lungs. Her eyes fluttered shut, exhaustion overcoming her in a rush. "I missed you."

"I missed you, too."

Perhaps she'd only imagined that soft response, because the next thing Ravenna knew was the comforting embrace of oblivion.

Eight

COURTLAND RAN A HAND THROUGH HIS HAIR, HAVING returned after a sleepless night on a hard couch to stare at the sleeping woman sprawled in his bed. His *wife*. His to protect and he could very well have lost her last night. His chest felt uncomfortably tight, his limbs brittle as though they might snap. The feelings that chased through him were unfamiliar.

And unwelcome!

All because of the fiery-tempered, shockingly direct, and intolerably vexing temptress currently ensconced in his bed. His fingers twitched, longing to drift over the satiny-soft skin of her shoulder just visible over the edge of her night rail. Memories of that lustrous skin flushing in the throes of orgasm assailed him—all rosy and delicious—she'd been the most exquisite thing he'd ever seen. He would treasure that gift forever, no matter how much she claimed to hate him.

Last night, she'd thought him Hades.

Hell, perhaps he was. The god of the underworld was far from a benevolent creature. He'd touched her and left her, avoiding her as much as he could. Coward that he was, he'd been holed up on the captain's quarters, poring over complex engineering diagrams and looking at the same steam-turbine prototype specifications over and over. The fine drawings and sheets of numbers had served to distract him for a good while. But then Rawley had brought word that the duchess was wandering about the ship, foxed out of her mind. Thankfully, Bingham had been the one to find her and not one of the other guests.

Lady Holding would have been irreparably scandalized.

And Sommers would have taken dreadful advantage.

Helpless fury flooded him, but having Sommers here was a necessary evil. Courtland was so close to securing his trust. The man was pure scum. He was a smuggler and a criminal with a cruel streak. The Earl of Waterstone had been tracking him for some time and had only recently enlisted Courtland's help to expose and arrest the man.

His marriage and the trip to England had come at an inopportune time…and so, he'd invited Sommers to visit his ducal estate in London. Like most of his ilk, the lure of hobnobbing with the crème de la crème of English aristocracy proved too big to resist. Though Courtland did not want his wife, or any of the other female guests, in any kind of proximity to Sommers, he'd had no other choice.

Waterstone had agreed it was the only way. The earl was a British agent who'd been on Sommers's tail for years for the illicit smuggling of undeclared goods under the guise of legitimate trade. Courtland had tried to get Sommers to use his ships to catch him in the act, but the slippery man had always refused. So the only alternative had been to befriend him and ferret out his secrets that way. It turned Courtland's stomach, but if his help put a criminal away, then it was worth it.

Not if it endangered his wife, however.

He glanced at the duchess, who moaned fitfully and shifted against the bedsheets before settling. God knew what had possessed Ravenna to pick up a bottle of spirits that had been left behind by a group of French poets and artists who'd been onboard the *Glory* some months ago.

He corrected himself. He knew exactly what had driven her to do so. Her brother had warned that she was not as tough as she pretended to be. Leaving her as he had after the intimacy they'd shared had not been well done of him by any stretch of the imagination.

Hell, he was a cad.

But if he hadn't left that room, if he hadn't stayed away, he would have finished what he'd started, and plowing his deliciously responsive wife wasn't an option. Divorce was expensive and difficult, even with the recent changes in British law, which made such separation legal without an Act of Parliament.

While mutual pleasure was a gray area, consummation would only make things harder, especially if he intended to let her go at the end of all of it. And he did. Courtland had no intention of keeping her trapped in a marriage she did not want. And worse yet, if a child resulted from an act of passion, she would be even more tied to him. Neither of them needed that kind of complication.

Therefore, he would keep his distance. He *had* to. Even if it meant he had to be as distant as possible so she had a chance to walk away with her dignity intact and reclaim the future he'd deprived her of. It was the least he could do.

The end of the season was only a few short months anyway. They would go to London and be seen, he would deal with Stinson and the dukedom, and then Ravenna could go back to Kettering to live her life, whereupon he would return to Antigua.

They would both get what they wanted, and go their separate, happy ways.

Easy enough, if he could keep his lust in check.

"Fancy a drink, little fairy?"

From her place on the happily empty promenade deck, Ravenna glared at the odious man whose smirk made her want to punch him in his smug face. "Call me that again, Mr. Sommers, and you won't be smiling."

"I can see why he wants you."

She threw an arm blearily across her face. "Who does?"

To Ravenna's absolute dismay, the man plunked his bulk down in the chaise that sat a few feet away from hers. "Ashvale, of course."

He settled in, to Ravenna's alarm. Even the slightest noise made her head throb. Peabody, bless his tiny, mouselike valet heart, had brought her a cure-all headache tincture early this morning when she'd woken up in the duke's wonderful bed, but the effects were already wearing off.

Sommers smiled unpleasantly at her. "You're quite a firebrand."

"I prefer to be direct, sir."

"Aren't all posh Englishwomen supposed to be demure and quiet?"

Are all American men so obtuse?

Thankfully, her reckless, brazen tongue did not communicate that. "We come in all shapes and sizes, Mr. Sommers."

"I see that."

This time she did not mistake the lewd gaze that swept down the fitted front of her modest walking ensemble. There was nothing to see, no daring décolletage on display. No, the Garibaldi shirt buttoned to her neck, but one would think that she was one of the puddings served at dinner, the way the man ogled her person.

She wished her husband was close by so he could put the man in his place, but the duke was not, so it was up to her. "It's rude to stare, Mr. Sommers."

His expression went hawkish. "I can't help admiring a beautiful woman."

"I am married, sir."

"So am I."

What a brute. Ravenna closed her eyes, once more with the hope that he'd take the obvious hint that she did not want company. How did one indicate one was *not at home* when out in public? She wished she had a fan. She could swat it open and place it on her left ear, clearly stating *I wish to get rid of you.* Or perhaps a slow, deliberate fanning movement, one that would indicate *Don't waste your time. I don't care about you.* Not that Mr. Clodhead would get it. She put a hand to her temples, unable to suppress a groan.

"Are you enjoying the voyage?" he asked.

"Most days."

Sommers laughed, and the sound was like cannons firing. Oh, good heavens, why wouldn't the dratted man *go*?

She tried to get the attention of Lady Waterstone who had just appeared on the foredeck and was giggling and leaning over the railing gazing into the depths of the ocean. Lord Waterstone appeared behind her, making her squeal. The blond gentleman whispered something to her that made her turn in his arms and then burst into laughter. The obvious closeness between the two of them made envy flood Ravenna's veins.

She wobbled to her feet, and her nemesis, Mr. Sommers, was quick to follow. "May I escort you back to your stateroom, my lady? Or perhaps to one of the lounges?"

The man was a slimy prick. She couldn't countenance that her husband was in any kind of business with such a man, yet here he was traveling with them like an esteemed guest. Despite her irritation, curiosity dug at her. Perhaps she could find out why.

"Walk with me, Mr. Sommers," she said, knowing she wouldn't be rid of him so easily and choosing to get some answers instead. "Let's take a turn about the ship." He offered her his arm, but she did not take it—a small breach of etiquette that she hoped he would not notice. His small frown appeared and disappeared in the same breath. "So tell me, how do you know the duke?"

"We've done some business together over the years."

"Business?" she inquired, though her stomach clenched at the implication.

"Trade and investments, among other things."

What other things?

Ravenna frowned. Courtland didn't strike her as a man who dabbled in illegal affairs. Then again, how well did she know the man she'd married? She had known the boy during her childhood, but she of all people knew how easily a person could change. And Courtland had deeply buried secrets that had to do with Stinson and his family.

Who *was* he?

Her gaze spanned the polished slats of the deck and the shiny, well-made railings that ran the length of the hull. This ship itself was worth a small fortune. How *did* her husband make his money? The old Duke of Ashvale had been by no means poor, but this kind of wealth was beyond what most of the peerage enjoyed.

Ravenna's stomach sank. Was Courtland truly involved with a man like Sommers?

"Is this your first time to England?" she asked.

Sommers grinned. "No, but it's my first time as the honored guest of a duke." An insolent gaze scanned her. "Duchess as well."

Oh no. Surely, he did not intend to stay with them. She would retire to Huntley House in London with her mother if that was the case. At least on this massive ship, she had enough room to thwart him. In a London town house, that would be impossible. And every instinct screamed that she would not want to be cornered by this man. As a matter of fact, he reminded her very much of the Marquess of Dalwood. They shared the same sense of entitlement and viewed people as things to own.

"Ashvale did not mention it."

"A man doesn't have to tell his spouse everything," Sommers said, voice lowering to a cadence he probably thought was seductive. All it did was make her skin crawl. "We all have secrets, darlin.'"

Ravenna came to a sharp stop and tilted her chin. "Mr. Sommers, you are overstepping," she said coldly. "I am happily married and do not keep secrets from my husband."

"Is there a problem here?" They both turned to see the Duke of Ashvale striding toward them.

Ravenna caught her breath, her heart tripping over itself at the welcome sight of him. Despite her lie to Sommers about being happily married, heaven knew Ashvale didn't feel that way. The only reason he'd put her in his bed the night before was because he didn't want her falling overboard and dying on his ship during his watch.

She didn't make him happy. She made him angry.

They were *unhappily* married.

Even now, his lips were a hard line, his eyes dark with a tornado of volatile emotion rolling through them. He was ever the storm around her, it seemed. Though it was the middle of the afternoon, he wasn't wearing a coat and his shirtsleeves were rolled up to expose tanned, muscular forearms. His inky hair was windblown, his cheeks ruddy, as if he'd been doing some form of manual labor. Ravenna liked that he wasn't indolent like other gentlemen and was willing to use his hands.

He'd used them well enough on her.

Goodness, where had *that* thought come from?

"All is well," Sommers drawled, annoyance flashing in his gaze. "Just accompanying the duchess for a turn about the deck. It's a lovely afternoon."

It had *been* a lovely afternoon until he'd interrupted it. Ravenna shook her head. "I was just about to go in. I fear I might've had a bit too much sun."

The duke's inscrutable gaze panned from her to Sommers. "Shall I escort you?"

"You look busy," she said, not wanting her neediness to show. "I can find my own way."

"Please, I insist."

She did not argue, resting her gloved fingers on the crook of her husband's elbow. Feeling the weight of Sommers's displeased stare, she was grateful to the duke for his timely arrival. Given his state of dishevelment, she wondered if a servant had fetched him in a hurry. She hadn't seen anyone on deck besides Lord and Lady

Waterstone, and they had been much too preoccupied with each other to have noticed Sommers's persistent attentions to her. But someone must have.

"Be seeing you, Duchess." Sommers drawled the address in the same way he'd called her *darlin'*, and that made her flesh crawl. Ravenna could not hide the way her fingers jerked on Courtland's arm, but she could have sworn every muscle in her husband's body went rigid. She didn't have to look at him to know that he was furious when he led her indoors.

Was he upset with her? Did he think *she* encouraged the odious man?

"Your Grace, I—" He silenced her with his body as he blanketed her against the wainscoting of the inside passageway.

"Did he touch you? Hurt you?"

She shook her head with a frown. "No."

Tension bled from him, even as his eyes searched hers. "Keep away from him."

"He's a friend of yours, is he not?"

"Far from it." Still looming in the empty corridor, the duke inhaled a deep breath and then exhaled raggedly as if the scent of her was too much to bear. His nose grazed the hollow beneath her ear as one muscled male thigh wedged between the skirts of her dress, making her gasp. "You smell of sunshine and the ocean."

"I was outside," she whispered, her knees instantly going weak at the gossamer pressure of his lips on her skin. Anyone could come upon them where they stood, but she didn't care. Neither did he.

"Why can't I keep my hands off you?" It was a tortured question, a rhetorical one she knew he didn't expect her to answer. Besides, she wanted his hands on her. All over her. Beneath her garments. *Everywhere*. Her body craved it. Demanded it. Her need was an insistent pulse in her head and between her legs. He shoved himself off the wall—off of her—with effort, his breath coming in harsh, hard pants. "Stay away from Sommers."

"Just like you want me to stay away from Stinson?" She hadn't meant to sound so waspish, but she was sick of his abrupt rejections. Sommers wasn't on her list of favorite people, and she'd gladly stay away from him, but Courtland's constant push and pull hurt. One minute he couldn't get enough of her; the next he was shoving her away. It was exhausting. "Who will it be next? Lord Waterstone?"

A muscle kicked in his jaw. "What did he do?"

"Nothing, he's madly in love with his wife if you hadn't noticed." She ground her teeth, inexplicably angry. "Then again, a blockhead like you wouldn't notice such insignificant things. Why don't you just leave me alone, Ashvale!"

He gave a harsh, desolate-sounding laugh. "If only I could."

Ashvale. She called him by his bloody title whenever she wanted to distance herself. It pierced him for no good reason. It was a name—*his* name. Surely he should get used to it! Courtland stared down at his impassioned wife, lips parted and eyes sparkling with hurt and rage. Hurt he'd put there. Yet again. He licked his lips, the honeyed salt of her skin resting upon them like dew, and suddenly, he wanted to taste every luscious inch of her.

He wanted to eat her alive.

She wants you. Put yourself out of your misery.

The thought was provocative. Sly in the extreme. Lust and fury battled through him like twin demons, but Courtland made himself see reason. He'd always been good at that. He could isolate a problem, take it apart, and solve it. His tantalizing wife was the problem.

With her, he could fight, fuck, or flee.

The last two were not practical—the second led to unnecessary complications and the third was an impossibility unless he planned to swim for England—which left only one option.

"You will obey me, Ravenna," he bit out, his voice hard. "Keep your distance from Sommers *and* Stinson, and anyone else I tell you to."

"*Obey?*" The reply practically vibrated with wrath. If looks could kill a man, Courtland knew he'd be skewered into tiny, unrecognizable pieces and flung into the dark waters of the Atlantic.

"You pledged your troth in your marriage vows," he said, folding his arms across his chest. "Do I need to remind you of it?"

"Do I need to remind you of your oaths?" she shot back. "How dare you make such demands of me?"

His look was coolly assessing. "I am your husband."

"Only when it suits you," she snapped. "Save us both the trouble and tell me what it is you want from me, Your Grace."

Your body. Your consent. Your surrender.

But none of those things were his to demand. Courtland blew out a breath.

"Stay away from Stinson and Sommers, Ravenna, or so help me, I won't be responsible for my actions." Face clenched, he ran a hand through his hair. "And all I want is to just to put this whole goddamned mess behind me."

"Were you always such a bastard?"

"Sadly no, or none of this fucking charade would be necessary, would it?" She reared back as if he'd slapped her, but Courtland dug the knife in and twisted it for good measure. "If I were a bastard, you would be ruined from your own folly, I would be living a life I love, and no one would expect me to fall on my unworthy sword to save a selfish brat from her silly, self-indulgent capers. Of all the goddamned luck, *you* had to crash into my life."

She flinched from the words as though they were blows. The anger drained from her starkly beautiful face, only to be replaced with a queer sort of distress. Her eyes, so full of life and fight before, went hollow.

Regret filled him and he reached for her before he could stop himself. "Ravenna—"

"Don't touch me."

Then she whirled in a flurry of skirts and dashed away.

Nine

Cold-blooded didn't begin to describe the stone of a man she'd married. For the hundredth time in two days, Ravenna wished she'd never married him. Wished she'd never crossed paths with him. Ruination would have been a pleasure cruise over being an unwanted, pitiful duchess whom he'd married out of *bad luck*.

"Are you well, milady?" Colleen asked shyly.

Ravenna glanced over her shoulder, throttling her resentment. "Yes, though I am quite ready to get off of this ship."

"I've never been to London," the maid said, looking up from her packing. "What's it like?"

"It's big and busy."

And fake and exhausting and suffocating.

Though in truth, she'd take town over her current circumstance in a heartbeat. Her husband resented her. Sommers stalked her at every opportunity. Lady Holding held her in silent contempt, criticizing everything from her short hair to her clothing choices to her impolite, unladylike views. God forbid that she dared have an opinion about anything that wasn't needlepoint. On top of that, Lord and Lady Waterstone were acting like a pair of besotted lovers every time she saw them.

Heaven help her, she was *this* close to murdering someone!

Thankfully, the end was in sight.

Rawley had informed her that they'd make landfall in less than an hour. And then the lies would begin in earnest, whereupon she would emulate the Dowager Duchess of Embry, exemplifying the impeccable hauteur of her mother. Ravenna had married a duke and they had come to London to put on a show.

At the sound of the stateroom door closing, Ravenna turned to find her husband staring at her. Her heart caught in her throat and she fought the instant physical reaction to him. She wondered if he felt the same elemental spark that made her acutely aware of him whenever he entered a room. Probably not. Since the altercation in the corridor what seemed like an eternity ago, he'd avoided her like the plague. She'd done the same with him, distracting herself with the pleasures to be found onboard the luxurious ship: entertaining musicales, games, extravagant dinners, dancing…anything to avoid seeing or thinking of him.

It had worked during the day.

At night, however, her efforts failed her miserably. Her dreams left her hot, bothered, drenched between the legs, and utterly deprived of sleep.

The duke cleared his throat. "We'll be arriving soon."

Even the deep tenor of his voice tormented her, giving her starved senses a hollow thrill. Ravenna wished she was immune to him. Wished he wasn't so absurdly appealing, impeccably dressed as he was in rich, dove-gray trousers and a navy waistcoat shot through with silver thread. The colors brought out a light sheen in the darkness of his eyes—a warmth that had been subdued since they'd left Antigua.

Because of her.

Ravenna bit her lip. It was done now; this was their fate. For better or worse, they were the Duke and Duchess of Ashvale.

Ravenna inclined her head. "Thank you for telling me."

"You look well," he said stiffly.

Colleen had dressed her in one of her new traveling dresses—a pale-blue ensemble with floral embroidery. Ravenna wondered whether the maid had planned for their clothing to match so splendidly, or maybe it was wishful thinking on her part. She smoothed the front of her skirts with a self-conscious palm. "Thank you, so do you," she said.

"We'll continue to London via my private rail car," he said, retrieving his pocket watch. "I've sent some staff ahead to make sure everything is ready for our arrival."

Ravenna eyed him, knowing full well that Stinson and his mother would be at the London residence. She couldn't remember the exact ages of his sisters, Bronwyn and Florence, but she had a feeling one of them would be of age. Both girls were more than a handful of years younger, though Stinson had come one year and nine months to the day his father had finished mourning his late wife and remarried. Lady Borne had wasted no time producing a son of her own.

"Where are we staying, may I ask?"

Unfathomable dark-brown eyes met hers. "I own several properties in London. One of those, I presume. Rawley handled the details."

"Naturally."

Silence spun like a web between them, thick and uncomfortable until he cleared his throat again. Uncertainty flashed over him. "Ravenna."

"Yes, Your Grace?"

He flinched at the formal address, his mouth flattening, but then he wiped all expression from his face and drew himself upright. His voice was quiet. "I never intended to marry, but here we are. I intend to honor those vows for your sake, and for the sake of my sisters."

His matter-of-fact tone gutted her, but this was their reality. "I am aware of your reasons for this marriage, Your Grace."

"In town, I trust you will conduct yourself as befits the Duchess of Ashvale, no matter your personal feelings toward me. It has come to my attention that it will be Bronwyn's first season. You will smile and charm, and pretend to be pleased with your new position as my wife. Evidence of a strong, caring union will put gossip to rest and ensure suitable offers."

Swallowing hard, Ravenna nodded, keeping her spine locked. The ache in her stomach rippled and grew, the urge to weep stinging the backs of her eyes. *A strong, caring union.* What a sodding joke. *Here* was the ruthless indifference he was known for.

"As you wish," she managed to say. "I won't disgrace you, if that is your fear. You've made your expectations of this marriage perfectly clear. As you've said, I am in your debt."

"It's not like that," he said with a frown.

Ravenna raised a palm, heart splintering for reasons beyond her control. "I will make it my mission to see your sister happily launched by the end of the season." She did not meet his eyes. "You've made it more than clear, Duke…when I am to speak, when I am to smile, when I am to breathe. As your faithful servant and obedient wife, I will do as you require." Ravenna curtsied low, catching sight of his shaken, embittered expression before he stalked away, leaving her alone.

Her limbs gave out and she sank to the floor in a pool of pastel-blue skirts. The tears she'd been holding back broke free. She rarely cried. Not when her mother took her to task for not being a proper young lady. Not even when Rhystan had left her alone to go on his travels.

But this man…her husband…he could eviscerate her with a few well-chosen words. Shatter her with a look from those hard, emotionless eyes. Break her unconscionably.

Because there was no way she was going to survive this.

Or survive *him*.

He'd lied to his wife. Twice.

The first was when he'd told her that a strong, united front would put gossip to rest. That had been purely selfish on his end.

Courtland simply couldn't stand the thought of her looking at him with apathy in front of their peers, even if he'd been the one to hammer the wedge between them in the first place. But instead of making things better, he'd only made them worse. Now she was intent on *obeying* him to death.

The second was that Courtland had known exactly where they were going. The house in Mayfair was one of the first he had bought when he'd made his fortune, mostly as a slap in the face to Stinson who had commandeered the family's town house as though it was his right. Courtland hadn't even come back to England to canvass the location. He'd bought it sight unseen for an exorbitant sum. Primarily because it sat directly opposite Ashvale Manor.

He was a vengeful soul.

Stinson likely didn't know that the property had been bought by him because Courtland hadn't made the sale public knowledge. The transaction had been private. But his brother would swiftly learn who his new neighbors were now that they were in residence.

He wondered what his sisters were like now. He didn't fault them for their egregious bloodline on their mother's side, but he would not be surprised if they had turned out just like the marchioness—greedy, blinkered, and arrogant. Seven and eight years his junior, he had no idea what they looked like either. Bronwyn would be nearing eighteen, and Florence, sixteen. He would withhold judgment before deciding whether he would consider them family.

Their brother's sins weren't theirs.

Pacing the floor of the well-appointed study, Courtland pressed his fingers to his temples, feeling the beginnings of a migraine. He hadn't had one in years, but London brought out the worst in him. Breathing in the thick, smoggy air had felt like inhaling soup through his nostrils, unlike the clean tropical air of the island. And London stank. Between the reek of the Thames and the filthy, clogged streets, he'd wanted to turn right back around, head for the *Glory*, and go back home.

One devastating kiss had set him on this path. He'd always been a big believer in small movements having big ripple effects, particularly in his study of commerce, but this was altogether something different. How had one small kiss taken on the power to change multiple lives, to impact the futures and hopes of so many? To get him to set foot on these shores when he'd sworn on his mother's grave never to return. It was inconceivable.

His head pounded with renewed force.

"Rawley?" he called out, the sound of his own voice echoing off the walls sending stabbing pains through his temples. "Inform Peabody that I require some of that Collis Browne's tincture."

The voice that answered wasn't the deep male one he expected and every nerve in his body leapt at the husky feminine notes of it. "Chlorodyne? Are you not well, Your Grace?"

"A headache," he said as his wife appeared in the doorway.

Curiously, the sight of her did much to dispel the dark fog stewing in his brain. Her windblown hair was an auburn cloud about her face, disobedient ringlets escaping their pins, and her porcelain cheeks were flushed a becoming rose. Her copper eyes sparkled with health and vivacity. Dimly, he registered that she was dressed in a smart riding habit and had evidently just returned from a ride. "Were you out?"

"Oh, I wanted to check in on Athena, my mare, and the weather was so lovely that I decided to take her for a quick turn about Hyde Park." She took a few hesitant steps toward him, bringing with her the scent of crisp air and that underlying fragrance that was uniquely hers—plumeria with a hint of peppery spice. London seemed to suit her. A concerned sherry gaze traveled his face. "You do look rather pale. Shall we fetch the doctor?"

"No," he said, moving behind the huge desk to put a barrier between them, lest he reach out and wind his needy fingers in that soft, unruly mass of curls that begged for him to touch it. "That's not necessary. Peabody will attend to me."

His wife eyed him, sidling closer, her own indecision clear in her eyes. Courtland's chest clenched. He resented that it had come to this. That they tiptoed on eggshells around each other, barely able to have a conversation lasting more than a minute beyond the standard greetings and platitudes. He hated them like this. He hated that he'd caused her any injury at all, made her feel as though she was beholden to him. The truth was that he missed their sharp-edged banter.

He missed *them*.

His regret must have shown on his face because she nodded once and gave him a tentative smile. "Do you trust me?" she asked softly.

It was a loaded question. In business, he trusted no one. In life, he'd fashioned himself a home somewhere safe, one which did not require much interaction with others, apart from a select few that included his man of business, his valet, and most definitely not his wife.

"Why?"

"I have an alternate remedy," she said, though irritation flashed in her stare at the curt question, followed by a defiant toss of her head. "Do you trust me not to poison you in the hopes of breaking the bonds of wedlock at your death, I mean?"

A choked laugh rose in his throat. Was she serious? Her unreadable face said she might not be, but he nodded, grudgingly. "I suppose so."

"Very well, I shall return shortly."

She left the study, and the dull throb in his skull resumed. Courtland slid into his chair and propped his aching head onto his hands, only to look up as someone entered the room with a tentative knock. Not his wife...his valet.

"The tincture, Your Grace," Peabody said, bringing the small

medicine bottle toward him. He rarely used it as it contained laudanum and other mixtures that acted as a sedative and clouded his
wits, but sometimes, he had no choice.

"It's all right, Peabody. The duchess is attending to me, but
don't fret, she promised not to murder me." The valet's eyes widened and Courtland fought back a laugh. "A joke, Peabody."

"You don't joke, Your Grace."

"No, I expect I don't."

One more change in disposition he supposed he had to thank
his wife for—the bold and thoroughly exasperating duchess. It
should bother him, but it didn't. Ravenna was...*Ravenna*. Fearless
in the extreme and curious about everything, she possessed a terrible sense of humor and was blessed with an unusually generous
heart. She always had been like that, even as a girl.

A forgotten memory rose to his thoughts.

Years ago, they'd once found a baby bird in the woods between
their estates with a wounded wing, and she'd insisted on ferrying
it back to its nest. It'd been a long shot that it would survive, but
she hadn't given up, climbing and returning it to its nest high up in
the boughs of an elm, even when a dour Stinson had sneered that
some things weren't worth saving.

They'd found the baby raven at the tree's base a few days later.
Its neck had been snapped.

"Oh," Ravenna had cried, dissolving in tears and dropping to
her knees. "Perhaps it tried to fly and couldn't. Do you suppose
that's what happened, Cordy?"

A young Courtland had stared at the dead bird and its glazed,
unseeing eyes. Birds didn't suddenly get their necks broken, especially not *this* specific bird. He suspected his brother had had
something to do with it. Stinson was known for his cruelty. He
would have done it for spite.

Courtland had gnawed his lip. "Sometimes they fall from their
nests."

"I thought most birds knew how to fly?"

"Ostriches don't," he'd said, trying to distract her. "And penguins."

It had worked. He'd buried that bird later and shed his own quiet tears in private. He had no idea why he'd been so sad. Perhaps his ten-year-old self had somehow seen himself mirrored in that poor little bird that someone decided hadn't deserved to live. Hadn't been deemed of worth. Like him.

Courtland shook himself from the bittersweet memory as Ravenna returned, a steaming cup of something in her hands. "Do you ever think of that baby raven we found?" he asked.

Her pretty eyes swam with confusion as she set the teacup in front of him. "The one in the woods between the estates in Kettering?"

"Yes."

She leaned one hip against the desk, her body close. Too close for comfort. One shift of his elbow and he'd be touching her skirts. Another shift and a tug, and she would be seated in his lap. His jaw clenched, adding to the vicious ache in his skull.

"It couldn't fly," she said. "Broke its neck, you said. I wept for days. What made you think of that?"

"No reason." He shook his head. How could he begin to explain that it was a metaphor? That London was the elm and he was the bird. That his own brother had sought to snap his neck and oust him from his nest. He reached for the steaming liquid. "What is this?"

"Willow-bark tea with crushed ginger and cloves," she said. "Sarani, Rhystan's duchess, taught me how to make it. It's better than laudanum for pain." Courtland sipped, the taste of it surprisingly not bitter as one would expect with willow bark. His wife smiled at his expression. "I added a touch of honey as well."

Without a word, she shifted off the desk and moved behind him. A discarded glove appeared, and then another. Cool fingertips grazed his temples and pressed gently. He couldn't suppress his groan of pleasure. "What are you doing?"

"Just relax and drink your tea."

"Wait, this is not…"

Fingers stilling, she blew out an aggravated hiss. "For once in your stubborn life, will you let someone take care of you?"

"So tyrannical," he muttered, eyes nearly rolling back when her fingers resumed their work and sank into his hair, massaging in small, firm circles. Without another word, he took a sip of the tea.

"Only when the situation calls for it." Her hands threaded through his mane, brushing it off his brow and temples. Pleasure lit up his nerve endings.

"Ravenna." He shifted and her fingers dug in to his scalp.

"Cordy."

He hissed out a breath. "Nobody has called me that in years."

"You haven't been this irritating in years," she said. Was it his imagination, or had her sensual voice grown a tad huskier? "Sit still and let me do this for you. It's no hardship and I've been told I'm quite good this."

The beat of jealousy took him by surprise. "Who told you that?"

"My harem of male lovers, who else?" she replied with a small laugh. It wasn't as funny to him and he scowled. Her fingertips smoothed over his furrowed brow. "My mother, silly. She suffers from frequent migraines. Massage helps."

He sighed at the firm ministrations. She *was* rather skilled, her hands moving in small, concentrated circles. Courtland opened his mouth to tell her so, but then lost all power of speech when those warm, strong fingers slid down his bare nape to knead into the tight muscles there.

"Damnation, woman." He breathed out, closing his eyes.

She laughed. "I suppose there's a compliment in there somewhere."

"Your hands are bloody magic."

"Thank you." Her voice was a liquid caress as her proficient hands stilled and lifted, and he mourned their loss. "Would you be so kind so as to remove your coat and waistcoat?" His eyes snapped open at the husky, nearly erotic command. She might have well commanded him to take off his trousers. The thought nearly unmanned him.

"It's not proper."

"How so? I'm your wife," she said from behind him, her warm breath gusting against his ear, and he had the abrupt desire to instantly strip himself bare. For some reason, the fact that he couldn't see her face added to the sexual tension currently flooding the study. "Besides, the door is closed. There's no one in here but you and me."

"Peabody and the servants will know." Courtland wanted to take the asinine words back as soon as he said them. When had he become so missish? He couldn't give a shit about Peabody, or anyone else, even if the house started to burn down around his ears.

Her laughter tickled his hairline. "Since when do you care?"

Since she'd turned him into a prudish henwit, apparently. Courtland was grateful the desk was covering most of his lap because his shaft suddenly had no intention of behaving. Against his own forewarnings, he shrugged out of his upper layers, not missing his wife's fine intake of breath. The soft lawn of his shirt grazed over his highly sensitive skin.

"Finish your tea and lean back," she said, and fuck if that throaty edict didn't harden him to forged steel.

Fingers reached around to unknot his cravat to reward him after he'd emptied the cup, and then slipped beneath the collar of his shirt to his bare skin. At her expert and divinely blissful touch, every nerve ending in his body went screamingly alive: his skin burned, his stomach clenched, and his cock wept.

Devil take it, he was going to purgatory.

Ten

GRACIOUS, SHE WAS A FOOL. AN IMBECILE. A DOLT. AN UTTER dunce.

Why on earth would she do this to herself? Torture herself thus? Hadn't she learned her lesson when it came to him? He would no doubt find some reason to push her away and then pretend he felt nothing. But clearly, she was a glutton for punishment. She should have brought the sodding tea and left it, but no…she just had to go and touch him. Revel in his thick, soft curling hair, delight in the strong, corded muscles of his neck, and now gorge herself on the spectacular glimpse of deliciously brown skin peeking from beneath the soft, white fabric of his shirt.

Ravenna couldn't believe that he'd removed his clothing after her scandalous request. She could hardly countenance that *she'd* asked, that such an audacious demand had even fallen from her lips! It was so shameless of her, though she wasn't complaining. Because here he was…her gorgeous specimen of a husband in shirtsleeves and entirely at her mercy.

And he had never looked more splendid.

An unrepentant Hades, and her, a salivating Persephone.

His shoulders were deliciously broad, his shape so palpably masculine that Ravenna couldn't stop from sighing. Her mouth watered indelicately, her blood running hot and her core clenching with need. She was glad she couldn't see his face and that he could not see hers, but there was something about it that was surprisingly intimate without the connection of their eyes. He *trusted* her, trusted her touch. And in truth, that made her bolder.

She resumed her attentions, digging her thumbs into the bunched, hard muscle. The duke's skin was hot beneath her exploring fingertips. She kneaded his shoulders and massaged down the sides of his spine. Soon, there was nothing but their combined breaths in the silence as she worked. His breathing had reduced to ragged sighs, and she could barely breathe herself, but still she soldiered on.

A few more minutes and then she would leave. All would be well, decorum observed, and modesty would be no worse for wear. On the outside, anyway.

"Fuck it," Courtland muttered, making her startle, and wrenched the shirt over his head.

Oh, for the love of things holy, Ravenna's knees buckled. She didn't know where to look. She wanted to absorb every single sinful detail of the masculine feast on display before her. Courtland was, by any stretch of the imagination, the most exquisitely built man she'd ever seen. The glimpse beneath the gap of his neckline had in no way prepared her for the glorious breadth of him or the muscles flexing beneath warm brown skin.

She wanted to lick him. *Devour* him.

In a mindless haze, she leaned down to press a kiss to his shoulder, and Courtland twisted in the same motion, capturing her parted lips with his. She gasped. He groaned. The kiss was not gentle. Teeth scraped against teeth. His mouth widened on hers, his tongue delving deep, taking control and claiming her with every demanding stroke. Undeterred by his ferocity, she leaned in, wanting more and giving him no quarter, her pent-up desires as greedy as his.

Courtland's hand reached up to cup her nape, holding her in place as he drank from her lips, drawing moan after ragged moan from the depths of her. With a smothered rumble of his own, he yanked her into his lap without breaking their carnal connection. Ravenna gasped into his mouth. Oh, good gracious, he was fully aroused, his stiffened length prodding through the layers of her riding habit to tempt the hot, simmering space between her thighs.

Her core ached, her nipples puckered beneath her bodice, and she hadn't even yet put her hands on him. *Touch him, yes*! Greedy palms traced down the carved planes of his chest, the ridges of his tight pectoral muscles as impressive as the ones on his back. Crisp hair tickled her fingers. If he ever released her lips, she'd feast on that sight as well…see if her nightly fevered imaginings matched up with the reality.

"How I want you," he muttered against her mouth.

Want. It was such an ineffective word to describe the sheer need barreling through her body with the force of a torrent, but Ravenna nodded, unable to do anything else. Courtland's eyes glowed like pools of midnight. She'd never seen them so full of reflective light, so full of melting desire. If he wanted to strip the dress off of her, she'd agree to that, too.

"Then take me," she said. "I'm yours."

"Mine."

Ravenna blinked. Was the whispered word a question? A rhetorical one? His eyes ravaged hers, so many emotions barreling through them: need, confusion, worry, sadness, and finally, the creeping arrival of the grim, implacable resolve she was used to.

"Don't, Courtland, please," she whispered. "Be with me."

"Fuck, this is impossible!" The cry was bitterly furious as one hand fisted in her hair and the other in her skirts. His forehead pressed against hers, his heady male scent surrounding her. "I can't. We *can't*."

"Why? I'm here…willingly. I want this, too."

"This is lust, Ravenna," he replied through his teeth. "That's all this is, and we both know that."

She blinked her confusion. "So what?"

"It's a fool's cause. The sooner we accept that, the better off we will be."

The blunt words were shocking, but nothing could hurt as much as when he lifted her off of him in one swift move and stood, reaching for his discarded shirt. She watched in silence as he put himself to rights, covering up that beautiful body of his…hiding himself from the world—from *her*—once more.

"Why would you say that? Surely, we can make the best of this, even if it means we seek comfort in each other? We've married for better or for worse."

"We might be husband and wife for now, but I am not the man for you, Ravenna." He ran a hand through his hair. "Getting more deeply involved with me will muddle things for both of us. It will ruin things for you and the future you deserve. I won't take that from you."

Ravenna blinked, trying to understand. Was he talking about his birth? She shook her head. "You know I don't care about any of that, and besides, that's my decision to make."

His eyes were bleaker than she'd ever seen them. "You should care. Blood makes a man."

"Blood is a bodily fluid that keeps us alive. It has little to do with who we are and what we make of ourselves."

"Said like a woman who has lived a charmed life."

The words were soft but gutting, and her breath hissed out on a pained exhale. "I might not walk in your shoes, Courtland, but please stop treating me as if I'm incapable of learning. As if I have no hope of empathizing."

"You don't. How could you?"

His eyes widened as she whirled away from the desk. "I can try. And before you ask me why, it's because I care about you! I always have. This is about *you* and *me*. I think you're afraid, Courtland." She ignored the beat of the muscle in his cheek and the layers of hardness in his eyes. "You're keeping me at a distance because you're terrified to let anyone in. You're terrified to let someone get close to you, and you know it."

"Have a care, Ravenna."

She frowned at him. "Who hurt you so badly?"

"I am warning you, that is enough. Cease this."

"Why, Courtland?" Ravenna exhaled, her chest aching with a heart-wrenching need to comfort him. Whatever he felt about not deserving her didn't come from others, it came from *him*. From some place deep down inside that no one could breach, not even her. "Nothing you can say will push me away."

"Sure about that?"

The sharp rap on the door knocked them both from the intense standoff. "Your Grace?" Rawley called. "Your brother is here and insists on seeing you immediately."

Ravenna froze. What was Stinson doing here?

"Fine," the duke bit out. "Give me a few minutes and have Morgan show him in."

She blew out a breath, furious at being dismissed as though she didn't warrant any more of his attention. He'd already shut her out and closed down. It was in his very mien, in his shuttered gaze and taut mouth. She was tempted to rail and scream, and shake some sense into him, but this was neither the time nor the place.

"Lord Borne, Your Grace," the butler intoned.

Ignoring Courtland's derisive snort at the announcement, Ravenna turned as her brother-in-law walked in. Stinson looked the same. Tall, elegant, and handsome. There was a definite resemblance between the brothers, and Ravenna was struck by the similarities, some she'd never picked up on until they were in the same room side by side.

Notwithstanding Stinson's stark, pale skin and Courtland's golden-brown complexion, they shared the same bone structure in their high-bladed cheekbones and angular jaws. Though Stinson's hair was chestnut while his brother's was jet black, it was obvious to anyone that they were related.

She frowned at Stinson. The curious lack of joy at seeing

his brother alive struck her as decidedly odd. She was missing something, it seemed. Something that had to do with the chasm between them.

"So it's true then?" Stinson demanded without preamble, eyes widening and then filling with unadorned bitterness when they landed on her. "You've married."

"Yes" came the duke's eventual reply, his glacial gaze panning between them. "You are acquainted with my duchess."

Stinson tensed but then bowed. "I am."

Ravenna felt a looming presence and knew that the duke had come to stand beside her. Whether that was for her benefit or Stinson's, she did not know. A hand rested at the small of her back, his thumb brushing against her gown, and she bit her lip, cursing her body's instant and stupid response. This was part of the performance, nothing more.

Gnashing her teeth, she pushed a smile to her face and stepped out of his touch, moving toward her old friend. Ravenna felt her husband's glare against her back but she ignored it.

"Stinson," she greeted him fondly, hands outstretched. "It's been an age. You look well. How's everyone?"

Instead of kissing her hand, Stinson took it and leaned down to kiss her cheek. Ravenna heard the growl before her brain registered any hint of danger, but the look on Courtland's face was enough to make a grown man quail. "Get your damn hands off my wife."

Ravenna frowned. "My lord duke, what has gotten into you?"

He glared down at her, his eyes chips of stark black ice and his nostrils flared as though he was holding on to his control by the slimmest of margins. "Leave us."

Her temper blazed at the curt demand. How *dare* he order her about?

"Please don't depart on my account, dearest," Stinson drawled, clearly unconcerned by the murderous scene unfolding in front of him. "You're family now, after all. I admit the news took me by surprise, but you've always been precious to me."

Her husband's fingers flexed at his sides at the endearment and the declaration. Ravenna could have sworn there was a nasty edge in Stinson's voice, some unspoken communication passing between the brothers, but Stinson's face held the wide, unaffected, friendly smile he always used with her. A perverse part of her wanted to stay just to flout Courtland's demands, but she couldn't bring herself to defy him in front of others, even if it was only his brother.

"Perhaps another time then," she said with the most gracious smile she could manage given the simmering frustration beneath her skin. "It's good to see you, Stinson."

His lips curled upward. "And you. I look forward to catching up soon."

"It's *Lord* Stinson," Courtland hissed at her before glaring at his brother. "And definitely not Lord Borne as announced, considering his borrowed title of marquess is now obsolete. And no you won't see each other, not if I can help it."

Shocked at his vicious tone, Ravenna blinked up at the stone-faced duke and shook her head. His expression was positively glacial, rage emanating from him in thick waves. A stormy possessiveness also glittered in his eyes, which baffled her. A few moments ago, he couldn't wait to get away from her, yet now he was behaving like a lion whose pride had been trespassed upon by another.

Perhaps it was a different kind of pride. As in *male* pride. He didn't want her, but no one else could have her either. The man was simply impossible to predict! Ravenna gritted her teeth, stifling the burst of anger, and swept from the room before she did or said something she regretted. Perhaps when she was calmer and her husband was more amenable, she would revisit the subject of Stinson. Revisit the subject of *them*, too.

In the meantime, she had her own battles to fight.

"To what do I owe the visit, Brother?" Courtland asked after his wife had left, stalking over to the mantel and pouring himself a liberal drink. It probably wouldn't help with his headache, which had lessened a little, but he needed it so as not to decimate the man currently ensconced in his study. He did not offer his uninvited guest a drink.

He hadn't cared that Stinson had been throwing himself about as their father's remaining heir—or that he'd all too happily assumed the courtesy title of the Marquess of Borne with Courtland supposedly deceased—but seeing his hands upon Ravenna had awakened a primal deadly instinct inside of him.

"Why are you here?" The question from his half brother was blunt and belligerent.

There it was—the rub—as if neither of them could exist in the same country…as if the reality of his existence was only bearable when they were separated by an ocean. He eyed his brother. The last time he'd seen Stinson, he'd been fourteen, barely a man. Now a decade later, they were close to the same height, give or take a couple inches, and the distinctive features he saw in the mirror every day were evident in his brother's adult face.

Courtland had wondered if his younger brother would show signs of a dissipated lifestyle, but he seemed fit and hale. He'd filled out, grown up, and yet the hostility in his eyes had not diminished. Instead, it burned.

"Answer me, damn you! Why are you here?"

"I am now duke," Courtland replied evenly. "This is my place."

"You're not welcome." His brother's mouth twisted into a sneer.

Sipping his brandy, Courtland ambled toward the other side of his desk, taking his time. He'd known it would not be easy coming back, and especially dealing with Stinson's wild claims and his unfounded jealousy. Or his incessant attacks on Courtland's legitimacy. "I'm here to tend to my affairs. I think it best if we simply agree to stay out of each other's way." He steepled his fingers. "How are my sisters?"

Stinson scowled. "How dare you insult them? They're no sisters of yours, and none of us wants anything to do with you."

"Not even money from the ducal coffers?" he asked silkily.

"Wealth won't make people accept you," Stinson said. "And that money doesn't belong to you."

"Doesn't it? Grandfather's solicitor seems to think it does." Courtland smiled and waved a hand at their opulent surroundings. "Though I have no need of it. I have more than enough of my own, as you can clearly see."

"This place was sold years ago," his brother said. "It's not yours."

"It is. I was the one who bought it."

Stinson's gaze narrowed. "So you married Lady Ravenna for the same reason you acquired this house in secret. To prove that you're better than me. Here's a hint—you are not. You will never be. You're just the mongrel born on the wrong side of the blanket from your conniving commoner of a mother, and soon that news will be fodder for the masses, too."

His blood boiled in his veins at the insults, but Courtland kept his face composed and his hands occupied around his glass instead of his brother's neck. "Is that what you came to tell me? You made those feelings perfectly clear eleven years ago. I assure you I have nothing to prove to you or to anyone."

Stinson slammed his fist down on the desk. "Stay out of my way."

"Or what?"

"You'll find I'm not the boy I once was."

The threat was empty. Stinson was exactly the same as he'd been as a boy. Cowardly and hateful. Only now he was driven by greed and narcissism that had increased tenfold with adulthood. "Is that a threat?" Courtland drawled.

"Take it as you see it."

"Rawley!" Courtland called out, knowing his cousin would be close by.

"Yes, Your Grace?" His man of business appeared with two sizable footmen in tow. Courtland had to bite back his grin both at Stinson's expression and at Rawley's preparedness. His cousin knew him better than he knew himself.

"Show my dear brother out before he hurts himself with all his grandiose posturing."

After Stinson took his leave, his face purple with fury at practically being thrown out, Courtland sat back in his seat. Stinson didn't worry him. Courtland would do what he came to England for, and then quite happily go back to Antigua.

His headache still throbbed at the base of his skull, but his wife's recipe had worked better than he'd expected. The tea, at least. The rest of it… Well, thinking about what had very nearly happened made him groan.

Then take me.

He would have, too, if reason hadn't intervened, followed by a timely interruption.

He let out a low chuckle at Ravenna's statement that blood was naught but a fluid. Her cleverness and her unswerving loyalty astounded him. In another world at another time, perhaps he and Ravenna could have remained betrothed as children, married as adults, and perhaps life would have been different. Perhaps even he could have let himself love her.

His throat knotted. Love wasn't in the cards for him. Once more, his astute little wife was right. Loving someone meant letting them inside—letting them see the real him with all his flaws, all his fears, and all his faults—and that was something he would never again do. If his own brother by blood could barely stand to look at him, much less love him, how could he expect anyone else to?

Still, he owed Ravenna an explanation, at least, for his behavior around Stinson, as well as the irascibility arising from his own jealousy.

"Rawley," he called out. "Where's the duchess?"

The man appeared like a wraith. "Her Grace has gone out, sir."

He frowned. "Gone out where?"

"I believe she took the carriage to visit her mother, shortly after Lord Stinson arrived." Rawley cleared his throat. "She seemed quite…agitated."

Courtland couldn't begrudge her that, of course, and he knew why she was upset. He blew out an aggravated breath and scrubbed a palm through his hair, remembering the sublime feel of her fingers kneading over his scalp. He also knew he could not let her face the Dowager Duchess of Embry on her own.

Not if any of the gossip had reached London.

"Tell someone to get me a horse," he said.

Rawley grinned as though him riding to a damsel's rescue was an everyday occurrence. "Right away, Your Grace."

"And Rawley?"

"Yes, Your Grace?"

"Wipe that bloody smile off your face before I do it for you."

His clown of a cousin only smiled wider.

Eleven

Ravenna sat in the ducal carriage, currently stationed outside Huntley House, her hands in her lap. She'd needed to leave, escape Courtland's overwhelming presence for a bit, and clear her head. Heavens, the man was going to drive her mad! His constant hot-cold behavior, his sudden chest-beating possessiveness, and his deep-seated enmity with Stinson were mindboggling.

While his mercurial moods were starting to become routine, the second had shocked her, though she knew it had something to do with the last. Growing up with three brothers, she was no stranger to sibling rivalry. But what she'd seen between Courtland and Stinson had seemed to go far beyond mere competition. It was almost as if they truly *hated* each other. One would think that Stinson would be happy to see his long-lost brother well and alive, but he hadn't been. Men were strange creatures at times.

Ravenna wrung her hands and stared up at her family's London home. While she wanted to escape her husband, she wasn't looking forward to facing her mother's temper either. If only Sarani was in town, but she and Rhystan had yet to leave their love nest in Hastings on the southern coast of England. And besides, Ravenna wasn't sure her sister-in-law would travel so soon with her new infant daughter.

A smile broke over her lips. She could do with some sweet baby comfort, and it'd been an age since she'd seen her sister by marriage. She wondered how long the journey was to Hastings. It would be at least half a day by coach if she were to leave right now.

Would Courtland even know she was gone? That she'd left town? Would he even care?

A tentative rap on the coach door made her jump. Her coachman would not have let anyone approach unless they were known to her. "Yes?"

"Lady Ravenna? It's Fuller. Do you require assistance?"

The familiar voice made her heart squeeze. Fuller, their butler, had long covered for many of her escapades over the years. What would he have to say about her latest scrape? With a sigh, she opened the carriage door. "Hullo, Fuller."

The butler smiled and offered his arm. "It's good to see your face, my lady!"

Ravenna gave a wry smile before alighting with his help. "It's 'Your Grace' now, I fear." When his eyes widened, she nodded with a sigh. "Duchess of Ashvale, in the flesh."

"Ashvale," he repeated. "Did you marry Lady Borne's son, the new duke?"

She shook her head. "Stinson isn't duke. His brother is."

"I beg your pardon, Lady Ravenna, er, Your Grace, but I thought the elder brother was deceased."

"You, me, and the rest of the *ton*. Turns out he's alive and well, much to everyone's everlasting surprise." She paused at the top of the stairs, as Fuller turned to look at her, an uncharacteristic smile on his face. Fuller wasn't one to display any kind of emotion, being the efficient butler he was, even when faced with the vagaries of her past exploits. "I never thought the day would come I'd see you a married lady. God save the man who caught you."

"Fuller!" Her eyes went wide with indignation as she swatted him. "You're supposed to be on my side!"

"For once, I'm delighted that someone else is on your side." He pointed at the spate of silver at his temples. "These gray hairs are all your doing, young lady."

She huffed a disbelieving laugh, the frustration sitting like a boulder on her chest melting away. Fuller had always been able to make her feel good about herself, even when he disapproved of her actions. She should have come home sooner. "I shall have you sacked for your cheek, you dreadful man."

He grinned and opened the door. "You cannot. The duchess cherishes me too much."

"My mother cherishes no one."

The levity disappeared from Fuller's face as he adopted his stern butler persona once more. Over the past few years, he'd become more of a father figure than a butler, and Ravenna felt flattered that the stoic, very proper fellow had chosen to share his true self with her. If only her standoffish husband would do the same.

On impulse, she hugged him, not caring which servants might see. She already had a reputation for being untoward and unpredictable. "I'm sorry for scaring you."

Fuller nodded, fondness flaring in his eyes.

Smoothing her patterned burgundy and ivory dress, Ravenna took a deep breath and walked down the familiar hallway. She deserved what was coming and more. She rounded the corridor and entered the salon, where her mother was sitting like a reigning queen on the settee, her face imperious, with a tea tray situated to her right.

"Her Grace, the Duchess of Ashvale," Fuller announced in the most affected voice she'd ever heard.

"Good Lord, man," Ravenna muttered under her breath. "Since when do you sound like a thespian?"

"You deserve it for disappearing as you did without nary a word, don't think you're forgiven," he said through the side of his mouth.

Ravenna stopped herself from pulling a face at the last minute, knowing her mother could see her. At first glance the dowager looked the same—haughty, untouchable, cold—but upon closer inspection, Ravenna could see the fine lines of strain at the corners of her mouth, the pallor of her already pale skin, and the gauntness of her cheeks.

Guilt slammed through her. She'd left a letter saying she was visiting with Clara and not to worry, but that was hardly an excuse. If any ugly gossip about her exploits had reached London, there was no telling what state her mother would be in.

"Mama," she greeted softly.

The dowager's icy gaze swept her, noting the fashionable new gown she wore, before examining her face and then pausing on the mop of curls that she'd attempted to smooth down with a hot iron and pomade. Her mouth curled down. "You've cut your hair."

Not like Ravenna could reply with: *I was pretending to be a man on a ship full of men. I cut my hair so as not to be ravaged.*

"Possibly not one of my better decisions," she said instead with a wary nod.

The duchess sniffed and lifted her tea to sip it. "It suits you."

Ravenna blinked. Who was this woman and where was her mother? "Er, thank you?"

"Sit, wretched child of mine, and pour yourself a cup of tea," the duchess said with an irritated frown. "And stop staring at me as if I've grown warts on my nose or some such. Surely I'm not so awful as to criticize a perfectly charming coiffure."

"Of course not, Mama," Ravenna said, obligingly taking a seat on the sofa across from the tea tray. "But you're rather calm in the face of..." Her voice trailed off.

"In the face of your disappearance and your barefaced fabrications?" The dowager tutted. "Poor Clara, she was in such a state after my arrival. That poor girl being with child and all. To think any daughter of mine would be such an awful, insensitive friend."

There were so many things to parse in that speech, starting with the fact that her mother was the queen of ice herself and ending with the fact that she went looking for Ravenna in Scotland. "You traveled to Edinburgh? And wait, Clara's with *child*?"

"Of course I went to Edinburgh," her mother said. "My fool daughter was missing!"

"I was hardly missing, Mama."

"And then, when I arrived to be told that you weren't in residence and that you never had been from the start, I feared the worst had befallen us." Ravenna waited. The *worst* to the Duchess of Embry could mean any number of things. "I feared that you had been abducted by highwaymen or had eloped with that dreadful scoundrel."

Which dreadful scoundrel? There were quite a number of them. But Ravenna could only think of one who would deserve such a designation—the very man she'd run from.

"The Marquess of Dalwood?"

The duchess shot her a peeved look.

The hand holding the teacup shook slightly, a pair of steely eyes rising to hers, and Ravenna braced herself for what was to come with the tiniest inhale of breath. "But nothing, not even a runaway heiress, could eclipse the vile gossip that reached my ears a few days ago…that my only daughter, the *ruined* Lady Ravenna, had been on the verge of being dragged to the stocks in the West Indies, dressed in *men's* rags, no less."

Ravenna's heart quailed in her chest. "The clothes were a lark, Mama, and I wasn't in danger of being dragged anywhere."

"And the ruination?"

"All a terrible misunderstanding." She was stretching the truth to threads, she knew.

There was no misunderstanding when she'd crashed lip-first into an unmarried man in front of witnesses. But their plan had been to play it off that they'd been secretly engaged all along, and a stolen kiss between an affianced couple was just that. The reasoning sounded feeble to Ravenna's ears even now. Her mother would see right through it, given her daughter's long-standing refusal to marry and her recalcitrant views on the subject. Besides, the dowager had the memory of an elephant. Duke or not, she'd remember the boy next door.

"Was it thus?" her mother asked. "Lady Holding did not seem to think so."

Ravenna scowled. The one woman who had sworn to uphold her promise had wasted no time in seeking out the Dowager Duchess of Embry to spread gossip. "Lady Holding is a poisonous busybody."

"Lady Holding is an old friend, looking out for your best interests."

"And yours, too, I wager."

The dowager sipped her tea, regarding Ravenna over the rim with an unruffled expression. Her mother hadn't changed. She'd just been baiting her lure, making it seem like she was composed before erupting. This was merely the calm before the storm. "So tell me, this hasty marriage of yours that I only learned of as an afterthought from you, was that a lark as well?"

"No, that's real enough." Ravenna attempted to square her drooping shoulders, though for some reason the craven things refused under her mother's stare. She hoped her voice would not crack. "I am a grown woman, Mama, and now a duchess. You should be happy. It is what you've always wanted for me."

Her mother's mouth tightened, and Ravenna realized it was the entirely wrong thing to say, insinuating that her mother only cared about social position…which *was* true, but there was no need to declare it so baldly. "How did you get to Antigua, pray tell?"

Ravenna's bravado melted like ice on fire. She *knew*. Oh yes, she knew. How she'd found out was anyone's guess. Rhystan wouldn't have told her, and Courtland had sacrificed his freedom to save her reputation. Words failed her. "I…"

"She was a passenger on my ocean liner."

The voice of rescue came from the hallway where the immaculately put-together Duke of Ashvale stood, followed by an impassive Fuller who seemed to be hiding his mirth. He hadn't announced the duke on purpose, the old rotter. But Ravenna couldn't focus on that. She could only focus on the tall and elegant man who suddenly dominated the space, who made every single nerve in her body hum to instant attention. The man who had just *lied* to the Dowager Duchess of Embry to protect her. The pressure inside her chest increased.

Goodness, *why* couldn't she control her reaction around him?

He'd been an ass earlier...and yet, here he was, coming to her rescue like a knight in the rustiest armor imaginable.

Fuller cleared his throat. "The Duke of Ashvale, Your Graces."

The dowager scowled at the butler. "I can see that, you daft man. Rather unnecessary to announce him at this point, don't you think?"

Ravenna's heart leaped, but for an entirely different reason this time. Only a few years ago, her own mother had been dead set against Rhystan's fiancée. Of course, she'd changed her tune since then and since the arrival of her precious granddaughter, but that didn't mean her new soft disposition would apply to her daughter's choice in husband.

Her mother waved an imperious hand. "Come forward then, Ashvale, unless you intend to dawdle in the doorway like a statue for the rest of the afternoon."

Lips twitching at the dowager duchess's dry tone, Courtland found himself standing taller. Lady Embry had been a frightening terror of a woman when he'd been a boy, though he was far from that now, but muscle memory was a strange thing. As diminutive as she was, she quite terrified him. If he hadn't witnessed grown gentlemen quail in front of her, he would have been mystified by his own reaction.

"Your Grace," he said with a bow, his gaze touching on the bemused expression of his wife, who seemed grateful to see him but remained somewhat guarded at his arrival.

"You've grown up, Ashvale." The dowager's stare grew thoughtful. "Your late grandfather was close friends with my parents. I am sorry for your loss."

"Thank you. I did not know him that well."

"Sit, please." She nodded to a waiting footman, and a tumbler of brandy was brought to him. Courtland was surprised that she was aware of his preference of drink, but he accepted it with a smile before sitting beside his wife and lifting her knuckles to his lips in greeting.

"You left without me," he murmured.

"You were otherwise occupied, remember?" A shuttered copper stare met his, her voice cool, not giving away the barest flash of injury in her eyes. "Moreover, I did not think you would want to come."

"Then you were mistaken."

He did not release her hand but kept it gripped loosely in his. Courtland felt the dowager's eagle-eyed stare on them, but he did not let it bother him. Lady Embry would undoubtedly be their harshest critic…and their greatest champion in the days to come.

Regardless of how she felt about him as her daughter's husband, she was fiercely protective of her children. He was counting on that if things got worse with Stinson, which he fully expected them to. His brother's sense of entitlement had only grown, and Courtland's presence in London threatened everything he'd become.

"I suppose we should toast to your nuptials," the dowager said in a somewhat brittle voice. "I was sad to miss them, but you know, my health is not suited to such a capricious climate."

"It's not so bad once you get used to it," he said.

"I shall have to take your word for it. Do you plan to remain in London?"

The question was blunt. "For the foreseeable future."

"And the unforeseeable future?"

Courtland fought the urge to grin at her tenacity. "I don't make decisions based on what I cannot predict, Your Grace."

Lady Embry eyed him over her teacup and then nodded. He could feel Ravenna's tension beside him. She was practically vibrating with strain. Surely she wasn't that terrified of her own mother? He spared her a quick glance, noting the bright spots of color on her cheeks. She'd changed from her earlier riding habit into a maroon-and-white dress embroidered with tiny gold flowers that made her complexion seem luminous.

Courtland thought back to their first encounter as adults, staring across at her over that table at the Starlight, and the stark differences in both her appearance and her conduct. She'd carried off the part of a carefree young fop with charming ease. How confident she'd been! The fake mustache had done wonders to conceal her sex, along with the dapper men's clothing, but the sharp intellect and fiery spirit that had shone in her eyes had not changed.

However, that wild version of Ravenna was nothing like the one who sat here now, as demure as any refined, well-bred English lady. He longed to rake his hands through her painstakingly styled hair, muss those perfect skirts, hear her throaty, wicked laughter. She was so picture perfect that it *hurt* to see his vibrant sprite reduced to this shadow. This *illusion*. He was wrong earlier. Being in England did not do her any favors either.

"Is something amiss, Your Grace?" the dowager asked, peering at him. "You had quite a severe frown upon your brow just then. Is the brandy not to your liking?"

"The brandy is excellent," he said. "I was simply remarking on my wife's distress."

"Distress?" Lady Embry asked.

He met her direct stare, feeling Ravenna's attention flick to him. "With respect, do you have concerns about this marriage,

Your Grace? If so, you are welcome to address them to both of us." He sent his suddenly twitchy bride a reassuring look. "Though the circumstances of our meeting were quite unexpected with Ravenna's surprising arrival in Antigua, the fact that we have known each other from childhood made us realize how much we had in common."

The dowager's glare was astute. "So your marriage had nothing to do with my daughter traipsing around in men's clothing and courting ruination?"

"A mere lark, as she mentioned, one that was unfortunately ill-fated. Hence, our swift exchange of vows. Trust me, Your Grace, your daughter's reputation did not suffer a fatal blow. In fact, our wedding was quite well attended and lauded by many peers and dignitaries."

"Antigua is *not* town, dear boy."

Courtland smiled. "No, you're right, of course."

"We must rectify that with a proper ball at once." The dowager's shrewd stare sharpened. She cleared her throat. "Your stepbrother will not make this easy on you. Nor will the marchioness."

"I am aware, Your Grace." He leaned forward. "Which is why we need your help."

Twelve

THE COMING-OUT BALL FOR LADY BRONWYN CHASE, THE granddaughter of the late Duke of Ashvale and half sister of the current duke, had to be the most ostentatious event known to man. There wasn't even royalty in attendance, though it was rumored that Bertie, Prince of Wales, might attend. Judging by the size of the crowd, everyone else of consequence had been invited, and naturally, given the mysterious *island duke* was finally in town, everyone had arrived en masse.

It was a crush and not a single expense had been spared.

Ravenna could hardly take it all in.

Towering potted ferns had been brought into the hall, while enormous sprays of flowers in every conceivable color and rhododendron-filled porcelain urns adorned the corners. The ballroom was richly decorated with floral motifs and brightly lit, with a small orchestra at one end. The tables in the supper and refreshment rooms at the opposite end creaked beneath the weight of all their dishes—from game, ham, and fowl to jellies, cakes, and trifles.

By all accounts, it was such a vulgar display of wealth that it nearly made Ravenna feel somewhat ill. Even by London standards, it was over the top. The obvious grandeur had a specific purpose. Either Lady Borne definitely had something to prove to the denizens of the *ton,* or she was hoping to marry off her daughter as soon as possible by attracting the best title money could buy.

Ravenna had only met Lady Bronwyn in the receiving line for the briefest of moments, and apart from the beautiful debutante gown, she wasn't able to glean much about the younger girl's personality. In truth, the poor thing looked pale and overwhelmed. She hadn't seen Courtland's sisters in years, but to her, Bronwyn looked the same, just slightly older. Chestnut-brown hair like Stinson's and pale-blue eyes like her mother's.

Lady Borne was a different story. Though she could not express public distaste for her stepson, now duke, who had arrived on the heels of the influential Dowager Duchess of Embry, her lip had curled into the slightest sneer when they'd greeted her. Ravenna had recoiled from the venom in the woman's gaze as her eyes settled on Courtland. It was not something Ravenna had ever noticed before. Years before, she recalled the marchioness and her children mourning Courtland's death, observed all traditions and sorrowfully accepted condolences from their peers.

This seething contempt was new. Or perhaps simply new to her.

"What is Lady Borne's quarrel with you?" she whispered to Courtland as he escorted her down the marble stairs.

"Besides stealing her son's coronet?"

She paused midstep. "It's yours. You were always Ashvale's heir. Even if they thought you were dead, you're clearly not, and the title belongs to you."

"Haven't you heard a word I've said, Ravenna?" he asked softly. "They claimed me dead when I was not, and my stepmother has always hated me for taking the position she desired for her own son. The only surprise here is why it was never formalized. Perhaps they were waiting for the old duke to die. Trust me, my being out of the way was no hardship for either of them. It was a windfall."

Ravenna blinked. "That's not true."

"Is it so hard to believe? That she wanted me gone so her precious son could fashion himself as a marquess?"

"She mourned you." Ravenna hadn't been mistaken in her memory of the marchioness sobbing her eyes out, her face buried in her son's shoulder as if her heart would break.

His smile was cold. "A pretense by a gifted actress, mark my words."

Courtland drew her into the ballroom where the dancers were setting up for the next waltz. Ravenna was so shocked at her husband's reply that she barely noticed all the stares and the whispers about the Duke and Duchess of Ashvale. Though they'd already had their own celebration, it hadn't been in London. They would have one, with Lady Embry as avid hostess, but not for a few weeks. Invitations had already been sent out and most promptly accepted, but this was the first time they'd appeared in public together.

"People are staring," she murmured.

He lifted her gloved hand to his lips. "Let them."

And then Ravenna forgot everyone as her husband adeptly guided her into the first turn. She'd enjoyed his dancing skill before, and now she just gave herself over to the movements and his expert lead. She didn't even have to count steps! For such a tall man, he moved with such effortless grace, every turn executed with flawless precision.

Despite the show of support with her mother, he'd made it clear that theirs was to be the most amicable and agreeable marriage known to man. While she fully intended to play along, her traitorous body had other ideas, flushing hot, then cold at every brush of his muscled frame against hers. His hand flexed at her waist, the searing imprint of his fingers cutting through gauze and tulle and making her blood simmer.

"You are blushing," he murmured.

"It's warm in here."

His lips curled in a familiar way that had her dropping her gaze, her cheeks burning even more. "You look exquisite tonight."

"Thank you." Pleasure at the soft-spoken compliment drizzled through her. The gown itself was new, nothing different from the extravagant ball gowns she'd worn in the past, but tonight, she felt beautiful in the layers of emerald satin and blond lace. His eyes were glowing, she noticed. Whether that was out of appreciation or something else, Ravenna didn't care. She wanted that light to remain. "So do you."

And he did. Courtland Chase stood out. Notwithstanding his height, he simply commanded attention. His finely milled clothing followed the lines of his broad shoulders, tapering to his narrow waist, and the raven-black color and snowy-white cravat only served to set off his masculine beauty. It wasn't just curiosity that drove so many glances his way. It was also desire and envy. Courtland wore wealth and power like a second skin. Ravenna frowned at a nearby lady who gazed up at him with a coy smile.

"You're glowering now," he remarked. "Do I have to call anyone out?"

She sniffed, cheeks on fire. "If anyone's calling someone out, it will be me."

"So fierce."

"You still don't trust that I can take care of myself, do you?" she asked, grasping his arm for the next turn.

Midnight eyes bored into hers, a smile softening those stern male lips. "I have no doubt, Duchess," he said, her pulse leaping at the address. When others addressed her thus, the title chafed, but when he did it with that underlying hint of possessiveness, it thrilled. Not that she would ever admit it. "I am aware that you are quite accomplished in many things."

He led her off the dance floor when the strains of music ended, much to her enduring disappointment. In the past, she'd always been more than ready to move on to the next partner. Dances were a way of passing the interminable time. She enjoyed the movement far more than she liked the tiresome conversation that always descended into some form of empty flattery. They wanted her dowry or her name or her connections.

"Embry's duchess taught me how to fence," she explained,

when he handed her a glass of champagne with a quirk of one dark eyebrow. "She could acquit herself with the best of Embry's most lethal men and fended off an attacker in my own home. I insisted on lessons and practiced diligently."

"And your skill with a pistol," he asked. "Has that sharpened?"

She grinned. "Care to test me?"

"No, I quite value my life." The reply was gentle and fell over her like a soft cloud of approval. Ravenna basked in it. How she loved seeing him like this…almost human, a grin flirting over that indecent mouth, eyes lit with esteem…all those hard, roughened edges tempered by something she hadn't expected from him. Playfulness. Affection.

Or maybe she was imagining things.

Stop being ridiculous. He doesn't actually mean to seduce you.

A low rumble of laughter caught her attention. Mortified, she shot her husband a glance, hoping he hadn't noticed her distraction, but of course she wasn't that fortunate.

"What I would give to be privy to your thoughts just then," he said. "You seemed to be having quite the internal debate."

Her cheeks heated anew and she snapped open her fan to cool herself. "Was it so obvious?"

"It wouldn't be if your lips hadn't been moving. I think I caught the words 'ridiculous' and 'seduce.' I admit I am rather intrigued." Courtland grinned, propping one shoulder on a nearby marble pillar. Despite the relaxed stance of his body, the light in his eyes smoldered, leaving her in little doubt of what such intrigue meant. To her consternation, she felt her body respond, liquid heat gathering in her belly and coiling down between her thighs.

Surely he couldn't mean…?

No, of course not. He'd made it clear that nothing could happen between them. This was merely an act for everyone else, and she was the ninny misreading every little thing because she couldn't think straight around him. Ravenna slowed her erratic fanning, even though the puffs of air felt good against her scorching face in the stuffy ballroom. Her skin felt as though it was on fire and he was the tall glass of water that could put it out.

Gracious, her thoughts were as ungovernable as her body.

She could handle an angry, fractious Courtland. It was the flirty, devilish side of him she had to be wary of. *That* man was of particular danger to her, as was evidenced by her current state.

"I assure you it's not all that interesting," she replied, snapping her fan closed and suddenly remembering all the coquettish movements she and Clara had practiced. If only there was a fan movement for *I am curious and wish desperately to learn more of whatever wickedness you have to teach, sir.*

Such a thing would likely entail dragging the tip of the fan down one's neck and across one's décolletage. Maybe even lower for the right emphasis. She wasn't daring enough for any of those, not with him. It was curious. A year ago, she would have flirted unconscionably…dared to be so bold and more. She'd lived for provoking the sensibilities of the *ton*. Perhaps then it was because she hadn't cared what any man thought of her.

But now things felt different, and not just because she was married. She did care what Courtland thought of her. She always had, even when he was dressed in short pants, his knobby knees covered in dirt as he built a fort between their estates because she'd suggested it. As a boy, he'd been her only confidant, and despite their volatile relationship, the only boy she'd ever trusted besides her brothers. And then he'd vanished.

"Why did you leave Kettering without a word?" The question burst out of her before she could stop it. This was neither the time nor the place.

He stared down at her. "Not of my own accord, I can tell you that."

"Why didn't you come to me if you were in trouble? I could have helped you."

The light in his eyes dimmed, though his smile remained fixed. "You were all of fourteen. My only living parent sent me away. What could you have done?"

She bit her lip. Nothing. She could have done nothing. Even now, despite the illusion of independence she'd pretended to have, she'd always been impeded by the boundaries of her sex, of her station. She owned no property and wielded no power beyond what society had deemed appropriate.

Ravenna huffed a breath, horror filling her. "Wait, *she* sent you away?"

"Yes, with a purse full of money and a retinue of servants I fired the moment I gained my majority. I wanted no one telling her what had become of me. I was always a burden to her."

"That's not your fault. It's hers for being a hateful person without a heart."

He shrugged. "She was only doing what others in her place might have done, Ravenna."

"Why are you defending her?" she asked with a scowl.

"I'm not. She's dreadful, but I was the son of the marquess's first wife and she wanted me gone. In hindsight, I was probably lucky. She could have had me thrown on a boat heading to the penal colonies if she wanted."

She shook her head. "No, you're wrong. Not everyone thinks like that. Not me, or my brother, or even my mother, and you know how set in her ways she is. Your stepmother must account for what she did to you."

His throat working, he opened his mouth to reply, but then drew himself upright, eyes shuttering, and Ravenna wondered at the swift change. She didn't have long to ponder it when his brother staggered into view, accompanied by none other than Mr. Sommers. Her immediate dislike of the second man intensified the minute his gaze fell on her. She did not realize the two men were acquainted.

"Good evening, Your Graces," the rotund man drawled. "Did I get that right?"

Courtland canted his head. "Sommers. Stinson."

"What are you doing here?" Stinson demanded, his face flushed, the pungent waft of whiskey surrounding him like a shroud. "You weren't invited."

"Do I need an invitation to my own house?" Courtland said, eyes narrowing. "The property is entailed, if you want to check with your solicitors."

"You cunning bastard," Stinson wheezed, going puce.

The insult wasn't as quiet as he'd intended, if the nearby gasps were any signal. Sommers grinned a sly smile as though he were enjoying the spectacle. Curious eyes darted toward them, guests shuffling nearer in anticipation. Even Lady Borne's blue gaze narrowed on them from where she stood near the refreshments room, but that could have been because she'd been keeping an eye on the whereabouts of the uninvited.

Ravenna scowled—she and her mother had received an invitation—so the slight was intended. Again, she stared at Stinson. She had never seen this disagreeable, ugly side of him. The Stinson she knew was charming and courteous to a fault...ever the perfect, if slightly ingratiating, gentleman. But perhaps that had all been some kind of act.

"You're foxed, Stinson," she said, sensing the tension in her husband double. She placed a hand on Courtland's arm, the hard muscle flexing beneath her fingertips. "I advise you to stop and walk away before you say something you truly regret."

Stinson's blue gaze—so much like his mother's, though at the moment red and watery—fell to her hand, scorn swimming in his look. "*You* advise me? Forgive me if I refuse, *Your Grace*. Even as a child you were oblivious."

"That is enough, Stinson," Courtland bit out.

The music in the ballroom hadn't stopped, but necks were

craning to see what was causing the commotion. Nearby guests had abandoned even pretending not to eavesdrop. Everyone was salivating at the latest on-dit between the two brothers. Despite Stinson's unkind jab, Ravenna had to nip this in the bud before it escalated any more. Already, she could feel Courtland's fury mounting, if his bunched muscles and tight expression were any indication.

"I thought we were friends," she said quietly. "I valued our friendship."

"Friendship," Stinson spat out, a cold spiteful little sneer brewing on his lips. "Do you know who you've tied yourself to? He might have fooled you"—he waved an arm, nearly toppling himself in the process—"and everyone here. And Grandfather too. What a goddamned joke."

"Stinson, control yourself!" The warning came from a feminine voice so icy a chill seemed to blow through the room, but either Stinson was too drunk to notice, or he was too far gone in his rage to take heed of his mother's command. Lady Borne bore down upon them with two hefty footmen in her wake.

Stinson sneered. "Well, hear me, the jest will be on you. You and the frigid prize you married. Everyone knows about her. Even Dalwood says she's as cold as any stone."

A hard buzzing hummed in Ravenna's ears, her breath coming inconceivably fast as a dozen stares converged upon her. She barely felt the duke move nor saw the fast snap of his fist before Stinson's head was flying back. A spot of red marred the spotless white of Courtland's glove and Stinson's nose started to gush blood as he stumbled back into Mr. Sommers, Lady Borne's footmen arriving in time to keep him upright. Shrieks permeated the ballroom and the music screeched to an ungraceful halt. The altercation had been so swift that even for those watching, it'd been a blink of an eye.

"Escort my son outside for some air," Lady Borne ordered the footmen, and the stunned Stinson went, as meek as a lamb.

Mr. Sommers followed with a circumspect look over his shoulder to the duke as though he hadn't expected the vicious strike. Neither had Ravenna, for that matter, but that chary look from the American troubled her. "Carry on," Lady Borne said to everyone else and clapped her hands. "Music!"

The band was quick to comply, music filling the hall. The dancing resumed and most people pretended to carry on their conversations, though they were still shamelessly eavesdropping. Lady Borne turned to her stepson, her cold gaze giving nothing away.

"Courtland," she said with a practiced smile that stayed a far step from her eyes, considering her refusal to use his title. "I had hoped you would call upon me before today."

His mouth tightened, but he canted his head. "Apologies, my lady. I was detained by urgent estate business."

Though he did not correct her, Ravenna bristled on the inside and pasted a syrupy smile on her lips. "It's His Grace, Duke of Ashvale, now, Lady Borne, but I am sure you knew that."

That cold stare met hers, fury sparking before it was hidden behind a charming smile that made Ravenna want to scowl. The nerve of this woman. The utter cruelty of any mother worth her salt turning out her stepson to the mercy of the streets because of her own ugly biases. What mother could ever do such a thing?

One who wanted her own son to be duke, instead of the rightful heir.

Could Lady Borne truly hate Courtland simply because of who *his* mother had been? British lords married commoners more often than expected, and while society screeched its dislike, eventually the scandals died down. But those commoners would not have hailed from a place portrayed by British novelists as a one of savage inclinations and dissipation. Brontë's words, as Ravenna had discovered herself, were especially misleading.

"Of course," Lady Borne said to her. "It was with some surprise I found out the news of your nuptials from my son."

Though her tone was as sweet as spun sugar, there was an

underlying judgment in there that Ravenna did not take kindly to, as if she herself had made an unpardonable mistake. The underhanded slight that Ashvale wasn't *her* son also didn't go unnoticed. "Thank you, Lady Borne. We are rather happy."

Her gaze fell to her husband who had peeled off his bloodied glove and was in the process of removing the other. It was considered uncouth to be ungloved at a formal event, but evidently, he did not care. Lady Borne looked horrified, and Ravenna took great satisfaction in that fact.

"Please, excuse me, Duchess, I need a moment," the duke murmured in her ear, a steely dark stare flicking down to her, a dozen emotions brimming in them for the briefest moment before they were throttled to one. Anger. Not directed at her, she knew, but it affected her just the same.

Her heart shouldn't have felt that statement—or his dismissal—as hard as it did, but the organ felt like it was splitting in half when she watched her husband walk away, cutting a wide swath through the guests as though he were a king.

Or a pariah.

Not for the first time, Ravenna realized she had no hold over him. Not as a wife, not as a lover, not even as a friend. Courtland Chase was an island onto himself. Circumstance and fate had decreed it so. Lady Borne had had a hand in that as well. Ravenna couldn't conceive that his own family had conspired to chase him away from what was rightfully his, but she supposed intrigues like that occurred more often than not in the *ton*.

Prejudice and greed could turn people into monsters.

Case in point was the woman still standing at her side.

A deep sense of righteous indignation rose in her like a storm tide. Ravenna knew it wasn't the time or the place, but she simply did not care. Before she could stop herself and before the other woman could leave, she stepped into Lady Borne's space, lowering her voice. "How *could* you?"

"How could I what?" she replied.

"Destroy his life. Send him away. Break an engagement that wasn't yours to break."

Those hard eyes glittered with malice. "He was not fit."

Ravenna bristled at the dowager's disparaging tone, glad that Courtland wasn't here to take in any of her spite. "And yet I find myself quite content to be married to the man to whom I had been promised so very long ago, regardless of your judgment that he was lacking in some way."

"Stinson is Ashvale's real heir, and perhaps he should have been your husband." She sneered, thin nostrils flaring. "Not that he would ever take you now, tarnished thing that you are."

"I am not a thing to be taken, Lady Borne." Ravenna's fingers itched to slap away that smug smile, but she kept them firmly at her sides. "You and I seem to have different understandings of the laws of primogeniture. Courtland is duke, not Stinson." She exhaled, dissipating some of the rage that coiled within. "Why did you do it? Why did you tell my father he was dead?"

"You wished to be married to a bastard?"

"His father was married to his mother before she died and then he married you," Ravenna replied, keeping her voice low. "His grandfather knew he was legitimate."

"My father-in-law was not in his right mind, you silly girl."

Ravenna kept her mounting fury in check. "I am not a girl, Lady Borne, and I'd much rather be called silly than a bigot. The truth is I feel sorry for you. That hate in your heart is a rot, one that has been left to fester, and it will be the thing to eat you alive."

"How dare you speak to me so in my own home?" the marchioness snarled, gripping Ravenna's elbow. "I'll have you thrown out on your ear."

Ravenna lifted a cool brow. "This residence belongs to the Duke of Ashvale, the man you cast out as a child because of your own selfishness, because *you* felt he did not deserve his birthright.

Let's not mince words, Lady Borne. You and your children live here only at my husband's whim. Now please release me. I doubt the duke will be pleased with your threats to my person."

The marchioness's hand fell away, mouth opening and closing on an irate huff, and then her lips thinned with rancor. "You two deserve each other."

"Thank you, I think so, too." Ravenna frowned thoughtfully, tapping a gloved fingertip to her lip. "My sister-in-law—you know the Duchess of Embry, don't you?—well, she has a saying about the things we put out into the universe coming back around, an intriguing phenomenon she calls karma, and I'd be very afraid, if I were you, Lady Borne."

"Are you threatening me?"

Ravenna clapped a hand to her breast in mock surprise. "Of course not, my lady, it's just some friendly advice." Her smile grew fangs and she leaned in close. "However, in case such advice is unwelcome, then you should also know that Courtland is not a child and he is no longer alone. He has family and powerful friends, and we won't stand by and watch him be maligned by the likes of you."

"Dear me, you've become as savage as he is."

"If being savage means fighting for what's right and being a decent human being, then you are correct. Now, please do excuse me, Lady Borne, I have better things to do than sit here and try to enlighten the equivalent of a rock."

Swallowing an unruly snort at Lady Borne's affronted expression, Ravenna turned on her heel and left, the tension draining from her stiff limbs with each step she took. She recalled how things like prejudice worked—why Lady Borne thought she was better than the previous marchioness. She'd seen it for herself with her sister-in-law.

Most of the *ton* had sneered down their noses at her because her father had been an Indian maharaja, regardless of the fact that *she* had outranked *them*. Queen Victoria had welcomed her to court, where she entertained royalty from around the world all the time. Despite those things, Sarani's heritage had still rendered her lesser in the eyes of many.

Ravenna couldn't deny the similarities between Courtland and her sister-in-law.

But he was also a man, which meant he wielded more power than Sarani ever had as a woman. And he was an English duke, the highest rank of nobility. Ravenna understood that neither of those external things were of much consequence, however. Fear and insecurity ate away at a person from the inside. Courtland might be male and a duke, but he was still vulnerable.

And the truth was, no island, no matter how well barricaded, was unassailable for long.

With a determined breath, Ravenna went after her husband.

Thirteen

THE RAGE WAS SUFFOCATING.

It gnawed at him like a starving creature.

Hell, if he didn't do something, he was going to explode, and proper English society would not soon recover from the scandal. Courtland rubbed at his bare knuckles, barely bruised from the brutal punch to his half brother's face.

How dare that maggot insult his *wife*?

Fury and bitterness crashed through him in unforgiving waves. The fact that his brother had seen fit to insult a duchess in public was galling! And Courtland knew it was because of him. His brother and stepmother viewed him as inferior, so Ravenna was inferior, too. He'd seen the degradation in Stinson's eyes, heard it in his stepmother's crass insinuation that Ravenna had made the wrong choice of husband.

The sight of Stinson's blood had been gratifying, but Courtland ached to thrash his brother senseless. How dare he embarrass him in his own sodding home? How dare he humiliate Ravenna? For the first time in years, Courtland had felt utterly powerless, much as he had when he'd been a boy.

"Fuck," he swore aloud, raking his hands through his hair and demolishing Peabody's excellent work. Cursing a blue streak, he stalked deeper down the wide hallway leading to the unlit conservatory. He hadn't meant to head this way, but his agitated, wandering footsteps had led him here. This was the one place he'd secretly adored as a boy whenever he'd been allowed to visit Ashvale Manor. The one place he'd always belonged.

Plants and flowers never judged. They loved attention and bloomed in return for the smallest measure of affection. Rumor had it that his grandfather had had a similar affinity for plants, though he'd have to take the old head gardener's word for it that they shared the same green fingers. The man had insisted that the conservatory was the duke's quiet pride and joy, and so it had also become Courtland's secret haven.

The conservatory was deserted, though he could smell the variety of lush plantings of lemon and orange trees interlaced with the sweeter musk of night-blooming roses. Thankfully the gardeners had kept his fondness for this sanctuary a secret. If the marchioness had suspected his love for the place, she would undoubtedly have set it on fire or forbidden him from entering. Then again, without the splendid conservatory, she wouldn't have had an impressive venue to hold her lavish tea and garden parties à la Queen Victoria.

And impressions were everything.

He inhaled deeply, letting the peace fill him and chase away the remnants of his anger as it had done so many times before. Perhaps it was habit, something ingrained like muscle memory.

Fresh horse dung splattered on his clothing in the wardrobe? He'd come here.

His careful school notes scattered across the lake? He'd come here.

Worms dumped beneath his bedsheets? He'd come here.

And each time, he'd left his rage, his fear, his pain at the door. The fist around his chest loosened as the fragrant air enveloped him and the sweeping stained-glass panels crested above him. The flowers, shrubs, and vines were lit only by moonlight, giving them a silvery cast that was no less beautiful than their natural coloring. It felt as though he were inside some forbidden fairy-tale forest. A reluctant smile curled his lip. He hadn't had such a fanciful thought in a decade.

He wished Ravenna could see it.

A soft noise behind him made him turn, and there she was framed in the arched doorway, as though his unvoiced desire had summoned her. His wife. His *duchess*.

Gilded in opalescent moonlight, she was the undisputed fairy queen of this vale. Her burnished auburn hair looked dark, her creamy skin dappled in shades of silver, that stunning dress of hers draping her beautiful body in seductive lines. His heart climbed into his throat, the blood thickening in his veins. Courtland didn't want to speak. Didn't want to disturb the thrall of this place. For the first time since he'd arrived in England, his soul felt at ease.

"I followed you," his wife said softly. "Do you wish to be alone?"

"No."

"Good, because I'm afraid I might no longer welcome at the party."

He frowned. "How so?"

A smile trembled over those lush lips before she tugged the lower one into her mouth. "I might have called your stepmonster a bigot and told her karma was coming for her arse."

Courtland couldn't help it; he chuckled, and it felt like a huge weight had lifted off his chest. "You did?"

"I did. And *then* when she threatened to throw me out, I might have said you owned this house and everything in it."

"Is that so?" he said, smiling, his heart giving a slow, aching throb.

"There's more," she whispered, eyelashes falling. "*Then* I told her that I had to go find you because she has the intelligence of a rock."

Courtland barked a laugh. He'd have given anything to see his stepmother's face. After the rest of her confession, his wife didn't say any more, standing there like a woodland nymph, eyes darting around the space, catching on a wide-frond palm and then flicking up to the vaulted glass before returning to him.

"This is beautiful," she said softly.

"My grandfather built it," he said. "They said it was his favorite place when he was in town. It was meant to be a reflection of the gardens at Ashvale Park."

"I remember." Courtland caught the gleam of her eyes, the expression in them hidden by the dimness, but heard the amusement in her voice. "My mother was ever so jealous of the duke's grounds, constantly berating our gardeners to achieve the same level of splendor. She never succeeded, of course. Your grandfather had exquisite taste and an eye for design that no one could replicate." She gave a tiny laugh. "Not even horticultural experts brought in from France and Italy. Trust me, Mama tried for years to best him before giving up in defeat."

Courtland prowled toward her, noticing the slight hitch in her breath at his approach. When he stood an arm's length away, he held out his ungloved hand. Whether she took it or not would be up to her, but if she did, all bets were off. He *needed* her more than he needed breath in his lungs.

His wife stared at his calloused palm, the seconds trudging on, his pulse drumming in his ears. For a shaky heartbeat, he almost snatched his hand back out of reach. What was he *doing*? He'd promised himself to stay away and here he was…begging for her touch. He moved to retract his hand, curling his fingers into a fist.

"Wait, don't," she whispered.

Curious, he stared at her as she dropped her fan and reticule onto a nearby bench, and then proceeded to unbutton the tiny clasps of her left glove. In a daze, Courtland watched, mesmerized, his breath seizing at the pop of every button, his groin clenching at the inch-by-inch reveal of pale, unblemished skin when the ivory kidskin parted. By the time she finished the first and was done with the second, his entire body was on edge.

"There," she said, discarding both gloves with the rest of her belongings. "Now that's better."

With that, warm fingers slid over his, the bare rasp of skin against skin so erotic that a groan nearly spilled past his lips. She laced their fingers together. Courtland closed his hand around hers and pulled her in, hard enough to feel her intake of breath. "You shouldn't have done that," he growled.

"Done what?"

"Undressed."

"Then don't let my efforts be in vain." A wicked smile lit her beautiful face.

It was his turn to be confused. "What do you mean?"

"Follow me and find out, why don't you?"

His vixen of a wife yanked on his palm, pushed herself to tip-toes, and pressed a cheeky kiss to his mouth before veering off into the depths of the conservatory. Frozen, he stood there for a moment, forgetting to breathe, before touching a finger to his burning lips. Desire burst through him in like a tropical downpour.

Checking that the door to the conservatory was secured from the inside, he made to follow his wife. He knew every inch of the glasshouse like the back of his hand, but she wouldn't, which meant he had the advantage. At least, so he thought until he came upon something that did not belong in a such a place. An elegant, beaded dancing slipper.

He chuckled. Had she lost her shoe? *Again*?

Courtland gathered it up, mesmerized by its delicate shape. He smiled as he circled past an ornate trellis that boasted climbing wisteria and miniature roses rising above a multihued flower bed. Thereafter, he discovered a second slipper. Scooping it up, he studied the match to the first. One could be considered lost; two could not be a coincidence.

Unless she'd kicked them off in a hurry to aid in her flight.

It was only when he spotted the next item a few feet away on the ornate paving stones that his throat went properly dry: a lady's stocking…*Ravenna's* stocking. The slippers had been no error, and stockings could not simply come loose on their own, which meant one thing. *She* had removed them. Purposefully. His devious wife was undressing in the middle of his conservatory. Courtland's heart hitched, while blood rushed elsewhere.

To his groin, to be precise.

"Ravenna, where are you?" It was a miracle he could even speak.

"Come find me, Duke" came the reply, followed by hushed, decadent laughter. "I seem to have lost my undergarments."

Arousal spiked, making him grunt.

Devil take it, he now had to be sporting the most obnoxious cockstand in existence. Doubling his speed and attempting not to hobble, he came upon the second silken stocking near a sundial, and then a pair of flimsy petticoats resting on a decorative urn. The overlay of her skirts followed, and at the next turn, the rest of the gown itself.

The discovery of each garment made his breath shorten and his chest tighten. And by the time he discovered the last item—an unlaced lady's corset—he was so fucking hard it hurt. Because he knew that when he caught her, she would be wearing only a chemise.

The thought demolished him.

Though when he finally came upon her sitting at the edge of the ornate fountain at the far end of the conservatory, her fingers wading in the still waters, Courtland could only stare in captivated silence. He'd thought her a fairy queen before, clad in all her finery, but wearing only her shift, his wife was an otherworldly creature.

Her hair was unpinned, her feet bare. Moonlight danced across the water and limned her shapely form in silver. He could see the outline of one round, luscious breast and the decadent curve of a hip beneath the near transparent lawn. Courtland's mouth went unspeakably dry.

Her face turned, in profile. "Have you ever seen anything so magical?"

"Not until now," he replied softly.

She smiled up at him. "You're only trying to make me feel better as I've lost all my clothing."

"Good thing I've found them," he said, lifting the pile of garments.

"Good thing it's also rather warm in here."

"Special heating for the more sensitive plants," he said. Setting the bundle down on a nearby bench, Courtland approached his nearly naked wife, each step unsure as though she might be easily spooked. "What are we doing here, Ravenna?" he asked quietly, sitting beside her and trying not to react to her distracting state of undress.

"Forgetting. Remembering."

His brows gathered. "Those are two different things."

"I want to forget who we are while we're here and remember who we were on our wedding day on the island." A pair of beautiful glimmering eyes met his, the honesty in them almost taking him to his knees. "I know how things happened…wasn't perfect, but well, here we are. Married. You have a wife, and I have a husband."

"Ravenna." He sighed.

She reached out to push a curling lock of hair off his brow. "Courtland, can't we just take this moment for us? Regardless of what the future holds, I want a wedding night. I want the man I married for *one* night, even if we have to go back to pretending to being strangers."

He couldn't move a muscle at her soft touch, though inside every nerve ending came violently alive. He wanted that, too. But he was also afraid of what taking that step meant for both of them. Things would never be the same, no matter their intentions. Intimacy had a way of changing everything, and deep down, Courtland already knew that once he touched her, once would never be enough. Not for either of them.

He rolled his lips between his teeth, his face giving away nothing when she dragged her finger over his cheekbone to cup his jaw, her thumb feathering across his hidden bottom lip. "Let's pretend that we met each other here in this magical space," she whispered, pupils wide with pure desire. "No pasts and no futures. A man and a woman. In the now."

Her words were intoxicating, casting a spell about him, and for once, logic fell to feeling. He didn't stop to think that they were in a conservatory with a crowded ballroom a few corridors away, and even with a locked door, they could be discovered at any moment.

His wife pulled lightly down on his lip, releasing it from the hold between his teeth and skating over its tingling contours, eyes locked onto the movement of her finger as though she were bewitched, too. Courtland could hardly think, the soft press of her thumb maddening. He wanted to touch his tongue to it, suck it into his mouth, and feast on her flesh.

"Please, Courtland. Give me this."

The plea was his undoing. He bent toward her at the same time that she slid her fingers around his nape and arched up to him. The meeting of their mouths was *hungry*, nearly making his eyes roll back in his head as he molded his lips to hers, parting them and delving deep. Her tongue touched his, softly at first and then with more fervor when he growled his approval deep in his throat. Tremor after tremor of pure pleasure slid through him.

How had he kept himself away from *such* gratification? Kissing Ravenna was like diving from the highest of cliffs and soaring for an eternity before plunging into the balmy depths of a tropical ocean. All consuming, intense, and shattering. Courtland swallowed her moans, delighting in them, and groaned when she tugged at his hair. Breaking the kiss, he nibbled at her lip, kissed down her jaw to her throat, relished the sweetness of her taste, and dragged her body closer, filling his palms with her feminine curves.

He pulled away, staring down into passion-glazed eyes the

color of molten copper streaked with gold. "Are you certain this is what you want?"

"More than anything. I'm yours, Courtland."

Her lips met his again, sealing her words with another torrid kiss. Unable to resist the decadent feel of her, his palm slid up her ribs, the friction of the silky fabric of her chemise over her hot skin making him delirious, until he felt the underslope of her breast. Ravenna flung her head back with a strangled gasp when his thumb grazed over one tight, beaded nipple.

Hell, she was too lovely to be real. His nymph. His queen. *His.*

Courtland gathered her into his arms and stood easily, taking them both toward the back of the conservatory where a worn chaise lounge was tucked into a nook, hidden in an alcove behind an enormous fern. It used to be one of his favorite places to curl up and read, or hide when he didn't want to be found. Faint music and lights from the adjacent ballroom filtered through the trees, glittering across the panes and dancing over the glass roof.

He set Ravenna gently down on the embroidered cushions, coasting his palms over her bare ankles and calves, and feeling her eyes holding on to his. Slowly, he sank to his knees in front of her, grasping the seat on either side of her legs. Never one to deny herself, she bent down to steal a kiss from him, eyes bright and eager.

"You have exquisite feet," he told her in a husky voice, and she bit her lip, releasing a tiny gasp when his big hands skated over the delicate arches. They were so fine-boned and elegant, much like the rest of her. He wanted to kiss them, work his way up every single mouthwatering inch of her endless limbs...chart her with his tongue. He wanted to expose all of that velvety skin to the moonlight. See her for the ethereal sprite she was.

Soon.

On the ocean liner, Ravenna's long legs had been covered in stockings, but he could recall the beautiful lines of her with precision—her shapely calves, rounded knees, and soft thighs that all led to the warm heart of her. Visions of her coming apart just from the touch of his hands filled his brain. Courtland wanted to see her fall to pieces again and again. His fingers twitched against her skin, his cock straining against his falls.

He loosened the tapes of her drawers, drawing them down over her legs before lifting the hem of her chemise. With every inch of skin he exposed, her breath hitched. His was quick to follow, his heartbeat thudding in his ears. Courtland's hands trembled as the embroidered edge grazed the tops of her thighs, and then she was completely bared to him. He sucked in a ragged breath at the sight of those slender thighs and the tantalizing V of her groin nestled between them. A fiery thatch of hair greeted his hungry gaze, and a grin broke over his lips.

A huff of laughter had him looking upward. "Don't you dare," she warned, mischief and lust warring in her beautiful eyes. She'd been studying him carefully, watching him as he unveiled her, desire burning in that open gaze. A smile played over her lips, too.

"Don't I dare what?" he asked, his grin widening. "Call you *gingersnap*?"

A blush tinted her cheeks. "I have no idea why the hair on my head darkened, but *that* didn't."

"I love it," he said, lifting his hands under her plump bottom. He kneaded the soft globes for a moment before shifting her forward on the seat, and then settled himself between her legs. She fought him when the motion made her knees push outward, exposing her to his gaze.

"What are you doing?" she whispered, eyes going wide when he kissed the inside of her knee.

"Exploring."

Her breath caught as he trailed his lips upward, wedging his shoulders in between her thighs. Fingers clutched at the seat before coming to rest in his hair. His mouth was watering as her intoxicating scent filled his nostrils. Courtland stared up at his wife, her eyes half-lidded but fixed upon him. Curiosity burned in them, trepidation, too. Once more, he was struck by the opposing counterpoints of her innate sensuality and her obvious inexperience.

"Has anyone ever done this to you before?" he asked.

She blinked, voice hoarse. "Done what?"

"Kissed you." His fingers skated over her mound. "Here."

Ravenna shook her head, eyes widening with shock, though the curiosity in them intensified. "Why would anyone want to do such a thing?"

Courtland found himself smiling—another first that would soon be his. "Because it feels good."

With that, he set his lips to her body. His eyes nearly rolled back in his head at the first silken taste of her, and if he hadn't been gripping her thighs with his palms, she would have bucked off the chair. Warm color flushed through the skin of her thighs, suffusing her hips and torso. One of his hands drifted up to her belly, stroking gently and holding her in place, before he swiped his tongue from her entrance to the knot of nerves that made her gasp. Courtland barely held back his groan of sublime delight. She tasted better than he'd imagined, the tart sweetness of her bursting on his tongue like fresh, ripe mangoes. One lick and he was lost.

"You're fucking delicious," he muttered, inhaling deeply.

She moaned, trembling beneath him, legs falling open in hesitant invitation. He knew what she needed, and he gave it to her, settling down to feast on the banquet in front of him, his tongue gliding hungrily through the hot, wet folds. Within moments, her fingers were yanking at the roots of his hair, and he worked his mouth faster, flicking the bud at the top of her sex. The tightening of her limbs wound more with each stroke, her body reacting beautifully to his ministrations. She was so responsive, he couldn't help thinking about what it would feel like to be buried inside her. To be joined in such a moment.

Ravenna writhed against his mouth. "Please, Courtland."

When his finger slid into her sheath, her thighs clamped around his ears, her body shuddering uncontrollably as she cried out and shattered around him. Wringing the last drop of pleasure from her, Courtland climbed up her still quivering body and took her lips in a deep kiss before pulling himself to his feet to shuck out of his coat. He stared down at her, skin rosy and flush from her orgasm, eyes bright and fastened on his.

"What are you doing?" she asked.

"Looking at you."

And he was. He could look at her until the end of time and still not have his fill. Half-dressed and mussed, her body still quivering with pleasure beneath that gossamer scrap of a chemise, his wife was the most gorgeous thing he'd ever seen. Everything about her captivated him—her effortless beauty, that smart tongue, her razor-sharp mind, that dauntless spirit. She was twisting him into knots he never wished to escape.

Fuck. She could demolish him without even trying. He stood there uncertainly for a moment, his own arousal coursing through him, but his usual demons were not gone, just momentarily subdued. He would destroy her—destroy that incredible spirit. His unsteady hands stalled on his waistcoat buttons.

Blast, he couldn't do this.

Fourteen

RAVENNA SAW THE DOUBT AND THE UNWORTHINESS START TO
creep in like the poisons they were. She would not have it, not
now, not when this was the most unguarded and open she'd ever
seen him. Not now, when he was *real*. Pushing up to her elbows,
uncaring of her own nudity, her gaze held him. "Stay with me."

Panicked dark eyes shot to hers, nostrils flaring. "I—"

"No, stop. You promised me one night. No dukes, no heiresses.
Just you and me. Are you so faithless as to renege on your word?"

"Promise me you won't want more than this, Ravenna." His
voice was tortured. "I couldn't bear disappointing you. Can you
do that?"

"Fine."

Clearly torn, he let out a breath. "I don't want to hurt you when
this is over."

"You won't. Now strip, lover."

She *hoped*. Deep down, though, Ravenna had the feeling that
a man as closed off as he was would hurt her without even knowing it. The fortress that surrounded his heart would not let anyone
get too close. Not even his wife. But if she wanted him—and she
did—she would simply have to separate the two…the physical
desire from the emotional attachment. Not insurmountable, but
not easy either.

This was about pleasure, not intimacy.

Ravenna adjusted herself and crossed her bare legs, seeing
his hungry gaze instantly go to them. The pose was provocative,
though she hadn't meant it to be. Notwithstanding the fact that

she was nearly naked in a location that was not a private bedchamber and a man who had just pleasured her to infinity was staring down at her like she was his last meal, a beat of shyness pulsed through her. She almost giggled. Said man had just spent a great deal of time lodged between her thighs, his sinful mouth pressed to her most intimate place, devouring his fill.

At this point, modesty was laughable.

A devious smile curled her lips as she remembered what the boatswains on the clipper had said about mouths going *there*. It had seemed shocking, unpleasant even, but disgust had been the last thing on her mind in the moment. No, her mind had been teetering on the knife edge of pleasure until Courtland's sleek tongue had hurled her off into the abyss.

Summoning her inner temptress, Ravenna peered up at him, bringing a knuckle up to her lower lip and brushing it back and forth. An obsidian gaze lifted to fix on the movement. "One would think a man of your considerable…acumen could follow simple instruction." Her hand drifted down toward the ribbon at her throat, and his hot stare followed the teasing path of her fingers. "Do I need to resort to more overt tactics?"

Ravenna lifted her upper body off the bench, and in one swoop, tugged the fine lawn of her chemise off her shoulders. She resisted the natural urge to cover herself and, instead, stretched like a contented kitten. She felt herself heat from the force of the gaze snapping to her exposed breasts, but not with embarrassment. With pleasure. The way he looked at her was the exact opposite of apathy.

The growl ripping from his chest urged her on. Her palm skated across her stomach, inching up in slow, torturous strokes to the underside of her breast. With each ragged heartbeat that threatened to punch through her ribs, she felt his resolve lessen, saw the smoldering lust in his eyes rise. She gasped as her knuckles grazed over a taut nipple.

"Will you make me beg, Courtland?" she whispered.

It broke the spell holding him in thrall.

Within seconds, the buttons from the waistcoat scattered on the flagstones in his haste to get it off. A ripping sound followed, the cravat torn from his neck, before his trousers were shoved down and his shirt yanked over his head. Within seconds, the duke was as bare as he was born, and she'd never seen a more heart-palpitating, lip-smacking sight in all her life. She had to remind herself to breathe.

Because the man was magnificent.

Ravenna had seen countless other men shirtless *and* pantless before. One could not live on a ship with dozens of sailors without being exposed to bare chests and random sightings of a bare arse or two, but none of those men had been built like this. None of them had ever made her feel such uncontrollable yearnings, such bone-deep desire. She wanted to leap up and bear her prize to the floor, staking her claim over that splendidly sculpted body like a lioness on the prowl.

"Still wish to beg, Duchess?"

Registering the smirk on his lips, she wanted to retort with some smart response, but instead, she went with the truth. "I'm way past begging now. We're into the part where pouncing and having my wicked way with you seems more fitting."

His deep rumble of laughter was music to her ears. Ravenna lifted her eyes to his, seeing his soft expression. She couldn't have been more obvious if she'd licked her lips and wiped her mouth with a napkin. He had to know how attractive he was. Had other women seen him thus? She ignored the spike of jealousy that lanced through her. He was a man, and given his stellar performance earlier, was not lacking in either experience or skill.

"Do you often get this reaction from women?" she teased.

"I've not had complaints."

He wouldn't. Her duke fairly emanated masculinity. The

teasing hints of the strong body she'd glimpsed and felt while massaging him in his study had in no way prepared her for the banquet of sumptuous male flesh displayed in front of her now. She wanted to freeze this moment so she could examine his physique from every possible angle at her leisure.

Muscles upon muscles rippled from the top of his deeply bronzed chest down the stacked, ridged plains of his stomach. Crisp black hair curled over the top half, narrowing to a thin line at the start of his corrugated stomach and arrowing down, down, down. She hadn't wanted to gawk before, but she could hardly stop herself now. Breath and good sense deserted her.

That part matched the rest of him.

Long, thickly formed, and just as hard. She forced herself to take in his well-built legs below, though her eyes flicked back upward to the thatch of black hair at his groin and the mesmerizing piece of him that most interested her. Despite her own inexperience, thanks to her scandalous adventures on the high seas, she had a general idea of what parts went where.

According to chatter she'd overheard on the ship, a man's tallywag, prick, or broomstick was meant to enter a woman's lucky bag, prat, or cunny. She'd reddened and chortled at the scandalous names of the sex organs as well as the act itself: a bit of business, charver, swive, dip one's wick, and her personal favorite, horizontal refreshment. Heat and lust sizzled through her, a hysterical giggle breaching her lips.

"What's so amusing?" he asked.

Ravenna had a feeling that if she told him what she had overheard from the boatswains, it would not be as hilarious to him as it was to her. Biting her lip, she blushed. She really had no idea how Courtland was going to get *that* monster into her body. "You're rather well endowed."

"You can take me," he said, which made her only want to giggle more.

Courtland knelt, one knee bracing on the edge of the chaise, and all amusement fled from her as his tall frame came to hover over hers. His mouth lowered and claimed hers in a hot kiss, and for a moment, Ravenna was lost in sensation as his lips glided over hers.

The man knew how to kiss. His tongue speared into her mouth, tangling with hers, licking at her like he couldn't get enough of her taste. She couldn't get enough of his! Brandy and darkness and utter sin. Pleasure flooded her nerve endings as his mouth left hers to trail down her neck. He sucked at the spot where her collarbone met her throat, making her moan and arch backward, thrusting her pelvis up into his hips. The searing contact of his hard sex to her inner thigh nearly made her stiffen, but then the brush of his lips over her breast made her forget everything but the hot, wet seal of his mouth closing over her nipple.

Gracious, she nearly came off the chaise when he sucked, his hot tongue lapping around the beaded tip. Wanton heat streaked through her all the way down to her core, throbbing between her legs and making her ache to be filled. Ravenna had never imagined such sensations…that a man's mouth on her breasts could provoke such intense ribbons of need. Not any man's mouth.

Courtland's. Her *husband's*.

No other man had ever deconstructed her to this raw, carnal version of herself, transformed by his touch alone. She'd never let one get so close. Was this what Clara had meant when she vowed that Ravenna would one day find her match? That she would desire him in a way that was obscene, that went beyond anything she'd ever felt for anyone? Was this passion or was it something more? In truth, she feared the answer. Lust was acceptable. Anything else was…not.

She could not, *would not*, lose her heart to this man. It would be pure folly.

Ignoring her thoughts, she focused on the pleasure at hand.

And there was so much of it!

Courtland lavished her other breast, alternating between bites that made her toes curl and deep drugging sucks that she felt throb between her legs, until she was a roiling mess of want. Not one to lie idle, she wrapped her leg around his thickly muscled calf, digging her heel in to find purchase, to get more of the delicious friction she craved at her core. Her fingers scoured his hard back, the bunched strength there a testament to how careful he was being with her. Though she was not a small woman, a man of his size could crush her easily.

His mouth moved down her belly and she moaned, her body turning to cinders under his careful attentions. Courtland's hands roamed the rest of her—skimming her ribs, cupping her bottom, squeezing her hips—before landing at the drenched heart of her. If she had two thoughts to rub together, she'd probably be mortified at how wet she was, but she didn't care. Ravenna rolled her hips, seeking his fingers.

"Touch me," she moaned.

"Touch you where?" he said, glancing up at her from where he nipped at her navel, gray eyes almost black with passion. His fingers skimmed her inner thigh. "Here?" They lifted to her crease, teasing the curls soaked with her arousal. "Here?" Then, they reached down, sliding through her folds. "Or, here?"

With each teasing *here*, his voice grew huskier, and she grew bolder. With a wicked grin, her other leg wrapped around him and she rolled her hips up, gasping as his knuckles rubbed right against the center of her pleasure. "There."

Rocking against his hand and taking what she needed without shame, it took mere seconds for her vision to go white. Her body seized and bliss tore through her like wildfire. His mouth came up to swallow her cries, his talented fingers drawing every quake, every decadent ripple of her orgasm to its breath-stealing end. A moment passed before she realized that Courtland's hands were now gripping her hips and the thick part of him grinding against her sex was no longer his fingers.

It made her burn hotter.

"Courtland, now," she commanded against his lips, needing him to fill her.

"Demanding little thing, aren't you?"

"I know what I want."

He gave it to her, sliding home with one hard, slick thrust.

———————————

Ravenna went still beneath him, a sharp cry breaching her lips. Courtland forced himself not to move, to give her time to adjust. She was so fucking tight, he could barely move. He glanced down, seeing her mouth parted on a gasp, those pretty eyes glimmering with a hint of pain.

"I've never felt so full in my life." She broke off, eyes closing with mortification. "It's too much."

"Take a moment to breathe," he said through clenched teeth. Hell, she was a virgin?

A puff of laughter left her lips. "As if I could possibly fit anything more into me."

Her body tightened with the fervor of her words, and Courtland nearly spent then and there as her tight sheath clenched down upon him. He gritted his teeth, fighting for control. Being inside her was every bit as transcendent as he'd imagined it to be. "I should have taken more care."

She sniffed and met his gaze, her hips canting slightly as she adjusted her position. "It was more of a pinch than pain. I expected it to hurt the first time."

Courtland flinched. God, he was a thoughtless boor. He should have guessed, despite her confident command, and instead of going slowly, he'd rutted into her like an animal.

"Don't," she said.

He frowned. "Don't what?"

"Do whatever it is you're doing in that head of yours," Ravenna said. "It was my choice. I wanted this, and the truth is if you had known, you probably wouldn't have done it."

She wasn't wrong there—virtue was valued in their world—but she was also right in that it'd been her choice to make. Courtland was not of the opinion that a man should have any sway over a woman's body, unless it was by her express wish.

"How do you feel now?"

"Better." Her eyes dilated when he flexed slightly, not enough to move but enough for her to feel his fully seated length. She moaned. "Do that again. Now, Courtland."

He grunted. "Who knew my wife was such a tyrant in the bedroom? I was promised obedient and demure."

"We're not in a bedroom, and whoever told you that was a fibber."

Blushing wildly, she stuck out her tongue and he captured it with his mouth, making her gasp as the movement drove his body deeper into hers. Courtland claimed her lips, sucking and nibbling, showing her with his tongue exactly what he wanted to do to her body. Soon, she was kissing him back and jerking her hips in needy little pulses.

He rolled her nipples between his fingers, causing her to writhe beneath him. Leaving the haven of her lips, he suckled her breasts until her body undulated against his in a sensual roll, letting him know without words what she wanted. That she craved more.

"Do you wish me to move?" he asked with a tilt of his hips, his voice tight.

"It feels like I'll die if you don't."

He knew exactly what she meant. Moving as slowly as possible, he withdrew so that only the tip of him rested in her channel and then pushed back in. Her eyelashes fluttered closed on a sigh when he repeated the motion. "All right, love?"

Her fingers dug into his flesh. "Faster."

"As my duchess commands," he said and then groaned the moment he quickened his movements. There was no way he was going to last, not with how deliciously tight she was. With each drag, the pressure built. He found her lips again, making love to them as fervently as he was elsewhere. He couldn't get enough of her taste. Or the feel of her. Her untried inner muscles gripped him, cradled him, and Courtland's eyes drifted closed in utter pleasure from the torturous friction. She felt perfect, as if her body had been made for his.

This felt like home.

On the thought, he stilled for a moment, but he wasn't going to explore its deeper meaning right now. He was going to give Ravenna—and himself—this stolen pleasure. Tomorrow would be soon enough to move forward with the future of freedom from him that he had promised himself he'd grant her.

"What's wrong?" she asked.

His eyes flashed open. "Nothing. Why do you ask?"

"You looked like you were in pain."

Courtland forced a smile to his lips, unnerved at how easily she seemed to be able to read him, even in the midst of passion. "Far from it."

"Then be here," she whispered, reaching up a hand to cup his jaw. "Be here with me in this moment. At least give me that, Courtland, if nothing else. Let me see you, please."

He didn't know what she was asking. He didn't *want* to know, but the look in her eyes gripped him as tightly as her body did. He quickened his strokes, feeling the heat building between them, watching her eyes dilate and her mouth part when the hair on his chest abraded her sensitive nipples. Moaning, she arched wantonly against him. Within a handful of heartbeats, he was close to the edge.

She was, too, if her flushed face and shallow pants were any indication. Her eyes still had not released his, forcing their join-ing to something much deeper than he'd ever experienced with any other woman. It unsettled him, and yet, he could not release her gaze.

"Courtland, I'm close," she whispered.

He reached a hand between them, pressing at the bundle of nerves at the top of her sex and felt her stiffen beneath him. With a low cry, her entire body jerked as she shuddered, and then con-vulsed gloriously all around him. It was the most magnificent thing he'd ever seen. For a breath, Courtland reveled in her beauty, the gorgeous flush of color that suffused her pale skin while the tide of her orgasm dragged her under. Lost to passion, his wife was the most stunning woman on earth. This moment would be etched into his memory for the rest of time.

One more deep thrust and he felt his own paroxysm gather-ing upon him. Courtland withdrew from the haven of her body, pleasure convalescing at the base of his spine and making him see stars as he spilled his hot seed onto her belly. With a growl of masculine satisfaction, he collapsed on top of her, breathing hard. He lay against her, gathering his breath, his wits, and his scattered thoughts.

"Am I crushing you?" he asked when he could speak, shifting his weight a little to the side.

She shook her head. "Why did you—" She broke off, her cheeks red. "Do that?"

"Do what?"

"Spend outside of me," she said in a rush.

Reality was quick to return, along with all the feelings of who he was and everything he did not want or deserve in this life, one of which was children. "To prevent conception."

"You don't want an heir?" she asked, her face instantly shuttering.

"I already have one," he said, sitting up and reaching for his handkerchief, which he used to mop up the stickiness between them. A pink smear of blood lay on her thighs and on his staff.

"Who?"

Courtland did not meet her eyes as he cleaned them both, knowing what he would see there. Hurt, disappointment, anger. Maybe all three. They had never discussed children—having them or not having them. But he supposed she should know his position on the matter. "All of this,"—he waved an arm—"is a means to an end. For you, for my sisters. Stinson is next in line, and when I die, as my living heir, he will finally get what he has always coveted."

He reached for his clothing, standing to draw on his trousers and then his shirt. Ravenna pulled her chemise over her head. They dressed in silence, him finishing much faster than her. When he offered to help with fastening her corset, she declined pointing out the ingenious side closures, so he watched while she put herself to rights: undergarments, petticoats, stays, and lastly, her gown. The sight of her dressing was almost as provocative as the undressing, and he felt his sated cock stir when Ravenna slid on her stockings and retied her garters.

"What about what I want?" she asked, smoothing her fingers through her short mess of curls and repinning the pins that had fallen out.

"When this is over, you can do as you like."

Her gasp was loud in the wake of his cruel words, and Courtland felt the rage in her stare as she turned to face him. "We are married, Your Grace. I do not plan to bring any children born on the other side of the blanket into the world."

"That's not what I meant."

She stepped closer. "Then what *did* you mean?"

"I meant to speak to you sooner about this. About us." Courtland let out a frustrated breath, meeting her furious eyes. "I supposed there's no better time than the present, but once my sisters are settled, there will be no need for this pretense to continue.

I'll be returning to Antigua, but I'll grant you a divorce under any grounds you wish. Adultery, excessive cruelty, I don't care."

"A divorce?" Her reply was barely audible.

"Yes. You deserve to be happy, Ravenna. I am not the man to give you the future that you deserve, trust me on that." He shook his head, gesturing to the chaise lounge where they'd coupled, regret pervading him. "I knew we shouldn't even have done this. Sex needlessly complicates things."

She glared at him. "Every time we take a step forward, you insist on taking a hundred back. Well, you know what? You can take you, your divorce, and your needless complications right to hell."

There was no warning before her fist cracked into his jaw, nearly slinging his head sideways. Courtland had three consecutive thoughts before his wife stormed off and left him in the darkened conservatory.

One, his wife threw a mean punch.

Two, clearly, she wasn't keen on divorce.

And three, if he'd wanted to make her hate him, he'd well and truly succeeded.

Fifteen

RAVENNA PROBABLY SHOULDN'T HAVE LEFT LONDON. IN hindsight, she really, definitely shouldn't have done it without telling her husband. Because here she was in Hastings alone, having arrived by Ashvale's private railcar, one of the benefits of being married to a duke, she supposed. Although the sumptuous railcar belonged to Courtland *before* he'd become duke.

She was only beginning to understand exactly how wealthy her husband was. This railway car, while smaller than the one they'd traveled in after the *Glory* had put in to port, was no less luxurious.

No doubt Rawley had alerted his lord and master that she'd intended to purchase a public train ticket on her own, fully expecting to travel to Hastings alone, and he had been the one to insist on her use of the duke's railcar. Not to mention that Rawley had followed her hansom cab halfway across town. Ravenna bit her lip, feeling guilt slice through her.

Perhaps she *should* have informed her husband of her whereabouts or that she was leaving London. Her jaw clenched. No, that cold-blooded rotter didn't deserve to be told anything. It was too late to do anything about it now, and she was already there. Might as well push forward with living the wonderful life of Ravenna Chase, impetuous heiress and notorious hothead, estranged duchess and resounding dimwit.

Her fingers twisted in her skirts, her chin rising high. She would not think of *him* or the equal parts blissful and dreadful night they'd shared almost two weeks ago in the conservatory. Two weeks of complete and total avoidance. The first handful of days, she'd pleaded illness due to the arrival of her menses—which had saddened her for no particular reason though she bitterly imagined that her husband would be pleased after his thoroughly sensible and prudent midcoitus precautions. She had barricaded herself in her rooms, reading any salaciously gothic novel she could find. Besides sending a fretful Rawley to check on her once or twice, the duke had not seemed troubled by her absence or her silence.

After that, she'd enlisted her lady's maid, Colleen, who seemed to have taken a shine to the duke's dour and unwilling valet Peabody, to inform her when her husband had departed for his daytime activities so she could get some fresh air. She took breakfast in her chambers and filled her days by entertaining callers, practicing her pianoforte, and perfecting her needlepoint—Lady Holding would be *so* proud—all the tediously necessary accomplishments of a lady of her station. At night, she'd attempted to keep herself busy, though the endless whirl of musicales, theater outings, and soirees had left her miserable.

And unquestionably lonely.

The sad, pathetic truth was she missed Courtland, though he didn't seem to miss her in the same way. Her husband had fallen back to his hard, heartless ways with little care for anyone around him.

Not even her.

That had been made clear at the Hartford ball only last night. Peabody had delivered a curt message that the duke had been held up by business at the last minute and would not be able to escort her. In a rash display of temper, Ravenna had gone alone. Courtland had arrived sometime later, his blank-faced mien giving away nothing, though his eyes when they'd landed on her had burned with an internal fire. He hadn't danced with her or sought her out, and his aloof treatment had stung. Others had noticed, too.

In the retiring room, the whispers had reached her.

"Estranged already?" someone had tittered.

"It was bound to happen."

"I don't care what anyone says, he's not one of us." The last had been said with such scorn and disgust that Ravenna had almost leaped from the water closet to defend her husband. "I heard he's not even the real duke and that his brother is the true heir. So scandalous."

"Speaking of scandal, what of his lady wife?" a vaguely familiar voice had said. "I'm certain that little tart disgraced herself abominably and that's the only reason they married. It wouldn't surprise me if she was with child."

They'd broken into ugly chortles before someone else had snickered. "They're quite the pair, aren't they? The heathen and the hussy. They deserve each other."

"Oh, that's clever, Jane!"

Ravenna had been shaking with anger as the spiteful ladies departed. She'd known her past exploits and her reputation for being cold were food for gossip in the *ton*, but she'd never before been the target of such obvious scorn. Then again, she'd lost touch with most of her old set. She hadn't seen any of their faces, but had identified one of the voices as belonging to Lady Penelope, now the Countess of Halthorpe.

Penelope hated her, mostly because Ravenna had thwarted the girl's designs on Rhystan years ago. It didn't help that her husband, the Earl of Halthorpe was a score her senior, had the face of a toad, and was rumored to be a debauched profligate.

After the awful incident in the retiring room, Ravenna had attempted to find Courtland to put on a show of marital solidarity, but was informed by a gloating Penelope that the duke had departed. Without her. The sneer the countess had sent her, along with the pitiful glances from her former acquaintances, had been hard to ignore.

Ravenna couldn't fathom if they pitied her for the duke's obvious lack of devotion where she was concerned or the fact that she'd married such an unfeeling ogre in the first place. Her own husband couldn't find it in his heart to be around her or see her home safely despite his late arrival at the ball. He simply did not care.

Which accounted for Ravenna's sudden need to quit town.

She'd had to *run* somewhere.

And so she decided that morning to take a trip to Hastings to see Sarani and baby Anu, whereupon she'd been stalled by Rawley at the station and escorted to Courtland's waiting rail carriage. Now, as the hackney pulled up to her brother's beautiful seaside estate, aptly named Joor Royal Green after the duchess's childhood home in India, Ravenna felt instantly eased.

The scent of the sea filled her nostrils and she breathed in deeply. It wasn't quite the balmy tropical air of the islands, but it would do. Extensive manicured gardens with statues and fountains dotted the landscape and led up to the sprawling residence. Ravenna descended from the conveyance and, instead of the butler, was greeted at the doorway by her smiling sister-in-law, a swaddled bundle in her arms.

Surprise glinted in Sarani's hazel eyes. "Ravenna, darling, what brings you here?"

"I had to see you and my niece," she said. "And since Rhystan said you weren't planning on coming to London until later, I decided to come see you. I'm sorry for arriving unannounced. I suppose I should have sent a telegram or something."

"Please," Sarani said. "As though we stand on ceremony here. Family is always welcome at any time. And besides, I'm rather desperate for some female company. Rhystan has been gone for days, busy in the House of Lords with some American issue regarding supply of goods and shipping fees."

"American?"

"Liverpool trading issues from private merchants supporting

the conflict in the Southern states." She sighed. "It's intolerable that such atrocities still exist."

"Truly," Ravenna replied, reminded momentarily of Sommers and his nefarious shipping, but she shoved him from her mind. "I'm glad Rhystan is doing something about it."

"That's your brother for you," Sarani said.

It made her think of Courtland and his own work in Antigua, and how much the locals respected him and vice versa. But the thought of him made her ache, so she banished him from her head, too.

She and Sarani spent most of the morning catching up on gossip from while she'd been gone, which was broken up by luncheon, followed by a walk on the beach. Apart from a long nap, her infant niece remained with them, wrapped in a clever body sling made from a swatch of soft woven cotton. Ravenna was struck by how tiny and perfect she was. Baby Anu was the perfect mixture of both her parents, sporting her father's huge blue-gray eyes, her mother's thick dark hair, and delicious plump skin the color of sun-glazed peaches. She was a beauty.

Ravenna loved that Sarani chose to look after her baby herself, instead of depending on a wet nurse. Being the daughter of a duke, the child had a veritable army of nannies and nurses, of course, but Sarani wanted to do the bulk of mothering herself. Ravenna had to admit, cuddling her sweet infant niece had been an unpleasant shock to her system, knowing that her own husband had snatched that choice from her without any qualms whatsoever.

She hoped for children…not now, but someday.

Do as you like.

Courtland's cutting words rose to haunt her, making a lump gather in her throat. The callous beast! Given the fact that she wasn't the kind of woman to cuckold her husband, or conceive a child out of wedlock, it seemed unlikely that she would ever mother children of her own. Not to mention his offer of a divorce!

That deeply depressing thought sent a harsh stroke of hurt into her chest. Determined not to think of the dour duke she'd married, Ravenna continued to skillfully steer the conversation away from her disastrous nuptials.

Her shrewd sister-in-law, however, saw right through that ploy. "I take it you're not happy, then?" she asked, propping a hungry Anu to her breast as they sat on a blanket on the sand. The attending servants retreated a few feet away to give them some privacy. "Being married to the Duke of Ashvale? I'm sure the dowager is pleased."

Sarani didn't care that Queen Victoria had declared nursing one's child an unsuitable practice for refined ladies, or what anyone in the *ton* thought of her. Ravenna heartily agreed. Besides, there was nothing more natural than feeding one's baby, not that she would ever get to know. A pang filled her, but she ignored it. She would have to have an enthusiastic partner and a functioning marriage before even thinking of nourishing infants.

Ravenna shrugged, sipping Sarani's special brand of tea that one of the servants had brought along in a picnic basket. "You know Mama, of course she is. She despaired of me ever getting married." She let out a slow breath, wondering how much she should confess. "In truth, it's not what I expected."

"How so?"

Sarani would understand better than anyone, considering her own background and the challenges she'd faced in being accepted.

"Ashvale doesn't think he deserves to be married to me," Ravenna explained. She pursed her lips with a thoughtful frown. "I haven't gotten to the bottom of it, but I suspect it's a convoluted mess that has to do with Stinson's and Lady Borne's feelings toward the first marchioness. They are calling out his legitimacy as well as the late duke's state of mind, and I fear it's going to get much worse. They want to do anything they can to discredit him." With her voice trailing off, she stared down into the teacup as though it held answers, and then exhaled. "I've never seen this side of Stinson. So vicious and hateful. Lady Borne too. It's as though I've been living with blinders on all these years. The way they treat him is abominable."

"Because of his origins?"

Ravenna nodded, lips tightening. "I cannot countenance it. He is the legitimate duke."

Sarani gave her a small, understanding smile. "Prejudice is rampant in England. Though I have been welcomed at court and I'm lucky to be in the queen's favor, people still rant about me behind my back."

"How do you deal with it?"

"With courage and a good dose of humor. I try not to let the opinions of others affect how I choose to live or whom I choose to love."

"Courtland doesn't see it that way. I fear his scars run deep. Likely tied to Stinson, I suspect."

Sarani nodded thoughtfully. "Rhystan is not particularly fond of Lord Borne, either, or is it Lord Stinson now, considering your husband's rather astonishing return from the dead." She frowned. "Rhystan did mention that legal certification of his death had never passed through the courts, which is rather surprising, if you ask me. You would think they'd want to get approval as soon as possible."

"What do you mean?"

"I'm not an expert on laws, but the family of a peer must wait seven years before declaring him dead, and it would have to be legally sorted out before the title and entailed lands could past to the next heir in line."

Ravenna's brows drew together. "But Stinson was calling himself the Marquess of Borne, which was Courtland's courtesy title, because everyone believed his brother to be dead."

Sarani nodded. "Apparently, it was never corroborated in the courts, and for good reason since your husband is clearly alive and kicking. He would have had to go back through the courts and prove his birthright." A thoughtful expression crossed her face. "People will do anything in the pursuit of power. I should know—my own cousin tried to murder me!"

"It boggles the mind."

"Heavens, it's like a theater production, isn't it?" Sarani pantomimed fanning herself with the baby at her breast as though she was in the grandest of ballrooms instead of in the middle of nursing. "So Shakespearean."

Ravenna huffed a laugh. "Indeed. Drat, I do wish you were in town. It would make things so much more bearable."

"You're that unhappy?"

"I don't know what I feel. Ashvale is...guarded on his best day. And on his worst, well, suffice it to say that he offered me a divorce when this is all over because he thinks it's what I want."

"Is it?"

She bit her lip. "It was. I mean, I thought that's what I had wanted."

Sarani canted her head. "And now?"

"I don't know. He's trying to push me away, for what he believes to be my own good. It's not, though, but he won't hear it."

To Ravenna's surprise, her sister-in-law chuckled. "I'm not amused at your expense, sister dear, but what you are recounting reminds me so much of how I felt with your brother. We stubbornhearted fools do so love to bear our heavy burdens on our own. I felt that Rhystan did not need to be saddled with me or shoulder any hardship that marrying me would bring. But that was *his* choice, not mine to make for him."

"I remember," Ravenna said. It sounded very similar to what Courtland was trying to do. "What should I do, then? When I try to talk to him, he shuts me out."

"Don't give up."

"Easier said than done." The answer was simple, though maddening at the same time. Her husband was well practiced in pushing people away and keeping them at a distance. His heart was walled in and barricaded from any and all interlopers. Including her. "Did you know we were engaged once? When we were young."

"Rhystan mentioned it." Sarani deftly burped Anu by gently patting her rump and back, and then switched her to the other breast. "But it was called off?"

Ravenna's mouth twisted. "I was told he'd died of illness somewhere on the Continent. His family went into mourning. But what actually happened was that his stepmother was the one to send him away from England with a handful of money and a few servants."

"That's terrible."

Her shoulders lifted into a shrug. "We were children. Cordy and Stinson were the only boys outside of my brothers that I knew, and such a betrothal arrangement didn't mean anything real for either of us at that age." A memory of them danced into her head and she smiled. "He gave me my first kiss. I'd forgotten."

Sarani's eyes lit up with interest. "Did he?"

"Well, on the cheek. Completely innocent. I was all of six or so. One afternoon, I was chasing the boys, as I often did, to the fort they'd build between our estates, and I fell and turned my ankle horribly on a tree root. My brother Richard laughed. Stinson too. But Courtland ran back to where I was and carried me on his back all the way home. He wiped my tears and kissed my cheek, telling me to be brave and that even the best and bravest warriors got wounded sometimes."

"Sounds like he was a sweet boy."

Ravenna shook the bittersweet memory away. "Too bad he's the exact opposite now."

"That bad a husband?" A smile played over Sarani's mouth.

"Worse."

Sarani winked, her lip kicking up at the corner. "But is he a *dutiful* husband?"

Ravenna warmed. She should have guessed from the mischievous look on Sarani's face that the question would be forthcoming. It was obvious from her emphasis on *dutiful* that it had everything to do with marital congress, though said act had only been performed the one time.

"As far as duty goes, it's a marriage of convenience. Most aristocratic marriages are." She rolled her eyes, unable to contain the hot blush that would not quit spreading over her transparent skin. "Not everyone expects to have what you and Rhystan have, you know, a sickeningly happy love match with your marital *duties* taking up all your sleeping hours."

Sarani laughed, a bloom coloring her light-brown cheeks. "Waking hours, too, though not since Anu's arrival."

"I wouldn't know." Ravenna sniffed, loving that Sarani and her brother were so happy and envious of their obvious passion for each other.

"Jesting aside, it's not all sunshine and games. Both your brother and I are pigheaded to a fault. We quarrel over the smallest things. At my worst, I am not the easiest person to love. Ravenna dearest, you know that."

"I have no idea what you're talking about," Ravenna declared loyally. "You are the most lovable person I know, barring my new niece, of course."

"Thank you, sister of my heart, but my point is it took time for Rhystan and me to trust one another. We fought hard for what we have and almost lost it all along the way. I'm saying that if one of us had chosen differently, we might not be here. We might not have had Anu." She paused, her stare lifting from the baby to Ravenna. "Do you at least care for your duke?"

"I...have feelings for him, I suppose, but that's because of forced proximity."

"And when he touches you, how do you feel?"

She owed Sarani the truth. "Alive."

Sarani's eyebrows shot up at the despair Ravenna couldn't quite hide from her voice. "That's a start."

"It doesn't mean anything. He doesn't want any of this."

Sarani handed off the sleeping baby with milk beading on her perfect rosebud lips to one of the waiting nurses, and adjusted her clothing. Her hazel eyes gleamed in the sunlight as she turned her face up to it. "One thing I've learned is that most men rarely wear their hearts on their sleeves or say what they are truly feeling, but the right woman can read between the lines."

"This man speaks his mind," Ravenna said. "He offered me a divorce, Sarani."

"Perhaps he sees it as a way to spare you."

She scowled. "Spare me from what?"

"From being hurt."

"By hurting me in the first place?"

Sarani took Ravenna's hands and squeezed, her face full of empathy and understanding. "Trust me, if what you're telling me is true about his past, he doesn't see it that way. I don't know him, but my guess is that he's trying to protect you, albeit in a misguided way, from being married to him. He's offering you the out before you reject him of your own accord."

"But I won't reject him." She stared out at the rolling sea, remembering the moments of unguarded emotion on the *Glory*. "I like who I am when I'm with him."

"I'm sure you do, dearest, but he doesn't believe that."

What Sarani was saying made a strange sort of sense. Her husband was pushing her away because he didn't feel worthy of her. But she wasn't the problem. Courtland would never feel worthy of anyone unless he felt worthy of himself. How could she make him see what she saw when she looked at him? A man of such accomplishment and honor. A man who people loved and men admired. A man any woman would be proud to call husband. *Especially* her.

"How do I fix this?" Ravenna asked.

Her sister-in-law smiled. "By being the warrior I know you are. By fighting for what's yours."

"He doesn't want to be mine." She was aware she sounded peevish, but the doubts had crept in and wouldn't leave.

For an elegant princess-turned-duchess, Sarani's grin was decidedly wicked. "Since when has that ever stopped you from going after what you want? The only person you control is you, Ravenna. If you choose to let him go, that is your decision. But if you don't, you should move heaven and earth to make it happen."

"What if I fail?"

"You won't," her sister by marriage said firmly. "But you won't know that until you try."

Sixteen

COURTLAND DRAGGED HIS FINGERS THROUGH HIS HAIR, standing at the window in his study and staring mindlessly out to the moonlit gardens beyond. *Hell!* The bloody chit was going to drive him into an early grave. Notwithstanding his constant interest in his wife's whereabouts, which had not diminished as he'd expected it would after their coupling, he was a mess. He'd fucked women out of his system before, but apparently she was there to stay, lodged beneath his skin like a prickly burr because he couldn't stop thinking about her. *Fantasizing* about her.

Those long legs hitched over his hips.

Her gorgeous face in the throes of orgasm.

That beautiful body that fit his like a silk-lined glove.

Cursing his weakness, Courtland adjusted the instant swelling in his trousers. Every second sodding thought was of her. When he tried to do estate accounts, he was plagued with memories of her hands all over him at this very desk. A brisk walk in the small gardens was curtailed by erotic thoughts of what transpired in the conservatory. If he went for a ride in Hyde Park, all he could think of was *her* putting him through his paces…and riding him to grueling satisfaction.

It had been barely a fortnight, but the days had become interminable, even with his attempts to stay busy with the estate finances, investment meetings, and sessions in the House of Lords. He took his dinners at his club. Yet, whenever he set foot in the house, he pined for a glimpse of her. Yearned to hear the husky rasp of her voice. Longed for the musical notes of her laughter.

He'd become a besotted fool!

And then, his willful wife had left him without a word. If it wasn't for Rawley, who he'd put on her tail, he wouldn't have known that she was planning to visit Embry's duchess in Hastings or that the foolhardy chit would attempt to travel by public transport on her own. Arranging for one of his private railcars was the least of what he wanted to do…besides dragging her home and locking her in her chamber for being so reckless. Thieves and flashmen were rife in that part of town.

But Courtland knew that attempting to cage her would only lead to chaos. His duchess was a free spirit who wasn't meant to be confined. As such, he'd ordered Rawley to shadow her along with two men for protection whenever she left the residence. Courtland had many enemies, including one he was keeping close to his side in Sommers. Not to mention Stinson, who seemed to be nearing the end of his rapidly fraying rope. Ravenna was not safe, especially with those around who would have no compunction about hurting his new duchess to get to him.

Apart from a short telegram detailing her safe arrival at Hastings, there'd been no other communication from his cousin. It'd been a night and nearly two days. He didn't doubt Rawley's skill, but he also knew what his wife was capable of. And if she discovered she was being followed, who knew what the impetuous, contrary-minded hoyden would do?

A knock on the door made him swing around.

"The Earl of Waterstone, Your Grace," his butler announced and then paused, clearing his throat. "As well as His Grace, the Duke of Embry, and Mr. Rawley."

Rawley. Was his wife back, then? Ignoring the two large peers crowding the study, he met his man's eyes and was rewarded with a small nod. Relief flooded Courtland's bones in an instant, the heavy tension over his shoulders finally lifting.

"Ashvale," the earl said. "How's ducal life?"

"Oh, for God's sake, *Valentine*, it's Courtland. And you'll know soon enough when your uncle dies."

Waterstone gave a mock scowl. "Only my mother called me Valentine, God rest her sweet soul. And Uncle Bucky has promised to live forever." He shuddered. "Being a duke is too much work."

Courtland would agree with that.

"You look like shit," Embry told him grinning widely. "Anything to do with a little bird flying off to Hastings for a couple days?"

"Fuck off, Embry." Courtland tugged on a sprig of hair, and catching the amused look from the duke, dropped his hand. He was sure he looked a mess. His hair was uncombed, his clothing mussed, and he probably stank like a distillery. He cleared his throat, wanting desperately to find out *why* she'd left without a word, especially now that she'd returned. "Was all well in Hastings?"

Hell, even that sounded needy.

Embry spared him with an arch glance, but nodded. "Sarani said that they had a wonderful time. She was grateful for the visit, given how long I've been away." He poured himself a drink, his voice lowering slightly. "She said that my sister looked well, if not so elated with her change in situation."

It felt like he'd taken a blow to his midsection. Courtland didn't know why, but the fact that she was open about her unhappiness gutted him. Not that he'd expected her to pretend to be a content, radiant bride, but they were in this together. At least for the moment. He was to blame, however. He'd been an insensitive bastard and more, but the truth was that confronting his own feelings had terrified him.

"She's not happy to be a duchess?" Waterstone interjected. "Or to be married?"

Embry sighed. "My sister is…unconventional in her views. I suppose she's always had a bit too much independence for a young woman of her station. She gave me a devil of a time with suitors, refusing every single one. Dalwood was adamant in his suit, and I thought she'd have chosen him until she pretended to visit her friend Clara in Scotland. When I received word that she was wedding Ashvale, though I've yet to get to the real truth of that tale, I was at my wit's end."

Courtland forgot the ache in his belly, his rioting emotions finding a new, worthier target. "The Marquess of Dalwood?" Both men turned at the leashed violence in his tone.

"You're acquainted with him?" Embry asked.

"No," Courtland bit out.

Rage settled within him, replacing his frustration with himself, but rage he could handle. Anger had been his constant companion for years, and he knew how to throttle it into better use. His *grandmère* had taught him to fine-tune its edges and direct it toward a purpose. He'd let anger drive the accumulation of his fortune, let it shape him into the man he'd become.

Until Ravenna, he'd embraced no other emotion, *needed* no other emotion. Pleasure took a distant second, and affection didn't factor in his life whatsoever. However, he would take pleasure in destroying Dalwood, and not just for Ravenna's sake.

"What do you know of him?" he asked. "The marquess."

"He used to be leader in the younger set, but rumor has it that he's rusticating at his country estate recovering from a severe groin injury." Courtland fought back a slow and gratified smile. Ravenna would be delighted. "As far as his character, he's smug, arrogant, rich. Much like half the gentlemen in the *ton*." Embry sipped his drink. "As a matter of fact, he's good mates with your half brother."

Courtland scowled. Of course he was. Like attracted like. With friends like Stinson and Dalwood, who needed enemies? No wonder Ravenna had gone running as far away as she could get, only to tumble right into his arms. *She isn't happy to be married.* The reminder gutted him. When this debacle with Sommers was all said and done, he'd put the offer of separation to her again.

"What's the news on Sommers?" he asked.

The earl pursed his lips. "Still trying to get funds for his cause from various Englishmen. Palmerson hasn't been so stealthy in his support of the American South, but the truth is, no one wants to get entangled in an expensive overseas conflict. Sommers has many private business relationships with those who do support him, however, particularly in Liverpool."

Courtland eyed the government operative. "Any closer to catching him?"

"Close."

That was the best he'd get out of the closemouthed British operative. The truth was that Courtland wanted Sommers gone from London and away from Ravenna. He'd seen the way the man leered at her. Not that she couldn't handle herself, but Sommers was here because of him...because of a favor he'd owed Waterstone. He did not want Ravenna anywhere near that man's crosshairs.

He glanced at Rawley. "Any news from our contacts at the port in Liverpool? What of John Laird and his shipbuilding yard?"

"My men report that Sommers has been in communication with them by telegram."

That did not surprise Courtland. "What about associates in Hong Kong?"

"Russell and Company is alleged to have some illicit business in Canton, and Sommers is supposedly paying for a ship to put into port at Liverpool, whereupon its cargo will be arranged to go to his lands in the Carolinas for distribution."

Waterstone's eyes narrowed. "The shipment needs to be on your liner with him on it for us to have any chance of catching and detaining him."

Courtland nodded to Rawley. "Find out whose ship it is and pay whomever you need to get that rerouted. Make sure he has no other options but me."

"Yes, Your Grace," Rawley said.

"Are you sure you don't want to work for Her Majesty as a spymaster?" Embry asked him with a grin. "You'd make an excellent addition to Waterstone's ranks."

"No, thank you." Courtland lifted a brow. He wasn't cut out to be a spy. "Sommers is personal."

"Then I pray I never get on your bad side."

"As if neither of you would do the same," Courtland remarked. Notwithstanding that Waterstone was one of the queen's most cold-blooded infiltrators, the Duke of Embry also had a reputation for ruthlessness. Both men were honorable to a fault, however, and he admired them for what they had achieved.

Embry was a couple years older than he was, and he'd gone to Eton, not Harrow. Waterstone was a transplanted New York–born peer who'd come back to England because his uncle was dying. Rumor had it that he was a double agent working for the Americans as well as the British Crown, but with the earl, one could never be sure. Even his wife was fake—a necessary deception that made most people look the other way. After all, who would look twice at a dandified earl with a coquette of a countess on his arm? It was the perfect disguise. The perfect diversion. Even Ravenna had fallen for the ruse, believing them madly in love when they were little more than colleagues.

"Where's your better half?" Courtland asked.

"Working another angle for information." Waterstone arched a brow. "Where's yours?"

"My duchess is not a spy."

The earl's grin was so wide, it nearly split his face in half. He waggled his blond eyebrows. "As far as *you* know."

Courtland shook his head, dismissing the man's absurd ramblings, and then froze. He swiveled, frowning at the knowing look on his friend's face and shifted his gaze toward the closed study door. *No*, his wife would not be so bold as to eavesdrop, would she? As quickly as the idea came to him, he discarded it before laughing at his own idiocy.

Of course she'd be listening.

She was Ravenna, a rebel through and through. Now that he thought about it, he'd bet his entire fortune that she was standing just beyond those doors, ear pressed to the wood. For how long was anyone's guess, though he imagined it would have been from the moment Embry and Waterstone arrived. If his duchess was one thing, it was inquisitive. The appearance of her brother and the earl would have been lure enough.

"Care to make a wager?" Waterstone asked snidely, catching the direction of his glance. "On what's beyond that door?"

The ever ascetic Duke of Embry covered his laugh with a cough. "I can't take that bet because of…reasons."

"Reasons that have red hair and brown eyes?" Waterstone joked.

Courtland blinked. His wife's beguiling image appeared in head. Her hair was not merely red, it was auburn with streaks of russet and cinnamon. And her eyes were the color of rich, potent sherry until she was caught in the throes of passion…and then they became molten gold-dusted copper. Fuck, even knowing she might on the other side of that door flooded him with lust. Tamping down his desires, he strode to the door and opened it.

There was no one there.

With a small, satisfied grin, he turned to set the mistaken Waterstone in his place, and watched as his smug friend burst into cackles better suited to a witch than a grown man. Courtland froze, thought for a moment, and then a huff of self-deprecating laughter tore from his chest. He shook his head in defeat and closed the study door.

The clever little minx wasn't outside the study because she was already *inside*.

Ravenna had forgotten how much energy it took to stay perfectly still…to barely breathe, while keeping her entire body from cramping in misery. That Earl of Waterstone was distressingly sharp. She could tell by the way his hawkish eyes took in every detail, cataloged every move and every change, even something so small as a whisper of air on the other side of a room.

Perhaps that was a bit of a stretch, but suffice it to say that he was more observant than most. Rawley, she knew from experience, was also alert. Her brother was no slouch either; he very rarely missed anything. If she'd had to guess, at least two of the men in that room had been spies, were currently still spies, or were planning a future in spying.

Her husband, however, had seemed distracted for reasons unknown. Courtland was a mess, his hair rumpled, clothing askew, and he looked like he hadn't had a shave in days. She'd gotten an eyeful of that strong, bristled jaw when he'd walked past to the study door. Ravenna wondered what it would feel like to kiss his face…to feel those unshaved whiskers abrading the sensitive skin of her bare thighs.

No! *Not* the kind of thoughts to be having when she was seconds from discovery, peeping on a private conversation with two dukes, an earl slash spy, and her husband's man of business whom Ravenna was nearly certain might also be an active agent of the Crown. But she couldn't help it as her body flushed with heat and the faintest of exhalations left her lips. Her husband faltered mid-step, though he did not look in her direction.

Damnation.

If Waterstone hadn't heard the tiny gasp, she might get off scot-free. From what she could discern, the earl was currently half collapsed in his chair from mirth over a joke she'd missed, and her brother just seemed amused. But Ravenna should have been paying attention to her husband because the duke had halted in

place, face thoughtful. For a horrible moment, she feared immi-
nent discovery, and then, a bark of laughter broke from him.

Shaking his head, he strode past her hiding place, the alcove
where what looked like a broken decorative bust used to be, not
even sparing a glance in her direction. Ravenna fought back a
silent sigh of relief. It was tight, but provided just enough space
for her to wedge into without being noticed. The duke went over
to the mantel and poured two glasses of brandy. Since her brother
already had a drink, she assumed it was for the earl.

"You might as well come out, Duchess," Courtland drawled.

Goodness, was he referring to *her*? Ravenna stilled, not even
daring to breathe.

"If you stop breathing, you'll swoon, and that alcove won't hold
you."

Well, shit.

Ravenna considered her options. She wasn't ashamed of sneaking in behind Rawley, the footmen, and the butler. She'd only just
returned from Hastings and had donned a loose shirt and a pair of
her male alter ego's trousers, much to the horror of her lady's maid.
But truly, she'd been sick to death of petticoats and crinolines—
and becoming Raven Hunt if only for a moment had made her feel
less trapped. The dark clothing had been a boon, allowing her to
slip unseen into the dimly lit study.

And then she'd listened in on the most enlightening conversation known to man. She might as well own being brazen. Giving
her chin a determined toss, she stepped from her shadowy hiding
place to meet the expression of her irate if resigned brother, a
beaming Waterstone, an exasperated Rawley, and lastly, her blank-
faced husband.

"Gentlemen, my wife," Courtland said, lifting one of the glasses
and holding it out to her. "The extraordinarily crafty Duchess of
Ashvale."

At the veiled sarcasm, Ravenna opened her mouth and closed

it. She had no excuse and would not apologize for her choices. It was the only way she'd learn anything, after all. At the very least, she'd expected a few secrets, maybe about the closed-off man she'd married, though not the veritable treasure trove of information she'd been privy to.

Ravenna was still reeling from what she'd discovered.

One, Waterstone was, in fact, a British spy. Neither was he truly married. She could have sworn he and his countess were a couple from their passionate display on the *Glory*, but what did she know of love and marriage? Perhaps, Lord and Lady Waterstone were simply brilliant actors. However, if the kiss she'd witnessed had been a fraction of what kissing Courtland had felt like, there was no way it could be false. Perhaps they were lovers in addition to being covert associates.

Two, the Marquess of Dalwood was likely going to meet a dreadful end, given the deadly look on her husband's face, unless she could convince her husband to leave well enough alone. Though a tiny, furious part of her *wanted* the marquess to suffer and never again try to compromise a young lady.

And three, the least surprising news was that Sommers was a rat and smuggler. She'd known there was something off about the man, and the fact that he still supported such an evil, vile system, made her ill. She felt no pity if he got caught by Waterstone.

What, however, was perhaps the most astonishing revelation of all was that Courtland appeared to have missed her while she'd been gone. If his question to her brother hadn't been a dead give-away, the expression he'd tried to hide from the men by turning around in her direction gave her a first-row view of it. He'd looked devastated and desperate, and for an unguarded moment, his entire heart had been on his sleeve.

Ravenna risked a glance at her husband, taking in his now stoic but drawn features as he held out the glass of brandy. Light flickered in the unreadable depths of his eyes as he took her in.

Up close, that dark unshaven jaw made her want to graze her fingertips against it. She wanted to muss his clothes even more and, most of all, growl at everyone to leave.

Instead, she took the glass and sketched a jaunty bow.

"Mr. Hunt, I presume?" her husband asked.

Her cheeks heated as she remembered her change in clothing. Rhystan had seen her in breeches before, especially in Kettering, but she was certain Waterstone hadn't.

Her brother scowled. "Hunt?"

"Mr. Hunt. Captain Hunt. I knew there was a connection."

"You dreadful liar," Ravenna blurted out. "I told you who I was to save my own skin from the bloody stocks."

The confession was out before she realized her mistake. She didn't dare look at her brother.

"What stocks?" Rhystan asked.

Courtland gave a sly grin and propped his body against his desk. The action pulled his fawn-colored trousers tight across his lean hips. Ravenna had to forcibly avert her eyes and then expunge the salacious thoughts that crowded her mind...of those very same hips driving her to obscene heights of pleasure. She should be angry with him for goading her into giving up what should have remained a secret to eternity, instead of the lascivious direction her thoughts were taking.

Avoiding her brother's gaze, she sipped from her glass, nearly choking as the brandy went down the wrong way. Once the liquid courage kicked in, she put her attention on her brother instead of the man who made her want to tear her hair out and her clothes off in the same breath. "A misunderstanding, nothing more."

Rhystan scowled. "That dismissive attitude might work on everybody else, but not me, sister dear. Explain what you meant."

"I was playing vingt-et-un at his tables, if you must know!" she burst out. "And he tricked me after I won fair and square. When he accused me of cheating and threatened to throw me into the stocks, I had to confess my identity."

Waterstone guffawed, clapping his knee. "Bloody capital!"

"Have a care, Waterstone," her brother growled before spearing her with a flinty blue gaze. "Did you cheat?"

"No!" Ravenna went hot; she'd only thought about it for half a second, but that wasn't cheating.

Courtland tapped his fingers against his glass. "She held nine cards totaling twenty. Those odds are suspect so what was I to think? And besides, other gentlemen had been complaining about her emptying their pockets for weeks."

That part *was* true. She'd made a killing, but she hadn't cheated. She'd counted...then lost count...then bluffed.

"I didn't cheat, for the love of God, but I needed the funds to live and those men were easy pickings," she grumbled and glared at her husband. "But then, you had to show up and ruin it all, didn't you? I could have been done and gone in a day."

"Gone where, Ravenna?" Courtland asked silkily.

"Another island, damn it. Somewhere far from you!" She peeked at her brother when she felt the spike in temperature, the room brimming with two very displeased males. "Can we drop my paltry transgressions and focus on what you've all been hiding? That you're gentlemen vigilantes trying to entrap a criminal?"

Waterstone sniffed. "I take offense at the term 'vigilante,' madam! I'll have you know that I have every confidence of Her Majesty, the Queen."

"Noted, and while I'm certain I don't know everything there is to know about my husband, I would know if he were a spy. Rawley, I would bet, used to be a spy or in the military. And Rhystan has always had his fingers in as many troughs as he could manage though he is not currently employed as a spymaster, or his duchess would have his hide."

"How would you know that I wasn't?" Courtland asked.

"You wouldn't serve the monarchy of a place you feel betrayed by," she replied quietly, watching when her husband's body went tense, though she'd kept her voice low. "You value your financial worth above all else, and you much prefer to remain king of your island of isolation instead of answering to anyone. No, the only master you serve is yourself unless it suits you, as it does because you have a personal vendetta against Sommers."

"He killed some laborers who left Antigua to work on his lands. When they refused to work without fair compensation, he beat them to death. Word got back to their families in Antigua and that's how I learned about it." Courtland tightened his lips. "Add that to possibly smuggling people under the guise of merchant goods. Sommers is a poor excuse for humanity."

"I agree, which is why you need my help." Ravenna gave a grim smile. "As bait."

Seventeen

COURTLAND GLARED AT HIS WIFE AS THEY STOOD TOE-TO-TOE in her dressing room, her face resolute, and his wreathed in anger and frustration. The argument about her involvement had not waned from the study earlier that evening, all through dinner, and it now threatened to go well into retiring hours. He dismissed Colleen, who had just finished brushing her mistress's shining curls into some semblance of submission, and stared at his wife through the mirror above her dresser.

"Ravenna, Sommers is much too dangerous."

"I agree," she replied mildly. "Which is why you need my help to speed things along and get him out of our hair as quickly as possible. I'm the last person Sommers will suspect of being involved. And he…desires me."

Courtland's fingers clenched at his sides. Oh, he'd seen the gluttonous looks Sommers had sent his wife. He'd had to remind himself to focus on the greater goal of incarcerating Sommers, but having that brute get anywhere near Ravenna made Courtland's blood boil.

"No. This is absurd. You're a civilian, a woman."

His wife sent him a cool stare. "Lady Waterstone is a female."

"She's a trained operative. You are—"

"A useless heiress?" Ravenna interjected. "A vapid henwit who should only worry about her soirees, her needlepoint, and her pianoforte? Yes, yes, I know exactly what society expects me to be, Courtland, but that's not me. I cannot stand by while a disgusting excuse for a man treats human beings like they're nothing.

If I don't act when I have the power to do so, then that makes me complicit."

He shook his head, frustrated and unable to refute her admirable argument. It was one of the things he loved about her—how fiercely devoted she was, from befriending an islander on the streets of Antigua to going after a dangerous blackguard who threatened her family. She was passionate about everything she touched. "That's not what I mean. If the countess is in danger, she can get herself out of it. She signed up for that. You did not."

"I'm signing up now. I can shoot a pistol, wield a sword, and defend myself, if need be. I can handle Sommers."

The name was a fan to his fury. Ravenna had no idea what Sommers was capable of, and it wasn't just murder. He had a perverse enjoyment for cruelty, especially toward women. Courtland could not—*would not*—expose his wife to that, no matter how capable or daring she was. The thought of her in danger left him cold. If anything happened to her…

"I forbid you to do this."

A pair of sparking eyes drilled into his. "You *forbid* me?"

"I am your husband, damn you, and it's my right. You vowed to obey, remember?"

She lifted a brow. "I'll obey a reasonable man, Courtland, and right now, you're not being reasonable."

Ravenna rose and turned to face him, her body draped in nearly transparent lawn and lace. He was too agitated to appreciate how perfectly her body was limned by the low light of the candelabra on her bedside table. Normally, the sight of her long legs, trim waist, and the luscious curves of her breasts would send him into instant arousal, but Courtland tried to keep a firm hold on his libido. She wasn't getting out of their spat so easily.

"And besides," she went on, closing the distance between them and making the embers of lust spark in his veins, "you've insisted time and time again that this marriage is doomed, so I don't think we have to worry about the vows, do we?"

"I'm in no mood for games, Ravenna," he grunted, her nearness and heady scent serving to distract him—the king of reason and good sense himself—from even forming a logical reply. "You're not doing this and that's final."

"Our safety is not a game."

"I mean it. The answer is no."

"Very well, Duke," she replied and then turned toward her bed, affording him a wonderful view of her rounded buttocks before she blew out her candle, and then they were shrouded in darkness.

Courtland barely registered the creaking noise of the bed and the rustle of her blankets as she situated herself. Wait, did his headstrong, unruly wife just capitulate to his demands? Frowning, he blinked. And also, did she get into bed while he was still standing there?

He approached the side of the bed, his eyes adjusting to the gloom, to make out her female shape right in the middle of the bedclothes. "What are you doing?"

"Going to sleep."

"We were talking," he said.

"*You* were talking," she replied, the slight rasp in her voice adding to the sexual desire flooding his body at the tantalizing sight of her body in the middle of the mattress. "I was finished. And unless you intend to join me here in bed and do things while *not* talking, I'd rather discuss this tomorrow."

He blinked. Did she just make an indecent proposition?

His swelling cock went fully hard, but instead of doing what his body so obviously wanted and accepting what she'd so casually offered, Courtland stepped back. And then back again until he was a safe enough distance away, at least to stop himself from diving groin-first into his wife's body. Sex wouldn't solve anything.

"There'll be no discussion tonight or tomorrow," he ground out.

And then he left. Because he could not take one more second of her alluring scent.

Or the sight of her in that goddamned bed.

Or the echo of her husky invitation.

Courtland stormed into his own chamber and slammed the connecting door, meeting the alarmed eyes of Peabody, who approached him as one would a skittish and very unpredictable horse. He said nothing as the valet removed the coat from his shoulders and then the rest of his upper layers of clothing, ending with yanking off his boots. Tearing his shirt over his head, Courtland sighed.

"Shall I run you a bath, Your Grace?"

"Yes," he said, hoping it would do the trick.

But the only trick was the one played on him as he lay in the hot water and was plagued with erotic thoughts of his wife just beyond the door that led into her chamber. Despite his anger at her refusal to listen, his fevered imaginings tortured him. She tempted him to folly. Courtland had never met anyone who could slip under his ironclad control so easily.

He washed himself quickly, groaning when the cloth passed over his aching groin. Relieving himself wouldn't hurt—at least then he'd be able to think. Discarding the cloth, he reached beneath the surface of the water and fisted his engorged length, hissing at the contact. He stroked from the root to crown in hard, purposeful strokes. A guttural sigh escaped him as he closed his eyes, imagining it was his wife's delectable body that clasped him…her wet, silky depths that sheathed him, taking him deep.

"Fuck, Ravenna."

A strangled gasp made his eyes fly open.

And there she stood in that indecent night rail, like a sprite come to tempt his sorry heart. Hooded copper eyes burned into him. They fell to his lap, where his hand gripped his staff. Her tongue darted out to lick her lips as her stare lifted to entangle with his. Not a single word was exchanged, and yet, a thousand things were said in that single glance. Courtland watched with bated breath as one elegant hand lifted and went to the ribbons at her throat.

His cock swelled impossibly when the ties released and the neckline went slack, displaying the full curve of one breast. She did not stop there, however. No, his brazen bride stepped into the bathing chamber and shut the door behind her. Eyes bright, they held his, daring him to tell her to leave. But Courtland could barely breathe, much less speak as her fingers drifted to her hem, tugging the fabric up inch by torturous inch. With a deft movement, she dragged the night rail over her shoulders and discarded it to the floor.

He took in a clipped breath at the uncovered beauty that greeted him.

Heavens, she was exquisite.

Miles and miles of gorgeous blush-infused skin met his hungry gaze, from the tops of her graceful shoulders, past the plump curves of her breasts tipped with rosy, taut nipples, to her gently flaring hips and long, slender legs. His avid gaze fastened to the fiery patch of curls at the apex of her thighs and a smile tilted his lips. She *was* fire, his wife.

Fire and perfection and salvation.

Courtland held his breath as she closed the distance between them, until she stood right in front of him before sitting on the lip of the bath. A sultry, wicked smile curved her pink lips. "You summoned me, Duke?"

"You weren't meant to hear that."

Her hand slid through the water, her gaze dipping to where he held himself like his cock was his deliverance. "Do you wish me to leave?"

Whatever incoherent reply he'd been about to make was smothered by the feel of her slim fingers wrapping over his. "What are you doing?" he asked.

"Teach me to please you."

With a groan, Courtland gave in and slid his palm down, squeezing his stiff rod, and almost growling when she interlaced her fingers with his to mimic his movements. Before long, his own hand fell to the side as she worked him up and down. Her thumb slid over the head of him, and he could barely hold back the needy thrust of his hips.

"Do you like that?" she asked, her voice husky.

"Yes."

She twisted her fingers on the downstroke, nearly making him growl and pump into her fist. "How about this?"

He let out a sighing snarl. "That too."

When he felt his body starting to respond to her teasing strokes, he reached over to grasp her around the waist, dragging her into the water with him. Courtland swallowed her gasp with his mouth, his lips claiming hers with a ferocity that stunned them both, even as her hips settled over his. His tongue teased hers, drawing it into his mouth. He suckled and tasted every inch of hers, learned the places that made her moan and arch into him...the roof of her mouth, the inside of her lower lip, the tip of her tongue.

"What do you do to me?" he bit out, breaking from her.

"The same you do to me." Her fingers threaded through his wet hair, those singular eyes on his, molten and wanting. She tugged, a devious smile on her lips. "Kiss me again, Duke."

He acquiesced with a grin of his own, taking her sweet lips in a hard kiss she wouldn't soon forget. With a moan, Ravenna twisted in his arms so that her beaded nipples brushed against his chest. Her searching hand found his length again, jutting up at her hip. His duchess was a quick study, pumping him to perfection with the perfect amount of pressure, but he wanted more than her hands. He wanted inside her.

Courtland broke the hungry kiss, setting his hands to her waist and lifting her up so that she settled over his throbbing cock, knees on either side of him. "Take me this way," he breathed. "Ease me into you."

Her heavy-lidded eyes widened. "Here, in the bath?"

"Yes."

"Is that done?" she asked, brow pleating.

Hell, he loved how innocent she was. "Trust me, this bath is the best place for all the filthy things I'm planning to do to you," he murmured, delighting in the radiant flush suffusing her wet skin. "Besides, I thought you liked adventure?"

She fought to the last. "I'm not sure about this. Wouldn't the bed be more comfortable?"

Instead of answering with words, Courtland canted his hips, feeling the tip of his cock brush the hot heart of her. Ravenna's lips parted when his thick crown prodded the tiny bundle of nerves at the top of her sex. "*Oh.*" She breathed out, spine arching. "I suppose this can work."

Chuckling, he shifted against her, their slick flesh meeting and rubbing, the warm water providing an added level of sensation between them.

"Guide me in, love," he whispered.

Ravenna lifted her pelvis, notching the head of him to her entrance, and then she sank down. Courtland had never felt anything so gratifying in his entire life as the silken feel of his wife's body swallowing him inch by heated inch. When she was fully seated, they both groaned from the exquisite friction.

"Bloody hell, you were made for me." His eyes met hers as he fought a primal urge to thrust upward. "Are you well? Still want the bed?"

Eyes promising retribution for his teasing, his wife grasped his shoulders and rolled her hips, pushing up onto her knees resting on the floor of the bath on either side of him. Her passage clung to him and when he was nearly all the way out, she let gravity do the work. Her body hurtled down, taking him deep. A groan ripped from his chest.

She looked like a sybarite perched on top of him, a sensual smile curling her lips, her face flushed with pleasure. Fuck if she wasn't the most sublime sight he'd ever seen. Her heavy breasts hung at mouth level, their nipples hard and rosy. Courtland lifted her to take one pebbled peak into his mouth, sucking hard and drawing an agonized whimper from her.

"The taste of you," he whispered. "I could devour every sweet morsel of you."

He turned his attention to the other breast, filling his palms with the globes of her rounded arse. The water sloshed with their movements, and soon, there was only the sound of their mingled breaths and the soft splash of the water in the bath as she rode him. His orgasm built at the base of his spine as she rocked against him, but he needed to see her get there first. He wanted to see her beautiful face when the paroxysm took her over the edge.

Courtland slid a hand in between their wet bodies and rubbed his thumb against the knot of nerves, relishing the gasping moans falling from her lips. Her movements turned jerky as she chased her pleasure. "That's it, Duchess. Take what's yours."

Head thrown back in ecstasy, a flush climbing her porcelain neck into her cheeks, his duchess did as she was bid and shattered around him with a cry, his name a silent scream on her lips. Courtland had never seen anything so fucking perfect in all his life. Moments later, he found his own release with a hoarse cry, jerking out of her still pulsating channel to spend in the bathwater and clutching her toward him.

Breathing hard, Ravenna collapsed in a heap against his chest. He stroked the length of her back with his fingers, marveling at her impossibly soft skin. After a while, he felt himself soften and slip from the notch of her body. He reached for the cloth, breaking the comfortable silence when he drew it down her back and up her arms.

"That was...educational," his wife whispered.

A chuckle broke from him as he worked the cloth in small circles. "And exceedingly practical, don't you think?"

"I had no idea one could…well, perform one's marital duty that way."

She peered up at him, and he gave her a lusty smile. "It is an act that can be enjoyed in many places. Even outside, in the ocean, if one so desires."

"In the ocean? You must be joking!"

"Oh, my sweet innocent I have so many wonderful things to teach you," he said, tilting her chin up for a quick kiss. "Wait until we do it outside *and* in broad daylight."

———

A sated and intensely curious Ravenna goggled at him, unable to grasp that men and women coupled in public. "You're jesting with me."

"I look forward to corrupting you anywhere and anytime you let me, Your Grace."

"But how?" she blurted out and then flushed. He must think her impossibly naive, though she could not fathom how they could do this outside or in the ocean.

Courtland sat her up, the cloth briskly moving over her limp body. "Sitting, like this," he said. "Perhaps on a bench in the arbor with you straddling me, much as you are now." His hands moved down each leg, past the bend of her knee to her sensitive calves. "Or standing, with these gorgeous limbs wrapped around my waist while I take you up against a tree or a garden wall."

She blinked, the lewd images he was painting assaulting her. The sailors had all nattered on about the act itself, not really places, so she'd only imagined it occurring in their private berths, behind closed doors, in the dead of night. The thought of Courtland taking her in such a bold manner had her body tightening with need again.

Goodness, she was turning into a wanton.

"Here, let me," she said, taking the cloth from him.

Ravenna returned his care in silence, marveling at the breadth of his shoulders that nearly dwarfed the large tub, and the bronzed expanse of wet skin. She had the sudden urge to lick the place where his neck met his collarbone so she did. That wasn't nearly enough so she worked her way up to his clean-shaven jaw. A part of her missed the thick stubble. He'd obviously been groomed to within an inch of his life by a dedicated Peabody. Ravenna snorted a giggle—the poor valet must have been beside himself with joy.

She bit Courtland's chin, grazing her questing fingertips over his skin. "I liked your whiskers."

"Did you?"

Heat filled her cheeks. "I had such depraved thoughts."

"Tell me about them."

Ravenna hid her hot face in the crook of his neck. "I imagined how they would feel between my thighs."

She felt *that* part of him jerk to life beneath her at the bald admission.

"Already?" she asked on a breathy sigh.

"Always around you, it seems." She gave a soft shiver, and he peered down at her. "Shall I refill the tub with more hot water, my duchess?"

Torn, Ravenna bit her lip. While she wanted nothing more than to enjoy the pleasures of her husband's touch and body in the bath, the very pleasant interlude they'd shared didn't change the fact that she was still cross with him. Or that they needed to clear the air.

"As tempting as the thought is, we need to talk." With reluctance, she lifted herself out of the cooling water and reached for a nearby length of toweling.

Unfathomable eyes watched her as she dried herself and pulled her night rail over her head. It wasn't much of a covering, but it was better than being naked, especially when the look in his gaze made her want to do unspeakable things. She folded her arms over her chest and took a seat in the chair. With a long-suffering look, Courtland followed her example and stepped out of the bath. Despite her very satisfied needs, Ravenna couldn't help gawking.

Water cascaded from his shoulders, all the way down the stacked muscles of his back to the lean indents at the base of his spine. The muscles in his bottom flexed as he bent to dry himself, giving her an unobstructed view of the impressive part of him that had brought her to such bliss. Even at half-mast, it made her breath hitch and a fresh surge of arousal course through her veins. Ravenna blushed and busied herself with the ribbons on the edge of her night rail. Licking his very delicious frame from head to toe was not an option.

She'd come to find him because she hadn't been able to sleep, and while their passionate joining had taken the edge off, the mountain between them would only grow. She waited until she heard the rustle of clothing and groaned when she saw him leaning against the wall. The black silk robe he'd donned hung loose and barely covered his front.

"Don't you have a nightshirt?" she asked, averting her eyes from the bronze vee of his chest and the dark hair that arrowed downward to more interesting pastures.

"I sleep in the nude."

Ravenna swallowed as her cheeks went hot. She'd walked right into that one. Well, now she had *that* image to contend with when she was in her own bed. She would simply have to dress him in nightclothes in her dreams. Maybe even full evening wear, just to be safe…and a greatcoat. Perhaps two.

She bit her lip hard and cleared her throat. "I know you're afraid for me with Sommers, but I will be in good hands. Even if I found myself at a disadvantage where I couldn't take care of myself, neither you, nor Embry, or even Waterstone would let something happen to me."

"Sommers is not a good man."

She nodded. "I know. But he's also smart. If you go after him too obviously, he will see through the ruse and you'll never catch him. This is how I can help. He's the sort of man who thinks women are only good for the use of their bodies, not their minds. If I can steer him to use your ship, chances are he will think it's his own idea."

Ravenna risked a look at her husband's expression. He seemed conflicted, his features twisted in some sort of visible distress, but he was quiet. He was thinking and when his reply came, it was quiet. "If something happens to you…"

She stood and walked over to him, placing her hands on his forearms. A muscle in his cheek flexed, his dark eyes shadowed with indecision and what looked like real fear. "Nothing is going to happen to me, Courtland. Let me do this. I want to do this. A man like that deserves to pay for his crimes."

"You don't understand." He let out a breath, face working in agony. "If something happened to you, it would… I wouldn't…" He trailed off with a vicious snarl and wrenched out of her grip, stalking toward the doorway to his bedchamber.

"You wouldn't what?"

He halted without looking back at her. His voice was the softest and yet the harshest she'd ever heard it, scraping along her nerves with ruthless precision. "You will not interfere in my affairs. You will conduct yourself as my duchess and no more. If I have to restrain you from doing something foolish and lock you in this house, Ravenna, I will do so without a qualm."

Shock blazed through her. "You can't do that."

"I can and I will." Body rigid, he was resolute. As cold as stone. "Are we clear?"

Everything inside of her rebelled at the mandate, but firing back at him would do no good in this instance. "As clear as Venetian crystal, Your Grace."

Eighteen

COURTLAND STUDIED THE MAN SITTING ACROSS FROM HIM AT his club and fought not to grab him by his ostentatious teal lapels, throw him bodily into the street, and then proceed to beat the living spit out of him. Everything about Sommers made Courtland want to resort to violence.

It was a good thing that he had decided to put Sommers up at Claridge's rather than in his own town house. Cold slithered through him at the thought of the man in any proximity to his wife. Courtland never would have wanted to put any woman in danger, but Ravenna had become…precious to him.

"A man could get used to this," Sommers said, flinging back his third glass of expensive brandy served by an efficient footman and patting his rotund stomach. "Why would you want to give all this up and live in Antigua?"

Courtland lifted a brow. "I like living there."

"You're cracked." Sommers laughed and shook his head. "Look at this! You are treated like a king. As a duke, people practically fall over to do your bidding. Men want to be you. Women fall into your lap." He paused, a nauseating smile curling his lips. "Or just one in particular, eh? Where is the lovely duchess?"

Courtland refused to display any emotion, though his fingers clenched in his lap. "Busy being a duchess, I expect. Ladies aren't allowed in this club."

"As it should be. A woman's place is at home." Sommers grinned, showing crooked and stained teeth that demonstrated his dissipated lifestyle. "Tending the hearth and seeing to my needs.

Though I imagine that your spirited wife might require some breaking in. She's a firecracker. Heard about some of her exploits. She's as rebellious as they come." He smacked his lips. "I envy you the task of bringing her to heel."

Anger spiked in his blood, but once more, Courtland gave no outward reaction. "We seem to have different opinions on women, Sommers. I do not require forced submission."

Only blind obedience, his irritating mind reminded him.

He bit back a sigh. The man was foul in the most depraved of ways. Courtland wouldn't even want his breath sullying Ravenna's air.

Though the idea of using her as bait had merit, there was no chance in hell. Embry had agreed, of course. He knew exactly what kind of man they were dealing with, and he declined to put his sister in any danger. Waterstone had been on the fence—he'd seen the value of what she could offer. A woman could always get closer to a man by appealing to his vanity. It was the reason the Countess of Waterstone was so successful at what she did. Her beauty, her intelligence, and her sensuality were all honed weapons.

Ravenna was a lady, however, and not a trained spy.

"How's business?" he asked Sommers casually, leaning back in his seat. "You mentioned you had some investments you were working on."

"Ah, yes, shipping. It's not as economical as I'd hoped, and the man of business is being difficult. He wants to increase his price because of some asinine bill that just got passed forbidding the taking of bribes. You English are such rule-followers. What's wrong with bending the rules a little to line one's pockets?"

"No one wants to go to prison. They've been cracking down on trading practices." Courtland frowned. He dimly recalled hearing about the bill from the Duke of Embry that was passed by the Commons and sent for approval in the House of Lords, aimed at reducing bribes. It was no wonder Sommers was frustrated, and if Rawley had been doing as he'd been asked, Sommers's contacts would be unforthcoming with the ships he needed.

"You know that I'm here if you need anything," he said.

Sommers nodded. "I have it in hand, don't you worry. There are always ways around naysayers. If it's not money, it's something else."

"How so?"

"I have a philosophy about the carrot and the stick. If the carrot doesn't work, then I'm willing to bring out the stick."

Courtland's eyes narrowed. "Physical threats?"

"Tell me you don't do the same at the Starlight," he drawled. "You abhor rule-breakers and swindlers in your establishment, and I've heard the rumors that you deal with them swiftly and ruthlessly. Let he who is without sin cast the first stone."

"You're quoting the Bible?"

Sommers grinned. "It can be quite useful, I find. People have an absurd fear of that tome. I find it enlightening."

It spoke to the levels of Sommers's depravity that he would use people's faith against them or use the teachings of the Bible to justify his own actions. The man was twisted, there was no doubting that. There was a special place in hell for man who condoned abusing humans for his own gain. Courtland's skin crawled with distaste that he was even insinuating there was any similarity between them. As ruthless as he was, he was nothing like this disgusting swine. He couldn't wait to get rid of the man, but he forced himself to focus on the task at hand.

"Cheaters and thieves must pay the piper his due."

"You're the piper?" Sommers asked.

"When I have to be."

The man leveled an unruffled stare at him, but didn't reply. Instead, his eyes darted around the room, taking measure of the gentlemen crowding in, some clustered in groups and some now arriving. It was the hour for luncheon after all. Courtland frowned as he recognized one of the men entering through the massive doors. What was his brother doing here? Apparently, he had the same question because his brows snapped together and Stinson crossed the distance from the foyer to their table in a few swift steps.

"What the devil are you doing here?" Stinson spat out.

Courtland's brow lifted. "Having a meeting, not that it's any of your business."

"This is my club."

"Is it?" he said softly. "I rather think it's the club of the Marquess of Borne, now the Duke of Ashvale, neither of whom are you."

"You are—" Stinson's voice spluttered and broke off.

"Generous that I've ensured my esteemed brother is also a member or you would not have been granted entry? Quite so." He smiled. "I assume that is what you'd been about to say, is it not? Or perhaps even, thank you, brother dear. I'm not deserving of your charity."

Stinson turned a dark shade of puce, his eyes spitting his hatred. He didn't bother to take notice of Sommers, who was intent upon the charged exchange, and turned on his heel to dash away.

"You two don't get along?" Sommers asked.

Courtland gave a small nod. "Our relationship is strained for reasons I'd rather not go into. That reminds me, how are you acquainted with each other? I noticed you at Lady Borne's coming-out ball for Bronwyn."

"That's your sister? She's a pretty little thing."

"Set your interests elsewhere, Sommers," Courtland said, the threat in his voice clear.

The odious man just smiled. "Maybe I should find myself a demure little English lady and marry into some blue blood. Make myself a spiffy lord like the rest of you nobs."

"That won't make you a lord. Titles are hereditary."

"Is that why your brother is in such a tiff?" Sommers asked. "Because you inherited the title and he didn't?"

"Something like that." That was the least of it. His brother despised him. It was a hatred that ran bone-deep, no doubt indoctrinated and nurtured by his mother over a lifetime. Still, he could not change a man's nature. At the end of it, Stinson was a weak man who wanted the easy way of things. Briefly, Courtland wondered if things might have been different had their father not died. Would Stinson have accepted him then? He clenched his jaw. That didn't matter.

"Aren't you worried that he's going to make a scene with the rest of his friends? Seems to me he was the kingpin here until you arrived and stole all his thunder."

"It won't matter because I'm not staying. He can have all the thunder he wants."

Courtland watched his brother standing across the room with a small frown. He wasn't worried about what Stinson would do—the man was all bluster and no brains—but he felt an odd twinge in his chest nonetheless. He should have felt nothing when Stinson had been the one to strip everything from him, but he felt only pity. His sometimes sweet wife might be rubbing off on him.

Though she wasn't remotely sweet at the moment. No, she was exceedingly so, to the point that his teeth ached as if he chewed on a mouthful of sugar. Earlier this morning, she'd acted the part of the demure, biddable wife, bringing him his slippers and fussing over his every need before he'd taken a step out of his bedchamber. Even Peabody had made himself scarce, a suspicious frown marring his normally impassive features. The curtsy worthy of Victoria's ballroom should have been a warning of the performance that was to come at breakfast.

Was the ducal bacon crispy enough?

Did his eminence have enough coffee?

Were the newssheets pleasing to His Grace?

She'd looked lovely, too, dressed in a stunning rose-colored muslin day gown with white stripes and dainty ribbons. If it weren't for the occasional sparks of lightning he saw in her copper eyes when she wasn't pandering to his every demand, he would have fallen for the act.

Because his darling, biddable wife was absolutely furious.

He hadn't been able to get out of the house fast enough. The brazen little chit had had the audacity to bow to him, every single tooth on display in the biggest mockery of a smile he'd ever seen. In truth, he'd wanted to laugh the minute he got into his carriage. He was tempted to relent, but his mandate was for her own safety. She was much too obstinate and impulsive for her own good. Suddenly, he frowned. She would listen, wouldn't she? She wouldn't dare disobey, not when he'd made his position clear. He thought back to her sneaking into the study and bit back a growl.

Courtland stood, nearly kicking over his chair. "Apologies. I have to go."

"Trouble in paradise?" Sommers asked, drawing him back to the present moment.

"What?"

Sommers laughed. "A man only gets that look on his face for one thing in my experience and that's a woman."

"No. You're mistaken."

Grabbing his gloves, hat, and coat, Courtland practically ran from the club, summoning his carriage and gritting his teeth all the while.

He'd told Sommers a lie.

His departure had *everything* to do with one infuriating, meddling, defiant little harpy.

"Quick, Waterstone," Ravenna hissed. "You're supposed to be the greatest spy among spies, and you're fumbling like the greenest lad of all time."

"Ashvale will strangle me if he finds out that I've involved you."

"Then hurry up!" she said. "And I involved you, not the other way round, so if anyone's getting murdered, it's probably me."

"I'm the man and I should know better." He flinched at the look in her eyes. "I meant I'm the operative, that's all, not that you're female or don't know your own mind." With a sigh, he shook his head and focused back on the keyhole. "Button it, Waterstone."

Huddled outside Sommers's rooms at Claridge's, Ravenna bit back a grin as she watched her husband's trusted friend carefully working the lock of the hotel room with the key. She was tempted to shove him aside and do it herself, but she didn't want to aggravate him, considering his reluctance to let her come along in the first place.

Earlier that morning, she'd wheedled Peabody for the information on the duke's whereabouts, and then followed Courtland herself in a nondescript hackney to see that he *did* have a luncheon meeting with Sommers. Even though she was concealed by her Mr. Hunt disguise, the American man had made bile churn in her stomach, especially when she'd nearly bumped into him. She'd feel much happier when he was behind bars where he belonged.

And when she'd caught a glimpse of Waterstone exiting the building not a moment later, she'd had a stroke of brilliance. She'd buttoned her thick cloak and tossed her top hat to a street urchin with a grin. He'd sell it for a mint. Feigning sudden illness while running into the earl further down the street had been easy, though she was quite sad she'd lost her bonnet in an unexpected wind gust.

Waterstone had frowned—it was an usually beautiful, *windless* day, but had nodded nonetheless. Predictably, he'd offered to see her safely home in a hackney, after she made a quick stop to deliver a parcel to a friend that was of the utmost import. It wasn't until they were on the corner of Brook and Davies Streets that Waterstone had caught on when Claridge's came into view. It didn't help that her illness had miraculously abated and that she wore men's garments beneath her cloak.

"What are you doing, Your Grace?" he'd demanded.

She'd grinned. "Reconnaissance. Are you with me? Sommers is with Ashvale. I nearly crashed into him in front of White's." She'd grinned at a narrow-eyed Waterstone.

"This is not a game, Duchess."

She'd tossed her head. "I can get his key. Trust me." He'd gaped at her, but she'd surged forward. "What better opportunity is there to search his rooms while he's with my husband. At least let me try before you dismiss my ideas."

"Ashvale will have my head."

"What the duke doesn't know won't hurt him." She'd waggled her eyebrows. "Tick, tock, my lord, or I go in without you."

"Fine," he'd capitulated with a sigh. "But if you are successful in retrieving the key, you do exactly as I say when I say."

Which had led them into the fancy hotel, whereupon Ravenna had tottered in and pretended to be the loud and utterly obnoxious Mrs. Sommers whose husband had gone to some gaudy men's club called White's and shuttled her back here like a sad, unwanted lump, and *oh*, weren't husbands the absolute *worst*? It'd been absurdly easy to get the mortified clerk to hand over the key, just to stop her from wailing and causing more of a scene.

Ravenna had hidden her grin. No wonder women made such excellent spies. Tears and vapors made for unbeatable subterfuge. Biting her lip to keep from crowing with victory, she'd handed the iron key to a stunned Waterstone, who wore a suitably astonished expression.

"Where on earth did you pick up an American accent?" he'd asked, once they were out of sight.

"Why, from my husband, darlin'," she'd drawled. "He's a real peach."

Ravenna hadn't been able to ask the clerk where the room was located as that would have been much too obvious, but finding out the room number had proved remarkably simple after the earl spent a few minutes charming a housemaid. When he'd returned with a triumphant smirk of his own, Ravenna had shot him an admiring look for his persuasiveness, to which he'd rolled his eyes and turned red, while muttering, "Part of the job." Finally, they'd arrived on the third floor at the requisite suite of rooms, only to have the key not turn properly.

"Maybe it's the wrong one," Ravenna said. "Maybe your maid got confused."

"The maid was not confused and she's not my maid. She knew exactly who Sommers was because he's a cur with all the female servants. This is the right room."

With one hard jostle of the key, the door opened.

The room was a mess, Sommers's belongings strewn everywhere. Now that they were inside, she had no idea what to do, but obviously Waterstone did because he instantly headed for the desk and started sifting through the papers. Wrinkling her nose, Ravenna stepped around some discarded smallclothes. *Horrid.*

"What are we looking for?" she asked, her voice loud in the silence.

"Anything. Documents. Plans. Contacts."

Ravenna peered into a trunk at the base of the bed. "Opiates?"

"What?" Waterstone hurried over to her side, eyes widening at the sight of a dozen or so small tincture bottles packed neatly into a case. Some were empty, others tightly corked.

"Who has need of this much laudanum?"

Waterstone lifted a shoulder. "An addict."

He moved back to resume his search, and Ravenna wandered the room over to a small table near the small hearth. A crumpled-up piece of parchment caught her attention and she bent to retrieve it. Unrolling it, the first thing that caught her attention was *her* name. Ravenna frowned, an oily sensation crawling over her skin.

Beside it was Stinson's name with a question mark. Then mention of a ball, underlined twice, which she realized was the date of her own official wedding ball being hosted by her mother at Embry House. She was certain that Mr. Sommers had not been invited, so did he intend to be there? And *why*? What was he planning? She pocketed the paper without showing it to Waterstone, who swore under his breath.

"What's the matter?" she asked.

"There's nothing of note here. The man's careful, I'll give him that. Or he keeps his documents with him, which is what I would do." His eyes fell on her as though seeing her for the first time. "Come, we should get you home."

Once they'd slipped out through the servants' entrance and were ensconced in a coach, Waterstone narrowed his eyes at her disheveled curls. "How did Sommers not recognize you?"

"My earlier ensemble included a hat." She grinned, sketching her infamous bow and feigning another accent. "Pleasure to meet your acquaintance, sir. Mr. Raven Hunt of Kettering, ne'er-do-well and happiest of chaps. Always up for a laugh, a chit, and a pint of ale."

Ravenna lifted a brow at his slightly bemused, openly admiring expression. "I might have underestimated you."

"Most do," she said.

In short order, they arrived back at the ducal residence. As the coach rolled to a stop, something danced up Ravenna's spine and she froze. It was the sensation she always got whenever her husband was near…that raw awareness, the elemental *connection* that existed only between them.

She blinked. No, she had to be imagining it because of nerves. The duke would be enjoying a cigar after luncheon, not that he smoked but Sommers did. Still, her instincts were firing like fireworks over Cremorne Gardens.

And for good reason.

Because the forbidding Duke of Ashvale stood waiting at the top of the stairs, and he looked beyond furious. Ravenna gulped and met Waterstone's gaze. "Stay put. I dragged you into this. No need for both of us to get into trouble."

"Your Grace—"

"Don't you underestimate me now, Waterstone. *Go*, before I tell him it was your idea." When he paled, she gave him a small grin. "A jest, you silly man."

With that, Ravenna hopped from the coach to face her fate.

She watched as it pulled away before turning to her husband who hadn't moved from his perch, staring down at her like a falcon about to pounce on its meal. She fought back a shiver and mounted the stairs with false cheer. "Good day to you, Your Grace!"

"Get inside, lest you cause me to make a scene in the middle of Mayfair," he commanded.

Ravenna peered up at him. His face could be carved from granite, though the muscle flexing in that jaw proved that he was indeed human. Eyes the color of an inky lake met hers as she walked past him and into the house.

The servants were mysteriously absent, which only added to her unease. Had he dismissed them because he intended to take her to task? The door snicked shut behind her and she jumped, his intimidating presence crowding her.

"Go into the study, please."

Her heart quailed. *Blast it!* She wasn't some cowering miss! She couldn't—*wouldn't*—let him intimidate her. Thrusting her chin up, she sauntered over toward his study as though she didn't have a care in the world, even though her soles dragged like lead, whereupon she poured herself a finger of brandy. And took it like a sailor facing the strap.

"Where were you?" the duke asked in a soft voice.

The awful mouthful of brandy gave her liquid, if foolish, courage. "Out."

"I gave specific instructions for you not to leave this house."

"You told Lady Ravenna, your dutiful wife, not to leave and she did not." Affecting indifference, she gestured down at her clothing. "Mr. Hunt did."

The silence was thunderous, pulsing between them like a living heartbeat. Ravenna moved to pour herself another drink and found herself halted by a fairly seething duke. "You've had enough, and I want your mind clear for what comes next."

What comes *next*?

Ravenna inhaled his dark, sinful scent and nearly swooned. She was a lunatic! The man wanted to throttle her with his bare hands, and she was struck with the demented urge to kiss him.

Her desires must have been transparent because her husband moved away with a hurried step. If it hadn't been for the tiny noise escaping his lips, she'd have thought him unaffected. Ravenna swallowed her grin of satisfaction. No, if anything, she and her controlling husband were afflicted by the same extreme lust.

"You disobeyed me."

"No, I did not," she tossed back.

He pinched the bridge of his nose with his thumb and fore-finger. "Ravenna, you are trying my patience. You and Hunt are one and the same. Do not try to manipulate the truth. Now, where the fuck did you go?" Those last few words were punctuated with wrath.

Ravenna's shoulders stiffened in affront. "How dare you speak to me so?"

"What?" he asked, brow arching in a mockery of hers earlier outside. "Like a man?" His smile was easy, trickery, she knew. The tension in his body gave him away. "You can't have it both ways, Mr. Hunt."

"I was bored. I needed to get out of the house."

He stared at her, those glacial eyes boring into her like a pair of ice-shards. "I will find out the truth, Ravenna, and when I do, you will regret lying to me." The duke turned on his heel and stalked toward the door. "Do not leave this house, Lady Ravenna and Mr.

Hunt both." He paused at the threshold. "Or in any other disguise your clever little mind concocts."

Unwilling to let him leave without the last word, a seething Ravenna snapped a sailor's salute. "Yes, sir, yes!"

That gaze drilled into hers, as if he didn't know whether to bend her over his knee or the desk. Breath hissed through his lips, a thousand emotions flicking through his eyes—anger, desire, impatience, frustration, passion, vexation, fury. Ravenna recognized every single one, because they were the mirror images of hers.

When he finally left, her trembling knees collapsed and she sank to the floor.

If anyone cared to know, she'd have preferred the desk.

Nineteen

THE NOTE DELIVERED TO COURTLAND HAD ONLY AN ADDRESS on it. There was no sender's name, only a time and a place with instructions to go alone. It could be a trap, or it could be a response to the numerous requests he'd put out for paid information on ships that Sommers might hire or any dockyard men willing to risk dodgy employment for significant coin. Courtland had sent for Waterstone, but perhaps it would pay to be prudent. He stood, reaching for his brace of pistols. He'd instruct Rawley to inform Embry as a precaution.

On his way out, he caught sight of Ravenna in the salon, her fingers drifting over the keys of the pianoforte. Dressed in a lavender dress that complemented her coloring, she was so breathtakingly lovely that it made him falter. Courtland's pulse caught as the sunlight from one of the paned windows turned her auburn hair to liquid fire.

Her maid, sitting quietly on a nearby chair, caught his eyes but he shook his head as he approached on silent feet. "I didn't know you played," he said.

"Well, you don't know much about me, do you?"

"Touché."

She didn't sound surprised by his quiet approach, and he wondered if it was the same for her. Whenever she was in a room, he *knew*. It was the strangest thing, as if some deep part of him, some part of his soul, recognized its own counterpart in her. Scowling, he shook the whimsical thoughts from his head as her fingers glided over the keys in a somewhat familiar melody.

"Mozart?" he asked.

"Bach, actually."

Courtland hesitated. "Ravenna."

"Yes, Your Grace?"

"This restriction is only temporary. I don't want you to get hurt, and I can't keep an eye on you every moment of the day. You're safer here, at home."

Her playing halted with an abrupt, harsh discordant note. "Will you keep me locked behind closed doors for the ball tonight, then?" Eyes the color of warm brandy lifted to his. "Or will you keep me glued to your side like some missish, helpless twit who hasn't lifted a finger in all her life? I'm not made of glass, Courtland."

"Still flesh and bone."

She scowled up at him. "Before you came along, I was managing just fine, remember? And besides, if it's Sommers you're worried about, he wasn't invited this evening."

Courtland's eyes narrowed as something flashed in her gaze that looked disturbingly like guilt before she tried to hide it. What was she up to now?

"I'm going out," he said. "Stay put. Rawley will be here."

"Wonderful," she said, her fingers crashing down into an ominous sequence that sounded too much like an incensed Beethoven. "My favorite warden. I'm even starting to prefer your cousin's company to yours."

"It won't be for much longer."

But she didn't respond, her talented fingers flying over the notes with a skill he hadn't realized she possessed. Once more, his young wife astounded him. Then again, Courtland didn't know why he should be so surprised. The woman was an enigma, full of secrets.

Outside, he met Waterstone, who was waiting atop a plain black coach, one that Courtland preferred to use whenever he was going incognito. Since the instructions had said for him to come alone, the earl was acting the double duty of coachman. Courtland gave him the address and climbed into the carriage. As they rolled away, he caught sight of Ravenna's face peering down from the front window. Thankfully, he'd left Rawley behind. The man had strict instructions not to let her out of his sight.

No doubt she'd try to escape. Possibly follow him.

Because she was a menace to herself.

Courtland let out a breath, easing the growing tension in his lungs. Hell, he couldn't understand how easily she threw herself into danger. Even as Mr. Hunt, she trod a perilous path. And it wasn't that he didn't think she could defend herself, if push came to shove. He knew she was capable. He just didn't like what knowing she could be in danger did to *him*. His very being was consumed with her, and that wasn't sound.

Courtland scrubbed his palm over his face. He needed to get this business with Sommers done so that he could return to Antigua and put this all behind him. For an instant, he felt a fleeting ache in the vicinity of his heart at the thought of leaving Ravenna behind, but he ignored it.

Waterstone's hard tap on the roof reached him, letting him know they were nearing their destination in Covent Garden. He peered out the window. It was a seedy, narrow street that allowed little light from the crowded buildings, but he could see the crooked sign over the tavern indicated on the note—*The Spotted Hog*.

Courtland checked on his brace of loaded pistols and swung his greatcoat over his shoulders. He also had a pair of knives tucked into his boot, and if all else failed, his fists would be just fine. Hopping out of the carriage, he exchanged a silent look with the earl, who patted his own brace of pistols. The man gave a slight nod. If Courtland wasn't out of the tavern in five minutes, he was to follow.

But he'd barely gotten to the entrance before there was a shout and he was rushed by half a dozen men. "Footpads!" Waterstone shouted, leaping down into the fray.

Courtland took a fist to the gut and another to the jaw. He couldn't get a hand to his pistols, so he struck out, letting his training take over. Punch, jab, hook. Weave. And repeat. After a moment, he managed to clear space enough to take account of his assailants. There were more than six, he realized. Three of them lay groaning on the ground around him, one out cold. Waterstone had thrown another into the wall, while pummeling a fifth and sixth bloody.

Two others faced him, knives in hand. Courtland reached for his own knives and wiped the back of his mouth with one hand. They rushed him as one, but he ducked and lashed out, catching one of them across the ribs. The man's howl was loud, drawing more men from the shack of a tavern.

"Fight!" one of them shouted.

Fuck. He had to end this and get out of here before it turned into a free-for-all. He jammed the hilt of the knife into the last man's chin and swung around to shout for Waterstone. The man was already running for the coach and climbing up.

"Get in!" the earl growled.

Courtland reached for his pistol and shot it into the air, the sound crashing through the filthy alleyway. Screams abounded, but he didn't wait to see whether they would recover and rush him. He ran, jumping for the rail of the coach as Waterstone drove by. They made it out by the skin of their teeth, gaining speed as the crowd faded behind them. Only when they were nearing a safer part of town, did the earl stop, jump down, and slam open the door.

"Did you get hurt?" he demanded.

Courtland shook his head, patting himself down for injury. "Nothing lethal."

"That was an ambush," a grim-faced Waterstone said. "But by who? Sommers?"

"Not likely. He needs my connections. Could have been a coincidence. It was a dodgy part of town."

But he knew it'd been no coincidence. Courtland had an inkling that it might be his brother—he'd solicited bully ruffians at Harrow—but this felt different. These men had been paid to maim or even kill. Besides Stinson and Sommers, who else was he missing? He had many other enemies across the sea, but not here in London.

He stepped from the coach with a wince. His ribs ached and he'd taken a full fist to the jaw. His lip felt as though it was swelling to twice its size. That would go over well with his mother-in-law—getting into fisticuffs the day of his wedding ball. Perhaps he could come up with some excuse. Maybe he could blame his duchess. Courtland grinned. She had a mean right hook.

"Why are you smiling?" Waterstone growled. "You were nearly drawn and quartered."

"Stop being a milksop. I was smiling because I will look a sight tonight for the ball. Lady Embry will have conniptions."

The earl stared at him. "You're worried about a dowager at a ball after you just got set upon by footpads?"

"You'll understand when you get the chance to meet my mother-in-law tonight." He sighed, touching his fat lip and flinching. "Come, let's get back so I can figure out what to do with this and get some ice or a poultice on it before my wife sees."

―――――――――――

"What in the world happened to your lip?" Ravenna demanded.

It was the first thing she noticed, descending the staircase to meet the duke before they left for her mother's residence. Well, the second thing at least. The first was how distressingly handsome her husband looked in his elegant formal wear—from his

raven-black jacket and trousers to a dark-green waistcoat and pris-
tine white shirt and cravat. If there was one thing that could be said
for him, even when she was frothingly angry, it was that he wore a
suit of clothing exceptionally well.

He looks fantastic naked, too.

Ignoring that salacious inner voice, she focused on what was an
obvious and recent injury. Ravenna narrowed her eyes on the cut
at the corner of his mouth. His lips were full, but the lower lip had
a plumpness to its curve that was out of the ordinary. The more
she looked, the more she saw the purplish hue of a bruise beneath
the brownish-bronze glow of his complexion.

"Sparring with Rawley earlier," the duke said, eyes widening in
appreciation as he took in her diaphanous lavender gown with its
silver trim and overlay of spangled star-colored tulle. "You look
ravishing."

She preened at the compliment and the melting look in his
eyes, but she kept her expression composed. No need for him to
see any weakness from her. She had to stay strong. "Don't try to
change the subject. Since when does Rawley ever get the drop on
you?"

"Since my minx of a wife became a distraction."

She frowned. "I wasn't even there…if what you say is true."

He lifted her palm and drew his lips over her gloved knuckles. "You don't have to be far from me to have dominion over my
thoughts, Duchess."

Ravenna drew in a clipped breath, filling her tight lungs. While
his comment sounded like a compliment, she knew it wasn't. A
part of him resented that she was in any way, shape, or form on
his mind. Courtland was single-minded, and he was the kind of
man who hated distractions. It was the reason behind his draco-
nian demand that she stay locked up like a naughty child. Her hurt
returned in full force. She yanked her hand away and eyed him
coldly.

"We will be late if we don't leave. Let's get this evening over with."

She did not wait to be offered his arm, but swept past him to the waiting ducal carriage. A pair of matching horses pawed the ground restlessly, and she took a beat to admire them as well as the gleaming coach with the Duke of Ashvale's coat of arms. For all her husband's faults, he had style. Ravenna rolled her eyes, refusing to give him the satisfaction of knowing she was impressed. She'd been raised the daughter of a duke and was well accustomed to pomp, circumstance, and luxury.

"Thank you, Rawley," she said to her husband's man who helped her into the carriage. "Is it true what my husband said about you being responsible for that bruise on his face?"

Rawley froze, and the momentary dilation of his pupils before he nodded told her all she needed to know. The injury wasn't Rawley's fault, which meant her husband had lied through his teeth. How had he come by it? And why did he need to hide the truth from her?

Across from her in the coach, the duke glanced at her, his dark eyes conflicted as if he had something to say but couldn't find the words, and they stared at each other in interminable silence. Something inside clawed at her heart, and for one stupid moment, she wanted to throw herself into his arms and beg him to hold her. Thankfully, her bottom remained firmly planted on the seat. She arched a quizzical eyebrow. "Is something on your mind? You seem agitated."

He opened his mouth and closed it. "I don't like this distance between us."

"You put it there, Your Grace, when you forbade me to leave the house like a misbehaving brat."

Courtland flinched at the icy reply. "Ravenna, please, try to understand. I don't want this evening to be awful for you. I'd like for us...to be friends."

"Friends," she echoed and then glared at him. "We are *not* friends, you thick lummox! We are two strangers playacting at being husband and wife. At best, we are enemies with a common goal of hoodwinking the *ton*. So right now, all I am focused on is putting on a good show so that you can marry off your sisters, claim respectability, and placate God-knows-who before you divorce me and fuck off back to wherever it is you intend. Did I get that right?"

She sucked in a breath, her eyes inexplicably smarting. She would *not* cry!

"Ravenna."

She lifted a palm. "Just don't, Ashvale. There's nothing you can say that can fix this. You don't trust me. You lie about your injuries—"

"And you haven't lied?" he shot back.

"I wouldn't have to if you trusted me at all! But the cold Courtland Chase trusts no one, does he?" The duke glowered, his handsome face tight in the flickering gas lamps of the coach. Ravenna throttled her emotion, knowing this wasn't the time or the place to quarrel, but she couldn't help herself. She wanted to hurt him the way she'd been hurt. "The great Duke of Ashvale is an island unto himself, and God save the soul of anyone who gets close to those rocky shores. It's a wonder you have any friends at all."

Tension unspooled between them, ugly and thick.

She wanted to take back her harsh words, but couldn't bring herself to do it.

"Now you see," he said gently. "The real me."

Ravenna wanted to scream that that wasn't the real him at all. It was a mask he wore to keep himself apart from the world and everyone. He held people at arm's length so that they couldn't ever hurt him, and she'd just gone and proven that with her thoughtless, angry words. Why did he have to make things so difficult?

Two absurdly stubborn people should not be in the same room, much less confined in a coach as they were.

"I wish to call a truce for tonight," she said as they pulled up in the line of carriages in front of her mother's residence. "We have a job to do. I made you a promise and I shall deliver on it." She let out a breath. "And in the interests of transparency, I have a feeling that your friend Sommers will be here tonight."

A dark gaze slammed into hers, but she was already up and stepping down from the coach into the crush that crowded the marble steps.

———

After Ravenna's bombshell, Courtland kept a close eye on the guests, but there was no sign of Sommers, not that anyone was easily visible in this crush of the beau monde. Except for one, that was. He watched as his wife danced a rousing polka with her brother, her face alight and her mouth pulled into a joyous smile. She was radiant. There was something about her that outshone every other lady in the room. And it wasn't that stunning lavender and silver dress that made her look like a shooting star, flaring across the heavens.

"She's lovely, isn't she?"

Courtland tore his gaze away and glanced down to the woman at his side who was gowned in a heavily embroidered jade dress with intricate trim. He'd been introduced to her earlier, Embry's striking duchess with the insightful stare that had cut right through him. She speared him now with a similar shrewd regard.

"Quite, Your Grace. Or should I say Princess?"

"Please, it's Sarani. I'm not big on formality as you will undoubtedly learn." She sipped on a glass of champagne. "I've heard a lot about you."

"Not all of it dreadful, I hope."

"Not in the least." Her smile was quick. "Ravenna tells me

you're a bit of an entrepreneur in the West Indies, that you invest in land and property and shipping among other things?"

Courtland canted his head. "Liners mostly, for passenger travel. Engines have always fascinated me."

"She did mention your fabulous ship, the *Glory*," Sarani said. "I hope to travel on it one day and experience it for myself."

"You are welcome aboard any time."

They watched their spouses in companionable silence. Oddly, Courtland felt completely comfortable in the duchess's presence and without the pressing need to converse that he often felt with other aristocratic ladies. Although he remained aware of her occasional curious glances at him, particularly when Ravenna let out a peal of laughter at a twirl in the dance or when her eyes caught his and he felt his entire body twitch in visceral reaction.

"You care for her, don't you?" Sarani's voice was soft, and when he turned to her, she tilted her head, erasing the denial on his lips. "It's obvious, if one knows what to look for."

"What's that?" he asked.

"The way you follow her with your eyes. Even when you're looking elsewhere, they always come back for that reassurance that she's still there, as if you need to ascertain it. It's in the way it feels like your very beings are connected via some invisible tether. When she enters a room, you brighten, and when she leaves it, the world dims."

"That sounds quite poetic." He kept his expression composed. "If rather fanciful."

Her smile was soft. "No less true." She finished her champagne and pursed her lips in thought. "I haven't known Ravenna very long, but she's loyal to a fault. And she loves with her whole heart once she's decided that someone is deserving of it."

"I assure you she does not feel that way about me."

But as Courtland looked back toward where his wife was dancing, he felt the lie deep in his bones. They meant something to each other, that was for certain. Otherwise, the thought of ending things wouldn't hurt so damned much.

Sarani's gaze tipped up to his, a smile making her eyes sparkle with merriment. "Watching the two of you realize how perfect you are for each other is going to be fun."

On that amused note, the princess-turned-duchess wandered away in a flurry of brilliant skirts. Courtland didn't have the chance to disprove the absurd claim that he and Ravenna were perfect for each other.

Except in bed.

It was the only space of concord between them. What would it feel like to be loved wholly and unreservedly by someone like Ravenna? One would never be in any doubt. She loved wholly. *Fiercely.*

The arrival of Bronwyn on the arm of Stinson thankfully claimed his attention. Lady Borne was conspicuously absent, but that was no surprise. She would make a statement any way she was able. It surprised Courtland to see Stinson, however, though his mouth was pinched disagreeably as if the ball was the last place he wanted to be. Then again, given his mother's aspirations to secure a good match for her daughter, she wouldn't want to make *too much* of a statement by not having Bronwyn attend. He suppressed a chuckle. The marchioness's ambitions were all too transparent.

He made his way over to the other side of the ballroom where Bronwyn had been unceremoniously dumped by Stinson. Courtland couldn't help noting how lovely she was. The real question, however, was whether that loveliness matched what was on the inside. His first inkling came when her face lit up as he approached.

"Brother!" An instant blush filled her cheeks as she dropped into a curtsy. "Goodness, I do apologize. I meant 'Your Grace.'"

A stunned Courtland faltered. That she would address him as an esteemed relation spoke volumes. The cynic in him warned that it could be a ruse, but the earnestness in the girl's face was too genuine to be false. Or perhaps he simply wished it to be so. He smiled warmly. "I much prefer the first. How are you this evening, Lady Bronwyn?"

"Quite well, thank you. I've only just arrived, abandoned by Stinson who claims he has business to attend to."

Courtland frowned, and immediately tried to find his brother in the crowd. The man had disappeared from view.

Bronwyn gave a small shrug. "Don't worry about me. I'm used to it, and I'm well aware that my purpose is to acquit myself to my best advantage and ensnare a suitable husband with my overflowing beauty and charm." He gave a startled grin at her couched cynicism, and her already red cheeks flamed. "Do forgive me, Your Grace, er, I mean, Brother. I'm not usually so…outspoken."

"Don't worry, I'm rather attached to the trait myself," he said and offered her his arm. Little Bronwyn was turning out to be quite refreshing, much more like him than he'd expected. "Shall we dance then? Display you in the manner fit for a duke's sister?"

"I would be delighted, but you don't have to. I'm sure Stinson will return shortly."

"I insist. It's my duty as your elder brother."

Her smile was bright. "Then I accept."

As he led Bronwyn to the ballroom floor, it didn't miss his notice how much attention they were gathering from others, especially from the unattached gentlemen in the room tracking Bronwyn with interest. *Good.* Courtland caught the glance of his wife who was now dancing with Waterstone. Approval shone in her eyes. Approval and something else. Tenderness? When she saw him looking, she tore her eyes away. Whatever it had been, it did not explain the sudden surge of tightness in his chest as if she'd reached in and grabbed hold of his heart.

"Why didn't you come back sooner?" his sister asked when he led her into the first turn.

Courtland almost stumbled. "What do you mean?"

"Why haven't you visited us before?"

He frowned and cleared his suddenly thick throat. "I didn't think I would be welcomed. In fact, I'm surprised you're dancing with me. I'd expect your mother would have warned you away from me on pain of death."

"Oh, she has," Bronwyn said. "But I want to make up my own mind. I've heard such stories of you, you see."

Courtland blinked. "Stories?"

"From Grandpapa before he died. I visited him nearly every day, and we became quite close. Mama encouraged it, thinking it would set us into his good graces, which it did, but not in the way she hoped." Warm blue eyes met his. "People thought he was addled because of the illness, but it varied by the day. Some days, he was as sharp as a tack. Others, he didn't know me. On the days he was lucid, he spoke of you a lot."

The lump in his throat widened once more for his grandfather, who had never given up on him. The notion that not everyone had reviled him was like a fist squeezing around his lungs. "What did he say?"

"How smart you were. How much you reminded him of Papa. How tenacious you were." She laughed. "*That*, he said, reminded him of himself. He told me about your accomplishments in Spain, and then in the West Indies, and most of all, he spoke of how proud he was of the man you had become. At first, I was shocked because of course Mama and Stinson had told us all you were dead, and we were very young, but still the house went into mourning. But Grandpapa said you were very much alive and it was to be our secret. I hoped to see you for myself someday, and here we are. He was right. You are everything he claimed."

He did stagger then. "He didn't know me after I left England."

"I think he knew you better than you think."

He stared at her. How was his sister only eighteen? She spoke with the wisdom of someone much older than that. His mind was spinning in confusion and shock, underscored by a bone-deep yearning for acceptance he hadn't felt since he was a boy. It unsettled him.

They finished the dance, and he escorted Bronwyn over to where the Duke of Embry stood with Ravenna watching with mirth as Waterstone attempted to convince Sarani to join him in a rousing polka.

"Gents, ladies, may I present my sister, Lady Bronwyn. It's her first season."

"Embry," Ravenna said to her brother brightly. "You must ask the lady to dance. I'm sure Sarani wouldn't mind, if she's to dance with the earl."

"Certainly," the duke said with a gallant bow. "My lady?"

As they joined the other dancers, the attention of two dukes in Lady Bronwyn's favor would not go unnoticed, Courtland knew. Now that that was done, he had to get some air. He let out a shallow breath and tugged on his shrinking cravat.

His sister's revelations battered him. His grandfather—the late Duke of Ashvale—had been *proud*. For the first time since boyhood, Courtland's eyes stung.

"Your Grace? Courtland? Are you well?"

His gaze found Ravenna's concerned one. "I need—" His voice trailed off in a strangled gasp.

"Come with me." A slender hand grasped his, and all he could do was follow.

Twenty

ONCE THEY WERE OUT ON THE SMALL UPPER BALCONY TUCKED
away above the main terrace, Ravenna thrust a tumbler of whisky
that she'd grabbed on the way out of the ballroom into her husband's trembling palms. She had no idea what had shaken him so
badly. Had it been the dance with his sister? What on earth had
she said? From her own covert glances, after studiously ignoring
the warm twinge in her heart, their dance hadn't seemed contentious, and Courtland had introduced his sister to Embry, which he
wouldn't have done if Lady Bronwyn had been horrid.

Something wasn't adding up.

Ravenna watched as he took a bracing gulp of the whisky, leaning heavily onto his elbows atop the stone balustrade. The crisp
night air was cool, but not uncomfortable. She missed the balmy
breezes and the fragrant air of Antigua, though not the sweltering
ballrooms. Every place had its appeal, she supposed. Even London
with its tainted Thames and glittering charm.

Moving over to stand beside the duke, she stared down at the
guests milling out onto the terrace, smiling as one of two shadows
disappearing into the arbor caught her eyes.

"This was my secret place," she said softly. "I used to come up
here as a child to watch the parties. I always wondered why some
of those people would leave the beautiful ballroom to go into the
creepy old gardens."

"Did you find out?"

The rasp was low, barely audible, but Ravenna felt encouraged.
"Hardly." She huffed a self-deprecating laugh. "I was much too

busy thwarting suitors to be seduced by a midnight stroll. And besides, that would have been a sure way to ruination." She swallowed, her memory tainted by the thought of another here in this very house. "Darkness, whether in arbors or in deserted rooms, tends to bring out the predators."

"You speak of Dalwood."

The name sent a shudder through her. "Yes."

"Do you want to talk about it?"

Did she? Ravenna had never told anyone, not counting the sardonic confession in Courtland's office an eternity ago. Not even Rhystan. Perhaps it would help with the coiling nausea in her stomach. She reached for her husband's half-full tumbler and took a sip. The whisky burned a blistering path down her throat. Blowing out a breath, she stared into the fathomless depths of the night sky.

"It happened here, the night before I ran away on Rhystan's ship. Dalwood wanted my hand in marriage. I didn't want to give it. He approached my brother and was refused. But he wouldn't take no for an answer." Her voice softened. "No...it's such a small word, so easy to ignore, isn't it?"

"It should not be. It means no."

"I'm glad you think so, but for a man like Dalwood, it was not. He saw it as a challenge. I suppose I made it so by being so adamant in my refusal to marry."

Ravenna was shocked by the savage curse that flew from Courtland's lips. "Don't you ever think it was your fault, do you hear me? You did not do anything to make him so. Nothing you could have done would ever excuse his actions. *Nothing*. That's on him, not you."

Something loosened inside of her at his words—guilt, perhaps, that she had somehow incited Dalwood to behave as he had. On the ship to the West Indies, she had mulled it over in her head, wondering if she was to blame. Her husband's stalwart defense washed over her.

"One evening, he followed me from the retiring room and ushered me into the music room, saying he wished to apologize. I was worried, but not really afraid. I mean, what could he do to me in the midst of a ball at my own home with my brother, the powerful Duke of Embry, in attendance?" A harsh laugh tore from her throat. "I was so naive. What could a man do? Anything he wants, apparently." Ravenna took another sip of whisky. "He said his piece. I accepted the apology and made to move past him. I sensed the threat a heartbeat before his hand went over my mouth. To stop me from screaming for help, I suppose."

"That craven bastard."

She bit her lip hard. "When you're powerful and privileged, you think nothing can touch you, but depravity doesn't discriminate. I can still feel his hot breath in my ear and his sickening arousal against my back. 'You think you're such a prize,' he whispered. 'How dare you refuse me? A marquess?'"

Panting, Ravenna cut off, reliving the horrible moment. The tension in Courtland's body rivaled hers, his fingers flexing on the stone as though they were wrapped around Dalwood's neck.

"He asked whether I would accept him then. It was that or suffocate. I could only nod. *Yes* was my path to survival. Then he unclipped my earbobs and necklace, and said they were to be a token of my esteem. You see, he could ruin me, compromise me, but I'd already refused him publicly. The jewelry was his insurance. He told me I had to announce my change of heart and our engagement later that evening, or he would expose what happened in the music room with my jewels as proof. I agreed, only to save my own skin, and then I ran."

She swallowed. "I went upstairs, emptied my jewel case, changed, packed, and headed for the docks. Dalwood must have suspected I would run because he almost caught me, but I stabbed him in the ballocks with a hairpin. The rest you know."

"I'm going to fucking dismember him," Courtland swore and

then gawked at her as her words registered. "You *stabbed* him? I thought you kneed him."

"Credit me with some compassion, Duke. I didn't want poor Lady Holding to have a fit of the vapors." She sighed. "He put his hands on me. He intended to force me. It was the least of what he deserved. Who knew that a lady's hairpin held between one's fingers in a fist is more lethal than brass knuckles?"

"Remind me never to cross you." He glanced at her short-coiffed hair. "And maybe to give thanks that you've no need of hairpins."

Ravenna laughed softly. They stood in silence, leaning on the cool stone, the faint notes of the music in the ballroom reaching them. She peered up at him through her lashes. Some color had returned to his sallow cheeks, but his jaw still remained tight with strain.

"Your turn," she said. "What happened down there?"

At first, she thought he wasn't going to speak after she'd bared her deepest, darkest secret, but then he cleared his throat. "I did not expect to esteem my sister…or be esteemed in return. She said my stepmother did attempt to poison her against me, but she wanted to make up her own mind." He paused. "She was close to my grandfather before he passed. She said he…spoke of me. With affection."

"And that scared you?"

Courtland's anguished gaze slammed into hers, so many emotions there that she could barely sort through them. The most potent of them was regret. Raw, aching regret. "I didn't know. He sent letters that I never read. And until Bingham arrived with the news of his death, I'd kept him out of my affairs."

"Why didn't you read them?" she asked quietly. "The letters?"

He scraped a hand through his hair. "I suppose I was afraid. A part of me assumed he felt as Lady Borne and my brother had— like I was the bad son to be ignored and shunned. I couldn't bear knowing that he might be ashamed of me. I had Rawley destroy them."

"But why would you think that?"

"It was something Stinson said, that I would never belong." He sighed. "I should have known that it was a lie. And now, because of my own stubbornness, I lost the chance of knowing someone in my family who gave a shit about me."

"You still have a chance," Ravenna said. "With Bronwyn and Florence. You have people who…care about you, Courtland. You have to let them in sometime." She let out an uncertain breath. "I know you're worried about rejection. We all have insecurities. You don't want to need anyone, and I refuse to conform. We're sharp square-cut pegs trying to fit into smooth, round holes. That doesn't make us unworthy, it just makes us different."

"How did you get so wise?"

"I am often accused of being a woman with radical views."

"That you are," he said softly. "It's one of the things that drew me to you."

Something snapped tight inside of her then…a feeling of acceptance, of *rightness*. Courtland saw her for who she was. For all his faults, he had never tried to change her.

The duke pushed off the balustrade. "We should be getting back or we will be missed. As much as I esteem my mother-in-law, I do not wish to be on the receiving end of her wrath." Courtland took her palm in his, and though his usual shutters had now descended into place, a rueful smile curled the corner of his lip. They made their way back to the ballroom, where he paused at the entrance. "Ravenna, I know things haven't been great between us. I just…I want to thank you for what you did."

Her chest tightened, but she squeezed the fingers still twined in hers. She could not have ignored the pain on his face any more than she could have ignored a bleeding wound on her own body. She was still reeling that he'd trusted her with what had happened with Bronwyn. A man as fortified as he was didn't share or trust easily. "You're welcome."

Courtland led her inside, whereupon they were instantly met by her mother. "Where have you two been?" she scolded. "Good gracious, I've had the footmen searching for you everywhere. It's time for your dance."

Ravenna frowned. "Dance?"

"Your *wedding* waltz." Her mother shot her a caustic look. "I didn't plan all this to celebrate someone else's nuptials, wretched child. The least you could do is humor me."

"Of course, Mama."

She bit her lip at Courtland's muffled grunt of amusement, though she felt a chuckle bubbling up in her own chest. They took their places, and then the music started. The minute Courtland started to move, Ravenna felt everything inside of her relax and settle. Everything about this waltz felt perfect. *He* felt perfect. Other couples joined them, but Ravenna barely noticed. All she could see was him.

Two square-cut pegs. And yet they fit perfectly together.

She smiled. Even though he could be an imperious toad at times, it wasn't because he was overbearing. It was because he was protective. He'd tried to keep her at a distance, but she'd gotten close anyway, and that scared the daylights out of him. His little confession about his grandfather had opened her eyes. Despite his aloofness, Courtland wanted to belong. Everyone wanted to feel like they had a place somewhere.

Cast out at so young an age, he'd carved out a space elsewhere that was his alone, but knowing that his grandfather had held him in esteem—*had loved him*—was gutting. He'd never admit it—at least not in so many words—but, like her, he was desperate for acceptance. Perhaps that was why they were so alike…both searching for their places in the world.

"Why are you looking at me like that?" her duke asked.

She flushed. "Like what?"

"Like I'm a lost puppy you intend rescue."

"You're absurd."

Courtland spun her into a turn and brought her close. "I don't need saving, Ravenna."

Despite the fond smile on his lips, his eyes were as impenetrable as cold flint. If she didn't know better, she would have heeded the clear warning in their stony depths, but she wasn't much good at doing what was expected or what one should do. "But maybe *I* do."

"You've never struck me as a girl who needed any man to save her," he said.

"I'm not, but I've decided that 'saving' is a flexible word."

His lips twitched. "It is?"

"Yes," she said. "It's whatever one needs it to be—liberating, redeeming, extricating, protecting, defending."

"Extricating?"

Ravenna laughed. "From the webs of your own folly."

"Are you insulting my considerable and cosmic intelligence, Duchess?" he asked in mock affront, the shine of those midnight eyes doing unconscionable things to her insides. A bubble of laughter built in her chest. She loved him like this—uncaring of rules and expectations. Just *him*. The sightings of the boy she'd known were rare, but she treasured them ferociously.

"*Cosmic?* Your ego is enormous."

He arched a brow, yanking her scandalously close. Her brain nearly melted as his hardness grazed her belly. She gasped and he grinned. It was wicked and delightful, and she loved it. "See for yourself."

Ravenna stopped and threw her arms around him, ignoring the gasps that went up to the rafters. She'd never been one for convention and she wasn't about to start now. Her mother would be appalled, but she would get over it. They swayed together in the middle of all the dancers, not even remotely counting the steps for the waltz, but letting the music flow through them all the same.

"You are dreadful," she whispered. "We're in public, you awful man!"

"You like it."

He was right. She did. She loved it. Loved him.

Oh my God.

Her entire body stiffened in horror. Of all the things she could have gone and done, this was probably—*categorically*—the stupidest. Because deep down, despite their occasional camaraderie and their deepening rapport, it was clear that Courtland would never be able to love her back. He was too scarred. Too fractured.

She couldn't tell him. He could never know.

They'd always been friends though. Maybe friendship could be enough.

———

Courtland's mind wandered for the dozenth time since he'd propped up a pillar in an unobtrusive corner of the ballroom. He'd been ready to leave two hours ago, but knew he could not. He watched his wife dancing with Stinson of all people, and though his fists clenched at his sides at the sight, he forced himself to be calm. Stinson was family. As long as he did not overstep, Courtland would tolerate it. This *once*.

His thoughts weren't on his brother though. They were on his wife.

During the last part of their dance when she'd scandalized all in attendance by doing the unthinkable and embracing him, he'd felt the change in her like the first scent of a storm wind on the horizon. That glorious smile had remained fixed in place, but something in her eyes had shifted. She'd seemed…unsure and careful, as though she'd run headlong into a rose garden and was suddenly reminded of the thorns.

Usually, she was easy to read, but now, she had not been. It unsettled him. He tapped the side of his tumbler with a thoughtful frown.

"Looks like Lord Ethelrod is the new contender," Waterstone said.

Courtland frowned at his friend. "What?"

"Ethelrod with your sister," he said, jerking his chin to where Bronwyn was being escorted off the ballroom floor on the arm of a well-dressed young gentleman. "She's had an unending stream of fops lining up. I'll say that part one of your plan to see her wed is well and truly accomplished."

Courtland didn't know why that knowledge didn't bring him the satisfaction he'd hoped. His sister had been launched as beautifully as a ship taking her maiden voyage. He should be happy. The suitors would be lining up at Ashvale House, requesting permission to court her. Then why did he feel slightly panicked as though his lungs had seized and he couldn't draw in a single breath?

Waterstone leaned in, his voice low. "Sommers is here."

Courtland froze. "Where?"

"Leading your duchess into a dance."

He lurched forward instinctively, only to be held in place by Waterstone's firm grip. Everything inside of him froze as he watched the man he despised more than anything put his hands on the woman he...

Grunting, Courtland drew a ragged breath and yanked his shoulder. "Let me the fuck go."

"Don't make a scene. We're too close to endanger the operation now."

Courtland swore savagely. "I don't give a shit. That's my wife."

"It's one dance."

It was one dance, but the thought of Sommers touching her made him see red. He gritted his teeth, his rage simmering beneath his skin. Why would Ravenna agree to such a thing? She loathed the man. But the answer came to him as quickly as he'd asked the question. His wife's face was tight, indicating her discomfort, but her smile was all single-minded politesse. *Purposeful.* Damn her infuriating, stubborn ways!

"What is she doing?" he ground out.

"What you told her not to, I imagine," Waterstone said, relaxing his grip as though he was no longer worried about Courtland dashing off to play the hero. "Your duchess is…tenacious at the best of times."

"Reckless," he hissed. "Sommers is not someone to be toyed with."

"Nor is she," Waterstone said. "She's bloody dauntless. I swear, if you hadn't married her, I would have fallen head over heels in love with her myself. In fact, I might well be."

"Just do your job. Watch her."

"What are you going to do?"

But Courtland was already slipping around the periphery, keeping to the shadows of the ballroom like a shadow himself. He didn't stop until he was a stone's throw away from the dancing couple. His rage bloomed anew at the sight of the blackguard's grasping hand on his wife's waist. One day, when this was all over, he'd break those fingers that dared to touch what wasn't his to touch. But not now.

Ravenna's laughter rang out, and Courtland strained to listen to their conversation.

"You should visit my estate in South Carolina."

"Should I?" Ravenna asked. For a moment, it felt like her eyes swept over where he stood hidden in the shadows of a statue and a fern. "I find myself…bored of late. Perhaps a change in…situation might help. Are you planning to head back soon, then?"

Courtland's fists flexed as his wife gave the man a coy smile and Sommers licked his fleshy lips. Courtland's blood boiled. What the hell was she doing? The American's face twisted into a faint scowl, and Courtland's foolhardy little wife was quick to pounce on it.

"Is something amiss, Mr. Sommers?"

"A minor inconvenience. Nothing to worry that pretty little head about."

"Perhaps I can help," she said.

He gave her a patronizing smile. "Not unless you own a ship."

Courtland froze in shock. Could it truly be that easy? He felt his wife's satisfaction from where he hid, rolling through her like a cat discovering the biggest bowl of cream known to man.

"But I do, Mr. Sommers. After all, what is my husband's is mine to command."

Sommers stared at her, eyes narrowed, but then he smiled as the last strains of the dance ended. He lifted her hand up to press a kiss to the back of it. Ravenna lowered her gaze, quick to hide the flash of revulsion, but Courtland still saw it.

"Perhaps I will take you up on that offer. Thank you for the dance."

Once Sommers was out of sight, Courtland lost no time in dragging his rebellious wife off into a deserted room down the hall. He slammed the door shut and opened his mouth to give her the blistering she deserved when she rose up on tiptoes, crashing her lips to his. Her sweet tongue invaded his mouth as she clutched at him in frantic urgency. Ravenna arched her spine, gluing herself to him as much as their cumbersome clothing would allow. She demanded his participation and he gave it, matching her ferocity as his mouth claimed hers, tongues dueling for dominance and then gentling to something less like war.

"I need you, Courtland," she rasped, breathless and breaking away to fumble at the fly of his trousers. "Erase the memory of his hands on me with yours."

Panting, he stared down at her, reason returning with fury fresh on its heels. "Why would you do that? Engage him?"

"He needs a ship. I offered him one."

Courtland blinked. "I think he's expecting a lot more to come with that offer."

"I don't want to talk about Sommers." He groaned as her hand found him, hot and hard and pulsating. "In fact, I don't wish to talk at all." She shoved him back onto a nearby settee, the backs of his legs hitting the frame. With a yank of his buttons, his trousers slid over his hips, baring his obscenely jutting length to his wife's hot gaze. A bead of arousal gathered over his aching tip. To his utter shock, his wife bent, gathered it with a heated swipe of her tongue over the head, and then shoved him backward.

She moaned, as if savoring the taste of him. "More of that later, I promise."

His cock jerked at the hunger in her eyes.

"Someone could come in," he rasped, falling back onto the cushions. He hadn't locked the door. Anyone could discover them. It wasn't in him to care about scandal, but for some reason, he did.

"They could."

But then he forgot all protest as his wife lifted those shimmering lavender skirts and climbed onto the sofa to straddle him. Her hands disappeared under those yards of fabric, and the sound of ripping drawers filled the room. It was the only warning he had before she sank down onto his cock. Courtland's eyes nearly rolled back in his head at the silken sensation of her blanketing him, *owning* him.

"Fuck," he groaned. "You feel so good."

He stared into Ravenna's molten copper eyes, her pupils blown with lust and need and something else that she tried valiantly to hide. Her lashes dropped as she increased her pace, her movements jerky and frantic. Courtland felt the tension building in the base of his spine as his duchess chased her pleasure and teased him with his own. A wild sob fell from her lips, her pelvis grinding into his as she used him ruthlessly. She was close to breaking, and so was he. With a cry, she convulsed around him, the clenching of her sex fueling his own release.

Courtland stroked a lock of hair from her face as their breathing slowed and calmed. There was something decidedly erotic about the fact that they were both still fully clothed, and yet connected so intimately beneath her skirts. He felt himself softening inside of her, but he did not move, not wanting to relinquish the soft clasp of her body.

Ravenna worried her bruised lip. "You must think me such a wanton. I don't know what came over me."

"An orgasm?"

Her face flamed. "You're quite good at delivering those."

"I'm not sure I had much to do with that last one," he said, teasing her and loving the flush that spread over her glowing skin.

"Part of you did," she said gesturing down to where they were still intimately joined.

Courtland nodded. "A very happy part."

But as the haze of pleasure faded, neither of them could ignore what had brought them there in the first place. Ravenna stood, accepting the handkerchief he offered her with a blush, as he tucked himself away and put his own clothing to rights. When the last of her skirts fell into place, she gripped the square of damp cloth in her hand.

"That's mine," he said, reaching for it.

She frowned. "But it's soiled."

"Still mine." There was no way he was going to leave such an intimate thing lying around for anyone to find. He pocketed it and glowered at her as she made to leave the room without any explanation or apology. "Do you honestly have nothing to say for yourself about Sommers?"

His brazen wife opened the door and shot him a saucy wink.

"Yes, Your Grace. You're welcome."

Twenty-One

RAVENNA FROWNED. THE SERVANTS WERE UNNATURALLY quiet at breakfast and no one would meet her stare, not even her usually talkative lady's maid. Courtland was ensconced in his study with Rawley, her brother, and Waterstone, no doubt planning for the takedown she'd arranged. As expected, Sommers had written her the day after the ball a week ago, requesting use of her husband's liner. He must have been desperate, but it was an opportunity that everyone was grateful for.

When another silent footman dashed out of the breakfast room after clearing her plate, she scowled and stalked out into the hallway where the butler stood. "Morgan, what on earth is going on?" The distress on his face made her nerves tighten with worry. "Just tell me."

"It's the newssheets, Your Grace," he said.

"What about them?"

Silently, he handed her the neatly pressed pages. Opening them, Ravenna's eyes chased over the front page in absolute horror, her chest clenching with every single damning word. It was one of the gossip rags, but still, the scandal would be interminable.

THE DUKE OF ASHVALE IS A SHAM!
How a Lowborn Bastard Lied and
Manipulated His Way into the Ton.
A True and Unbiased Account.

Her heart ached at the vile and vulgar words. This had to be Stinson's doing. Unbiased, her foot! No wonder he'd seemed so smug during the ball when they'd danced, saying that the truth would come out sooner or later. Ravenna hadn't paid much mind to his ramblings.

"The dukedom was never yours, Stinson," she'd told him gently, hoping he'd see reason.

"Because he stole it," he'd snarled.

"He's your brother."

He'd shaken his head. "That lowborn bastard is no brother of mine. You'll learn the truth soon."

There'd been no convincing him then. She'd only accepted the dance out of a misguided hope to salvage what was left of their friendship. It was clear that that would never happen when he was still so consumed with jealousy...as was made obvious by the callous, erroneous evidence in her hand. It didn't matter if any of it was true; this was everything Courtland had feared. His origins would be exposed and he would be vilified.

She glanced at Morgan. "Is the duke still in the study?"

"Yes, Your Grace."

Folding the vile papers beneath her arm, she strode to the study and knocked. Without waiting for a reply, she entered. None of the men seemed surprised to see her, which informed her that they must already know. Courtland's face was expressionless.

"You've read them, I gather," he said eventually.

"They're lies."

Her brother cleared his throat. "I've dispatched my lawyers, but the damage is already done. Lady Borne is swearing on her husband's and the late duke's lives that the claims are true. She is stating that Bingham was paid handsomely by your husband to declare Ashvale the legitimate heir, when he is, in fact, illegitimate, lowborn, and mix-blooded to boot."

"But that's preposterous," she burst out. "What does the last have to do with anything?"

Her brother's mouth twisted. "You, of all people, know the narrow-mindedness of the *ton*. Sarani still faces their bigotry at every turn. They will champion a duke from their own ranks and class before exonerating one who is not."

"But he's the true duke!" she said.

"They won't care," Courtland said. "I will have already been tried, convicted, and sentenced, even though my parents' marriage was recorded in the local parish register. My grandmother took me to see it, and my father had to have made some record here. Unless there was some error in the filing."

"What about Bingham?" she asked. "He's the one who came with the documents of Courtland's succession. He must have proof of the marriage."

Waterstone looked grim, his perpetually amused smile missing from his somber features. "Bingham is in the hospital, fighting for his life. Thieves broke into his residence and ransacked the place, stealing a lifetime's worth of files before thrashing him to within an inch of his life."

"Who would do such a thing?" she murmured.

"Who, indeed?" Waterstone said. "But I'll find out, never you mind."

But Ravenna already had a sneaking suspicion. It had to be Stinson. No one else had anything to gain by discrediting the new Duke of Ashvale, and he'd all but admitted it. But Mr. Bingham? To set ruffians upon an innocent man? That seemed beyond the pale.

"What can I do?" she asked. "I want to help."

Her brother turned. "You can be the Duchess of Ashvale. Hold your head up high."

"She should separate herself from me," Courtland replied at the same time. "That was the plan anyway."

"That was *your* plan," she snapped. "Never mine."

Rhystan's eyes narrowed. "Plan?"

She exhaled, her hands fisting at her sides at the expression on Courtland's face. She could barely look away to answer her brother's question. Ravenna's heart felt as though it was tumbling from a great height, off a cliff to jagged rocks below. Those sharp edges loomed, taunting her with the end. *The end of them.*

Swallowing past the knot in her throat, Ravenna firmed her jaw and walked past her gaping brother to the desk where she met her husband's shadowed eyes. "Let me make this very clear. I. Do. Not. Want. A Divorce."

"Tying yourself to me was a mistake."

"Marrying you was the best thing I've ever done!" She felt the tears breach her eyelids, but let them fall. For once, she would not hide her vulnerability. "Go on. Ask me why."

His face was impassive. "Why?"

"Because..." Her voice trailed off, breath, strength, and hope rushing from her in a desperate attempt to save her poor heart from impending doom. "I love you."

The confession was strangled, whispered. *Raw.*

Light slivered in his beautiful, midnight eyes before it was suffocated by the sheer force of his will. "I warned you not to hope for more with me."

The night of pleasure they'd shared in the conservatory came back to mind. She had started falling for him long before that. A small, rueful smile touched her lips as she recalled the falsehood for what it had been. "Well, I did."

"Don't let this misfortune"—he gestured to himself—"ruin you."

She leaned over the desk, uncaring of the other men in the room. "You are neither misfortune nor ruin, Courtland Chase. You're the star...the light that brightens everything it touches. It's time you saw that."

His eyes widened, but Ravenna knew he wouldn't change his mind. Not just yet. She would have to show him. Turning on her heel, she stalked from the study, nodding to her brother, Waterstone, and Rawley, whose faces seemed suitably discomfited. It was good to see she wasn't losing her touch when it came to causing mayhem. As if a woman couldn't announce that she loved a man in her own home. It was laughable, really.

She had a plan. Well, the glimmerings of one. Ideas spun through her brain. If Stinson was the one responsible, there was a chance he'd have the documents from the thieves—the proof they needed. Grabbing a shawl and a bonnet, she tucked the foul gossip rag under her arm, left the house, and went across the street.

After knocking, she was greeted by a butler who peered down the length of his nose at her, surprise on his face at a visitor at such an early hour. Drat, this was London. She'd always been an early riser, even after late nights of dancing, but most of the *ton* stayed in bed until the afternoon.

"May I help you, miss?"

From the look on his face, Ravenna wished she'd worn something fancier than the plain morning gown she'd donned or remembered to bring her calling cards. But then she shook her head. She was a goddamned duchess!

She squared her shoulders. "Her Grace, the Duchess of Ashvale, to see Lady Bronwyn."

"Yes, Your Grace." He bowed. "I shall see if Lady Bronwyn is at home to callers."

His tone, despite the formal address, made it sound like it was an absurd request. Ravenna wanted to scowl. Rising before noon wasn't a crime. She only hoped that Bronwyn wasn't still abed.

Not long later, a smiling Bronwyn came down the hallway. Thankfully, it looked like she hadn't been dragged out of bed. "Your Grace, how lovely it is to see you. Humbold, send for tea in the morning room."

"Lady Bronwyn," she said. "I apologize for the early hour."

"Pish, posh, I've been up for hours," Bronwyn replied. "Though

Mama and Florence are both still abed. Stinson has not returned, though he hasn't been here for the last few nights." She lowered her voice as she beckoned for Ravenna to follow. "I suspect he spent the evening at his club or with his mistress."

Despite her shock at the girl's nonchalant statement, Ravenna did not reply. Once they were ensconced in the room, and the tea was served and poured, she closed the door. Bronwyn's eyes went wide, but she did not say anything. "I know you have no reason to trust me, but I need your help."

A pair of shrewd blue eyes assessed her over her teacup. "I'm afraid you'll have to give me more than that."

Gracious, it was like dealing with a mini-Courtland. She was his mirror in everything but coloring. Even the attentive expression on her face reminded Ravenna of Courtland. She hid her smile, but something like warmth filled her heart.

"My husband, your brother, confided that you thought... kindly of him."

She nodded. "I do."

"You might be the only one in your family who does."

Bronwyn sighed. "No need to couch your words. I'm well aware of my mother's and brother's opinions. Florence vacillates."

"He's in trouble." With that, Ravenna handed over the news-sheets. She watched as the girl scanned the front page, blue eyes widening with every breath.

"Goodness, this is dreadful. Courtland is duke; there's no contestation."

"Stinson doesn't feel that way."

Bronwyn folded the offending papers and, with a decisiveness that made Ravenna like her more, thrust them into the grate. "What is it you need my help for? My brother has no care for me, and I have little sway with him. If he's behind this, you know what he's capable of."

"Can I trust you?"

"If you're here, then you must already do so."

Ravenna drew a breath. It was a windfall that Stinson was not at home, one she couldn't afford to miss. She'd planned to speak to Bronwyn to find out Stinson's usual routine, *then* return with a plan to snoop. "Very well, I need to search his rooms."

The younger woman bit her lip, none of her thoughts visible on her face, but after an interminable moment, gave a firm nod. "If you think that will help."

Rising, she went to the door and crooked a finger to Ravenna. Together, they dashed up the stairs, stopping on the landing where Bronwyn put a finger to her lips. They tiptoed past several closed doors until Bronwyn stopped at one near the end. It opened with a creak that made Ravenna wince, but there were no other noises, from the door or elsewhere in the residence.

Stinson's bedchamber was dark and the bed was empty, thank goodness. It would have been a nightmare, and a shock, to discover that he had returned at some point. Ravenna crossed the room with swift steps, pulling back the drapes to let in some light. There was nothing on the table beside the bed, so she made her way over to a settee and a low table in front of a cold hearth. Nothing.

Her stomach sank.

She wasn't even sure what she was looking for.

Bronwyn must have wondered the same because she tapped her shoulder. "What is it you hope to find?" she whispered. In a few short words, Ravenna explained what had happened with the late duke's solicitor, letting the girl come to her own smart conclusions. "You think he stole the documents?"

"I don't know. I suppose I was hoping to find proof that Courtland was the true heir." She gnashed her teeth in frustration. "This was an absurd scheme. I'm sorry to have involved you."

Bronwyn frowned, eyes glinting in the gloom. "I think I can help, but I need time."

"How?"

"You're going to have to trust me a tiny bit more, Your Grace."

Courtland stared at the missive that Rawley handed him. The news from his cousins could not have come at a worse time. Three of the estates given over to the locals to farm had caught on fire, and while his men had done their best to contain the fires, they had caused significant property damage. Courtland wasn't too concerned with the loss of money—he'd make sure the families were compensated—but more about those who had been hurt. One fire might have been chance, but three at the same time suggested a plot.

"Arson?" he asked his man of business.

"I suspect so, Your Grace."

"I should go back and assess the damage myself," he said. "See to it that the workers and their families are cared for. Ready the *Glory* for travel now."

"And Sommers?"

Courtland frowned. "He will have to wait until I return. A delay won't hurt him. Alert Embry and Waterstone to the change in plans. Alternatively, we can arrange for another ship. But right now, the lives of those who depend on me matter more."

"What about the duchess?"

He sighed, the thought of her a hot lance to his chest. Since Embry and Waterstone had left, he'd been hard-pressed to get her urgent confession out of his head and the blatant defiance in her teary eyes. She *loved* him. "She should stay here in case there's danger. Inform her as well." He paused. "After I leave."

"Is that wise?" Rawley asked.

Courtland smiled wryly. "Probably not, but she's prone to disguise and stowing away when the situation requires it. I'd rather she not have the chance. You'll stay behind and keep an eye on her here."

"Very well, Your Grace."

After Rawley left to take care of everything, Courtland pressed his hands to his desk. Ravenna would not be happy, he knew. Nor would Embry and Waterstone. But he had a duty to those people who had gotten hurt because someone wanted to attack him. Showing up was the least of what he had to do.

He had a full wardrobe on the *Glory*, so it was only a matter of collecting some documents before leaving. Morgan had informed him that the duchess had gone out for a walk, which was a relief in itself. Facing her meant facing his own feelings, and he wasn't ready to do either. Thanks to Rawley's efficiency with the arrangements, he was quickly on the *Glory* and ready to depart in less than a handful of hours.

"How bad was the damage, Rawley?" Courtland asked his old friend, who had joined him on deck where he was waiting while the crew prepared the liner to leave the Docklands. He ignored the feeling resting like a boulder in the pit of his stomach. Something didn't feel right. Perhaps it was leaving Ravenna behind. At least Rawley would be staying with her.

"Extensive."

"Any deaths?" he asked.

"No, Your Grace. Minor injuries from smoke inhalation and burns."

He blew out a breath. "Thank God. They have care?"

"Yes, as you instructed." Rawley handed him a packet. "Here are all the names and the arrangements made as discussed."

"Good. Excellent work. Thank you." He cleared his tight throat. "Cousin, please take care of her. Tell her I said I'm sorry."

His man nodded. "Of course, you have my word."

Suddenly, a commotion on the docks grabbed their attention as a troop of mounted police surged onto the wharf. Courtland frowned, watching as they headed right for him and strode down to the gangway. One of the men dismounted and walked toward him.

"Are you Mr. Chase?"

Courtland's frown deepened. "The Duke of Ashvale."

"We received word that there are stolen goods aboard this ship. We have orders to search it. Permission to board?"

Courtland frowned. Stolen goods? That was preposterous.

Rawley stepped forward. "Cousin, do not allow this. This doesn't feel right."

"I have nothing to hide." He gestured to the policemen. "Go ahead."

Despite's his cousin's warning, he watched as the men marched onboard and proceeded to search every nook and cranny. Courtland wasn't upset, but he was irritated over the delay in his departure. He needed to get to Antigua—there were people who needed him there. Even with a dozen men, searching a ship of this size would take time. Not that they would find anything.

"Arrest this man," the main policeman declared.

Rawley moved to block the nearest man's approach, but Courtland shook his head, stalling him with a palm. He didn't need any violence or for Rawley to be locked in the stocks. "I am a peer of the realm, and you will explain yourself, sir."

The man closest to him spat. "You're a thief. We found the crates as described in the cargo hold, full of stolen goods, tea, and lace, and God knows what else, out in full view for anyone to find."

Courtland felt the blood drain from his body. "None of any of that belongs to me and I can prove it. Who claimed those goods were stolen and on my ship?"

A man from the wharf cleared his throat. Rage filled him as Sommers strolled into view. "I did. These good English people deserve to know what kind of cur they let into their midst, wouldn't you say, *Duke*?"

"You rotten, lying bastard."

"No, Chase, last I heard, that was you. At least, that's what was printed in the scandal sheets. Poor sniveling Stinson, all he needed was a little encouragement to tell his side. It's too bad you won't get to tell yours." He grinned. "Who will comfort your little wife now?"

Fury burst through Courtland's body in a blaze, and it was all he could do to hold himself back from shoving past the wall of policemen and taking the lying blackguard to the ground.

"Come quietly, Your Grace," the head policeman said.

But Courtland had no intention of going quietly, not while Sommers stood there with that smug smile on his face. Had he *planned* all of this?

"Out of the way!" Momentary relief sluiced through him at the sight of Waterstone, shoving through the now thick crowd. He was followed by the Duke of Embry. "I'm acting on orders from Her Majesty, and this man is under my authority. You will step back."

"This man is a criminal."

Waterstone glared. "*If* that is true, he will be in my custody. Now move before I make you move!"

As the policemen dispersed, Courtland tracked the crowd for Sommers, but the slimy snake had also disappeared. When the earl gave him a slightly sardonic look at his current predicament, he ignored it. "Sommers. He did this. Planted goods he claimed were stolen on my ship. He was just here."

"I gathered," Waterstone said. "Embry's on it."

"What happens now?"

The earl grinned. "You're under house arrest, Your Grace."

Twenty-Two

"HE *LEFT*?" RAVENNA'S VOICE WAS SHRILL ENOUGH TO BREAK glass as she advanced on the poor butler. She'd only just returned from a much-needed visit with Sarani and Anu, who were heading back to Hastings later that afternoon, only to be told by the butler that her husband had left the country. "To go back to Antigua," she said.

Morgan flinched. "Yes, Your Grace."

"And he told *you* to tell *me*."

He shook his head. "No, it was Mr. Rawley. He'll be back soon. There was a fire, Your Grace. Several fires. He had to go. There was no time to waste."

Ravenna fought the urge to scream. It wasn't Morgan's fault; it was her rotten husband's fault. She belonged at his side, not stuck here in England. He could have waited to tell her, but he'd chosen to leave, like a bloody coward. She was going to throttle the man. But first, she was going to hire the first passenger ship out of here.

"Colleen, pack our bags!" she hollered like a fishwife on the wharf. "Morgan, I need my carriage."

"Your Grace." The butler was begging now. "Please don't do anything rash."

Was murder rash?

She ignored him, but froze as her very quarry strode through the doors, followed by Waterstone and Rawley. Her husband looked...tense and angry, his hard features hard. Something had happened! Concern crept into her mind, but she shoved it aside.

Upon seeing her, Courtland stopped and stared as she crossed her arms, not even trying to disguise her wrath. "Back so soon? How was the weather on the sea?"

He opened his mouth and closed it, before scrubbing a hand through his hair. "I'm sorry I didn't tell you myself, Ravenna. I should have."

She blinked. "Yes, you should have." Frowning, she noticed the policemen who had followed before Morgan shut the door behind the others. "What's going on?"

"Sommers happened," he said. "He planted crates on the *Glory* full of goods and claimed I stole them from him. He also put Stinson up to the piece in the scandal rags. I'm being held by Waterstone, confined to this house until my trial."

"A trial? For what? You're a peer and his claims are false."

"Guilty until proven otherwise."

"But you *are* innocent." Her mouth fell open. Of all the things she expected him to say, that was not it. She glanced at Waterstone, the earl's solemn expression making her stomach sour. "He'll be cleared, won't he?"

"There's chatter of a forthcoming petition in court by Stinson that Courtland is not the true Duke of Ashvale because of illegitimacy. It might lead to a trial, and if he's stripped of his title, things could get ugly."

"But he *is* the duke."

Waterstone exhaled. "We know that. Our hope rests on a man who has not awoken. Who might not awaken."

"Bingham." This was catastrophic. "What do we do now?"

"Sommers is wanted for questioning, but I suspect he's gone to ground. We will find him and get a confession out of him."

She frowned. "How?"

"I have ways and means." At the deadly look in his eyes, Ravenna didn't doubt that in the least. "In the meantime, I'll avail myself of your cook's fine talent."

When he headed for the kitchens, she turned her attention

back to her duke, and all her anger drained away. He needed her, even if he wouldn't admit it, and there was no way in hell she was going to walk away now. In silence, she followed him up to his bedchamber, where he poured himself a liberal glass of brandy from the decanter on the mantel.

He gave her a tight smile. "Still want to be my duchess?"

"You'd have to pry my cold, dead hands away from you."

"That sounds dirty," he said.

"You prefer my hands warm and alive."

Courtland stared at her, his handsome face somber. "You are the best thing that's ever happened to me, too. I want you to know that."

"Why are you talking as though it's all over?"

"Because it is," he said. "I was never meant to be duke."

She shrugged. "And I was never meant to be a married duchess, but here we are—a reluctant duke and his hoyden bride. To tell you the truth, I've gotten used to us. I've gotten used to this. We make sense in a way that nothing ever has before. Tell me you don't agree with that, and I will walk out that door."

"I can't tell you that." He set down the glass and walked toward her. A lifetime swirled in those gorgeous dark eyes—showing glimpses of the boy he'd been and the man he'd become, and all the faces he'd worn in between. But above that, she saw raw honesty...the man she adored stripped down to his basic self. "I love you, Ravenna. I've loved you since I was ten and you wept over a baby bird in the woods."

His declaration wrapped around her like the softest silk. "You love me?"

"Since forever, it seems."

She frowned. "Then why would you try to push me away?"

"If your childhood nemesis stole your heart without your permission, wouldn't you do everything to get it back?"

"Maybe. Very well, fine. I can see your point."

Her duke gathered her in his arms, holding her close, and she reveled in the feel of his strong, lean, beautiful body encasing hers. She felt his lips against her hair and her eyes fluttered closed. Standing in his embrace was heaven. Courtland took her hand and placed it over the left side of his chest. "The truth is this heart has always been yours. What I didn't realize was that one cannot steal something that has already been gifted."

Ravenna stared up at him, her own heart filling to bursting. "So we're doing this, then? No more games. No more running?"

Her gorgeous husband laughed, the rich sound sinking into her nerve endings like honey, as his cheeky palm slid down to cup her bottom with a wicked squeeze. "Well, I'm not going to say *no* to games. They can be fun."

"You say this as if I know these things. I require detailed instruction, Your Grace." She tugged his head down to hers with a smile. "Now shut up and ravage me, Duke, before I expire from all this sexual frustration."

"Say that again," he rasped, skimming his mouth over hers in a move that had her panting and her nipples standing at attention. She knew exactly what he wanted her to say.

"Sexual."

His pupils dilated, his voice like gravel. "Again for good measure."

"Sex—"

The Duke of Ashvale swallowed the rest of the word and took her lips in the most erotic kiss known to man. Or woman. Or anyone with a working pulse.

And all she could do was succumb.

———

Courtland had never felt freer in his life, considering that he was incarcerated in his own home. Who would have thought that confessing a decade and a half of feelings would be so liberating? He was terrified and a part of him still wanted to protect Ravenna from the gossip storm he knew would come, but she was a grown woman with her own mind. She would choose the battles she wanted to fight, and she'd chosen to stand up with *him*.

He still couldn't quite believe it. Any sensible person would have run.

She had not.

He glanced over to where his wife sat reading a book curled up in an armchair near the fireplace. A tendril of auburn hair curled onto her cheek, her full mouth pursed in deep thought. She was beautiful. Over the past few nights, he'd made love to her until dawn broke over the skies, until they were nothing but limp sated bodies and whispered nothings.

Last night had been no exception. Nor this morning's invigorating ride that his lusty duchess initiated. His cock perked up at the image of her above him—breasts on display, lips parted in pleasure, all that riotous red hair spilling like a silken cloud atop her shoulders—but Courtland sent it a stern message to behave. It would not do to ravage his wife in the library.

"Your Grace," Morgan announced at the door. "Lady Bronwyn and Lord Stinson to see you."

His sister and brother. Why were they here? Ravenna met his eyes with a quizzical look. While the scandal caused by the account in the papers had not died down, Embry's lawyers had been successful in shutting down the scandal sheets that had published the sordid tale. The battle for the dukedom was still ongoing, and Bingham showed no signs of awakening. Doctors had said that some men remained in such a state for months. On top of that, Sommers had not been found, though Waterstone was confident he hadn't left London.

"Show them in," Courtland said.

Bronwyn entered first, to Courtland's surprise, and the determined look on her face as well as the pinched look on his brother's gave him pause. She held a sheaf of parchment in her hands. "Your Graces," his sister said with a curtsy. "Apologies for the intrusion. My brother has something he wishes to say to you."

A brooding Stinson glowered at her before stepping forward. "It was untrue. What was printed in the paper."

"And?" Bronwyn prodded.

"And I apologize," he gritted out.

Ravenna gaped at him, but it wasn't unlike the thread of surprise coursing through Courtland's own veins. What did his younger sister have on Stinson that would make him confess such a thing or *apologize*? The answer was revealed when Bronwyn's smug blue gaze met his. "Stinson has a mistress who's fleecing him by threatening to expose their child to Mama."

Stinson cursed under his breath. "Damn it, you promised you wouldn't say a word!"

"Yes, to Mama," she replied calmly. "This is our brother. We can trust him."

"He's no—" He cut off, lips pursed, as though he'd swallowed a bug, both Courtland and Ravenna watching in bemused silence as he snapped his mouth shut. His face turned dull red.

Bronwyn gave an approving nod. "Now the rest, Stinson."

Stinson glared at her high-handedness, but met Courtland's eyes, shame lurking in them. "Sommers approached me at my club and expressed interest in Bronwyn. If I were to arrange an agreement, in exchange, I'd be rid of you."

Bronwyn sniffed. "As if I would ever look at that overgrown toad."

"What did Sommers offer you?" Courtland asked, alert and eyes narrowed.

"He said if I agreed to the match as her guardian, he would give me Bronwyn's dowry as he had no need of it."

"That woman is the mother of your child, you imbecile," Bronwyn said, blue eyes rolling upward. "A baby is your responsibility. Good Lord, you'd think that we women shoulder all the burden for men's complete lack of brains. If you didn't want your ladybird to get pregnant, you should have worn a French letter."

"Bronwyn!" he snapped.

"What? I'm a modern woman. I have to know these things. How else will I protect myself from unscrupulous gentlemen? This body is the only one I have."

Courtland was sure that Ravenna's dumbfounded expression mirrored his. He'd never been prouder to call anyone family than he was at that moment. Underneath all the layers of feminine politesse, Bronwyn's spine was made of pure steel.

He cleared his throat, motioning for Stinson to continue. "Go on."

"As you can guess, the stubborn chit refused to even see the man, and had the audacity to say that as duke, you were the only one who could approve her marriage."

"I didn't lie," she pointed out.

"I called her names I'm not proud of." Stinson swallowed hard, lines of misery and shame making his face droop. "I begged her to reconsider, telling her that it would solve all our problems. If she would only agree to Sommers's suit, you wouldn't be a problem anymore—that he knew how to get rid of you for good. She told me that she'd never thought of you as a problem, but as a long-lost sibling, and that she wanted to get to know you."

Stinson let out a shuddering breath as though all the fight and anger had been leached out of him. With a groan that came from the lowest depths of his body, he sat heavily in the nearest chair. "I was so angry, and I was well in my cups when I went to Sommers and told him everything. He paid for the exposé in that gossip rag. He told me not to worry, that he had a plan to deal with you, and I could have back my life, if I told the world what my mother has always told me—that you were illegitimate and that you were of mixed blood. I'm ashamed to admit I didn't think twice. I wanted you gone."

"Why?"

His brother gave a hollow laugh. "You were always so…good at everything. Even Grandfather was *Cordy this* and *Cordy that. Why can't you be more like that Cordy lad*?" Courtland's eyes widened as Stinson dropped his head into his hands. "It drove me insane how sodding perfect you were. You were the brilliant heir and I was the nothing spare. Mama was the one who told me your mother was nothing but an island commoner. It's no excuse, but it was one I latched onto that you didn't deserve what you had. By default of my bloodline, I was better."

Courtland felt all his muscles lock as years and years of anger and bitterness descended on him. He'd always felt unworthy because of the way his own brother and stepmother had treated him. No child deserved that. *No one* deserved that.

"But I'm not better," Stinson whispered. "I'm worse. I blamed you for my shortcomings then, just as I blamed you for everything now. I convinced myself that if you went away again, it would all be better."

"You and your mother gave me no choice but to leave England," Courtland bit out.

"I know," Stinson said with the first genuine and repentant look that Courtland had ever seen on his brother's face. "I *know*. It only took my little sister to inform me of that fact. That I was angry at the wrong person. That I should be angry at *me*." He drew a shuddering breath. "When I saw the newssheets and heard about the false arrest, I never expected to feel so bleak at what I'd done. I thought I would be happy, but I wasn't. I was miserable."

"Because deep down, you knew it was wrong, Stinson," Ravenna murmured from her perch. "I won't lie. That was a prick of a move."

Courtland's lips twitched at his wife's candor even as his brother's face crumpled. "You have no idea how much I regret it."

She eyeballed him. "Well, I suppose that's a start, and you're here now, even if it was forced, and that counts for something. A very *minuscule* something."

Courtland exchanged a look with her, one that led her to rise from her seat near the bookcase and came over to stand near him behind the table. It was as if she could sense that he needed her before he knew it himself. Her hand drifted to the top of his shoulder and squeezed, letting him know she was there, no matter what he decided: hear his brother out or have him hauled from the room.

He stared at Stinson and saw the face of the boy who had relished his pain, one who had destroyed any hope of brotherhood. An image of him expecting his younger brother to back him up at Harrow and watching Stinson laugh instead as he was nearly pummeled to death by his classmates filled his brain. He swallowed at the memory that had yet to heal. Those childhood wounds still festered and burned.

Hurt and resentment boiled like acid through his veins. His fingers clenched into fists. This latest betrayal was layered upon so many others from a decade ago, tangling and twisting into something that threatened to demolish the fortress he'd built around himself. But something new battled to be heard, too, tempering that ruthless, unfeeling, *distant* man he'd been for so many years: his wife's compassion. Her fierce devotion.

Her *love*.

Ravenna squeezed her fingers again as if she could sense the chaos of his thoughts and sought to soothe the raging, wounded beast inside. At the heart of it, Stinson was a spoiled and overindulged man, but a part of Courtland understood that Ravenna was right. His brother wasn't completely rotten if he was feeling any remorse at all. If he was here and the apology was sincere—still to be seen—that was something. It was the only redeemable thing saving his skin.

"You hated me that much?"

"No, I envied you." Stinson did not look up. "Because clearly, you're the better choice…the better duke. The better brother, son, everything."

Courtland sighed. "I am neither better nor lesser, Stinson. I'm just a man, trying to exist on his own terms. Trying to survive. I've done ruthless things and I have some regrets, but even the worst missteps take us to where we need to be."

"Do you truly believe that?" Stinson murmured.

"I do." He frowned, staring at his brother as something occurred to him. "I have one question. Why didn't you and the marchioness go to the courts after seven years? You could have declared me dead and that would have been the end of it."

"Grandfather forbade it," he said.

Surprise flooded Courtland as Stinson continued. "He didn't care what I called myself, or the charades my mother insisted on, but she didn't dare defy him. He was still powerful in the Lords. She'd hoped to do it somehow after he died." He exhaled. "But then you came back."

"He wouldn't have if he hadn't married me," Ravenna said. "But everything happens for a reason. The dukedom was never yours, Stinson."

"I know," he whispered.

Courtland pinched his nose between his thumb and forefinger. "I'd have much preferred to have my brother"—he glanced at Bronwyn—"and my sisters than any empty title."

Bronwyn's eyes glittered with tears, and Courtland could feel his own eyes smarting. How was it that something like this could tear families apart? It was just like money, he supposed.

"Do you think you could ever forgive me?" Stinson's strangled plea was barely audible.

Courtland clenched his jaw so tightly his teeth hurt. *Could* he forgive Stinson? Could he let go of the hopelessness and anger that had driven him all these years? It had become such an ingrained part of him—the burning flame that had kept him soldiering on to build his fortune, to insulate himself from anyone who sought to tear him down. But things had changed. Courtland glanced up at his wife. *He* had changed.

"You destroyed my life once, and those actions are on you." He let out a heavy exhale. "You have to come to terms with what you did. Those demons are yours, they were never mine, and you have to do the work to be a better man. That said, I wouldn't be who I've become, the duke my wife believes me to be, if I didn't try to lead by example. I'm your elder brother, after all." He reached up to grasp Ravenna's fingers. "Are you willing to swear your account to the police and incriminate Sommers for his part in the deception?"

"Yes, I will."

Courtland's relief was tangible.

"And there's proof," Stinson added. "Sommers told me where his warehouse is. You'll find more of those crates with undeclared goods, enough to implicate him at least."

"That's good." Courtland breathed out. "As far as my forgiveness, that will take time. I can't promise anything, but I'm willing to try."

"Thank you." Stinson's suspiciously bright gaze panned to his sister. "You were right. I am sorry."

"I knew a better man was inside you somewhere." Bronwyn nodded, a small smile gracing her lips. "You can go now. I'll finish up here, but when I return, we need to talk to Florence. Mama is probably a lost cause, but I refuse to stand by and let our younger sister become twisted by lies."

Courtland watched in disbelief as his slip of a sister shot the brother that was several years her senior an uncompromising look, and hid his own proud smile. A dragon lurked beneath that demure exterior.

After Stinson took his leave, Bronwyn smiled at Ravenna.

"Thank you for trusting me." She held out the papers, closing the distance to the table. "This is for you."

"What is it?"

"Consider it a belated wedding gift." She gave a tiny shrug, her eyes meeting Ravenna's and spiking Courtland's curiosity. Why did it seem like they were conspiring? "Sorry it took so long. They were hidden away in Kettering, so I had to come up with a plausible story for my urgent return to Ashvale Park. As it turns out, one's favorite pair of gloves is enough to convince my mother, apparently." She wrinkled her nose with a disgusted look. "Anyway, this is a record of your birth, and your father's marriage, given in trust to me by our grandfather before he died. He told me to keep them safe."

In astonishment, Courtland glanced down at the documents, signed by the late duke and witnessed by several other names of peers he recognized as powerful men in the House of Lords. He sifted through them, spreading the pages out on the table's surface. Beneath those was a portrait of...his mother. Ravenna's fingers contracted on his shoulder, a soft gasp escaping her lips as she peered down.

Courtland's heart expanded behind his ribs as his eyes took in the thick black hair he'd imagined—exactly like his only longer—the huge, dark eyes that shone with intensity and intelligence, and the full curve of the mouth he'd inherited. He'd always wondered what she looked like, and now, he knew. She was beautiful. Underneath the portrait was inscribed: Lady Annelise Chase, Marchioness of Borne. There were a few other letters and documents that seemed to be written in his father's hand.

"I'm the damn duke," Courtland murmured.

Bronwyn grinned. "You're the damn duke."

He opened his mouth to chide his little sister on her dreadful language but was drowned out by the sound of his wife's earsplitting shriek. "Hell yes, he's the *damn* duke!"

"Wonderful," he said drily. "Now there are two of you."

But he couldn't hold back his laughter or the storm of emotions that filled him to the brim. He was bracketed by two absolute and unapologetic hellions, but he wouldn't have it any other way. He dragged a grinning Ravenna into his arms.

"Be my duchess forever?"

She kissed him and grinned. "As if you could get rid of me."

"Eww, find a bedchamber, you two," Bronwyn yelled out, covering her eyes and backing away. "A lady of quality does *not* need to witness her brother mauling his wife in public."

"Then you better run for the hills, sister dear." Courtland paused, swallowing hard against the unexpected tide of affection for a girl he hardly knew. He was responsible for that. Yes, he'd been chased away, but it'd been his choice to stay away. He hoped to change that for all their sakes, even Stinson's. "Thank you, Bronwyn."

"That's what family is for," she said and closed the door behind her.

Family. Courtland nodded to himself, throat thick. He had one, now, and it felt astonishingly, extraordinarily good. He turned his attention to the woman in his arms—the woman who had brought him back home, who had shown him that he didn't have to keep running from his past...or who he was. That love wasn't out of his reach.

Happiness was his—all he had to do was be brave enough to take it.

Twenty-Three

RAVENNA PACED THE MORNING ROOM OF HER MOTHER'S RESI-
dence, her fingers clenching and unclenching on her skirts. Once
more, she'd been left behind, though this time it was for a valid
enough reason. Courtland, her brother, and Waterstone were pre-
senting the evidence of her husband's birth in chambers to put to
rest once and for all that he was the Duke of Ashvale.

It should have made her feel a sense of peace, and it did, but
she wouldn't feel at ease until she *saw* Courtland with her own
eyes. Something felt unsettled in her gut and she wasn't one to
ignore her instincts. Earlier that morning when he'd accompanied
her here, he'd seemed preoccupied, understandably so, but something wasn't right. Her bones ached and her skin felt chilled. She
fingered the bulky reticule buried in her pocket, the presence of
the small pistol within not bringing its usual ease.

She paced anew.

"You're making me exhausted, dear," her mother said from
where she sat. "Do sit or at least move away from the window
so you don't keep catching the light like a miniature walking
thundercloud."

Ravenna let out a puff of laughter, glancing over her shoulder.
"I can't sit, Mama. I'm much too nervous."

"Nervous about what?"

"I want this all behind us, behind Courtland and me," she said
and bit her lip. "And I have an awful feeling that something terrible
is going to happen."

"Nothing's going to happen. The duke will prove he's Ashvale's legitimate heir, and all the squawking in the *ton* will fade away in time."

Exhaling again, Ravenna left her spot at the windows and moved to sit on the armchair adjacent to the dowager. "He's a good man. You believe that, don't you? No matter where he comes from?"

"I know," her mother said, peering at her over the rim of her teacup. "I see it in the way he treats you like you're something treasured. And you are a treasure, my daughter." She shook her head, touching her temples. "But willful, oh so willful. Fuller wasn't the only one you gave a set of grays to."

She flushed. "I wasn't *that* bad, Mama."

"No, you weren't," the dowager admitted with a fond smile. "But you always knew what you wanted and you went after it. You and Embry are the same in that kind of singular pursuit of something you love. You do love your duke, don't you?"

"I do, more than anything." She gave a wry smile. "Ever since we were children, I think." She toyed with an embroidered flounce on her walking dress. "Mama, you do realize I would not be the woman I am today, if you were not the woman you are, don't you? You might have your faults—we all do—but the biggest step is recognizing our flaws and doing what feels right in our hearts. You taught me that. Though your methods aren't for the faint of heart, I'll be the first one to admit," she said with a dry laugh, "you taught me to stand up for myself with three brothers, and how to be strong and heard in a world governed by men."

"Oh, you wretched girl," her mother said, eyes going glossy and her fingers lifting to quell the brimming moisture. "You'll make me get splotchy and have bags under my eyes."

"You're beautiful no matter what. I love you, you know."

The dowager smiled through her tears. "I love you too, Daughter, even though, by God, you try my patience and my sanity most days."

Unable to sit quietly, Ravenna stood and resumed her pacing at the window, waiting for the ducal coach to return. Courtland had given her—and her alter ego, Raven Hunt—strict instructions to stay put, and for once, Ravenna wanted to obey, even if it chafed. She pressed a hand to her chest and frowned. "Goodness, this is intolerable. My blood is racing and it's hard to breathe. Something is amiss. I can feel it."

The dowager let out an exasperated noise. "You've always had an active imagination."

"I'm not imagining this. I should do something."

"You should stay here."

Fuller announced his presence in the doorway. "Would you like more tea, Your Graces?"

"How about something stronger?" Ravenna said instead.

"It's much too early for spirits," the dowager put in. "But a splash of brandy in the tea would not go amiss."

After the tea had been refreshed and a small amount of brandy added, Ravenna sipped the warm liquid, hoping it would settle her nerves. She had no idea why she was so on edge, but her instincts had kept her safe from danger while crossing the Atlantic on a ship full of men, and she'd learned not to ignore them.

"I don't like this," she muttered to herself, peering past the drapes to the streets below.

"Exactly what do you think is going to happen?" the dowager asked. "Parliament is the most boring place known to man. A bunch of men in wigs and robes declaring the size of their egos and phalluses, and pretending they have all the answers to the problems in the world."

Ravenna gaped. "*Mama!*"

"What? It's true."

"That's beyond the pale for you," Ravenna said. "You don't speak about men's… Goodness, I cannot even utter such a vulgar thing in your presence."

"I never took you for a prude, dressing in men's clothing and gallivanting everywhere. You know, Lady Holding told me an interesting story of when she first saw you with Ashvale and your compromising…situation."

Ravenna's face went hot with mortification. Oh, no, she didn't. "Lady Holding was undoubtedly confused about whatever she thought she saw. It was quite a commotion. And I am not a prude, Mama, but this is *you* we're talking about."

Hiding an uncharacteristic grin, the dowager waved a hand. "How do you think I had four children? By miraculous conception? I'll have you know, your father—"

Hot-cheeked, Ravenna let out a choked noise and lifted a palm, stalling her midsentence. "I do *not* want to know about your bedroom life, Mama."

"Are you sufficiently distracted then?"

Oh. She had to laugh at her mother's tactics. "That was rather unconventional, but yes. I suppose I should thank you for putting those images in my head instead."

Ravenna was still shaking her head in smiling disbelief when a loud *pop* echoed outside, and at the same time the glass pane above her head shattered. Her mother's scream was all Ravenna heard before she hit the floor in a flurry of skirts. She knew what that noise was all too well and what it meant. She'd heard many a discharged pistol on the high seas for it to be any coincidence.

"Mama, get down! Fuller!"

Pure instinct taking over, Ravenna crawled over to where her ashen mother was covering her ears, her eyes wide with fright, and gathered her into her arms. She moved them both behind the sofa just as the butler skidded to their sides. "What was that?" Fuller asked.

"Nothing good," Ravenna said, her heart racing as she eyed the broken window. That lead ball had come much too close to her head for comfort, and whoever had shot it would want to make sure that the bullet had reached its target. There was a chance it could have been an accident, but Ravenna didn't put much stock in coincidence. "Are Papa's pistols still in the study?" she asked Fuller. When he nodded, she drew a breath. "Good, fetch them, and then gather the biggest footmen and get the duchess to safety. We should get the rest of the servants through the back as soon as possible."

But before the butler could move to do her bidding, the front door burst open, and the last man she'd expected to see sauntered in without a care in the world. Her stomach dropped. *Sommers*. "Come out, come out, little bird. I know you're here. Don't make this worse. I wouldn't want anyone else to get hurt. It's you I'm here for."

Damn and blast.

Fuller shook his head in warning, but Ravenna gritted her teeth. There was no choice here. The man was deranged enough to shoot through a window in the middle of Mayfair. Slowly, she stood. "Fine, I'm here. Don't hurt anyone."

Sommers stood there, his clothing mussed and dirty as though he'd been hiding in a hole down by the wharves, but his eyes glinted with triumph, the pistol pointed directly at her. "There you are, darlin'." His beady eyes found Fuller's as he lifted the pistol in warning. "One move and I'll shoot her, understand?"

"What do you want with me?" she asked, slipping her hand unobtrusively into her pocket.

"You're my ticket out of here," he said. His smile widened. "And besides, I heard a rumor from the desk staff at my hotel that a sweet little redhead was claiming to be my wife. I didn't think you had it in you, little duchess."

"So you tried to shoot me?" Ravenna's fingers worked furiously and furtively. The reticule's drawstring was proving to be a problem with one hand, but she wouldn't give up. Not now and never to a man like him. She'd fight with her bare hands if she had to.

He laughed. "I admit my aim was off. That would have ruined my plans, but I suppose the dowager would have done in a pinch." He scrunched up his nose. "Though I don't favor saggy flesh."

"You're a pig," Ravenna growled. "You won't get away with this."

"I will. Now, walk over here like a good girl. No one's coming to save you. Your husband and all his friends are locked away behind closed doors."

Bloody hell, the deuced knot was hopelessly tangled. Perhaps she could get close enough to bludgeon him with the reticule and distract him enough so the others could get to safety. She sent a reassuring glance to the butler, and then to the footmen she could see hovering in the hallway. She only hoped they would leave. Sommers could have more than one gun on him. Ravenna sucked in a breath and closed the distance between them. Her nerves had ceased their noise; the only thing in her head was a sense of quiet calm.

"You're right, but you're forgetting one thing, Sommers."

"What's that, darlin'?" he asked with an oily grin when she was a few feet away.

Finally. The strings went slack.

"I don't need anyone to save me."

And with that, she yanked her trusty pistol from her pocket— the very same one she'd pointed at Courtland a lifetime ago—and fired. There was no hesitation with a man like Sommers. But she was no killer. She aimed for the hand holding the gun and shot his shoulder.

When the slimy bastard dropped the weapon and went down mewling like the sack of shit he was, Ravenna bared her teeth. "I'm not your fucking darlin'."

———

If it wasn't the screaming aristocrats running down the streets with fear on their faces, the sound of the gunshot had Courtland nearly diving from the carriage before it came to a final stop. He was closely followed by Embry and Waterstone as they dashed up the steps of the residence through a door that lay drunkenly on its hinges.

Fear filled him in that moment, but the sight that greeted him would stay with him for forever—his magnificent wife standing like a vengeful fury over a moaning Sommers as he lay on the floor clutching his bloody shoulder. Her hair tumbled around her face in a halo, her beautiful eyes sparking fire at the man who dared enter her domain without permission. Courtland's mouth went dry. Fuck if she wasn't the most glorious thing he'd ever seen.

"God above, I leave you for one hour," he said, striding into the room and tutting under his breath.

Her eyes lit with happy relief. "In my defense, Husband, he shot first."

Courtland didn't wait to sweep her into his arms, his mouth finding hers with unerring accuracy. Neither of them cared as footmen poured into the room at Waterstone's direction and the wounded Sommers was secured. Embry hustled over to the dowager, whom Courtland dimly heard saying she was uninjured thanks to Ravenna.

He broke the kiss, his gaze searching his wife's, but he didn't release his hold around her body. "He didn't hurt you?"

She lifted a pistol he recognized. "I didn't let him."

"I thought you left that thing in Antigua," he said with a slight frown. "Though I'm glad you didn't. Just never point it at me again, please."

"I'd never shoot you, Cordy," she said grinning. "Unless you provoked me, of course."

He wrapped his arms tighter around her. "Remind me not to do that."

Courtland only deigned to release his wife when Waterstone's men swarmed into the room to collect the evidence and to listen to the accounts of what had happened. Embry escorted the dowager from the room to where the family physician had been summoned to make sure that she wasn't in a state of shock or in need of medical help. The duchess was a tough old bird, Courtland knew, but even the hardiest of men or women could be traumatized by a shooting.

His fists tightened as he realized how close he'd come to losing Ravenna when she recounted how the first shot had shattered the window and that Sommers had meant to shoot at her. As if she could sense his distress, she reached across to grasp her husband's palm and squeezed. He knew she was capable, as she'd clearly demonstrated with Sommers, but the thought of not having her in his life was unbearable.

It didn't take much longer for Waterstone and his men to clear out, and after Embry confirmed that the dowager had taken a tincture and was resting comfortably, Courtland escorted his wife to their waiting carriage. She stared at him in the coach as they headed for home. "Stop looking at me like that."

He shifted guiltily. "Like what?"

"Like I'm a fragile piece of glass."

"It's not that. I know you're not fragile and you can take care of yourself." He let out a breath. "You're important to me and the thought of losing you…"

"You won't lose me." She shot him a wicked grin that went straight to his groin. "I'm a flesh-mongering beetle, and we don't give up our delicious prizes so easily."

Courtland's mouth fell open. He'd never actually *told* her that, had he?

"Rawley, that loose-lipped shit," he muttered, just as she burst into laughter, confirming his suspicion. "In my defense, that was before I knew you."

"Don't worry, I'm certain I called you much worse when I was in my cups on the *Glory*."

He let out a chuckle. "Like Hades?"

"Precisely, so consider us even. I'm a greedy beetle and you're a vengeful god who steals maidens away to his domain."

"If it's any consolation, you're the most fearsome beetle I've ever encountered."

Smirking, she stuck out a pink tongue, making his blood heat. "It's not, but I know of a way you could make it up to me."

When they arrived at their residence, Courtland couldn't help taking her into his arms again in the foyer. For some soul-deep reason, he could not stop touching her and reassuring himself that she was all right. It was because of the earlier incident, of course, but he had an inkling that it would be a good while before the restlessness in his body settled and accepted the fact that she was safe. Nuzzling into him, she didn't seem to mind.

Breathing in her scent, he kissed her again until she pushed at his shoulders, questions swirling in her eyes. "Wait a moment, I forgot to ask in the heat of things, is it all settled, then?" she asked. "The legitimacy thing?"

"For now."

Ravenna frowned. "What do you mean?"

"The documents are proof enough, but the seeds of gossip are hard to uproot once they've dug in, and you know the kind of battle I'm facing."

He gave a small shrug. Most of the lords had agreed, but there were some peers whose sentiments would not let them accept the evidence right in front of their faces. Even with solid proof signed by the former duke, he'd earned the majority of support by a hair.

"Sometimes, I hate this place," she murmured.

"It's not just here, love. Intolerance is everywhere. People refute and fear what they do not know."

"Will you step down then?" she asked, copper eyes meeting his. "Give up your seat in the House of Lords?"

"No. That seat is power, and I want to use it. Even one voice can make a difference. I'd rather not lose mine because people don't want me there. Others might distance from me, and there's inherent privilege in that, but I'm always going to be me." He lifted a palm. "Brown, island-born, and proud of it. If I won't fight for myself, who will?"

Her arms tightened around him. "I'll never stop fighting for you, Courtland. I hope you know that."

Choked by her fervent promise, he buried his face in her fragrant hair. How on earth did he get so lucky?

His duchess cupped his cheek, coppery eyes glinting with so much love that it almost undid him. "I can feel your mind whirling like a child's top, Duke. What are you thinking in that head of yours?"

"How lucky I was to catch you cheating."

Eyes full of mischief, she gave an indignant huff. "*Alleged* cheating. I will have you know, there was never any evidence of such charges, sir. Thinking the crime is not doing the crime."

"So you admit you did think of it?"

"For a hot minute," she said.

He gathered her in his arms. "You still lost fair and square."

"I did not!" She blinked. "Wait, what did you have?"

"A natural."

Ravenna stared at him. "You have no proof of your terribly baseless claims, my lord duke."

Smugly, Courtland reached for the queen of diamonds and the ace of hearts resting in his breast pocket and waved it in front of her face. "This evidence?"

"You had those cards in your pocket all along?"

He nodded sagely. "A wise man keeps his enemies close."

She couldn't help it. She burst into peals of laughter. With a devious glint in her eyes, Ravenna's hand drifted down to the bulging front of his trousers. "What about lovers?"

"He keeps them even closer," he said on a shallow groan when she gripped him through the fabric. "Sometimes in his lair, tied to his bed, preferably without clothes."

Copper eyes blew wide with desire. "Is that a fact?"

"A promise."

Her answering gaze was so sultry, it was a wonder they both didn't combust then and there. "Then why are we still here in the foyer, Duke?"

Courtland scooped his smart-mouthed, intelligent, and supremely fierce duchess into his arms with a devilish grin of his own. He would give her everything she desired, everything she deserved. To the unabashed delight of their proper London staff, he ferried his duchess up the stairs to his bedchamber like the precious treasure she was. "I love you, my duchess."

"Not as much as I love you."

"That is not possible," he said, halting on the threshold.

She wrapped her arms around his neck, argumentative and contentious to the last. "Then we shall have to agree to disagree."

He kissed her nose. "Are we quarreling already?"

"I am about to win this argument because I have two words for you, Duke." She rolled her eyes impertinently. "*Sexual. Frustration.*"

His blood ran licentiously hot.

It was a wonder they made it into that room at all.

Epilogue

RAVENNA DESCENDED THE STEPS OF THE TERRACE LEADING down to the sandy beach overlooking the azure waters of the Caribbean Sea. A balmy island breeze caressed her skin, the faint smell of citrus teasing her nostrils. She was glad she and Courtland had elected to return for a few months every year. While most of their time was spent in London during the season, and sometimes for part of the little season, the rest of the months were split equally between Kettering and Antigua.

After the debacle with Sommers in London, with Stinson's testimony of the foiled plot and the location of the warehouse containing the man's illegal goods, Sommers had been arrested for attempted murder, thievery, and smuggling, and summarily deported. Waterstone had received the queen's own commendation.

In the aftermath, Ravenna and Courtland had remained in London for the better part of that first year, while he got his affairs in order. Bingham had finally awakened and corroborated Courtland's status as duke, which had helped to strengthen his position. In his role as Duke of Ashvale, Courtland had been very vocal in championing bills that made for better living conditions and wages for free peoples in the British colonies.

He'd also used the time in London to get to know his family, including Bronwyn and Florence. Courtland's and Stinson's relationship, however, had needed effort and care to repair. When Stinson had asked to be part of the family business, Courtland had put him through his paces as a lowly deckhand for months. To everyone's surprise, he'd borne the drudging work without complaint. Ravenna had always felt that it'd been a sort of penance—Stinson's way of showing his brother that he was sorry, instead of just saying it.

Her husband had never said anything, but she knew it'd meant something to him.

With a man like him, actions always did speak louder than words.

In due course, Courtland had relented and pulled Stinson into his shipping businesses and railway investments. Stinson had inherited their father's knack for numbers, and he'd proved to be an invaluable asset. Though it had taken her husband some time to truly trust his brother, eventually he had. As for Stinson's love child, eventually the truth had come out when his mistress had admitted her infidelity with none other than the Marquess of Dalwood. It helped when the child looked exactly like his sire. Stinson was off the hook, but for some reason, he still sent money for the care of the boy.

Lady Borne, however, had been another story. She was much too hardened in her views to see things differently. Not everyone wanted to listen or learn, or change. Ingrained bias could not be dismantled so easily, and while Bronwyn was determined to keep trying with her mother, Courtland saw no reason to keep the marchioness in their lives. Her burdens and her choices were hers to bear.

Digging her bare toes into the crumbly sand with a delicious sigh, Ravenna lifted her arms and turned her face up to the sun. Her mother would shriek to high heavens that she needed a parasol, but Ravenna loved leaving the trappings of London behind. The joy was worth every second of a burned nose and a few freckles.

"Praying to the sun gods?" Her husband's lips tickled her hair as a pair of sun-browned forearms wrapped around her curved belly. He rubbed the small bump gently. "How's baby doing today? Still causing havoc?"

Ravenna leaned back into his lean frame. "Honestly, I don't remember it being this bad the last time."

"It was," he reminded her. "You simply put it out of your mind the moment you saw our beautiful girl."

On cue, a screaming toddler raced toward them, followed by a hapless nurse who looked like she was on her last reserves. Ravenna swallowed her smile. At nearly two, Isla was a handful and a half, always curious, always daring, and always getting into everything. If there was trouble, she'd proved that she was more than capable of finding it. She grabbed her daughter and kissed her nose, grimacing at the dusting of sand covering her skin. "You need a bath."

"No bath! Come see, come see!"

"What is it, my teeny mermaid princess?" Courtland said after plopping a kiss on Ravenna's head and collecting the tiny bundle of chubby arms and legs. He made her squeal with delight as he tossed her high into the air. "Come see what?"

"Shells!"

He propped her up on one shoulder, and Ravenna marveled at the similarities between them. Born with a head of inky-black hair, Isla had also inherited her father's dark eyes, and even with her button nose and cherub lips, they were like two peas in a pod. Her mischievous and rebellious nature, though, Courtland had insisted was all Ravenna's.

"I was never so willful," she'd insisted after discovering Isla in the pantry covered in sticky jam.

Courtland had shot her a wry look. "You forget who chased after you all day long in Kettering. Trust me, you were worse."

"I think you're going addlebrained in your old age."

He'd shown her just how old he was by flinging her over his shoulder and carting her to bed, whereupon she'd been thoroughly convinced of his youthful prowess. A fond smile slid over her lips. That virility was probably the reason that baby number two was so swiftly on the way. Ravenna rubbed her fingers over the protruding swell, humming softly underneath her breath.

Their first baby had been a bit of a surprise, but when her breasts doubled in size and her bedroom appetites increased indecently, Sarani had been the one to discreetly suggest that she might be with child. And so Isla had arrived and promptly charmed everyone within arm's reach into submission. At first, Ravenna had been worried, given her husband's earlier assertions about children, but Courtland had fallen irrevocably in love the minute her tiny fingers had curled around his.

The duke's laughter drifted back toward her as their daughter pointed out a pink and white shell with fringed edging that was bigger than her head. He crouched down beside his pint-sized princess to investigate. At the sight of the linen trousers stretching tight over the flexed muscles of his thick legs and firm behind, Ravenna's mouth went instantly dry.

She groaned as a heated ripple of desire surged through her right to her core. Apparently, this pregnancy was going to go the way of the first. It was truly scandalous. She only had to see him or smell the man, and her entire body would go on alert, nipples pebbling beneath her shirt, thighs going damp, brain dissolving into a useless chant of want. She needed a dunk in the ocean. Perhaps *that* would cool her overheated body.

Courtland met her eyes over the top of Isla's head, his teeth gleaming in his tanned face, and froze as if he could see the need etched in every line of her body. He nodded for the hovering nurse to take Isla in for her bath, then stood, shirt pulling taut over his chest, those corded forearms doing things to her libido that should be outlawed. The man was beautiful—all sinuous limbs and sculpted muscles. As he prowled toward her, Ravenna couldn't look away if she tried. That sultry onyx gaze impaled hers, holding her prisoner.

"Don't you do it," he warned.

She arched a brow at his imperious warning. "Do what?"

"Run."

Her breath hissed through her lips, muscles bunching. Ravenna whirled and ran down toward the beach, hearing him give chase behind her, his huge strides eating up the distance between them. She had no idea where she'd intended to go, but he caught her around the waist before she could even make it more than a dozen steps.

Her husband's lips closed over her nape, his teeth grazing her damp skin and biting down just hard enough to make her whimper with need. "I told you not to run," he said, lips traveling up her neck to her ear.

She gasped as he sucked her lobe. "You like the chase."

"That's true."

He drew her into his arms, his hands finding her full, aching breast as his mouth sought her lips. "Courtland," she gasped. "Someone will see."

"Who will see?" He pinched her sensitive nipple, and an indelicate moan tore from her throat.

"The servants."

"I've dismissed them all except for Isla's nurse for the afternoon, and she just went inside to give Isla a bath and put her down for a nap." He nipped at her lower lip, his tongue soothing it and then chasing into the depths of her mouth to tease hers. "We are quite alone, Duchess."

Eyes nearly rolling back in her head, she ground herself onto the straining length of him as his delicious mouth devoured hers. It was erotic and exciting...the fact that they could be discovered at any moment. Even if the servants were gone and theirs was a private stretch of beach, they were still out in public. In the *open*.

Worry interspersed with pleasure warred inside her, but Courtland took the decision from her when he walked them both into the waves. And then his hands were roaming her body, touching her in places that made her gasp. When they stood waist deep in the sea, standing past the small breakers, he shifted her slightly to free his stiff length and yanked up her sodden cotton skirts. Even submerged, she was so wet it didn't take much for him to slip into her sheath. They both groaned in unison at the tight fit and the unexpected friction of the water.

"Fuck," he growled against her ear when she wrapped her legs around his waist.

Ravenna's cheeks went hot. *Fuck*, indeed. They were in the middle of the ocean with no one around for miles and half-hidden by the water, but they were still exposed. Anyone stumbling upon them would know what they were doing, glued together as they were.

"Stop thinking and enjoy it," he told her.

"What if someone comes?"

His smile was downright sinful as he fisted handfuls of her bottom, shifting in and out of her with three shallow thrusts that made her forget every coherent thought. "Someone *is* going to come, if I have anything to say about it."

"That's not what I meant." Was her voice always so breathless?

He rolled his hips, making her gasp. "What did you mean?"

"Nothing, you awful man. Just move!"

He complied with a smug grin. Ravenna's body was so sensitive that pleasure built and roared through her in a matter of strokes. She cried out, her body clenching around him, and Courtland followed with a deep thrust and a growl of his own. He wrapped his arms around her when his body slid from hers, and sank them both into the cool water, his lips sealing over her temple.

"You are stunning," he murmured, licking the salt from her skin.

She pulled a face. "If the *ton* and Lady Holding could see me now. Frolicking in the sea like a wanton."

"I quite like this side of you—a siren come to life."

Ravenna kissed his nose, and let her body relax into the heavenly water, her cotton clothing floating about her. "Do you know you're the only man who has ever accepted me for who I am? Everyone else always wanted to change me in some way. Mama, Rhystan, Lady Holding, everyone but you."

"They're fools. You're perfect as you are."

She stared at him, love brimming and overflowing in her heart. "You're perfect, too, you know."

"I wouldn't say that."

Ravenna grinned. "Are we quarreling, Your Grace?"

"No, no. I surrender," he said with a mock sigh of defeat, dragging her toward him for a kiss. "Fine, suffice it to say that we're perfect for each other, jagged edges and all."

As she gave herself up to his tender kiss, Ravenna couldn't agree more. They were made for each other—there was no other man in the world who could ever fit her so well. She was wild and unconventional, and he was contrary and uncommon. If there was ever a match made in the stars—a star-crossed bond between two lonely, kindred souls—this was it. She wouldn't trade the chance of a lifetime of happiness for anything.

Not when she'd finally found the one worth staying for...her sinfully handsome, deeply infuriating, and extremely kissable island duke.

If you loved *Rules for Heiresses*, don't miss

THE
PRINCESS
STAKES

Available now from Sourcebooks Casablanca

India, 1861

THE COPPERY SCENT OF SPILLED BLOOD COILED INTO PRINCESS Sarani Rao's nostrils as she fled down the corridor toward the courtyard, her slippers soundless on the polished marble. She tugged on her maid's arm, hefting the carpetbag she'd stuffed full of jewels, weapons, and clothing over one shoulder. Bombay. They had to get to Bombay, and then find a ship. *Any* ship.

Her stomach roiled with nausea and nerves.

"Hurry, Asha," she whispered urgently. "Tej is waiting."

"Where are we going, Princess?" the maid cried when they stopped to make sure the second, less-used courtyard was deserted. Most of the noise had come from the front of the palace, which gave them a few precious minutes, and Sarani had sent Tej, her longtime manservant, with a hastily stuffed portmanteau to ready any transportation he could find. She was well aware that her life could end right then and there, just like her father's. This was a royal coup.

Sarani let out a strangled breath. "Anywhere but here."

She'd just seen her father—the Maharaja of Joor—lying on his bed and in his nightclothes with his throat slit. Bile crept up into her throat and she retched helplessly to the side, tears stinging her eyes. The distant sounds of shouting and the clang of steel filled her ears, the acrid smell of smoke permeating her nostrils.

She hadn't expected the attack. No one had, not even her father or his advisors, despite the fact that India, and in particular the princely state of Joor, had been divided in turmoil for years. Things were becoming precarious with feudal nobility and hostile laborers fighting against British rule, annexation, and cultural practices, and the sepoys in the British army were getting restless.

But Sarani felt deep in her gut that this had been an assault from within. No one but family could get into her father's private quarters. Her cousin, Vikram, had the most to gain from eliminating the maharaja, and even if Vikram took power, he would always view her—the crown princess—as a threat.

The minute she'd found her father, Sarani knew that she would have to run if she hoped to get out of there alive. The only reason she hadn't been in her own quarters was because she'd snuck out with Tej to go down to her favorite childhood spot by the river. One last time, for memories' sake. To do something *normal* before she was married off like chattel the next day to Lord Talbot, the local regent and a decrepit English earl, whom she'd managed to thwart with an unnaturally long five-year engagement...until time had finally run out.

The single moment of whimsy had been the one thing to save her.

Sarani had known something was off as soon as she had returned. While climbing the trellised vine up to her chambers, she'd seen shattered glass on her father's adjacent terrace. And then she'd discovered him. Only her years of training with her weapons master had kept her from screaming or fainting at the sight of so much spilled blood.

Her room had been disturbed as well—sheets overturned, doors askew—as if a search had been made in haste. It had struck Sarani again that the assassin had known exactly where to go… exactly which suites had been hers and her father's.

She'd packed and woken her maid, blessedly unharmed in her own adjacent chamber. "The maharaja's been killed," she'd told Asha. "We have to go."

Tej was their only hope of escape. Locking down her grief and terror, Sarani searched the gloom for her loyal manservant, blood chilling with alarm, until she spotted him waiting with one of the smaller coaches a little way down the drive in the shadow of a cluster of banyan trees.

The boy waved, eyes wide from the driver's perch. "Get in! They're coming."

She and Asha sprinted down the drive and tumbled into the conveyance. It was moving before either of them could sit. Listening to the sounds of Asha's quiet weeping, Sarani forced back her own tears, her body tense with fear, as the carriage rolled off into the night.

Would they be followed? Had she left quickly enough? Would they be *safe*? If Vikram was the murderer—or had orchestrated the murder as she suspected—who knew what he might do? He would certainly not leave her alive. He might be a weasel of a coward, but he wasn't stupid.

The first leg of the journey took several hours. When they stopped to change horses, Sarani felt her dread start to ebb and stopped looking over her shoulder as often. No one chased them, and they'd made excellent time. After they were back on the road, the tears she'd been holding back came like the monsoon. They spooled hot and earnest down her cheeks, and she allowed herself to cry in the privacy of the carriage.

Asha offered her a lace handkerchief, sobbing quietly herself. "What will we do?"

"Go where they cannot find us." Sarani clasped her maid's fingers. "Asha, do you wish to come with me or stay? Tej has no family, but you do. We can secure lodgings for you in Bombay until you can safely go back to Joor."

"No, Princess, my place is with you."

With a sad nod, Sarani dried her tears and straightened her shoulders. They were on their own now and survival was tantamount. Money was no object—she had a fortune in jewels and priceless heirlooms in her portmanteau and carpetbag—but they would have to leave India until it was safe to return. A tiny voice inside acknowledged that could be never.

With the instability and political unrest, the safest place for her would be off these shores. As far away as possible…which left her with only one option.

Her mother's birthplace.

The thought of faraway London, known only from second-hand stories, made a knot form in her throat, but the alternative was much worse. If she stayed here, her fate would be the same as her father's. No, she would go to England and take on her mother's maiden name of Lockhart.

Pretending to be an English countess wasn't the worst thing in the world. She had fortune enough to last a lifetime. She had her wits. She had her training. And she was of aristocratic blood. Mostly.

She could do it…be English.

Sarani caught a hint of her reflection in the carriage window. A wild-eyed woman with dark-lined eyes and a bird's nest of black hair stared back at her, arguably more a mess of a girl than a highborn lady. She bit back a choked laugh. Her old French governess would be in a lather at the sight of her. Even with the aid of a bath and a comb, she wouldn't pass muster. Thanks to her mixed heritage, her complexion had changed throughout her life, and right now, it had taken on a brown glow from recent days spent outdoors. *She* might love it, but English aristocrats were more critical.

And they were quite dependably so…

Over the years, she'd witnessed many curious and disparaging looks by other English lords and ladies in her own court…ogling her as though she were an oddity. A princess of hybrid origins led to scrutiny, and not always the good kind. People saw what they wanted to see. Once, when she was twelve and sick of such intense observation, she'd hollered *boo* and made three visiting ladies spill Madeira all over themselves. Their reaction had been hilariously gratifying, but her punishment wasn't—she'd been forbidden from riding for a month.

Sarani blew out a breath. Plenty of Europeans had darker, olive-toned complexions. She would brazen it out if she had to. Besides, Lockhart was a common enough English name, and Sarani had been raised as a royal, if not a lady of quality. With an English earl for a great-grandfather, she had *some* claim on her mother's family—even if her half-Scottish, half-English mother, Lady Lisbeth Lockhart, had fallen in love with an Indian prince and renounced all ties with her home of birth.

The thought of England was daunting, but there was no one else she could turn to, at least not in Joor. Her father's relatives didn't accept her, not truly, and she couldn't put her trusted handmaidens in more danger. And besides, she had no idea who her enemies were or who supported her cousin. Though she despised the fact that the British had barged into her people's lands like conquering heroes, ironically, to escape a murderer, Britain was her only hope.

Sarani inhaled a brittle breath, folding her hands in her lap. She could do this. She would get the three of them to safety.

She would just have to hide Princess Sarani Rao.

And not yell *boo* to any frail English ladies.

"Your Grace!"

Rhystan looked up from the length of sail he was inspecting aboard the *Belonging*, brushing a clump of sweat-soaked hair out of his face and squinting into the hot Indian sun. He scowled. Not at the person addressing him but at the use of his title. Two years and he still wasn't used to it. One would think as the youngest of three sons, he would have been spared the monstrosity, but no, sodding fate had had other plans. His scowl deepened as the identity of the man approaching became clear. The harbormaster.

"Thornton," he said, wiping damp palms on his breeches, one hand curling lightly over the end of the flintlock pistol tucked into his waistband. He walked to the edge of the rail and propped a booted foot onto the rigging. "What can I do for you?"

The man was red and sweating profusely when he came to a stop at the gangplank. Rhystan noticed a wiry local hurrying behind Thornton's bulk but did not recognize him. "It's of grave import, Duke."

"Captain," Rhystan corrected through his teeth and fought a sneer. The man was full to the brim with his own consequence, though he wasn't above taking extra coin to line his own pockets from time to time. "Spit it out then, this matter of grave importance."

"Immediate passage is required," he said. "To England."

"We will make it worth your while, sir," the boy standing behind Thornton piped up.

Rhystan frowned, his eyes on the harbormaster. "The *Belonging* isn't a passenger ship. And might I remind you that you have your own steamship, Mr. Thornton, which I suspect is much better equipped for comfort than this one."

"Not for me, Your Grace," Thornton spluttered, wiping a handkerchief over his perspiring cheeks. "For Lady Lockhart."

"Lady who?"

"Lady Lockhart, Captain," the small manservant replied. "She needs passage to England and can pay handsomely."

Rhystan frowned, racking his brain for a face to match the name, but none came to mind. Either way, the *Belonging* was no place for a lady. The ship was fickle enough as it was, having once been a converted auxiliary steam warship that had belonged to a dodgy American privateer, and the living quarters were less than lavish. Enough for him, of course, but nothing compared to the guest accommodations on the rest of his fleet.

He waved an arm toward the rest of the ships docked in the harbor. "I don't care if she's the queen herself, I'm not taking any passengers. Find someone else."

Thornton shook his head. "None of the other packets are due to leave port tonight for England. Yours is the only one. She must depart without delay."

He glanced at the houseboy behind Thornton. "Why can't she leave tomorrow or the next day?"

"It's a matter of some expediency, sahib, sir," the boy stammered, and Rhystan frowned at the Eastern form of address he'd heard frequently when he'd been stationed as an officer.

"Who is your lady? Lady Lockton, you said?"

"Lady Lockhart, Captain."

The name sounded vaguely familiar, though he could not place it. Then again, he hadn't set foot on English shores in a while. All the names of the peerage sounded the same. "Tell your mistress to speak with Captain Brooks. He sails the day after next."

"That's too late."

"Why does she wish to leave so desperately?"

"There's been a death in the family. Your ship is the soonest on the ledger."

The reason struck an unexpected chord of understanding and sympathy within him. Death had a way of upsetting everything. This unknown lady was racing against time for closure, while he was doing the same, only he was trying to beat the clock to get to his purportedly ailing mother in time. Rhystan could empathize more than anyone.

The boy must have noticed his hesitation because he started forward and bowed deeply. "I implore you, sahib. Please, reconsider."

"Where are you from?" Rhystan asked, curious.

"Joor," the boy replied and then gulped as if it was something he shouldn't have disclosed.

But Rhystan was too stunned to dwell on his reaction. *Joor.* What were the odds?

Unwanted and unwelcome memories, long buried from Rhystan's youth, rushed up to greet him. He shook himself hard and ground his jaw. What was in the past was in the past. He hadn't thought about Joor—or what had happened there—in years. And for good reason.

A feminine lilt rose in his head: *I'm yours, Rhystan.*

He throttled the recollections with brute force. Sarani Rao had never been his, not when she'd jilted him for an earl. Rhystan appreciated the irony, considering he now held the most venerated title of the English aristocracy, a half decade too late. Joor and that faithless princess were parts of his past that needed to remain dead and forgotten.

"Captain Brooks of the *Voyager*," he said to the servant, dismissing him and turning on his heel. "Tell him I sent you."

———————————————

Sneaking onto a ship in the dead of night wasn't ideal. Or ladylike. Or sane.

Especially for one newly nascent Lady Sara Lockhart. But Sarani was desperate, and since the *Belonging* was the only one on the manifest leaving Bombay for England in short order, she didn't have much choice.

Tej had explained that the captain had been inflexible. Sarani would have gone herself to beg, cajole, or argue, but she was short of options and time. And she couldn't shake the sensation that one of Vikram's men had followed them from Joor.

"Where is the captain now?" she whispered to Tej.

"At the tavern with his men."

"Are you certain the ship is unguarded?"

Tej shrugged. "He's a duke. No one would be foolish enough to board this ship."

Except for them, clearly.

A half hysterical chuckle rose in her throat. She'd questioned Tej thoroughly, but the boy had been adamant that this was the only way if she wanted to leave Indian shores in short order.

"Won't those men waiting onboard stop us?" she asked as they crept up the footbridge where two deckhands were waiting.

Tej's pale teeth glimmered in the gloom. "I told them it was all arranged with the duke earlier and that he gave orders to settle you aboard in the meantime. I also learned that they were hired here for the journey so I convinced them to give up their places."

Sarani worried the corner of her lip. "And they agreed?"

"They'll live like kings with what you gave me to pay them," Tej whispered when the two men in question took their trunks.

Sarani winced. If this recalcitrant captain-duke found out that members of his recently added crew had absconded with a better offer, he'd be furious. He would be even more furious to discover his new, unwanted passengers. But Sarani hoped the ship would be long at sea before that happened. In any case, the amount of money she planned to settle upon him would be enough to convince him not to toss them overboard.

She hoped.

Sarani sucked in a breath, the briny waters of the harbor carrying a hint of salt on the wind. It smelled like rain. Though it was two months shy of the start of the monsoon season, if a cyclone was brewing, they would be stuck here for who knew how long and at the mercy of whoever had murdered her father. She shivered. No, this was the only viable alternative.

Then again, this duke might kill her, too, once he discovered the deception.

Sarani swallowed her fear and hiked her skirts. Better to beg forgiveness than ask permission.

The two scruffy-looking men led the three of them down into the hold and deposited them in a cabin the size of a closet. A lumpy bed took up one side, a small chest and a chair the other. The lodgings didn't matter. She and Asha could sleep together, and she hoped Tej would find a space in a hammock with the rest of the crew.

A frisson of doubt assailed her as she thought of the weapons she'd packed in the base of her bag: a brace of pistols, several daggers, a pair of polished sabers, and her precious kukri blades. All deadly, should she need to use them. And she might. Four months on a ship she had no right to be on and whose captain already sounded like an unforgiving sort.

Goodness, am I doing the right thing?

England was an entire world away, and fitting into life there would be a struggle. But she had no choice.

It was either that or die.

Author's Note

Research for this novel was fascinating. While delving into colonialism and British rule in the West Indies, where I grew up, I also had to research the American Civil War, which occurred during the time period of the novel. It was eye-opening to comprehend the significant differences in race relations during the period both in the United States and the wider Caribbean. Slavery was abolished in 1834 in the West Indies and not until three decades later in the United States of America in 1865. As a result, the racial dynamics, especially in the islands, were very different. People of color owned businesses and property, formed families, and forged lives for themselves.

That said, colonialism was a very fraught period in history, and many terrible and unforgivable atrocities were committed during this time. Having been born in a colonial country and having grown up on an island where old plantations were taken over and farmed by locals and descendants of former indentured laborers, I have an intimate idea of the harm that was caused by colonization. However, living on a West Indian island is part of my history and my own experience. Trinidad and Tobago gained its independence from Britain in 1962, but I decided to set this novel in Antigua, a smaller colonial port, though I used references from my own travels to other West Indian islands to deepen the narrative.

The inspiration for my hero came from the movie, *Belle*, which I recommend to anyone who likes historical films. In this novel, the hero is the one of mixed race. In my previous book *The Princess Stakes* where the heroine was biracial, I wanted to emphasize that feelings of unworthiness or displacement because of race aren't limited to gender. Living and thriving as a person of color has its unique challenges, even if one is a duke and in possession of all the power and influence that comes with such a title. While my hero pretends to be impervious, he is still deeply vulnerable, and I loved being able to craft these different layers into his personality.

In the story, I also mention the novel *Jane Eyre* and Brontë's account of local island women. Much of Bertha's characterization is derogatory—her madness and savagery attributed to her time in the islands and the fault of what the author claimed to be a hot, terrible climate. She isn't given much of a voice, and I wanted to have my character point that out. As much as I love *Jane Eyre*, I always felt that Antoinette got the short end of the stick while Mr. Rochester was unfairly romanticized. If you're interested in reading a different version of Bertha/Antoinette, please read *Wide Sargasso Sea* by Jean Rhys. It gives such an interesting alternate perspective to this story.

I also had an interesting time researching ocean liners. Obviously, the early-twentieth-century *Titanic* is the most famous of the luxurious passenger liners, but there were some lavish liners in the second half of the nineteenth century when marine steam engines and passenger transatlantic travel had just begun to gather popularity. I took creative liberty with some of the designs and had so much fun with my hero and heroine's first honeymoon love scene.

Lastly, I'd like to point out that there are so many facets to a diaspora. One POC's experience will not reflect another's. My experience as a woman of West Indian descent will not be the same as someone who was born or raised in the United States, England, India, the wider Caribbean, or elsewhere. This means that as a writer, I might not be the perfect representation for members of another diasporic community. I can only write from my own mixed-race, Caribbean-born experience and through the knowledge of my own sphere of existence. I do hope that more diverse voices will be called to the publishing table to represent the amazingly rich narratives in the world.

I hope you enjoyed Courtland's and Ravenna's journey to their happy-ever-after!

XO, Amalie

Acknowledgments

I have so many people to thank for this book. As always, a huge thank-you to my awesome editor, Deb Werksman, for all your notes, care, and insight on this book. Thank you for taking a chance on this diverse historical romance series. Thanks also to the entire production, design, sales, marketing, and publicity teams at Sourcebooks Casablanca for your efforts behind the scenes—I'm so grateful for everything you do. A special thank-you to Stefani Sloma.

To my incredible agent, Thao Le, thanks for everything…your advice, your support, and all your superstar agenting skills. I'm so glad to be on this publishing journey with you!

To the women who hold my hand on this publishing rollercoaster, take off their earrings, or read my scrappy first drafts under duress, Katie McGarry, Wendy Higgins, Angie Frazier, Aliza Mann, Sienna Snow, Sage Spelling, MK Schiller, Shaila Patel, Vonetta Young, Kerrigan Byrne, Lisa Brown Roberts, Jen Fisher, Stacy Reid, Ausma Zehanat Khan, Jodi Picoult, and Brigid Kemmerer, I have nothing but love and gratitude for you. Your friendship means so much to me.

To all the readers, reviewers, booksellers, librarians, and friends who support me and spread the word about my books, a tremendous thank you for all you do! I definitely would not be here without you. Thanks for reading!

Last but not least, to my beautiful family—Cameron, Connor, Noah, and Olivia—who are my bright stars and the moon in my sky, I love you deeply.

About the Author

Amalie Howard is a *USA Today* and *Publishers Weekly* bestselling author of *The Beast of Beswick*, "a smart, sexy, deliciously feminist romance," and one of *O, The Oprah Magazine*'s Top 24 Best Historicals to Read. She has also penned several award-winning young adult novels, critically acclaimed by *Kirkus Reviews*, *Publishers Weekly*, *VOYA*, *School Library Journal*, and *Booklist*, including *Bloodcraft*, an IPPY silver medalist and Moonbeam award winner, and *Alpha Goddess*, a Kid's INDIE NEXT pick. Of Indo-Caribbean descent, she has written articles on multicultural fiction for the *Portland Book Review* and *Ravishly* magazine. She currently resides in Colorado with her husband and three children. Visit her at amaliehoward.com.

THE PRINCESS STAKES

Smart, sexy, and beautiful Regency romance
from bestselling author Amalie Howard

Born to an Indian maharaja and a British noblewoman, Princess Sarani
Rao has it all: beauty, riches, and a crown. But when Sarani's father is murdered, her only hope is the next ship out—captained by the man she once
loved...and spurned.

Captain Rhystan Huntley, the reluctant Duke of Embry, is loath to
give up his life at sea. But duty is calling him home, and this is his final
voyage. Leave it to fate that the one woman he's ever loved has stowed
away and must escape to England on his ship...

**"Vivid, sensual, and beautifully written—
impossible to put down."**

—Lisa Kleypas, *New York Times* bestselling author

For more info about Sourcebooks's books and authors, visit:
sourcebooks.com